HER HEARTLESS SAVIOR

THE SYNDICATES BOOK 2

R.G. ANGEL

Her Heartless Savior

Cover: Fay Lane Cover Design

Editing: Silvia Reading Corner

Her Heartless Savior By R.G Angel

Copyright © 2022 R.G. Angel

This book is a work of fiction. Names and characters are the product of the author's imagination and any resemblance to actual persons, living or dead is entirely coincidental.

This book is licensed for your personal enjoyment only.

If you're reading this book and did not purchase it, then please purchase your own copy. Thank you for respecting the hard work of this author.

WARNING: 18 + only. Please read responsibly. THIS NOVEL CONTAINS TRIGGERING CONTENT.

CONTENTS

Dedication	V
Prologue	1
Chapter 1	9
Chapter 2	21
Chapter 3	49
Chapter 4	59
Chapter 5	77
Chapter 6	99
Chapter 7	119
Chapter 8	135
Chapter 9	153
Chapter 10	173
Chapter 11	189
Chapter 12	211

Chapter 13	229
Chapter 14	255
Chapter 15	271
Chapter 16	297
Chapter 17	311
Chapter 18	327
Chapter 19	347
Epilogue	361
About R.G. Angel	370
Also By	371
	373

To Angel (AKA David Boreanaz),
You are the first anti-hero/villain I fell for, paving the way for an embarrassingly long list of them.
You are the source of my inspiration. I don't think all my morally gray heroes would have existed without you and that moment when I saw you walk onto that screen in that black suit of yours.
And come on readers, let's admit it - villains truly do it better :P

PROLOGUE

LILY

I straightened my accordion dark green skirt, throwing another irritated glance at the clock on the wall.

Three hours late! Who the hell makes you wait three hours for an interview? Mr. Bossman asshole, that's who!

I narrowed my eyes toward the closed black door leading to the office of Alessandro Benetti, CEO of Datasole Corp.

I'd been a little surprised to even be invited to take place in the process. I only had one year experience being a PA and it was for my uncle's construction company.

I had been even more surprised when I'd stepped into this waiting room to see that most of the PAs seemed to have been broken from the same mold—the bimbo factory.

I waited as they were called, one by one, and then they'd come out giggling some time later. I was getting more and more irritated as the scheduled time of my interview came and passed, and my name had yet to be called.

The last bimbo, who I called Bimbo number eight, had left the office of Mr. Asshole over an hour ago, yet I was still sitting here like a dumb fool.

I extended my leg and winced at the pain shooting up from my knee to my hip. Today was not a good day for my chronic pain, especially with the amount of rain.

The pain only added to the exasperation caused by this man's rudeness.

I threw a look toward the secretary, though I knew it looked much more like a glare than anything else. I was not in the mood to fake anything anymore.

If I had half a mind, I would just take my bag, flip them off, and take my four-hour train trip back home, but part of me refused to let him off that easily. He had to face the consequences of his dismissal; I wanted him to look me in the eyes as I made him waste time as he made me waste mine.

The woman sent me an uncomfortable smile before typing furiously on her keyboard—her long, pointy, blood-red nails on the plastic the only noise in the deadly quiet waiting room.

Her phone rang, startling me.

"Mr. Benetti."

I turned a little on my seat to listen more closely as I grabbed my bag from the seat beside mine to rest it on my lap, expected to be called any second now.

I took a deep breath, trying to rein in my irritation. It wouldn't do me any good to tell him off right off the bat, even though I knew I would eventually do it.

"Ms. Matthews?"

I stood, slipping my bag on my shoulder.

She gave a sheepish smile, which looked more like a wince. "It seems Mr. Benetti ran out of time for his interviews and now has a full schedule for the rest of the day. He'd like to extend his apologies and will contact you to organize another interview."

I remained locked on the spot for a few seconds, too shocked about the rude dismissal to react straight away.

"However, we'll be happy to indulge for a taxi back to your hotel or to the train station."

Indulge? That got me out of my stupor as fast as a bucket of iced water. "Indulge?" I scoffed, hardly believing the nerve of this man. "You made me travel four hours in a beat-up train and stay in an overpriced hotel for an interview your boss doesn't even have the *decency* to conduct, and you are ready to *indulge* in a taxi?"

She pursed her lips, looking from her screen back to me a couple of times, clearly not used to people expressing their disapproval.

"Miss—"

"No," I shook my head. "I don't think so." I had nothing left to lose, and hell if I let this CEO with an overinflated ego treat me with such disdain. I wanted him to look me in the eyes when he sent me away; he needed to see I was not a commodity he could just dispose of as he saw fit.

I grabbed the cool metal handle and pushed the door that barely moved, destroying my dramatic entrance in his office. Damn it, that thing was much heavier than I had anticipated.

I pushed again, this time using all my strength, and I kept my face impassive despite the pain shooting down my leg.

The man behind the desk, Alessandro Benetti, was laughing at something someone said on the phone, and that annoyed me even more. He was clearly not that busy if he had the time to exchange jokes over the phone.

My brows furrowed even more as I hugged my folder closer to my chest and walked into the room uninvited, hating that my occasional limp decided that exact moment to make itself known. Based on the way his eyes flickered down, he didn't miss it either.

He said something in Italian and hung up the phone before looking at me with his eyebrows raised, expectantly. "Yes?"

Yes? Was that all he had to say when faced with my intrusion and murderous glare.

Completely at a loss of words at his reaction, I opened my mouth and closed it.

"I'm sorry, sir. I tried to send her away!" his secretary said breathlessly from behind me.

"You did a stellar job, Annabelle, as usual." His sarcasm was biting, and it angered me a little on her behalf. He'd been the one asking her to do the dirty work—something I suspected he probably did quite often. "You can go now. I'll deal with this myself."

"Yes, sir. I'm sorry."

He connected his eyes with me again. "We're losing daylight, dear. I suggest you get the words out."

Dear? I pursed my lips. *Patronizing asshole!*

His mouth quivered at the corner, as if he could read my annoyance and it was amusing him.

Be ready for the full show, Mr. Bossman.

"You owe me an interview."

His eyebrows shot up. "I *owe* you?" He snorted. "I don't owe *you* anything."

"You do!"

His smirk vanished as a frown appeared on his face. I didn't think he was contested often.

"Do you think that just because you're rich and good looking, with your expensive suits, fancy office, sharp cheekbones, and chocolate eyes, you can treat people like commodities?" I asked, my ears burning with anger under the mass of my unruly red curls.

"I do," he replied with a placid tone, but the muscle pulsating on the side of his stupidly well-defined jaw showed me his anger was simmering.

Instead of calming me down, as it would have any normal person facing a big powerful man, it actually pushed me further.

"You don't make people take a godawful four-hour train ride and leave them to wait for three hours while you make *social calls* to whoever, and then don't have the decency to keep your side of the agreement. You weren't even *man* enough to send me away yourself; instead, you hid behind your secretary."

His nostrils flared as his eyes tightened at the corners. I had touched his virility by calling him a lesser man, and I was bracing for impact.

"I've no qualms sending you away myself. I just thought Annabelle would do it more gracefully than I would have."

He rested his big hands on his desk and leaned forward. "You don't fit the profile."

I frowned. That wasn't really the comment I'd been expecting. "And yet you asked me to come, forcing me to face a crowded train that smelled like burned cheese and take an overpriced hotel room to just—"

He waved his hand dismissively, as if my grievances were insignificant—and they might have been for him, but not to me. I was not being disregarded this way again.

"Is that why you're whining?" he asked with an eyebrow arched in derision

I gripped the leather strap of the bag I had dangling on my shoulder. I had half a mind to swing it at him and wipe that grin off his face. "I—"

"The agency will reimburse you for the expenses; I believe it's part of our contract with them." He snapped his fingers toward the door. "I'll even throw a little extra if you leave now and stop wasting my time. I'll have Annabelle draw you a check for a thousand dollars. Tell me, dear, would that be enough to mend your tender little heart?"

I took a step forward, pursing my lips. I'd never considered murder as a solution for anything before, yet I could see myself stabbing him repeatedly with the silver paperknife on his desk. Would his blood even show on his dark wooden desk?

"No," I replied firmly, doing my best to ignore the slowly building burning pain in my thigh. It wouldn't be long until the pain went down my leg, making it spasm. I was not supposed to stay up for too long, but I'd be damned before I showed that man the extent of my weaknesses. "I want to know why?"

He rolled his eyes. "Fine. The only reason you're here is for quotas. Happy?"

No, I was obviously not happy. I had been the 'quota girl' for years now. Just disabled enough to fit the category, but not too much as to be seen as a hindrance. At university, I was invited to clubs that didn't even want me, I was named spokesperson for 'diversity' without making the request, and I ended up shying away from everything as the attention didn't make me feel better—if anything, it made me feel worse.

I stood straighter, moving my weight from foot to foot, hoping to delay the spasms just a little longer. "The agency said you had eight assistants in less than a year... Maybe it's because *your* profile is flawed."

"Are you criticizing my judgment?" he asked with a surprised scoff.

I shook my head a little. "I don't need to; your retention rate is enough."

He leaned back in his seat with a sigh. "Why would you even work for me? You seem to find me aggravating."

I couldn't deny that, and it must have been written all over my face. I shrugged. "To prove you wrong."

He laughed. "You won't last a week," he said with a little shake of his head.

"Let me prove you wrong," I insisted. "And if you're right... Well, just imagine the joy you'll feel by telling me '*I told you so.*'"

A mischievous glint lit his dark eyes, and I knew he was imagining the pleasure he'd have when he'll send me away.

"Fine. Monday, nine a.m. Don't be late," he said before turning toward his screen, silently dismissing me.

"Yes. Monday nine a.m. You won't regret it."

"I highly doubt that," he replied, though he didn't even bother to look at me.

I exited the office, meeting the secretary's eyes challengingly.

"See you on Monday," I told her as I passed her desk toward the elevator, my damn limp taking away from my victory procession.

I let out a sigh of relief after the doors closed behind me, letting go of some of my bravado.

I had won—I had the job—yet the glint in his eyes and his twisted smile made me believe that I'd lost... and lost big.

I shook my head with a snort.

"Don't be silly, Lily!" I muttered to myself, looking at my reflection in the elevator's mirrored walls. *He's just a powerful CEO; what's the worst that could happen?*

So much... SO. DAMN. MUCH.

CHAPTER 1

Alessandro

I let out an irritated sigh as the car stopped in front of the iron gates of Matteo Genovese's compound in New York.

I had no time for whatever they were working on behind the scenes, but when you were summoned by the *capo di tutti capi,* the only reply you could give was 'I'm on my way.'

The gate opened and the car took the first path to the right, far enough from the main house.

That also aggravated me. I was important enough to be summoned for whatever they were planning, but not enough to be welcomed in the sanctity of his home where his pregnant wife and two-year-old daughter were staying.

Can you blame him? a little voice taunted as the car slowed in front of the ugly concrete structure Matteo used for his *famiglia* reunions.

That thing was an abomination, more akin to a secret military base than anything that should be part of this stunning property.

I stepped out of the car as soon as it stopped and took a deep breath, the air heavy—another prediction of the impending storm about to hit the city.

I let out my breath in a huff, buttoning my suit jacket. It was lucky my jet landed before the low gray clouds delivered what they were promising. I'd been in a storm once before, and I was man enough to admit that it was something I never wanted to experience again.

The door opened to reveal Gianluca Montanari, the head of the East Coast mafia.

He gave me a quick nod with a small smile, and I gave him the same as I walked toward him. I didn't have to fake it with him. I genuinely liked and respected the man; I also trusted him, which, in our world, was a very rare commodity.

"Thank you for coming on such short notice," he said after I passed him to enter the building. "Third door on the left." He indicated as my pace slowed down in the dim corridor.

I walked in to find Genovese sitting at the end of the table, and Fabrizio sitting at his right.

I bowed to Matteo as a sign of respect and nodded my acknowledgement to Fabrizio, trying my best to keep my face devoid of the annoyance and irritation I felt at seeing him here.

He was the head of the small territory we had in California, and I didn't think he'd ever get over the fact that my sister married a *yakuza*, and that I allowed it.

I sighed internally, as if I could have stopped those two from doing whatever they wanted to do.

"I hope I didn't create too much havoc in your busy schedule," Matteo said, gesturing me to a seat on his other side.

We both knew he couldn't care less about creating havoc in anyone's life, but I decided to play along.

"It's nothing Matthews can't handle," I said, taking my seat and waving my hand dismissively.

"Matthews?" Fabrizio cocked his head to the side. "The cripple is still working for you?"

I pursed my lips, my hand twitching to grab the back of his head and smash his face into the wooden table. I hated when people insulted my staff, and even though I knew he was not saying that in a true mocking way, it still aggravated me.

"Don't call her that. If my wife hears you, she will stab you," Luca said with a shake of his head, taking the seat beside mine.

Fabrizio turned toward Matteo, as if he expected help there. He must have been truly desperate.

Matteo shrugged. "I'll hand her the knife."

I knew it! I rested my hand in front of my mouth to hide my smile. Matteo held grudges, no matter how ridiculous they were. And he was mad at Fabrizio because, in what seemed to be a lifetime ago, his wife Elena had said that she liked Fabrizio.

Matteo Genovese was the iceman. He barely showed any emotions, and I suspected that he didn't feel a lot of them, but one he felt was love for his wife, which bordered on insanity and a jealousy that could cost a man his life.

"What do you need?" I asked, trying to redirect the conversation. Matthews could reorganize my whole day—even a week, I had to give her that—but the more I caused her trouble, the more annoyed she got. I had to admit I enjoyed the fire, but I was not a fan of her being mad at me. The sooner I could get back to Chicago, the better it was.

"We've got issues with the ports," Matteo started before throwing a look at Luca for him to continue, since New York was his city, after all.

"I'm just not sure why you called the *yakuza* sympathizer."

I rolled my eyes with a sigh. *Here we go again.* My half-sister marrying a *yakuza* boss did stir some shit in our *famiglia*, especially in the older generations, until we managed to strike an alliance that benefited both sides. To be honest, I was pretty sure that Fabrizio didn't care, he just didn't like being the weakest of all the territories—a territory that was owned by my brother-in-law. I didn't look too favorably at their relationship, not because of the mafia he was a part of, but because he was mafia and that usually meant heartbreak and death for the people you loved.

"We're not our fathers; our sisters and daughters are not commodities we can sell. They have their own mind and make their own choices," Luca interrupted.

"It's easy for you to say," Fabrizio insisted. "Your sister married the *capo di tutti capi,* not the enemy."

"Hoka Nishimura is *not* the enemy." Luca shrugged. "And my sister was free to marry whoever she wanted."

A dark chuckle made me look into Matteo's icy blue eyes. "No, Gianluca. No, she wasn't. Your sister has always been mine. There was never another choice for her."

Luca rolled his eyes, but I believed that. Matteo was a hound when he wanted something, and I didn't think he ever wanted anything more than Elena Montanari.

"So, what's the problem?"

"The problem is that a few of our recent shipments have been stuffed when they shouldn't have. Even with randomness... three in a row seems highly unlikely."

I frowned and nodded. "Don't you own the port authority?"

Gianluca raised an eyebrow. "Obviously, we do." He let out a heavy sigh. "Well, until now. We had enough people there, but some of our highest agents have been replaced recently and the new ones are a little harder to..." he rubbed at his jaw, "convince."

Matteo snorted. "If you let me deal with it, it'll be faster."

"Yes, and the sea would turn red with their blood."

Matteo shrugged but remained silent.

"It's nothing I can't *fix*," Luca insisted, keeping his eyes on Matteo. "But I need time to fix it." He turned his eyes toward me. "Time I don't have, as we have four shipments on the way."

"Ah, you know my port is not the biggest. Depending on the shipping location, it may not be risk-free."

"I know, but I should have it fixed soon. We've got one of the instigators in this."

"He may not talk."

"Oh, he's in my playroom, he'll talk." Matteo's smile turned into a twisted grin that made me shiver. I knew what usually happened in Matteo's playroom, and it was not a place I ever wanted to be in.

"Wouldn't Boston be easier?"

"Much," Luca agreed with a sigh. "But we don't own the port in Boston, the Irish do, and Killian Doyle is asking for more than I'm ready to give." He shook his head. "He doesn't grant favors easily."

I looked down at the table, hoping they could not see with their trained eyes that I knew how to make Doyle give in. I just wanted to keep this card up my sleeve for something important to me, and the shipping issues from another part of the *famiglia* wasn't it.

"I don't mind you using the port as long as you need. Matthews managed to get all the maritime permits I needed for the business. Not sure how she did it, to be honest; there are strict quotas set by the state but…" I shrugged. "I don't expect your boats to have too many issues, as long as you give us a few days' notice to smooth everything up."

"Matthews, huh?"

I cursed internally, turning my head toward Matteo. I slipped up and we both knew it.

His phone beeped on the table, and he quickly glanced at it before looking at me again. "How much does she know about the business?"

"Which side?"

He raised an eyebrow that seemed to say, 'The only one I care about.'

I shook my head. "Nothing at all."

Matteo snorted. "How long has she been your assistant? A year?"

Eighteen months and he knew it. He was just testing me. Everything was a fucking test, a sadistic game for him.

"Eighteen months."

Matteo nodded silently as his phone beeped again. He glanced at it before grabbing it and putting it in the inside pocket of his jacket. "Is she slow? I've heard she has a disability. Is it mental?"

I pursed my lips into a fine line as he threw his words with such careless disdain. I was heartless—fuck, I knew it—but I was a fucking *Care Bear* compared to him.

"She is *not*," I spat through gritted teeth.

He stood up. "*Bene*, then that settles the situation. She knows things." He sighed, buttoning his suit jacket. "Nobody can work closely with one of us for that long without figuring it out. You're not James Bond or Batboy."

"Batman," Fabrizio corrected. Yep, that man was a moron.

Matteo turned his emotionless, icy eyes toward him. "Thank you for your input. You can shut up now." Matteo was married to the geekiest woman in North America; he didn't need Fabrizio to question his education in pop culture.

Matteo let out a frustrated sigh before turning toward me again. "Batman, batboy, batdog, *che importa*?" He knocked on the table with his knuckles. "The assistant comes with you next time. She and I need to have a little chat."

Cold sweats ran down my back at the thought of Matthews in the same room as Matteo—she was just too confrontational for her own good. I found that amusing, even endearing, but Matteo Genovese would not see it like that.

His phone beeped in his pocket. "Now, if you excuse me, my wife needs me." He gestured toward Luca. "I'll leave it to you to wrap up the details of the shipments."

"Is she okay?" I asked with genuine concern. I really liked his wife—she was funny and sweet... everything her husband wasn't.

He gave me a sharp nod. "It's a second trimester issue that only I can fix."

I frowned. "How—" I started, just as Luca interrupted me with a loud, *"Don't!"* but it was too late.

"She needs my cock," Matteo replied as Luca made a gagging sound.

I looked at Luca horrified, knowing only too well how traumatizing it was when you were faced with your little sister's sexuality. I've been suffering a lot with Hoka and Violet, so I felt for the man.

"Okay, fine." I nodded. "Sorry I asked."

"No, no, don't be sorry. You'll know when you'll have a pregnant wife. The second trimester is delicious, they're just so... horny, and man," he rested his hand on his chest, "they take it any way you want to give it."

Luca grunted, hanging his head low, resting his hands on each side of his face.

Matteo laughed before swirling around and leaving the room, knowing full well he'd caused Luca some emotional damage.

"I'm sorry, man. I really am. I know the pain you're going through."

"I don't get it." Fabrizio shrugged. "It's just sex."

Luca looked up to him with one eyebrow raised, at least the stupidity of his comment helped him get out of the traumatic state.

Luca shook his head before turning toward me. "This is the list of the shipments about to leave. Three will be leaving Trieste, two from Cagliari, one from Gioia Tauro, and two from Dar Es Salaam."

"Tanzania?" I cocked my head to the side, twisting my mouth. "That's regulated trade."

Luca nodded before turning toward Fabrizio. "Could you go see Dom and have him give you the list of the shipments' contents?"

Fabrizio nodded briskly and almost jumped off his seat, way too happy to go order Luca's second-in-command around.

"Domenico's here?" I asked with surprise. Dom belonged in this room much more than Fabrizio did.

Luca's lips quivered in a half smile. "No, he's following a lead on a port official, but it'll take Fabrizio a while to figure that one out, which will give us enough time to finish this without him."

I snorted, leaning back on my seat. "That's why you're the boss."

He sighed. "Anyways, the Tanzania shipment is quite sensitive."

"Gold, stones, oil?"

"All the above."

I let out a low whistle, impressed.

"Do you think it'll be an issue?"

I shook my head. "Matthews did a fine job. As long as we get the right products in the ship, along with what you need, we'll be okay. I'll send you a copy of the list of what you need to declare and put in it for a smooth sail."

Luca looked at me silently, tapping the end of his pen rhythmically on the table.

"What?"

He threw a quick look toward the door and sighed. "I hate to admit it, but Matteo is right. She's lasted much longer than any assistant you ever had, and she seems really involved in your business."

"That's what assistants do, don't they? They are here to facilitate your life. I hate to admit that she's not just good at it, she's amazing. What am I supposed to do? Fire her?" I hated how defensive my tone was, and also the ridiculous pinch of something very close to sadness at the thought of sending her away.

He tilted his head back, a frown forming between his eyebrows. "No, I'm not saying that, but I'd try my best to keep that defensiveness out of my tone if I were you—it shows you care, and it'd give Matteo a field day. Trust me, I know."

"I don't care, and she knows nothing," I insisted.

Luca looked at me for a couple of seconds before shaking his head, as if he was having some internal debate and decided it was not worth it.

"Okay then, I presume you are in a hurry to get back to your life, so this is the shipment numbers and date of sail. Make sure you send me the type of goods we need to put in the export docs."

I nodded and reached for my phone, opening the encrypted folder and looking at the color-coded filing Matthews had put in place. That small change had infuriatingly changed my whole life in the best ways.

I'd admitted to myself so many times how much she'd improved my work environment and my life in general. She was funny in her stuck-up ways, and it was so easy to get her fired up.

I couldn't help but smirk at the thought of how much she must have cursed me when she received my text this morning asking her to reschedule everything. The only thing that annoyed me was her complete radio silence. I'd expected a passive aggressive email from her—well, not so much passive, and much more aggressive about my lack of consideration. I enjoyed these in a very masochistic way. Her righteous fire was entertaining.

"What are you thinking about?"

I blinked a couple of times and met Luca's curious look. "Nothing." I jerked my head toward him. "I just emailed you the list." I leaned over the paper he'd put on the desk with shipment numbers and the additional information, then snapped a quick picture.

"I'll make sure these ships won't encounter any problems." I looked at my watch, though I wasn't sure why—it's not like I was expected anywhere right now. Matthews was so efficient, I knew she'd managed to clear my whole schedule, but I was still itching to go back to my kingdom.

And see why Matthews is ignoring me too, right? the taunting part of my brain reminded me.

"Good, and..." He sighed, as if he thought better of it.

I walked to the door but cursed myself as I took the bait. "What?" I asked, turning my head to the side to look at him.

"Matteo has probably forgotten already, but he won't forget forever. The next time, we both know it won't be a request, so act now. Make sure she knows nothing; either take her completely in or let her go. She's too close."

"I'll take that into consideration," I replied evasively, hoping deep down that Matteo would forget long enough for the decision to make itself.

CHAPTER 2

Lily

"So, these are all the revenues from each department?" I asked, pointing at the screen. Line after line of green and red numbers were making me cross-eyed.

"Yes..." Alex trailed off, probably thinking I was stupid. "The red are the losses and the green the profits. This is why it's titled 'P&L Spreadsheet'."

I nodded. "Makes sense. So, you take all that and send it to Mr. Benetti?"

He frowned before removing his glasses and wiping them with the untucked side of his green dress shirt. "Did you say you used to help Matt before?"

I leaned back in my chair, trying to make myself relax. Alessandro Benetti was only away for the day, and it couldn't have been a better day. Any normal day I would have cursed him and his stupid male ego for forcing me, once again, to deal with frustrated people because he had decided on a whim to just change his whole day around.

But today was the last day before the financial reporting was due, and it was a godsend for me to gather the proof of what I'd suspected for a while.

"Yes. I don't know if I told you, but I'm studying accounting remotely, part-time." At least I used to, though my books have been covered in dust for the past eight months. "Matt and I used to date." Date was a bit of a stretch, unless you counted the two disastrous meals and a sloppy kiss as dating. "I often helped him when Mr. Benetti was away."

"Uh." He put his glasses back on and detailed me. "His promotion was a lucky break. Do you know how it came about?"

I quickly glanced at the clock. I'd been down there for over two hours now and I couldn't allow myself much longer—losing precious investigation time in idle chit-chat with a man who was the epitome of boring. Even if Alessandro was away, I knew his nosey secretary was keeping tabs on me.

"It was a lucky break for sure, but he was very dedicated to the tasks and letting me assist him really helped his work get noticed by the higher-ups. I could help you too, if you want."

To be fair, his promotion came as a shock to everyone, Matt included. He'd even whined a couple of months before saying that his performance assessment had been unfair, and that he didn't get the five stars he deserved. Yet, not even two days after our second disastrous date, he was offered a position as the head of special accounting projects in the London office. I didn't even know there were special accounting projects in the company.

"Oh! I'd like that."

Of course, you would, I thought with a degree of cynicism. Men were all the same. If I didn't need him right now, I'd probably tell him to review his expectations. What had happened to Matt—going from junior accountant to the head of special accounting projects—was close to impossible, and Alex was just a junior accountant, the bottom of the barrel and only in place for six weeks.

"Okay, so explain how you do it again?" I asked, tapping my short, neon green nail against the screen.

He rolled his chair closer—visibly more motivated now. "Every division is providing us with a P&L document from their regional offices across the continent each quarter." He rested his hand on top of mine and clicked on a tab at the bottom. "See this one, urban division, which is basically the commercial construction branch of the company. These are all the profits and losses of the urban divisions in the seventeen locations across North America. They were put together by the divisional accounting team, and then they were sent to us in the head office. My job is to take the main numbers of each division and put them on the front sheet, then consolidate all the numbers on one page so Mr. Benetti and the board will have just a high-level view."

"Oh." I had to admit, I was a little disappointed. "So, this will be the list you send me tonight, right?"

"Well, yes, after Mr. Byrne's approval."

I straightened up on my seat, perking up immediately. *Now we're talking.* "How is that?"

"I'm about to send this list to him now. I mean, he's the CFO, you know." He let out a little chuckle that seemed to say, 'bless you.' "He has his say."

I chewed on my bottom lip. What I suspected had the potential to be so much worse than I had first thought.

Don't get into this mess, it can only splash you along the way, I could hear Victor warn me with the same underlying exasperation he used to do at school. Victor used to call me 'Lily Matthews, the woman to right the wrongs'. But I'd never listened to him back then, there was little chance of me listening to him now, especially when he was nothing more than a memory. My heart squeezed with sorrow, but I quickly smothered it before it became too much to bear.

"I'll help," I offered and pressed print. "Oh shoot, I'm sorry. I pressed print instead of send. I didn't—"

He raised his hand. "It's okay. I'll deal with it."

I stood and grabbed the pages from the printer, then folded them and slid them into my handbag.

I sat back down, fully aware that having these highly confidential documents in my bag would create more trouble than anything else.

I turned to Alex and forced a smile, hoping he could not read the guilt on my face at the idea of potentially throwing us both into the deep end.

Alex smiled back, pulling his chair closer to mine, apparently oblivious to my scheming but assuming I was his key to a promotion.

I opened my mouth to ask him more questions about what happened once the CFO sent him back the numbers but was interrupted by a deep voice that both aggravated me and made me shiver with anticipation every time I heard it.

"Are you working for accounting now and nobody told me?" Alessandro Benetti asked, his arms crossed over his wide chest. "Should I pay you two wages?"

I pursed my lips but didn't reply or remind him that about six months ago, I did, in fact, consider applying for the junior accounting position. Within two hours of mentioning my interest in the position to the team leader, I was sitting in HR with a contract offering me double my salary, along with a sneaky clause that stated I was not allowed to apply for any other position in the company due to my insider knowledge.

I'd signed it with a little smile and lots of pride, because even if we drove each other crazy most of the time, I knew what that contract meant. Alessandro loved my work and didn't want to lose me, but I also knew he'd probably choose to get stabbed rather than admit he'd been wrong about me.

"Oh, s-sir! Mr. Benetti." Alex jumped from his seat, completely flustered. "I... What an honor to meet you, sir, Mr. Benetti, sir."

I couldn't help but roll my eyes and cringe when I met Alessandro's amused gaze—he'd not missed that.

"Obviously, it is," he replied haughtily as he turned toward Alex again. "What's your name?"

"Alex... Alex Albright, sir," he replied, still standing by the corner of his desk.

"Well, Alex Albright. Do you mind if I take my assistant back? I'm not sure she's suited for this... *environment*."

The environment in question was a windowless shoebox-sized office caught between the noisy and overheating central processor room on one side and the toilets on the other. It had once been Matt's office and now was Alex's. This was what you got when you were at the bottom of the food chain.

Alessandro arched an eyebrow as I stood, throwing him a glare that didn't faze him, not even a little.

"I... N-no, of course, she's the one who came here."

I threw him a side look. *Wow, way to throw me under the bus, asshole.*

A furrow appeared between Alessandro's eyebrows as his eyes narrowed. "I see. Well, maybe she realized you were out of your depth. Matthews has a thing for pathetic, lost causes. It's annoying, but what can I say?"

I winced as Alex's face fell before he looked down at his desk, running his forefinger along the edge.

Alessandro took a step to the side and gestured for me to move to the door. "Let's go, we've got *actual* work to do. Alec," he added with a sharp nod.

"It's Alex," I whispered as we walked down the corridor to the elevator.

"No one cares," Alessandro replied with a heavy sigh as he pressed the call button.

"You didn't need to be that unkind to him," I insisted as the elevator beeped, announcing its arrival.

He snorted, throwing me an exasperated look. "That insignificant bug threw you under the bus like you were nothing more than a commodity! I defended your honor," he exclaimed as we stepped in, and he swiped his card to take us to his floor.

I couldn't help but laugh. "You treat me like a commodity most of the time!"

"I do." He reached up to straighten the knot of his tie that was already perfect. "But I pay you for that privilege."

"You were not even supposed to be back yet! You said you wouldn't be in today."

"Oh, I'm sorry my schedule as the CEO of this company, and subsequently your boss, ruined your attempt to gallivant in the slime."

Gallivant? Was he stuck in Victorian England?

I rolled my eyes and turned toward the golden metallic doors, and despite the ridiculously deformed reflection it was giving us side by side, it was impossible not to see the striking differences between him and me.

"I didn't know that boring, lanky, and pasty, with disproportionately big glasses, was your go-to type."

I turned my head toward him again, but he was looking up at the floor-indication panel on top of the door.

"What?"

He looked down at me, his mouth a thin line, his dark eyes flashing with an irritation I knew well but was rarely directed toward me. How did I even manage to annoy him today?

"First Max, now Alec. I'm not paying you to flirt with the nerds."

"Matt and Alex." I chewed on my bottom lip as his icy look turned into a scowl. "What if they are my type?" Challenging him, I felt my irritation with him crawl back up. "We can't all want stupidly tall Italian gods."

His face morphed into a cocky smile. "And thank heaven for that! We're a rare quantity," he offered haughtily before exiting the elevator.

My pace faltered as I followed him out, and I glared at the back of his light gray suit. *Damn it! I did it again.* I wanted to insult the man, and I ended up complimenting his looks.

He opened the door of my small office, which was directly across from his secretary's desk, and turned his head toward me.

I kept my composure as I walked there as confidently as I could under the judging eyes of the woman who clearly didn't think I'd last as long as I had working for him.

I kept my eyes on him all the way to my office, and as always, there was a little light of approval in his. It was something I'd learned quite early in my time working for Alessandro Benetti. He found it annoying when you challenged him, but you were also rewarded by a type of respect few people received from him.

"What can I do for you, sir?" I asked, sitting behind my desk.

"Your job?" I knew he was trying to get me fired up again.

I simply pursed my lips, waiting for him to stop playing his game.

He sighed after a second and removed a folded piece of paper from his pocket. "Can you send me an updated version of my calendar?"

"Already done. If you refer to today's calendar, the ones highlighted in green have been rescheduled for this week, the amber ones are for the week after, and the red ones didn't want to reschedule because you're too rude canceling at the last minute."

Alessandro let out a snort. "Oh yeah? And please, do tell, who's the delusional idiot?"

I couldn't help but smile. "Mr. James."

"I see." Alessandro nodded. "Guess someone's balls have finally dropped. Give him a week; he'll come crawling back."

"I'll actually wager two days. He was acting way too offended to be taken seriously."

"What would you bet on it?" he asked teasingly, but I knew better by now than to play this game with him. There was nothing I could offer that he'd want or need, and I knew he'd be cruel enough to let me know that.

I pointed at the paper in his hand. "Is this for me?"

"Huh?" He looked down to his hands. "Oh yes, that's the list of additional shipments that will be coming in over the next eight weeks. I just need you to prepare the registration for them. You'll get the list of contents in the next couple of days." He extended the piece of paper.

"What are these for?" I asked, unfolding the paper and looking at the shipments list.

His body tensed, his back straightened, his usually impassive face taking an edge of wariness. "Why do you ask?" His voice sounded much colder than usual.

"I..." I was taken aback by his hostility. It had been a while since I'd been on the receiving end of it.

"I just need it for the allocation number to give the port authorities." I hated how feeble my voice sounded, but I had somehow forgotten this version of Alessandro Benetti existed. Even though I knew he was a well-respected CEO, there was an edge in him that raised all the alarm bells and scared me. "I-I'm sorry I asked. I—" I looked at the clock and could have thanked all the angels in heaven when I noticed it was almost five. "There's no rush. I won't have the time to complete those forms today anyway, so I can sort that out tomorrow when I get the actual listing."

His shoulders relaxed almost immediately, burying his hands in his pockets before giving me one of his sheepish half-smiles—the one he used on the rare times he pushed further than I appreciated.

"It's been a long day," he started as a way of apologizing. I was pretty sure this man had never used the word 'sorry' and actually meant it. "Just do what—" He cocked his head on the side and looked at the clock on the wall before turning toward me again. "What do you mean you don't have the time? I thought you were an expert at those now?"

"I am..." I trailed off, unsure where he was going with that. "But there are eight shipments here, and just to log the initial forms will take me about an hour and half."

He kept staring at me, his face completely impassive, as if he still couldn't understand what the issue was.

"My day finishes at five, which is in fifteen minutes."

His scowl deepened. "I've only been back in the office for an hour, and I found you flirting in the basement. You can hardly call that a fruitful and honest day of work, can you?"

I would have never pegged myself as a woman with a temper before working for Alessandro Benetti; I'd been meek and soft—the total opposite of Victor—but it seemed this man had the ability to summon this part that must have been buried inside my whole life. Or maybe it was something that Victor had given me the day he'd died.

"I beg your pardon?" I asked him, pushing my office chair back to give me more room.

He removed his hands from his pockets and crossed them on his chest. "You heard me."

I stood, my whole body humming with indignation as my hands shook slightly with anger.

"How dare you?" I hissed through my teeth, trying to keep my voice at a respectable level so as to not attract the attention of his secretary, the queen of gossip, who I could see through a small sliver between Benetti's massive form and the door. She was already throwing us questioning looks every so often, and I knew how words spoken too loudly, would be enough for Alessandro and I to be the source of tomorrow's lunch gossip.

I raised my forefinger. "Firstly, if you had the *decency* to inform me of your absence with more than, oh let's say, ten minutes notice, then I would have actually been able to organize my day differently and optimize my time without you. Two," I raised my middle finger, "I'm always here before everyone and usually leave at the same time as you. I'm paid for a forty-hour week, but I usually work closer to sixty hours, and I *never* complain!"

With his scowl still settled in place, he opened his mouth to reply, but I was not having it this time. I was going to finish my tirade, whether it pleased him or not.

"*Thirdly,*" I pressed on and raised my hand to show him three fingers. "I have done everything I was supposed to do today, and until ten minutes ago, I was leaving the office with a cleared inbox and a clear desk. And last, but not least, I have plans tonight because, contrary to you, some of us have friends, and it's one of my dearest friend's birthdays—not that it has anything to do with you. I do not owe you *any explanation* of what I do or don't do outside of work."

I stopped talking, my chest heaving with my angry, shallow breath.

He looked at me defiantly, his eyes so infuriatingly placid, as if this man had no emotions, as if he was just an empty vessel.

Maybe that's just what he is, a high-functioning sociopath, Victor's voice warned me.

Everything in me wanted me to look down, to bow my head, but I refused as I kept my eyes locked with his. Using all the strength I had, I concentrated on the pang of pain my short nails were causing to my palm instead of the apprehension that made my heart speed up in my chest.

"I'm not sure what the deal with celebrating birthdays is." He finally said after a few seconds of silent standoff.

"What?" I looked around the room as if I was missing something. I'd just lashed out at him, and he was acting like we were just having a normal conversation.

"I'm just not sure what's to be proud of." He shrugged. "Congratulations, your parents had sex and you got expelled from your mother's birth canal." He waved his hand dismissively. "If anyone should be celebrated, it should be the mother for the pain she went through to get her child here."

I opened my mouth and closed it again a couple of times, probably looking like a fish out of water. How could I even answer that? *Nothing, Lily. You say nothing and you just leave his cynical ass behind.*

"I'll do it tomorrow. I'll come in early if need be." Drats, why did I offer that? I didn't owe him anything more than what I was already giving him. I grabbed my bag just as he stepped to the side, blocking my exit completely.

I couldn't help the apprehension that settled in the pit of my stomach as alarm bells rang in my head. I looked around as I grabbed my bag tighter, as my palms were getting sweaty.

"Where are you going?" he asked, taking a step closer.

I took a step back, my back connecting with the cool window, and I shivered as the cold seeped through the thin material of my royal-blue button-up cardigan. "Home..." I let out on a breath, all my previous bravado gone.

"No, tonight. Where are you going?" he asked, taking a step forward, hovering over me, his overbearing presence sucking all the oxygen out of my space.

I opened my mouth and closed it again. He was going to spoil my fun and punish me for not staying. I knew that; he'd done it before. The only time I went out with some girls from work, he showed up at the club with two of his friends, effectively killing the mood and causing every single female to seek his and his friends' favors. No, thank you.

I reached up to fidget with my dice pendant. "Please just let me go." I hated how pathetic my voice sounded.

He blinked a couple of times and widened his eyes before taking a few quick steps back.

"I..." He stopped and reached for the knot of his tie, then cleared his throat. "Yes, well, just make sure you're on time tomorrow." He moved from his spot in front of the door.

"Of course, sir, have a good evening," I replied quickly as I rushed out of the room and to the elevator without looking back.

I felt like I was able to breathe again once the door closed and the elevator started its descent to the lobby.

I leaned against the back of the elevator, resting my hand over my racing heart, grateful I was alone in the confined space with no witnesses to my mini meltdown.

I was not even sure why I reacted so erratically. It was not like I'd never been exposed to Alessandro's temper or his mood swings before, but it felt different today, as if he was on edge about something; and for the first time since I started working for him, it seemed like it was directed toward me.

I grabbed the silver double dice charms around my neck again and took a couple of deep breaths. I needed to shake this feeling or I would not go back tomorrow.

I had to be logical. There was no reason for Alessandro to be on edge with me. No, it was probably my own worry and anxiety reflecting the situation. It wouldn't be the first time it happened, and even though it had been rare over the last couple of years, I knew this anxiety always had the potential to rear its ugly head.

I couldn't let whatever feeling that was going through my head spoil Katia's birthday. It was important, and my presence at her celebration was always so important to her.

By the time the L-train had stopped at Roosevelt station, I was much more myself and even if I didn't particularly look forward to socializing with people I barely knew, it felt good to be normal for once—to experience what would probably have been if things hadn't turned the way they had.

I stopped at the Starbucks across my building for a coffee, knowing I'd need the extra caffeine as I usually stopped functioning by nine p.m. How sad was that for a twenty-four-year-old?

I'd been living in this area of Chicago for almost a year, even before the insane raise Alessandro Benetti had given me. Sheer luck, or maybe a Christmas miracle, had allowed me to move from Englewood to The Loop in this providential, fully furnished, gigantic one-bedroom apartment in a three-story building. The Loop had all the amenities one could dream of, for a rent that was about the same as what I paid in Englewood.

I was a defier of odds, always had been. It had also been why Victor had bought me the double dice necklace for my sweet sixteen.

That apartment had been posted on the company ad board in the lunchroom. It was a sublet of a colleague who would be working abroad for the next couple of years. He had already been gone by then, and HR helped with all the paperwork, but part of me still thought it was given to me due to my health issues and ability to be in the office in twelve minutes instead of thirty-eight.

I hung up my coat, discarded my shoes, and let out a little sigh of relief as I wiggled my tight-covered toes. I was just going to sit and relax a little before getting ready. I sat on the comfortable cream sofa and grabbed the bright pink knitted blanket my grandma had made me when I was in the hospital and snuggled into it while sipping my coffee.

I turned my head to look at my fish tank—the only pet my lifestyle allowed me to have. If it had been up to me, I'd have many dogs, but it took time, money, and space—three things I didn't have. I looked at my two mollies swimming around, completely unbothered by my presence.

My phone beeped and I looked at the screen to see a text from Katia, asking me once again if I was coming.

I'll be there. 8 p.m. at Britannia. I would not miss it for the world.

I grunted as I got up from my cozy place. Yep, I was definitely twenty-four going on seventy.

I stopped by the fish tank and dropped a little food in it. "Well Sam, Dean, Mommy's going out tonight, so there's no need to worry. I know it doesn't happen often, but sometimes you have to bite the bullet." I sighed. "You boys be good, okay?"

I went to the bathroom and turned on the hot shower. I did some of the physio exercises I had to do for my leg and back as the steam started to fill the room. I'd been neglecting them recently with work being so busy, but Fall was well underway and now that the cold and rain had really picked up, my lack of diligence didn't go unpunished.

I let out a painful grunt and winced as I rested my foot on the toilet cover and pushed forward—both my muscles and scar tissue reminded me that they were there and not happy to have been ignored.

"Urgh." I pulled back and pushed, trying to relax my hip joint. "I promise to be better but please," I winced again when I switched legs and did the same, "just be good tonight."

I knew the effect my limping or slight arm tremor had on Katia—how unjustified guilt always took over, and how it would, without a doubt, spoil her birthday.

I got under the very hot water—it was not comfortable, but I hoped this hot shower, followed by some soothing balm, would help keep the soreness at bay for a few more hours.

If not, I'd have to settle and take some tramadol, which I only took on rare occasions. If I took the medication,

I would not be able to drink even one glass of alcohol. I would not repeat the disaster from last Christmas. Maybe it was a blessing in disguise because after being put in a taxi way earlier than justifiable and sleeping it off the whole weekend, I was given the opportunity for this apartment on the Monday morning.

The shower helped a lot, as well as the ibuprofen cream, and even if I knew I wouldn't be able to dance all night, it was enough to pretend, for one evening, that everything was a long-forgotten memory.

I walked back into my bedroom and retrieved the only fashionable dress I owned. Hooking the hanger on the door of my wardrobe, I took a couple of steps back to really take it in as I tightened my wet hair into a tight braid, which was the only way I could tame my unruly curls.

My mother had bought this dress for me just two weeks ago when she'd come to spend the weekend with me. She'd pretended she wanted to come to do some shopping in the city, but we both knew she and my dad hated Chicago. I knew she was just coming to see how I was doing and report back to my father, uncle, and everyone else who worried about me.

I smiled as I sat at the foot of my bed and my heart pinched with a little homesickness. It had been bittersweet to leave Greenhill, of course. It was familiar, safe. The place where I'd grown up, and where everyone knew everyone. The place where all the people who loved me were. But it was also the place where I had lost myself for a while, a place of loss and grief. A place where I was not Lily Matthews. No, it was the place where I was *poor* Lily Matthews; the place where most eyes contained pity and wariness when they looked at me. A place where most of them averted their gaze, as if staring at me for too long would make them catch the pain and stigma I was carrying. I missed home, but I could not go back, not yet.

The dress was really pretty, but not something I would have bought for myself. I'd never been the epitome of fashion, and since the accident, I simply vanished in the background, becoming invisible... well, more invisible than I'd been before.

I grabbed my bottom lip between my teeth as I pondered wearing that dress tonight. It was long enough to cover most of my scars and didn't reveal too much, despite being quite form-fitting. My décolletage was a lot more predominant than what I was used to but wearing it would kill two birds with one stone.

For one, this dress would please Katia a lot—it'd show her that I was 'out there,' that my life had not been destroyed as thoroughly as she thought. I could also send a couple of smiley photos to my mother, so she could see there was nothing to worry about and I was living my twenties to their full potential. In all honesty, the dress was probably something I wouldn't have worn even before the accident, but it was just for one evening.

I removed the lilac mousseline from the hanger, and I slipped into it, my heart constricting with love for my mother as I noticed she hemmed it to stop just over my ankle to prevent me from having to wear any type of heels with it. Heels caused me the worst pain, even after a couple of hours.

I zipped the dress at the side and slid into my black ballet shoes, then rolled my braid around but could not find any pin to secure my bun.

I let out a frustrated grunt as I walked back into the living room, holding my hair up to get the little emergency pin pouch I kept in my bag. I swore I spent way too much money on things to tame my crazy mane. I sometimes thought I should just let it all flow freely and embrace my inner Merida.

"Damn it!" I cursed after I popped open my bag and noticed the rumpled pieces of paper I had shoved in there.

I let go of my braid, not really concerned about my appearance anymore, and took the papers out, putting them on the counter, smoothing it the best I could. I'd forgotten about the accounts when Alessandro came back much earlier than usual, being his asshole-ish self.

I looked at the time on my phone. I had to leave in less than twenty minutes if I hoped to make it to the restaurant on time. I could take a taxi, which would allow me a little leeway, but I had to see these numbers through tonight. I needed to check my suspicions before Alessandro's board meeting tomorrow.

I looked down at my dress. If I got caught walking in the office dressed like this, at this time of night, I'd have a lot of explaining to do—things I was not even sure I could explain yet, if ever. Worst of all, what if I'd been wrong? These were very serious accusations.

Maybe I could go early in the morning and... I shook my head, shutting down the idea. Alessandro arrived before seven in the morning on board meeting days. I would never have the time to do everything I wanted to do if I actually did that.

"Shit," I muttered as I quickly retrieved the hairpins from my bag, settling for a quick bun.

I booked an Uber, forgoing the full makeup look and settling for only a little mascara and pink lip-gloss applied using my reflection in the metal door of the microwave.

My phone beeped, announcing the arrival of the car. I grabbed my small handbag and put the pieces of paper, my wallet, my pepper spray, and my pass for the office inside before exiting the apartment.

I hesitated for a second in the corridor. Taking the stairs would be faster, but the pain had just barely subsided, and I was scared of overdoing it yet again.

I sighed, pressing the down button on the elevator, feeling somehow self-conscious taking it when I only lived on the second floor. There were moments where my limitations aggravated me more than others, and tonight was one of them.

I got into the car, stopping myself from apologizing for taking longer than anticipated. That had been something I had done a lot—apologizing for my shortcomings, real or not, but I was working on that, too. Why should I apologize for who I was?

I grabbed my phone just as the driver merged into the traffic and called Katia.

"You're not coming," she announced in a resigned sigh as a way of greeting.

I grimaced at the hint of sadness in her tone. It was not crazy for her to assume that—I'd canceled on her way too many times.

"I'm coming," I assured her. "I might just be running a little late."

I heard some laughter and cheers behind her—her roommates, no doubt, the friends she'd made at the sorority when she had been a student.

"Do you—"

She stopped and I frowned at her hesitation.

"Katia?"

"Do you... Are you okay, I mean? Do you need anything? I can ask Tessa or Lizzie to come and pick you up, or you know what, I'll come and help you just—"

"No." My voice was a little colder and sharper than I intended it to be. She had a good heart, I knew that, and I knew that whatever she wanted to do was coming from a good place, but I also hated how all these little moments of attention were making me feel so much worse about everything.

I took a deep, calming breath. "I'm already on the way, but I forgot I had something super important to drop at the office. It will not take long," I added quickly. "I just wanted to let you know."

"Oh."

I heard someone call her name. "Well, I better let you go back to the pre-party. I'll—"

"It's only work, Lil. Can't you just let it go for once and think of you? Of me?" Her voice carried a little exasperation and somehow, it made me feel better instead of worse. She was letting the mask slip for once—not walking on eggshells around me but treating me more like she would have done before the night of homecoming.

"I know, it's just—"

"No, it's my *birthday*! You're not paid enough for this."

You'd be surprised... I'd never dared to tell her the salary I made because she would either assume I lied or slept with the boss.

"It really can't; I should have done it today. Listen, my Uber just stopped in front of the office," I lied and met the driver's eyes in the rearview mirror with a sheepish smile. It was not such a big lie, since I was only three streets away. "I won't be long. Go ahead and start without me."

"Don't bail on me," she said, and her begging tone almost broke my heart.

"I won't. I'll be there, I promise."

She sighed. "I love you, Lil."

I closed my eyes. "You, too." I put the phone back into my bag and tried to shake off the weird combination of feelings my old life caused in me. It was a very weird mix of nostalgia, pain, helplessness, anger, frustration, and sorrow that didn't belong in my life anymore.

I had closed the lid on that box as the car stopped in front of the building.

"Do I need to wait for you?" the driver asked as I reached for the handle, clearly showing that he'd listened to my conversation and the fact I told Katia I'd only be a few minutes. Something that both her and I knew was a lie.

I shook my head. "No, thank you. I'll call another Uber when I'm done."

I swiped my card on the side door and was welcomed by the security guard's low whistle.

"Sweet God, did I die and go to heaven? Because, Miss Lily, you look like an angel," the night security guard exclaimed from behind his desk.

I rolled my eyes and snorted, though I couldn't help but blush at the compliment despite the cheesiness. It was obviously a courtesy compliment, but those were rare and far in between. I couldn't deny I enjoyed it just the same.

"You're such a flirt, Dave! What would your wife say?" I joked as I walked past his desk.

Not many people were well-acquainted with the old security guard working the night shift. He started at eight p.m., which was well after the building had been emptied. Staying late at work was a common occurrence for me, and I knew him just as well as the day team.

He frowned, glancing at the time on his screen, and pursed his lips.

"Is Benetti asking you to come on nights when you have things planned now?" He let out an irritated sigh. "You need to set boundaries, sweet girl. That's exactly what I'd say to my daughter, you know."

I couldn't help but smile at him as my heart filled with warmth. Dave was such a sweet old man—probably way too old to still be working, but with six children and fourteen grandchildren, I guessed he needed the extra income.

"No, he didn't make me come; I just forgot to do something. I won't be too long." I stepped into the elevator but reached out to hold the doors as his words hit me. "Wait. Is Mr. Benetti still here?"

He nodded. "I haven't seen him, but his car's still here." He pointed at one of his security screens.

"Okay. See you in a bit." I reached up to make sure my hair was in order, and I cursed my treacherous heart for skipping a beat at the thought of seeing Alessandro while I was dressed to impress.

I shook my head and looked down. I didn't have to impress Alessandro Benetti with anything other than my work. It was all that mattered, and all I could really shine at.

He didn't see me as anything other than his human diary and personal assistant. It was as it should be. I was neither female nor male for him—I was just a tool to facilitate his life.

And despite the ridicule of it all, my most shameful secret was that sometimes I wished he'd notice I was more, like how I noticed him in spite of myself. How his playful grin always made my heart beat a little faster, or how his deep voice always seemed to rumble all the way through my body.

That man was a condescending asshole, I'd known that from the day of my interview and the little regard he'd shown me, yet I couldn't help but find him both charismatic and insanely good looking.

"You should have your feminist card revoked," I muttered to myself as the door opened on the dark floor.

"Hello?" I called as I took a tentative step, the furniture barely discernible under the faint lighting of the safety lights leading to the emergency exit.

I took another step. "Mr. Benetti?" I called louder before wincing, all too aware this looked a lot like the beginning of a very low budget slasher movie. I held my breath as I trailed my hand along the wall, looking for the light switch.

I pressed the switch and jumped with a startled cry as a dark shape caught the corner of my eye.

I turned my head briskly and let out a relieved laugh as I saw it was only the office Ficus and not Michael Myers.

I rested my hand on my chest just to make sure my heart was still firmly in my body and not on the floor like I half-expected it to be.

I took a deep breath as my phone beeped in my bag. I grabbed it and read the text as I walked to my office, grateful for the distraction.

We're at the restaurant. I saved you a seat next to me. Text when you're on your way.

I glanced toward Alessandro's office, but there was no light coming from under the closed door. He must have been on his way down when Dave looked at his screen. It was probably for the best—seeing him now would have opened the door to a lot of questions I had no answer to.

If that's true, then why are you so disappointed? my stupid brain taunted.

I'm almost done here. I'll text you.

I turned on my computer as I retrieved the pages from my bag. I opened the first email I forwarded to myself from Alex's computer, and the numbers seemed to match.

I wrinkled my nose as I logged onto the main server using Alessandro's access code. He never used them, and I knew he'd given them to me by accident, not knowing that with this, I had the ability to access the central drives for all the company, including the email servers.

I took a deep breath, my fingers hovering over the keyboard. Chances were, nobody would even know what I did and what I checked on the server, but if they did and I had nothing to show for it...? I could probably kiss my job goodbye.

I connected to the email server for the California office and logged into the construction division junior accountant outbox as he was the only one I knew who would have the primary access to the number based on Matt's constant chatter about their rivalry. *Accountant rivalry... how riveting.*

I pulled the email he'd sent with the original numbers, and I held my breath as I leaned forward. I looked at the paper on my desk and the one on my screen. The numbers didn't match. The difference wasn't massive—only $3000, which, for a six-digit net profit was barely noticeable.

This finding encouraged me to go further, and I scribbled the correct number on the paper I had as I searched for the names of a few more junior accountants across various divisions and regions.

I stopped after five more discrepancies, which was more than enough to prove to Alessandro this was not a fluke and more than enough for him to investigate further.

It wasn't much each time—between $1500 and $4000, depending on the profit—but assuming it was the same from every division and location, I was sure that everything put together would be an astronomical number.

My phone beeped just as a chat box with Alessandro's name popped onto the computer screen.

What are you doing in the office so late? I would have thought he would be thrilled. It's not like I wasn't doing this often.

I glanced at the clock and grimaced. It was almost ten, and I'd lost track of time. I didn't need to be a mind reader to know what the text would say.

I disregarded the text, figuring I'd deal with the guilt and reproach later.

I found something important I'd like to show you. I frowned as I looked toward his office which was obviously empty. ***Where are you?*** I added, knowing the only way for him to use the company chat was for him to be somewhere inside the building.

Sub-basement 2.

I scoffed. ***You're joking right?*** No way he was on the maintenance and basement floor. What would he even do there?

Do I have a habit of making jokes?
Yes, actually, he did.
If you need me, I'm in sub-basement 2. If not, have a good night, Miss Matthews.
I arched my brows. *Miss Matthews?* Why was he acting so formally all of the sudden? I shook my head; I was not interested in trying to decipher his little moods tonight.
On my way.
I took all the papers I just printed, as well as the one I wrote on. I tried to come up with a coherent speech to explain why I broke about twenty corporate rules with diverse degrees of gravity to discover a serious case of embezzlement, which I was sure had been going on for years.
"Mr. Benetti, I know I've discovered something that... No." I shook my head. That was not the right way to start. "Mr. Benetti, I've been suspecting something for a while and—" The elevator beeped, announcing its arrival. "Here goes nothing," I muttered on a sigh, pulling my bag higher on my shoulder, then turned left, following the echo of voices and faint light.
I seriously needed to have a conversation with him again about boundaries and what was acceptable professionally. Making a woman go to the basement in the middle of the night definitely wasn't cool.
And yet, you went... Who's the idiot here?
"Seriously, I think—" I started to chastise him as I opened the door, but the words died as all rational thoughts escaped me, replaced by an immediate, vicious dread. I watched, horrified, as Alessandro Benetti put a bullet right in the middle of a bloody man's forehead, who then slumped while tied to a chair.

Alessandro turned toward me, and he didn't look like my haughty, condescending boss anymore. No, he looked like death.

"You were not supposed to see that," he said with a tone that was eerily calm for someone who had just committed murder.

He nodded at something behind me, and I felt a sharp pain before everything went black.

CHAPTER 3

Alessandro

Fuck! I thought as I stared at Matthews' unconscious form on the floor.

I wasn't sure if it was all by karmic design, but I should have known better than to expect a bad day to end in nothing less than disaster.

I looked up and glared at Lorenzo, who stood behind her, his gun in his hand.

He shrugged. "What? I had to do something!"

"I'm not sure hitting her on the head with your gun was the solution," I commented. I knew I was not being fair; hell, I'd probably do the same if I'd been in his position and if it hadn't been Matthews.

No, actually, I would have probably shot the person, and I should have felt grateful that she was only unconscious.

My nostrils flared with annoyance as I looked down at her, making sure there wasn't any blood gushing from her head.

I put my gun back in my holster and turned toward the man leaning against the back wall, hiding in the shadows... Domenico Romano. Matthews' fate was sealed now; there was no turning back.

When I came back today, I'd been aggravated when my secretary told me way too gleefully that Matthews had vanished to accounting 'once again.' I wasn't sure what her deal was with pasty, gangly, boring, vanilla, bland boys, but it seemed they were her taste of choice.

I'd been pissed on my way down there; I couldn't afford for her to have any distractions. I needed her full attention, her whole time. She was a crucial part of my organization and she seemed to be hellbent on looking for distractions.

It had already been a pain to get rid of the stupid baby accountant and send him across the sea for a job that didn't even exist. I just didn't think I could pull off something like that twice.

I was angry at her for not appreciating what she already had in her life. Seriously, she had everything she needed to be fulfilled! A prestigious job with an insanely high salary, and an apartment way above her means. What more could she possibly want? Why did she need a boyfriend, too? Especially the kind she was sniffing around. These men had nothing to offer her, but she was blind to all of it.

Then she gave me attitude, refusing to stay late to work, which added some aggravation to my anger. I snapped just a little, just for a minute, but I didn't miss the fear in her eyes as she took a step back. I'd shown her a glimpse of my other side—the one that belonged in the darkness I lived in—and I realized it was not something she could have handled. Matthews would never know about our mafia connections.

She was able to deal with the cold, mean, unfeeling corporate king. That was something I honestly didn't think was even possible when she stormed into my office trying so hard to hide her pain and limp.

In retrospect, it should have been a hint that she could. She stood tall in my office and told me everything she thought, chastising me as if I was a naughty little boy, not a man so rich and powerful that I could destroy her just for fun. And she did all that while in pain and feeling apprehensive. That woman was a warrior, and for that, she'd always have my endless admiration, even if I'd rather get shot in the kneecaps than admit it out loud to anyone.

I balled my hands into fists when she left, forcing myself to remain in place as my whole body hummed with frustration and the desire to grab her and force her to show me the admiration and respect she owed me.

I felt the muscles in my jaw tremble almost painfully as I ground my teeth. She refused to tell me where she was going. What did she have to hide? I'd have to put one of my men on her trail, if only for security reasons and to ensure Matteo's suspicions were unfounded.

Matteo... That brought me back to reality really fast. There was no way that tonight's events didn't go up to his ear before the night was over—especially not when Domenico Romano, who was both Gianluca's *consigliere* and Matteo's brother, happened to have witnessed the whole thing.

I turned toward him, and he was looking grimly at Matthews' limp form on the floor. His dark eyes carried a certain compassion that would never have been found in his brother's eyes.

I had no choice. I had to kill her or induce her, and knowing Matthews, she'd refuse to be induced quietly and would end up being shot.

I tensed as the hint of dread for the woman on the floor unexpectedly took grip of my heart. I would not hurt her, but nothing stopped them from doing so, and with Matteo's immunity, I could not even do anything.

If only Domenico had not been here, but as I got ready to put my man on her, my phone rang and it was Domenico. He told me the lead he'd been following concerning their port issues had actually brought him to Chicago, and a low-life New Yorker loan thug who was drooling on the daughter of a rich arms dealer with a few very lucrative government contracts located in Chicago. The same arms dealer who was the brother of the freshly elected Governor of New York... A little bit too convenient for a coincidence, if you asked me.

As the rules dictated, Domenico asked me permission to seek justice on my territory, and I offered my assistance. That was the reason why I was in this basement, having just put a bullet in the head of the idiotic thug in front of my way too innocent assistant.

I ran my hand over my face. *What a fucking mess.*

"Should I ask the team to get rid of her at the same time as the body?" Lorenzo asked, looking down at Matthews

My frown deepened as my hand twitched to reach for the gun at my side and shoot him, *consigliere* or not.

"*Attento,*" Dom warned me, letting his gaze go from my hand to the holster, showing me that my pulsion was showing. "We'll deal with her." He then turned to get Lorenzo's attention. "Go get the cleaning team."

Lorenzo straightened, his jaw ticking visibly, letting me know he was more than annoyed at being ordered by a *consigliere* of another *famiglia*. Technically, since they were both *consiglieres,* Lorenzo had authority over Domenico in this territory.

I shook my head. I didn't have the time to deal with his fragile ego today.

"Do as he says, and I'll deal with her."

Lorenzo threw one last poisonous glare at Dom before he picked up his phone and muttered something in Italian as he exited the room. The only word I picked up was *cavolo,* which basically meant bullshit.

"He's clearly a fan of mine," Dom said placidly, obviously not fazed to be on Lorenzo's shit list.

I waved my hand dismissively. "Don't worry. Lorenzo hates everyone."

"Even you?"

I laughed. "Especially me." It was true, Lorenzo and I never saw eye to eye. He had been my father's *consigliere* after his own father died, and now he was mine. I didn't think he approved of my more modern ways to direct the *famiglia*, especially agreeing for my sister to marry a *yakuza* when he thought that honor should have been his.

Dom arched an eyebrow. "Yet you keep him as your *consigliere.*"

I shrugged. "He was already in place before my father's death, and I'd rather have him since I know what to expect. He's predictable, defenseless."

Dom nodded thoughtfully. "Be careful with the ones who seem to be harmless… they're usually the most dangerous. We learned that the hard way," he added while subconsciously rubbing the side of his stomach.

I was not sure what the full story was, but I knew there had been some turmoil in New York a couple of years ago.

A moan made us both turn toward Matthews, and I felt an abnormally large relief at seeing her stir.

"I'll handle it," Dom said, taking a syringe out of his pocket.

I grabbed his arm firmly as he moved in front of me. "Do not hurt her."

His lips quivered at the corner in a little knowing smirk. "I wouldn't dream of it."

He crouched beside her, and I held my breath as he uncapped the needle and stuck it into her jugular. "Sleep tight, little one," he murmured with such gentleness that I barely recognized his voice. "I know she's an innocent," he kept his position beside her, "but it doesn't change anything. I'll have to tell Luca and Matteo."

"I know. I'll deal with it."

Dom cocked his head to the side, detailing me. "I can give you a day or two."

I nodded. "There's no need; don't get yourself into trouble." I had no clue what to do with her and having an extra day or two would not make any difference.

I had to take her away, somewhere where Matteo would not see her as a threat and where he couldn't reach her. I needed to take her someplace where I'd have time to figure out what to do about her. A place where she couldn't escape while I tried to make her understand that she didn't need to always be so self-righteous.

"Why do you look so defeated?" Dom asked, standing as the cleaning team rushed in to take care of the body still tied to the chair.

"Do I?" I asked as he came to stand beside me. We both watched as the team efficiently erased any trace of what happened here.

Dom chuckled but it lacked mirth. "It's easy to see when you've been there too, but you know, for what it's worth, women are much more resilient than you may think."

I frowned, turning toward him. "Do you mean about the whole mafia thing?" I knew Matthews was resilient. Fuck, she worked for me and stood up to me; she carried her disabilities and pain with so much strength that it left me in awe sometimes.

He shrugged. "About anything." He buried his hands in his pockets. "Women are a force of nature, and I can tell you they are so much more understanding than we give them credit for... especially in the name of love."

I took a step back in surprise. "What does love have to do with anything here? She's my assistant, a damned good one, and I'm not in the business to hurt innocents."

I spoke before thinking, and I knew the blow landed as Dom's face morphed into a wince for a second.

"Dom, it's not—"

He cleared his throat with a shake of the head. "I have to go. I still have a lot to cover, and Matteo will be waiting." He reached into his pocket and gave me another syringe.

How many of those things did he have readily available?

"It's easier and less messy when you don't attract attention," he said, replying to my unspoken question. He jerked his head toward Matthews on the floor. "Based on her size, I'd say you're good for five, maybe six hours. I don't know how long you need her out of commission, so use this one just in case—half would be enough but beware of the headache."

I nodded, rolling the syringe around my fingers as I went through all my options.

"Why was she even here?" I asked more to myself than anything else. She had no business being in this basement; she never should have witnessed what she just did. Nobody came to this basement in the eight years we used it. It was too impossible to be just sheer bad luck.

"I'd say that's something you need to figure out... and fast." He straightened up as Lorenzo came back, the room now clear of the dead body and any trace of what had happened, except for the innocent woman asleep on the floor.

Lorenzo still sported his dark glare as he looked at Dom, who straightened his jacket, buttoning it slowly as if he were immune to Lorenzo's animosity. Truth be told, I suspected he really didn't care.

"I'll go now. I assume the security cameras are still playing on a loop?" he asked me.

I looked at Lorenzo for the answer.

Lorenzo snorted. "Of course, it is. Who do you take us for? Amateurs?" He curled his lips, baring his teeth at Dom like a rabid dog.

I cocked my head to the side. Maybe this one needed to be put down after all...

Dom's lips lifted into a little smile, which I knew irked Lorenzo even more. "I'll see you soon, *amico*," he said before patting my shoulder in a friendly gesture.

He took off in the direction of the door, stopping a couple of seconds beside Matthews, giving her a thoughtful look tinged with pity.

And she deserved that pity, because now, one way or another, her life would never be the same.

He looked back at me. "You can expect a call from Matteo in the next day or so."

"I don't expect anything less."

I waited for him to leave before I approached Matthews and crouched down, sliding my arms under her body and lifting her. Damn, she was light. So much lighter than I expected.

I nudged her up a bit so her head rested against my shoulder before looking down at her, finally taking a few seconds to really detail her. Why was she even wearing such a sexy dress? That was not like her, and it grated me the wrong way to see her be anything other than herself. Who was she trying to entice by dressing like that? Who was the fool who thought she was not good enough as she usually was.

"Why did you let him order me around?"

I sighed internally. I should have known better than to expect something less from Lorenzo.

I looked up from the load in my arms to Lorenzo, who had his arms crossed on his chest.

"I had other things on my mind," I replied as calmly as possible, nudging Matthews a little for emphasis.

"Still, she's only an insignificant assistant; I'm *consigliere*, Sandro." He looked down at the floor with a deep scowl.

Oh god, was he actually pouting? I would never understand why my father picked him, even if he was the heir apparent of his father. He was my age, with the behavior and sensitivity of a rowdy teenager.

"I'm sorry, Lorenzo. I will have a word with Luca about Domenico's behavior." *When pigs fly.*

"What are you going to do with her?" he asked with obvious disdain.

"That's for me to worry about," I replied with authority, reminding him of his place.

I exited the room and carried my cargo to the elevator. Once I was in, I released my facade and closed my eyes, letting the full extent of my weariness wash over me.

I knew what I had to do—something I swore I'd never do for *anyone*. I had to take her where I kept my biggest weakness, my most treasured gift. I had to take her to my secret Eden...

I was taking her to the island.

CHAPTER 4

Lily

I turned in my bed as a dull headache resided at the back of my skull, despite the soothing sound of the ocean in the background and the cooling breeze gently brushing my legs.

I stopped mid-turn and fell back on the bed. Since when did we have the ocean and cooling breeze in Chicago? The breeze in Chicago was angrier, the honking sounds more aggressive than the sounds of the ocean, and the hotdog smell was noticeably absent.

I had to be dreaming, that was the only explanation. But if I were dreaming, would I even be conscious that I was dreaming?

I opened my eyes with difficulty, as if I'd just been woken from a deep sleep. My vision was blurry, and I blinked a few times, concentrating on the ceiling above me.

I sighed. Yep, definitely a dream because that wasn't my plain white ceiling, it was a beautiful wooden ceiling with a matching fan. I turned my head, looking at the cream walls and the open French doors leading to a balcony that seemed to overlook the bluest ocean I'd ever seen.

I moved my hand and something that was beside me fell with a dull *thud*.

I sat up suddenly as the sound brought back the events of the night before. The party I missed, the embezzlement I discovered, and worst of all, my boss being a cold-blooded killer.

I sat on the side of the bed, my heart hammering so hard I could feel it in my throat, deaf to any other noise than the furious beat in my ears.

I stood and swayed a little as nausea hit me. It felt like I was getting seasick while standing firmly on the ground.

I grabbed the canopy with the mosquito net to steady myself and padded to the door, uncaring that I had no shoes, bag, or even the slightest idea of where I was. All I wanted was to get away from here.

I pushed the handle, but the door remained closed. I tried again and nudged it a little with no more success.

I am locked in?! I let out a little tearless sob as I took a couple of steps back, staring at the offending door standing between me and freedom.

I turned toward the opened French doors and ran to the balcony, barely noticing the hot tiles under my bare feet and the stunning view of the deep blue sea.

I leaned over the railing, trying to figure a way to climb down, but a straight cliff was below me.

I leaned over the other side, knowing it was futile one way or another. And even if there was a way to climb down, I was not even sure I could even climb over the high railing with my legs.

I let out a little frustrated cry as tears started to prickle my eyes and run down my cheeks.

I pressed my body against the front of the railing and considered, if only for a few seconds, grabbing a chair from the room and just jumping down. How far of a drop could it be? I used to be an excellent swimmer; I still was actually, since water always eased the pain in my legs. What was this? A hundred feet? Would I even survive the plunge?

"The fall would most likely kill you."

I swirled around at the familiar deep voice that had just answered my unspoken question.

Here was my boss, Alessandro Benetti, dressed in a way I've never seen before. I let my eyes trail up from his bare feet, his pair of khaki shorts revealing tanned, muscular legs, and a matching linen shirt, half unbuttoned, that revealed a similarly tanned chest that was even more perfectly sculpted than in my most secret fantasies.

I stopped at his face, taking in his wet hair—probably from a recent shower—and easy side smile. He looked like someone I'd never met before. He was not Alessandro Benetti, the cold, calculating millionaire and killer.

I gripped the railing behind me as I took a step back, the wood biting painfully into my back.

His gaze quickly flicked to my hands before looking back at me again. "It would be a shame for you to fall and die after all I did to save you."

He took a step toward me, and my heart stalled as I tried to take another step back.

"Don't," I said, my voice cracking with fear.

He stopped immediately and frowned as if I offended him. "I'm not going to hurt you."

I let out a humorless laugh as I looked around the balcony and only saw water. "I-I saw you…" I said and winced. I was not used to so much sun and heat, especially wearing a dress that was not appropriate.

"Just come in. You're turning red."

I shook my head as sweat dropped into my eyes, making them burn. I blinked furiously a few times, not comfortable with not seeing him.

"Matthews, just come in," he ordered, his tone matching the CEO I knew.

"No!" I replied stubbornly, knowing I was probably minutes away from heatstroke.

"Manageria miseria!" he muttered, running his hand through his hair. "Listen, if I wanted you dead, you'd be dead."

I opened my mouth and closed it again. Despite how messed up it was, I could not deny his logic.

He took a few steps back, raising his hands. "I'll stand by the door. What do you say? It's the same distance." He rolled his eyes. "*Dai*!" He gestured me in. "I'll be really angry if you pass out, and then who will be protecting you?"

That set me into motion, and I took a few quick steps forward and stopped just when I reached the blissful shade of the room.

"See?" He smirked. "You're still alive."

"You killed someone!" I hissed, pointing an accusing finger at him.

He shrugged. "He was a bad person."

"I... Are you a criminal?" *Of course, he is, you dumbass. He shot someone right between the eyes!*

"It depends on what you mean by 'criminal.'"

Fear subsided, making room for irritation. I hated when he did that. Give me all his elusive answers that make me question my own intelligence. In retrospect, maybe it has been for a good reason.

"Someone who commits a crime."

"It's a bit reductive, don't you think? Even a little offensive, I'd say." He crossed his arms on his chest."

"Offen—" I snorted. "Oh, I'm *so* sorry!" I sneered, walking further into the room and closer to him without even thinking about it.

He shrugged. "It's okay. Give me a kiss and I'll forgive you."

"I—" I started. Did he really say that?

"A kiss... tongue optional."

He can't be serious. "You kidnapped me and took me to God knows where!" I shouted, throwing my hands up in exasperation.

"Oh, you mean a paradise island in the middle of the Pacific Ocean. Ugh, what a prison."

"I'd never kiss you, anyway," I finished rather lamely.

"Oh really?" he asked, arching an eyebrow.

His undertone made me pause, as if he was baiting me, which made me wary. This man was obviously much more cunning than I gave him credit for.

"Yes, really, and that's not the point." I started to pace the room. "You... you killed someone and now you're keeping me locked against my will. Kissing was never, and never will be, on my mind!" *Again...*

"You didn't say that when you kissed me last Christmas."

I stopped my pacing and looked at him, my mouth open with shock.

He grinned. "You remember, don't you? Because I do." He brushed his fingers against his lips.

I kept staring at him silently, the thought of my abduction put on the back burner for a minute. It was impossible... it had not been real. I woke up hungover, with a killer headache, remembering the most awkward dream.

I narrowed my eyes. No, he would have teased me tirelessly if it'd been true.

He let out a loud chuckle. "You do remember." He sighed. "I thought you were too drunk to remember." He twisted his mouth to the side. "You're a real lightweight, though. Who would have thought two glasses of champagne would have made you drunk."

It was probably because I'd never had alcohol in my life—not after I saw it destroy my world in a minute. I was awkward at parties but Alessandro made it mandatory for me to go. I'd been so nervous that I'd barely eaten anything that day, and then...

"I don't know what you're talking about."

"Let me tell you, then. You were not walking straight and got much too comfortable with the pasty accountant's filthy hands." His upper lip curled for just a second as his nostrils flared. "I kept an eye on you; I wanted to make sure your honor remained untouched."

My heart warmed at his attention. I'd never thought he would care for my wellbeing.

"I mean, I could not have an assistant with the reputation of a slut, could I?"

Ah yep, that was more like it.

He shrugged. "So, I came and swept you away, and as I secured the seatbelt..." He took a step toward me that I mirrored with a step back. "You leaned forward and brushed that little freckle-covered nose against my jawline. When I turned around to look at you, you kissed me... twice." He raised two fingers with a taunting smile. "And then you said, '*Alessandro Benetti, you are too sexy for my sanity. My panties get all wet every time I see you. Please take me now,*'" he added with a ridiculously high-pitched voice I presumed was supposed to be mine.

I blushed crimson, both for the kiss I thought had been nothing more than a dream and for his words, which despite being untrue, did reflect some of my nightly thoughts.

"This is *not* what I said!" I snapped, stomping my foot for emphasis.

"No, you didn't." His smile turned predatory. "But your eyes did, and now I know for a fact you remember everything."

I was mortified because I believed his words.

I moved to the side to help myself to a glass of water from the pitcher on the console, and he took a step to stand right in my line of sight, reminding me that, despite the banter, I was here against my will.

"Let me go, please?" I asked with all seriousness.

His smirk faded and his face took on a seriousness I've rarely seen. "I can't."

"Of course, you can! You can just move out of my way."

He shook his head. "I went to quite some length to keep you alive. And I'm not about to let you leave this island and get shot."

I opened my mouth to tell him that I'd take my chances on whatever he thought was a danger to me. *He* was the coldblooded killer here; he could pretend to be the savior as much as he wanted. *He* was the only one to blame for the situation I was in.

"Dad?"

We both turned toward the door at the small voice.

"Dad?" the voice called again, getting closer.

I looked at Alessandro, my brow etched in confusion. *Dad?* I mouthed.

"Dad, are you in here?" The little boy's voice was directly behind the door.

Alessandro paled, his eyes wide with an apprehension I've never seen before—which actually made him look even more human.

"He doesn't know anything... Please, Lily, I'm begging you," he whispered with urgency before turning toward the door. "Yes?" His voice was rougher than usual as he directed his voice to the door.

I was too shocked to even compute everything. Alessandro had a child, and I didn't even think he realized that he called me Lily—something he had not done once in the eighteen months I'd been working for him.

The cutest little boy opened the door and wheeled himself in, throwing a curious, speculating look from his father to me.

There was no denying that this little boy was Alessandro's. He had the same dark hair, the same air of authority—probably due to his matching high cheekbones and straight nose. Yep, that boy was a mini-Alessandro, except for his big green eyes.

He stopped his wheelchair beside his father but kept his eyes on me. "Hi, I'm Pietro," he said, holding his head high.

I couldn't help the thawing of my heart at the fierceness in his face.

Alessandro sighed. "Matthews, this is my son, Pietro. Pietro, this is my assistant, Matthews."

The little boy's eyes widened. "You're Matthews?!"

I nodded slowly, unsure what he'd heard about me.

"Matthews is a *girl*?" Pietro asked his father, finally breaking eye contact. "I heard you talk to Aunt Violet, and you said Matthews was a hard-ass who drove you crazy but was much too good at the job—"

"It's fine, Pietro!" Alessandro interrupted him.

I narrowed my eyes a little before looking down, unable to contain my smile at the light flush on Alessandro's face.

"What did I tell you about listening to conversations that you are not a part of?"

"Don't do it..." Pietro mumbled.

"Well, sharing what you hear should not be done either, and..." he looked at his watch before crossing his arms on his chest, "what are you doing here? Aren't you supposed to be in science class?"

Pietro's green eyes stayed on me as he shrugged. "The internet connection is not working."

"Isn't it? Is it because there's an actual problem or because someone used his aluminum trick to make the modem go off."

I couldn't help but smile at that, even if I knew that it would only encourage Pietro's naughty behavior.

He gave me a little matching smile and Alessandro let out a frustrated sigh.

"Don't encourage him! It stopped being funny a long time ago."

My eyes paused by the control of his wheelchair, and I smiled again at the Starfleet badge logo sticker he put there.

"You know how in *Star Trek* they use teleportation to go everywhere?" I started to relax a little more and finally grabbed the glass of water I'd been craving.

His eyes widened and his features lit up at the mention of something he was so obviously a fan of. The more I looked, the more it was obvious—even his wheels have been designed to look like the Enterprise.

"Yes!"

"Would you believe me if I told you that it's actually possible?"

He rolled his eyes and shook his head. "You're pulling my leg."

I couldn't help but laugh. Who even said things like that anymore? "No, I swear. You see, all living organisms emit a constant current of photons as a means to direct instantaneous nonlocal signals from one part of the body to another and to the outside world."

"Okay…" He leaned forward on his chair, clearly engrossed.

"Well, in 1993, an international group of six scientists showed that perfect teleportation is possible in principle, or at least, it's not against the laws of physics. More recently, scientists both in the US and China have been trying. Chinese scientists were able to 'teleport' photons to a satellite 300 miles away, using a phenomenon called 'Quantum Entanglement'."

He narrowed his eyes at me, not sure if he could believe me or not.

"We can't move people yet, but now they know how to move not only photons, but also electrons, so who knows?"

"How come they didn't teach me that during my course?" he asked, his eyes narrowing to slits.

I had to do my best not to laugh at the suspicion in his tone. This kid was not Alessandro's child for nothing.

I gave Alessandro a look and saw he was watching me and Pietro with a light of amusement in his eyes and a little carefree smile on his lips. I had to admit, seeing him like this made him even more beautiful, if that was at all possible.

"Can you tell me the difference between a photon and an electron?"

"No," he said with a scowl on his sweet face.

"Ah, and can you tell me what quantum physics is?" I asked, knowing it was unfair as it was something I knew only because I took AP physics back in high school.

His scowl deepened and he crossed his arms over his chest. "No."

I nodded. "See? You need to know all the boring stuff before you get to the cool stuff. So," I twisted my mouth on the side and gave him a little shrug, "it's up to you, but if you don't get the boring stuff, you'll never find out about all the cool stuff, like teleportation and time travel."

"We can't do time travel!" he exclaimed, throwing his arms up in the air. His leg slid down his footrest from the sudden movement, but he lifted it back up before I even had a chance to help.

I tried to keep the surprise out of my face at his ability to move his leg. Maybe his handicap was more similar to mine than I thought.

"Yes, we can. We did it with the Large Hadron Collider in Switzerland, but you know what, that's a conversation for another time. Go to your science class."

He nodded, visibly much more eager to go now. "We'll talk later, right?"

"Yes, of course!" I replied, not even having to force the smile I was giving this little boy. "We can talk about all the cool *Star Trek* stuff."

"I like you!" he exclaimed.

I took a couple of steps toward him. "I like you, too."

He turned toward his father. "I like her. She's so much cooler than your other friends."

"So, it seems," Alessandro replied, looking down at his son but throwing me a sideways look.

"See you later, Matthews!" Pietro said with a wave before leaving the room.

Once he was gone and the door clicked shut behind him, Alessandro turned toward me

"Thank you," he said before pursing his lips. I didn't expect it to be something he often said and meant.

I waved my hand dismissively. Now was not the time for this. "How old is he?"

He remained silent for a couple of seconds, obviously not expecting the question. "Ten. What do you know?"

I suspected he was back at the conversation we were having before Pietro's interruption. "Nothing. How come I never knew you had a child?"

He raised an eyebrow, probably taken aback by the accusation in my tone—a tone I had to admit, surprised even myself.

"I don't remember us being friends or anything. Now answer the question."

"I'll answer if you answer mine." I jutted my chin in challenge. "You don't just... hide a child! Are—" I stopped, hoping that what I feared was not true. "Are you ashamed of him because of his challenges?"

His face morphed from mild annoyance at my difficult attitude to plain anger, and I took a step back in apprehension.

"What did you say?" he hissed between his teeth, taking a threatening step toward me.

I was seeing him again... the killer from last night.

"I-I..." I took another step back. "I just thi—"

"You don't know anything!" His nostrils flared as his dark orbs burned with so much offense that I felt like cowering and apologizing all at once. I didn't know if it was by miracle or sheer stupidity, but I forced myself to keep my eyes locked with his. "That boy is probably the most precious thing in my life, my greatest pride, and I will kill anyone who even considers causing him any pain."

My heart stalled in my chest, but it was not in fear—despite the barely veiled threat. No, I was in awe at seeing Alessandro Benetti's human side, and seeing how powerful that man could love when I had suspected for many months that he was heartless.

"Now tell me what you know because if you don't—"

"You'll kill me?"

He threw his hands up in exasperation and started a full rant in Italian that I couldn't understand, though based on his gestures and budging muscles in his jaw, it was enough to hint that it was a tirade about how idiotic and irresponsible I was.

"You were not supposed to be in that basement."

I cocked my head forward as if he was missing something. "You made me go there."

"No, I didn't." He shook his head

"Yes, you did!"

"No, I didn't. I—"

"You sent me a mes—"

"Can you just stop arguing for two damn minutes?!" he snapped. "It will go a whole lot faster if you just, for once in your life, shut up and let me speak."

I opened my mouth and closed it again. "I don't always argue, do I?" I winced. *Maybe I did...*

"You received a message from my private chat, but it was not me and frankly, I was even a little offended you could have presumed it was from me. Since when do I call you Miss?" He snorted.

I pursed my lips, crossing my arms on my chest. "I thought maybe you had some manners."

He rolled his eyes. "The person who did that to you wanted you dead. We never leave witnesses behind; we don't leave loose ends. We're careful, which is why we have been around for much longer than most and will last when others fail."

"Who is '*we*'?" I asked, already knowing the answer.

"You know... of course you know."

I shook my head. *Mafia, of course*. It made so much sense.

"I didn't sign up for this! I didn't sign up for any of this!"

"I know, and I'm sorry. I knew that—" He stopped and looked behind me at the sea. "I should have done something before, but I never thought you'd last so long. I'm quite insufferable."

Understatement of the year! But it was not the time to discuss his qualities as a boss or a human.

"If that person wanted me dead, then why am I still here?" I blurted out, wishing I could kick myself almost immediately. I was still very good at defying the odds it seemed, but there was no need to tempt fate.

"Do you *want* me to kill you?" He let out a sigh when I remained silent. "I brought you here instead."

"Where is *here*?" I asked, turning around to look at the stunning sea. "I'm not..." I turned around to look at him again. "I'm not saying I'm not grateful that you didn't kill me." That was a messed-up sentence if I ever heard one. "But I can't stay, I have to go home. My parents will be worried, Katia will be worried. I..." I shook my head. "I have to go."

He waved his hand dismissively. "Don't worry. Everything has been handled."

My heart stalled in my chest as the heat of the room was replaced by the icy chill of cold sweat. "Did you...?"

"Kill them?" He nodded. "Of course!"

All the blood drained from my body, causing a wave of nausea so powerful that I lost my balance and had to grab the console beside me to stay up.

"Are you ser—" He let out a growl of frustration. "Of course, I didn't kill them! I used the voice system to send them a voicemail with your voice to tell them you were traveling with your boss and only had access to emails for the next few weeks. Seriously, who do you think I am?"

"A killer, and obviously a fucking sociopath!" I shouted, my eyes prickling with tears of relief. "Who even jokes about killing people?!"

"Come on, it was funny." He grinned, burying his hands in his pockets.

"No, it wasn't."

"A little funny?" he asked, bringing his forefinger and thumb close to each other.

"*Humph*! I'm out of here!" I tried to pass him, but he grabbed my wrist—not enough to hurt me but enough to let me know that I was not leaving this room anytime soon. I looked down at his hand around my wrist; I couldn't really remember the last time he'd touched me.

"Even if I let you get out of this room, there's nowhere to go. This is my island, and we're in the middle of the Pacific Ocean. We're twenty miles from the mainland and the boats are heavily protected. You're welcome to try to swim to the mainland, some people probably could do it. Well... that is, if you don't meet one of our friendly sharks."

I looked up from his hand. "You know I can't stay here forever, right? If that's the case, I would rather choose death."

He let go of my wrist and ran his hand in his hair, looking at me silently, a sort of resignation in his eyes that concerned me.

"I-I won't say anything," I offered, sitting at the foot of the bed. "I swear I won't." I looked straight into his eyes, hoping I was conveying the veracity of my words. I'd never be stupid enough to speak against organized crime. "If you bring me back to Chicago, I'll just go home. I'll disappear from your life and forget we even met. I swear I will."

He rubbed his stubble, doubt and something I could not quite pinpoint flashing in his eyes.

He let out a weary sigh, then sat on the chair across from my bed, showing me a little gesture of trust—allowing me to run out of the room but trusting me not to.

My body was tense, the damaged muscles in my leg twitching painfully as my fight-or-flight instinct screamed for me to run, despite my rational mind knowing I had nowhere to go.

"Even if I believed you and, honestly, I'm having a hard time with that." He raised his hand to stop me from contradicting him. "I know you think that now, you may even believe it, but Matthews, I know you, I really do. I know that after a couple of weeks, you'll start questioning your choice. You're one of the most outstanding, fair, and aggravatingly good people I know. I'm not sure you could go against your grain, but even if you could, the big boss won't see things like that. He'll kill you and everyone else you might have spoken to just because you're a potential threat, and there will be nothing I can do to protect you."

Despite everything, I felt a pinch of pride in my heart. I never thought he had such a high opinion of me, and he'd just said that so casually, as if it was evidence.

"The only way I could help you is if you told me why someone within our organization would want you dead."

"What about the boss who wants to cut loose ends?" I winced.

"I'll deal with him in due time, but first, I need you to talk to me. I know you don't trust me, but honestly, you're out of options."

I nodded. I was on a deserted island with my criminal boss and his son with no way to reach anyone, and even if I did, I'd put them in danger, too. And most of all, even after everything that man had just done to me, I still trusted him, maybe even more than I did before.

Does this mean I'm crazy? Without a doubt.

"Okay." And then I told him everything I'd suspected.

CHAPTER 5

Alessandro

Embezzlements. Of all the things I could have expected, that was not one of them. It was just so... common, so basic, and so very, *very* stupid.

It had been three days since Matthews admitted what she knew, and I was not closer to really understanding this whole mess.

Somebody wanted Matthews dead for something as silly as a white-collar crime. Something that, if you were rich enough, wouldn't even cause jail time anymore, but this one was so much more complicated because even if the perfect suspect—my CFO—had so conveniently disappeared, he could not the source of it all.

Firstly, because he was too smart to instigate something like that, and secondly, because he had no way of knowing I'd be in the basement that night. Few people knew, but the ones who did were too high within our organization for me to just go out, all guns blazing. I needed a plan, and I needed Byrne alive at least for a little while—long enough for him to tell me, on record, who he was partnering with.

I leaned back on my chair, letting out a growl of frustration. I'd acted on impulse, deciding to take her to the island and to this side of my life. I was now stuck here with barely anyone I could trust in Chicago. I had a rotten apple close to the top, and who was to say how many others were infected?

I rolled my eyes, knowing I needed to ask one of the only men outside the *famiglia* I trusted implicitly for help. The man who would never cause me any harm—not because he liked me or respected me, but because he was in absolute adoration with my sister, who luckily, loved me dearly.

I scrolled down my contact list and stopped on my brother-in-law's name, *Hoka Nishimura*, head of the *yakuza* across the whole US.

"Here goes nothing," I muttered, pressing the dial.

"*Ani*, I think you dialed the wrong number," he said as way of greeting, but his voice was light and amused. He knew how it irritated me when he called me Ani, which meant brother.

I took a deep breath, fighting the urge to correct him again. "No. I actually wanted to talk to you."

"Oh? I am quite entertaining, I agree."

"I've got a rotten apple." It cost me to admit it, but somehow, it was easier with him, especially knowing he went through something similar not so long ago.

"What do you need?" The amusement was gone from his tone and he was back in the *yakuza* skin. "Do you want us to take Pietro earlier this year?"

"No, Pietro's safe, but I need you to find someone who conveniently disappeared from Chicago."

"No problem. Just give me a name and I'll get the east clan on it."

"Fitzgerald Byrnes, my CFO." The words 'former' and 'deceased' will be soon added to his fancy title.

"A civilian?"

"A dirty one," I admitted, not wanting to give too many details over the phone and while my office door was open.

"I always told you never to work with the Irish; they're slimy."

I shook my head. It was hilarious how different mafia families could be prejudiced toward the others. "You never said that."

"Well, I thought about telling you, which is basically the same thing."

Pietro's loud laughter drifted into my office, and I froze on my seat with surprise. I've heard my son laugh before, but never like that.

"Is that the little man?" Hoka asked, his voice tinged with soft affection. It was another reason why I would go to war with that man if he asked me to. He loved my sister and my son, and I knew that when Pietro was going there over the summer, he was treated as one of their own.

"It was…" I replied with confusion as I stood and walked to the door, trying to peek as to what could make him laugh like that.

"Who's there?"

I frowned. "Why can't I make my son laugh like that?"

Matthews suddenly laughed too, and against all odds, my spirits lifted almost immediately at both their joy, leaving all the worry and poison of my world behind.

"Is that a woman?" Hoka asked with a tone that seemed to suggest it was impossible.

"It's a long story," I replied gruffly.

"It's okay; I've got the time... Lay it on me, big boy. Does little Sandro have a girlfriend? Oh, I'll need to tell Violet; she'll be so happy!"

I muttered a string of Italian insults I knew he wouldn't understand to ease my irritation. "Find Byrne and then we talk."

"You'll tell me about the girl?"

"Sure." *Nope*.

Matthews said something to Pietro, and they laughed again.

"Oh my god! It's Matthews, isn't it?! I knew you had the h—"

"Goodbye, Hoka!" I hung up before my brother-in-law managed to dim the levity I felt.

I slid the phone into my back pocket and padded to the source of the voices and laughter.

I stopped a few steps from the open space kitchen, half-hidden behind one of the wooden pillars.

Pietro was using his standing frame instead of his wheelchair—something he usually hated to use. He said it made him feel even more different than his wheelchair did, and yet...

My heart tightened in my chest to the point of pain at seeing my little boy looking so happy, so carefree, and part of me was shamefully jealous that the woman he met only three days ago was the one who managed to bring him a piece of his much-needed childhood.

"Are you sure that's what the recipe says?" Matthews asked, tapping the wooden spoon against the side of the big glass bowl full of batter. She looked like a complete mess with her hair in a messy bun and dressed in one of the ill-fitted yellow summer dresses I'd bought for her before we boarded the boat from San José de David. I really needed to find her something better, and soon.

She leaned toward Pietro, who rested his phone against his chest.

"Don't you trust me?" he asked with a giggle.

"I think you went too far when you said two cups of chocolate chips. Rookie mistake." She winked at him and popped a chocolate chip into her mouth.

I took a step back and to the side to get a better look at her face spattered with batter and flour. I shifted and knocked over one of the stupid plant Rosita insisted on leaving around the house.

They both stopped laughing and turned toward me.

"Dad, tell Lily that the more chocolate chips in the muffin, the better it is."

I felt a sense of relief at the fact that my arrival didn't spoil the moment, at least not completely, because even if my boy still sported the brightest smile I'd ever seen, Lily tensed up as soon as she saw me. That bothered me a lot more than I was ready to admit.

"I'm not an expert, *cucciolo*, but I think you still need a bigger ratio of batter to chocolate."

Matthews nodded as she sucked her finger covered in batter, which stirred something both in my stomach and in my pants. I scowled; my stomach and below my belt didn't have any business stirring because my son was in the room and also because it was Matthews—the *perfect* Matthews, the *unattainable* Matthews.

I also didn't miss that he called her Lily. These two were bonding fast, maybe a little too fast, and I feared my little boy would be crushed when it was time for her to go back to the world, because she'd been right, of course. I couldn't keep her here forever, even if a part of me wanted to.

"What are you doing? A food fight?" I asked, pointing at the mess in the kitchen.

Matthews looked around and twisted her mouth to the side. "Oh, don't worry; I'll clean everything, I just—"

"No, this is not—" I sighed with a shake of my head. That joke failed with epic proportions. She was always so businesslike with me, except for that night at the Christmas party when I saw the intriguing little vixen she had the potential to be. I'd stayed away that night and didn't touch what she was wordlessly offering me. Firstly, because she was intoxicated, and despite what people thought of me, consent was and always would be a prerequisite; and secondly, because it would have changed everything, and that was not something I could have afforded.

"Lily let me do most of it." Pietro beamed, moving his standing attachment with a little step. "Didn't you, Lily?"

My heart burst with so much pride and love for that boy that a lump formed in my throat as unexpected tears clouded my vision.

I looked away for a second, blinking them away before turning toward them again and meeting Matthews' all-knowing eyes. Her face looked less guarded as she gazed at me with something I'd like to think was akin to tenderness and understanding.

"I did… until you tried to trick me into making chocolate with muffin instead of the other way around."

Pietro giggled as he left his phone on the counter and my smile vanished for a second as I looked at it. She had access to a phone with internet for hours now. Did she do anything? Had she called anyone? All I wanted to do was grab the phone and look through it, but I knew that it would not help my case.

"You're staying longer, right, Dad? Lily said she'd show me more recipes."

I nodded silently. I couldn't commit to any real period of time; I didn't want to scare Matthews or give Pietro false hope.

"Did Mr. Pietro here tell you that he has a video call with his doctor in fifteen minutes?" I asked, trying to change the subject and keep the lightness in my tone while still giving Pietro a stern look. I knew he hated therapy, but it was advised by all the medical professionals. I was already dreading the weekly visit of the physio tomorrow. Would I have to lock Matthews in her room to stop her from raising the alert on her captive situation? If I did that, I knew she'd never forgive me.

She glanced at the clock. "Yes, he did, which is why we're hurrying to finish the muffins. We wouldn't want Dr. Julie to wait, now would we?"

Pietro shook his head and grabbed the wooden spoon she was loosely holding and put it in his mouth.

She laughed and winked. "You're too fast for me, my padawan."

I frowned. What the hell was a padawan? Was it something from her town?

"Come on, go to your appointment, and then once you're done, you can have a warm muffin."

"Okay, but you better give me one that's extra chocolaty."

She grabbed more chocolate chips and put them on top of the muffin in the corner of the tray. "Here, we're good."

Pietro gave her his mischievous grin—one I only saw once or twice before, reminding me that my son was still just a boy.

He undid the strap around his left leg, and I moved to help him, but Matthews raised her hand to stop me. While her face was still directed toward the tray, her eyes were directed to the side, looking at him. How could she have guessed what I was about to do without even looking?

I tightened my hands into fists as I looked at my little boy, the love of my fucking life struggle to unbuckle himself and move his legs carefully, tentatively, with a certain degree of uncertainty.

It would have been so quick for me to ease everything, to make it better for him. Anger rose at Mathews letting him go through all that, and at myself for even listening to a woman who knew nothing about him and me.

I let out a little growl of frustration as I decided not to wait any longer, but she took a quick step back, standing in my path, stopping me from reaching my son.

I suddenly felt a little less remorse at locking her up in her room.

These few seconds were enough for Pietro to pull his chair closer, and he used the handle of both his stand and the wheelchair armrest to help himself into his chair.

He let himself plop on his chair with a little huff, but as he looked up, I knew his pride and joy mirrored mine.

Matthews finally turned to him and ran her finger through his hair—it was such a tender, motherly gesture.

"I'll put the stand away. Now, chop-chop, leave your phone and don't forget your juice!" she added, pointing at the fridge.

"On it!" he called and grabbed the juice before stopping beside me and giving me a half hug before going down the corridor to his bedroom.

I couldn't remember the last time Pietro reached for a hug.

I turned back toward Matthews, but I was a little deflated to see that she had her back to me, having already put the muffins in the oven and now wiping all the flour from the counter.

"It seems like there's more flour on the counter than there was in the bowl."

I saw her shoulders tensed a little at the sound of my voice as she stopped wiping the counter.

"Yes. I've got to admit, I got carried away by Pietro's enthusiasm," she said, still keeping her back to me.

I looked at her silently as she efficiently took care of the mess. I let my eyes trail down her shapely calves and bare feet. I couldn't remember ever seeing her in anything other than her ugly long skirts and oversized tops. She reminded me of the old austere headmistress from boarding school, but then I saw her in that dress the other night and the dress she was wearing today was just a little too small, showing curves I didn't know she had.

I took a couple of steps closer, as if hypnotized, wanting to let my fingers trail from the curve of her slender neck to the slope of her shoulder to see if her skin was just as smooth and soft as it appeared to be.

"I saw you look at his phone, it's on the counter. Feel free to check it. I didn't call anyone."

I blinked a few times, getting out of the weird trance the view of her skin put me in. "I didn't think you would," I lied.

She threw me a quick, knowing look over her shoulder before concentrating on putting the dirty dishes into the dishwasher.

"Why didn't you?" I couldn't help but ask. It was a fair question because, despite doing it for all the right reasons, I had abducted the woman.

She closed the door of the dishwasher and turned to face me. "I thought about it," she admitted with a nod as she threw the dish cloth over her right shoulder and leaned against the counter. "But You've done a lot of things in the time I've worked for you, but I don't think you ever lied to me. Well..." She cocked her head to the side. "You hide things, sure, but that's for obvious reasons, which I'm now regretfully aware of."

I knew she hadn't meant it as a jab, but it stung even more *because* she didn't say it for the purpose of hurting. She was just admitting, oh-so casually, that she rejected everything I was.

She waved her hand dismissively. "So, if you are telling me this was the only thing you could do to keep me safe, I believe you. I just want to be part of it all. I want to know what's happening, and how long things will take. I'd also like to call my parents, if at all possible, just to check on them."

I nodded silently, not committing to giving her access to technology. I trusted her, more than I ever trusted an outsider, but that was what she was at the end of the day... an outsider. One not committed to our values, our rules, our laws. Nothing prevented her from rethinking her shaky trust and calling the authorities, putting not only the *famiglia* in danger and a target on my back, but she could also reveal Pietro to the ruthless world I lived in, and that was not something I could ever allow. He was much too precious to be thrown into our world.

Pietro...

"He did well today, moving from his stand to his chair."

She let out a little sigh as her mouth tipped down at the corners. She was disappointed, and I wasn't sure why.

"I know," she replied, turning from me as she started to organize all the baking ingredients back into the cupboard.

"I really thought he needed help," I continued, taking another small step toward her. I was close enough now to see the faint freckles marking her shoulders.

"I know. You're his father, and it's normal for you to want to help him, but he needs to try things, he needs to find his limit. He needs to see he's much more capable than he thinks he is." Her soft tone was laced with the resignation coming with the familiarity of his situation.

I wished her back was not to me. I wanted to see her face when she said that. Matthews was an open book, so easy to read, and it frustrated me more than it should have to have lost access to her face.

If I wanted her to open up to me, I had to open up to her, too. "He has cerebral palsy."

She nodded. "He told me."

That was something else that took me by surprise. Pietro hated talking about his condition, acting like if he'd ignored it, then it would just disappear.

"He—" She cleared her throat. "He also told me his mother died giving birth to him."

"And you wondered if it's true, or if I put a bullet in her brain like the heartless killer I am." I couldn't contain the bitterness in my voice.

"It has nothing to do with me."

"Matthews, turn around, please?" I asked, barely recognizing my voice based on how deep it was. It was too much all at once.

She turned around warily, her eyes widening at my proximity.

I took a breath, but it got caught in my throat. How hadn't I noticed before how eerie her eyes were? I always saw them as muddy brown orbs judging me, but here, with the sun at this particular angle, I could actually see so much gold in them.

"I did not hurt or kill her," I said, keeping my eyes locked with hers. I wasn't sure why, but I needed her to believe me and see that the darkness and negativity she'd witnessed up until today wasn't all there was.

"Did she die giving birth to Pietro?" she whispered with uncertainty, as if she feared I'd snap. I couldn't blame her, though; I'd never been very forthcoming about anything.

I shook my head and leaned back just to make sure the corridor was empty and that Pietro's bedroom door was still firmly closed.

"I was young. Well," I cocked my head to the side, giving her a small smile, "I guess I was still older than you are, but I was twenty-five and she was a stunning model coming from Italy for a fashion show. I just…" I shrugged. "She was not who she pretended to be; she was a money grabbing drug addict, looking for a permanent wallet to feed her very expensive addiction."

"We all make mistakes," she replied gently, resting her hand lightly on my forearm. I didn't think she'd done it consciously, she was just trying to give me comfort, but I was too aware of her cool touch on my warm skin. It felt like all my nerve endings were on fire with just this innocent touch.

"I found out about her addiction and wanted to kick her to the curb, but she was already pregnant by then and we claim our blood, always." We might have been criminals and heartless most of the time, but we still had values and we were not the kind to let a child be raised without a father.

She was looking up at me, her face full of this gentle patience I'd only seen her show Pietro. It was lovely to be on the receiving end of this look... It was the kind of attention you could very easily become addicted to.

"She started to blackmail me for the child, and my father demanded I have her abort the child—it was always his first solution, his quick fix—but I couldn't. I think it's the first time I ever went against my father's will." I buried my hands in my pockets and looked away despite how good her eyes made me feel.

I was about to admit a few things I was not particularly proud of... well, no, that was untrue. I didn't care about what I did, it never weighed on my conscience; at least not until a few minutes ago when I realized how Matthews may perceive it and how the gentle patience and understanding I could see in her big eyes would most likely dim again.

"I told her I would not marry her, but if she could stop using drugs until the baby was born, I'd give her the money she wanted to keep feeding her addiction." I sighed, doing my best to keep my eyes trained on the terrace instead of looking back to gauge her feelings. "She started to play the card of the loving mother, how she could never be parted from her child. I suspected that it was just a ploy to get more money, but I was willing to give her a chance." I let out a humorless chuckle. "I'd been so naive."

"Where is she now? Is she really dead?" she asked tentatively.

I grimaced as I reluctantly turned back to look at her, and while there was a certain wariness in her eyes, there wasn't the complete rejection I had expected.

"The thing is, you see, I was busy establishing my place, and I had no affection for her. I only cared about the baby she was carrying."

There, I saw it, the little glint of disappointment in her eyes, and it stung a lot more than I'd thought it would, but I was also surprised I could still disappoint her.

"I got the call while I was taking care of a r— *business*," I stumbled on the word. There was no need to tell her exactly what I'd been doing then, because it was irrelevant. "The man I'd put in charge of her security called me; she was having the baby and for the first time, I felt it, you know?" I tapped at the center of my chest. "That unconditional love and elation, but also a fear so intense, it was almost incapacitating. He was not due for another five weeks, and it was too early."

I took a deep breath before continuing.

"It took me over four hours to make it back—the four longest hours in my life—and then suddenly, I was there, in the hospital. They shoved a weird blue robe and cap in my arms, and then pushed me into a room with a gigantic plastic incubator. My baby boy was so little and connected to so many tubes—" My voice broke and her small hand was back on my arm, her eyes back to the soothing patience they'd reflected before. "They told me he had little chance of making it… He was withdrawing from drugs. She had kept using while pregnant, probably going for cheap stuff cut with God-knows-what or sharing needles. Either way, her habit gave her an infection, and that had caused Pietro's cerebral palsy. He was a junkie, premature baby with a disability. They told me the odds were low."

She rubbed my arm gently. "Pietro is the type of boy to defy the odds, I can tell that much." She flashed a small secretive smile that seemed to say a lot more than she was.

She reached up with her free hand and played with her double dice necklace—something I'd seen her do quite often. It was obviously a tell, but I was just not certain of what yet.

"I wanted her dead," I admitted, feeling so much more comfortable with her than I'd anticipated. "I honestly did, but when I finally made it to her room two days later, she was already gone." I shook my head. "She'd left a letter about how she could not deal with a broken child." I tightened my hand into a tight fist, my muscles jolting under her hand.

She squeezed my forearm and I let out a huff, as if this was enough to ease the anger.

I concentrated on her face, forgetting for a second the story of what was both one of the best and worst moments of my life, as I detailed her features. Her eyes, which now I noticed were just a little too big for her face, her little snub nose covered with a faint dusting of freckles, and her fleshy full lips that women paid good money to have.

"Then?"

"What?" I asked, my eyes quickly going back up to connect with hers.

"What happened?" she asked again, thankfully not too aware of my growing interest in her features... all her features.

"I let her go. I had enough fault to make up for as far as this little boy was concerned, and I didn't need to add the blood of his mother on my hands." That didn't include the blood of the guard I'd trusted with her sobriety during her pregnancy. A guard who had started fucking her as she was expecting *my* child. A guard who turned a blind eye when she left the luxury apartment I had rented for her, only for her to go into the slums and get high with the street junkies. No, his blood was on my hands, and his screams had been delicious, like a soothing balm on my soul, just as Matthews' gentleness had. I was a man of contradictions—a man who found solace in the blood and screams of my enemies, in revenge and retribution, but also in the honey-brown eyes of my *five-foot-nothing* rebel assistant who I wasn't sure even liked me very much.

She nodded as if she understood, and maybe she did in her own way... maybe she could relate.

"She died of an overdose eight months later in Brazil, but the news didn't bring anything more to me, good or bad. I was more focused on taking care of my son and keeping him away from my father's poisonous existence, who—" I stopped talking and leaned my head back just to peek down the corridor to make sure Pietro's door was still closed. "He considered my son a waste of space, a disgrace to the Benetti genes." Indignation filled my veins with raging fire against the man who'd been rotting in the ground for almost four years. "Pietro is all that's good with the Benetti genes." I smiled. "He's the best thing I've ever done."

And then something I didn't expect happened. She wrapped her arms around me and pulled me forward into a hug. I stayed frozen for a second with shock before I sank into the gesture, wrapping my arms around her and pulling her even closer. I leaned down over her, as if to wrap her into this comfort cocoon she'd created.

I closed my eyes and let this attempt to comfort sink into me. I couldn't remember the last time anyone other than Violet reached for me like this, and to be honest, I wasn't sure I could find anything—even my mother had been nothing more than cool efficiency. It was not as if I could blame her; I'd been nothing more than the mandatory offspring issued from a loveless marriage.

I wrapped my arms around her tightly and buried my face in her neck. She let out a little gasp as I brushed my nose against her racing pulse, somehow satisfied that this seemingly innocent embrace had just as much of an effect on her as it did on me.

She removed her arms from around me and pulled back a little. Reluctantly, I loosened my hold but kept one of my hands on her back, stopping her from taking the steps back I knew she'd wanted to take.

I looked up and saw the little frown of confusion between her eyebrows, her eyes filled with so many unspoken questions.

I let my eyes trail to her cheek and brought my free hand up, brushing my thumb over the flour that speckled the corner of her jaw.

"You made a mess," I whispered as I kept brushing her jaw despite the flour being gone.

She tilted her head up a little. "I know." She was so close to me that I could smell the faint chocolate on her breath. Chocolate had never been my favorite flavor, but I never wanted to taste it more than I did right now. "I shouldn't have..." she added, and I knew she was not talking about the food mess anymore, but the emotional mess I could see swirling in her eyes, making them look more copper than honey.

A mess I was also experimenting to a certain degree; and she only stirred more by providing me comfort by seeking a physical contact that only served to cloud the reality just a little more.

I let my thumb trail back from the corner of her jaw to her chin, but instead of going back or breaking the contact as I should have, I brought my thumb up and brushed the seam of her lower lip.

She froze, holding her breath, but I was encouraged by her immobility. I was not holding her too tight—she could have broken the contact if she'd wanted to—but I suspected she was just as reluctant as I was to walk away from this intimate, yet confusing, moment we were sharing.

"Did you mean it?" I asked, keeping my eyes on her rosy lips that reminded me of the coral dawn climbing roses that used to grow on the west-facing wall of our family home. The lips that had been so soft and plush when they'd pressed against mine for barely a second almost a year ago.

"Mean it?" she asked, her warm breath brushing my finger and waking up the most primal part of me, causing my dick to stir.

I used all my willpower to control its reaction. This was not the time; it probably would never be the time. The situation was already messed up, and there was no future in this for her or me, and it would cost me the little I had if I let this go too far.

Matthews was the only constant in my life, and she obviously shared a priceless bond with my son. I could not risk damaging us further than I already had, I knew that. I knew what my conscious mind was ordering me to do, *Let go of her lip and take a step back*, yet I heard myself say…

"When you asked me to kiss you that night, when you asked me to give you the kiss that would make you forget every kiss you ever received… Did you mean it?" I'd been flattered at the time, knowing I had the skills to give her that kiss, but I was also aggravated at the words 'every kiss.' How many kisses had she received? How many insignificant boys had kissed her? Has she kissed the boring accountant? I'd been unsettled at the thought, as well as shamefully jealous, which was unfamiliar territory for me. I had to nip the jealousy in the bud. I also had wanted to give it to her, I really did. I'd convinced myself at the time that it would have been to satisfy my ego, but I was wondering now if it had not been something else that had made me crave the kiss.

"I did." Her cheeks and nose turned red, making her freckles even more apparent. "But I'm grateful you didn't," she added as I leaned down to finally give her what I knew we both wanted.

I stopped, my lips barely a couple of inches from hers, and I stayed there, waiting for her to make the decision to either close the distance or pull away.

I felt her body tremble under my hand resting on her lower back, and I gripped the material of her dress in a tight fist, stopping myself from pulling her forward.

"Because if you did, things would be different, and I'm not sure I'll ever be able to go back to the way things were before, and I don't think m-my heart would be the same," she added, her face turning even redder before she looked down.

I looked at the crown of her head for a few seconds, unsure how to process this because what she'd just admitted as a weakness was one of the biggest strengths I'd ever witnessed—something no one in my world possessed. She admitted her true feelings, she made herself openly vulnerable by admitting this, and she was brave enough to take the risk and expose the throbbing nerves to the surface. This would be inconceivable for me, and it made her braver than any of the men I've ever encountered.

My heart stalled in my chest as I leaned down and kissed the crown of her head in a gentle, tender gesture I'd never given anyone other than my son or sister. I'd never been tempted to soothe anyone, and these new feelings were both exciting and terrifying.

I kept my lips there for a few seconds as she leaned forward a little, as if to seek the comfort of my arms again.

I took a deep breath, but I realized I was more attuned to her scent than I'd thought because this shampoo didn't smell like her... it was all wrong.

I lifted my head, and she looked up at me again but this time, there was not only doubt and confusion in her eyes, but also this yearning I'd seen that night, a want I was not sure she fully understood and one I craved to satisfy.

I leaned down again, slowly enough to let her move away if she wanted to. I held my breath as my lips were about to touch hers and...

"Done!" Pietro shouted from down the corridor.

We both took a couple of startled steps back, and she hissed as her back connected with the kitchen counter.

I cleared my throat and took another step back as she quickly swirled around to check on the muffins in the oven.

"I'll send one of my men to pick up some supplies from the mainland. Please go to the shop website and buy what you need." I ruffled Pietro's hair as he stopped beside me. "Pietro will show you how, but don't abuse your power, my son, I know how much chocolate you'll try to sneak," I added in an attempt to ease the tension with some humor.

"Okay, I'll have a look," she replied, keeping her back to me but she didn't fool me. Her voice was saying it all, just as her eyes had a few minutes ago. I'd unsettled her, and not only because of the fear she might be feeling about who I was, but also with an attraction she was trying to smother.

Maybe it would be for the best if I let her try. Maybe I should just keep away and deal with the shit at hand.

But you don't want to, do you? Because you feel it too, don't you?

I swirled around and disappeared into my office, realizing now even more than before the mistake it had been to take her with me.

I didn't have to only protect my son and my way of life, but I needed to protect myself, too.

CHAPTER 6

LILY

I somehow fell into a routine over the next few days after the kitchen incident. I was calling it the 'kitchen incident' because I was not sure how to process it, not from my feelings or his reaction to me. I'd never expected Alessandro to look at me any other way than as his young, nerdy, and aggravating assistant, who he enjoyed annoying as if it was an Olympic sport. But he had switched in the kitchen, and he'd seemed just as confused as I was. I didn't think either of us had expected we'd open a door that could only complicate things and muddied my decision making about the whole situation.

I'd been convinced after seeing what he did and being kidnapped that I would escape the first chance I got and go to the closest police station to tell them everything I knew. But then I met Pietro, and I fell in love with the little boy in less than a day. He was everything I could ever hope my child would be, and I'd realized then that even when I was gone, I could never tell on Alessandro and take him away from Pietro. However, I was still planning to leave all this behind and go back home.

I might have been good at defying odds from the moment I was conceived, but I also knew that you could only tempt fate so many times before it gave up on you. I was convinced that staying in Alessandro's orbit, knowing what I knew, would not be good for my health.

But then there was that moment in the kitchen; the moment where I realized that my attraction to Alessandro was not only the lustful part of my brain reacting to a gorgeous, masculine, powerful man, but I was also attracted to the man himself. And I knew the more I saw the real Alessandro here in the cocoon of this island, the more I'd risk falling for him.

The man had already stolen my freedom—for good reasons or not—I would not let him steal my heart in the same breath.

I've been doing my best avoiding him since then, and he'd spent most of his time locked in his office. Was he avoiding me or was he trying to find a solution to our problem? I suspected a little of both.

I reached for my phone on the nightstand and felt a new wave of tenderness for the man I should only feel concern and wariness for. When woke up yesterday, I found my phone on the nightstand, fully charged with a Post-it note stating, '*I trust you.*' It meant so much more than he could probably imagine.

He didn't realize what this phone meant, especially today. For the call I just took from my mother and all the others I'd let go to voicemail. Today was a heavy day, one I needed distractions from. I shook my head and slid the phone into the pocket of my linen pants I'd ordered online and walked to Pietro's room. I felt bad for the kid having to hide on the island during fall break because I had to hide until the threat was gone.

I knocked softly and opened the door a little when he called for me to come in.

I tried to keep my face blank as I saw him, leaning on the sides of his exercise bars—the ones the physio told me he refused to use. I wanted to let out a woot of victory at seeing him try, but I knew it would not help. I knew how he would hate for me to make it a big deal because if he failed, it'd be even more disastrous.

"I was wondering what you usually did during fall break. Since you're stuck here, I can maybe try to make it fun. What do you say?"

He cocked his head to the side, wrinkling his little nose up as if my words made no sense. "I've got no fall break, Lily," he said with a little chuckle as if the idea was ridiculous. "I only leave during the summer to go to Uncle Hoka's house in California for a month." He shrugged, but I didn't miss the hint of sadness and longing in his voice.

I opened my mouth and closed it again, hardly believing what I was hearing. That was not being careful; that was being cruel.

"D-do you like it? California?" I asked, walking into the room and sitting at the foot of his single bed covered with constellation sheets.

"I like their house; it's nice, and now I have a cousin, Yuko. He's only a baby, but he is funny."

I nodded, looking around his room, my mind reeling with so many emotions. Part of me was back six years ago, when I was placed in my own bubble intended to be a protection but didn't feel much different than a prison.

His room was almost the size of my whole apartment and had all the luxuries any boy in the world could only dream of, but it was not what Pietro wanted, not really. I knew that because I could see the look in his eyes, the longing for a life he believed he'd never get. I saw it because I used to see the same look in the mirror all the time. The desire for more mixed with the guilt of already feeling like a burden.

"You know what? We're going to have our own pre-Halloween party, you and me, this weekend. What do you say?"

His whole face lit up like Christmas in July, and I felt a wave of pride at being the reason behind his joy. I was growing more and more attached to this boy as the days passed, and consequently, to his infuriating father, who seemed to do everything wrong whilst he only wanted to do the right thing.

Talk to him, adult to adult. Help him understand what his little boy can't tell him.

"But it's hot here. On TV, Halloween is always cold."

I shrugged. "We'll crank up the AC. It'll be colder than a Polar bear's butt."

He giggled. "But Halloween is in three weeks," he added but he was bouncing a little on his feet. I wondered if he even realized he was putting more pressure on them.

I was about to answer, to tell him that we'd need at least three weeks to make up for all the Halloween activities he missed, but his smile and good humor vanished almost just as quickly as it appeared as he turned his head toward the massive window giving a breathtaking view of the green island and the mainland far in the horizon.

"It's because you won't be here in three weeks, right?" he asked, his voice neutral despite his rapid blinking which I knew was a way to keep the tears at bay.

My heart broke. He was too young to already be able to hide his emotions the way he was; he was too young to feel so... lonely. But I could not deny it, and I could not lie to him. If everything went well, I would probably be gone and back to my boring life in my small town, doing the accounting for my uncle's business, but I was not even sure that would be okay anymore. It was barely fulfilling before, and I was not the same girl who had left—I was even more different since I came here.

I loved this little boy, as incredible as it was, and I was not sure I would ever be okay with being fully out of his life.

"It's okay," he continued, like he was trying to convince himself. "Dad never stayed that long before. We talk every day on the computer, and he usually comes for two or three days, two or three times a month, so it's already good, and he brought you along." He turned and his smile was back on his face. It was genuine, even though it was not as bright as the one before. "And I really like you."

I brought my hand up to my chest, his words filling my heart with bittersweet happiness.

"And I like you so much, little prince. So, so much." I stood and kissed his forehead. "I don't know how much longer we'll stay, but we'll make the best of it, deal? Tomorrow we'll start our Halloween special. What do you say?"

"Yes! And we're baking cupcakes tonight, right?"

"Of course, we will, it's tradition." I pursed my lips, unsure as to why I'd let that slip. "I love you, Pietro," I let out, not able to stop myself.

"Why are you crying?" he asked, reaching up to touch my cheek.

"Ah..." I wiped under my eyes. I had not even realized I had shed a few tears. His pain and loneliness were probably the catalyst of a pain I tried so hard to move past from. "Probably my allergies." I tapped my hand on his desk and the half-drawn DNA, which I was sure was way more advanced than what a normal ten years old learned in science class.

I walked to Alessandro's office as soon as I was done with Pietro, before I lost the righteous fire that would allow me to confront him about something that had nothing to do with me.

"I understand, but this is not your territory... it is mine."

I stopped, leaning against the wall by his slightly ajar office door. I knew I should not have been listening to whatever he was discussing in there, but if the door was open, then it could not have been that sensitive.

Sure, Lily, keep lying to yourself.

"Thank you for what you did... It's more than enough. I'll take it from here. Bye."

I took a deep breath, trying to think of what I should say to him.

"You know it's not polite to listen to people's conversations, Miss Matthews. I expected better from you," he called with a mocking tone. "You might as well come in; I know you're there."

I felt my face grow hot with humiliation and my defensive streak kicked in.

"And I expected better from you than being the prison guard of a little boy you keep hidden in this golden cage like a shameful secret," I spat, entering the room. I hoped he'd attribute my red face to only anger.

He remained very still, almost unnaturally so.

"You know the physio told me yesterday how impressed he was with Pietro, and how he's made more progress in the past week than he did in a year, and you know why? It's because he knows he can, because he gets the chance to try."

"Excuse me?" he hissed through clenched teeth. "I'm well aware of the physio assessment about *my* son. However, I'd appreciate it if you didn't go around and flirt your way into the man's bed while he's here to concentrate on Pietro. Frankly, it's pathetic."

That stung and unfortunately, put some more oil on my righteous fire, making me lose all rationality and cross the line in ways I'd never would have dared otherwise.

"And I'd appreciate it if you treated your son as an actual human being, instead of the bubble boy. I can't believe he's stuck here all the time. How horrible! Have you ever noticed how miserable he is here? How damaging it is to be stuck with your thoughts as your only companion? Do you even care enough to notice in the few days a month you *actually* see your son? Of course, he's not trying because he doesn't think he can, because his own father doesn't bel—"

"Enough!" he bellowed, jumping from his seat and slamming his fist on the desk.

I jumped back, my heart in my throat. *Yep, I'd gone too far...*

"Who *the fuck* do you think you are? His mother?" He snorted. "You've been here five fucking minutes, and you think you can give me life lessons on how I should or shouldn't raise my son?"

His hands were now balled into fists on his desk, so tightly that his knuckles were bone-white.

"Do you have any idea what it's like to live in the *Cosa Nostra*? Do you know what they'd do to me, to Pietro, if they smelled one ounce of weakness?"

"It's just—"

"Let me finish!" he roared, slamming his fist on his desk so hard that his half-drunk glass fell on the floor.

I looked at the dark liquid spreading slowly across the black and white rug as my eyes prickled with tears at his cruel words.

"You know nothing about anything. You're not the one who's been worrying for ten years, you don't know what it's like to reign over a syndicate, and you have *no idea* what it's like to have a child. Spare me your fucking two cents on the situation; I could not care less." He gestured toward the door. "Now go before I start regretting sparing your life."

I took a step back under the blow of his words. I rested my hand on my chest, half expecting to find it coated with blood.

"You're right... I don't know what it's like to raise someone like Pietro," I said barely louder than a whisper. "But

I know what it's like *to be him*." I left the room just as the first sob escaped my throat.

"Wishing upon a star?"

I startled, almost letting go of the cupcake I was holding, and turned my head to look at Alessandro standing in the threshold of my French doors.

"Hoping I'd drop dead for being a horrible person to you?"

"No... Pietro needs a parent."

"Ouch, is it the only reason you'd keep me alive?"

I gave him a little smile and blew the candle, wishing for this man to heal and for his son to thrive. "I wished for my life back."

He sighed and took a seat on the lounger I occupied. "I knocked, but you didn't answer."

"I didn't hear you, but I don't think it allows you to just walk in... even if it's your house."

He grimaced and reached up, as if to adjust his tie. He let out a sigh as his hand touched his open collar, and he let it fall on his knee. It was his tell, his show of discomfort.

I put the cupcake back on the plate on the floor and looked straight ahead, letting the nice evening breeze play with my crazy mass of unruly curls. I was not going to ease the tension—I was doing that way too often, sweeping everything under the rug, but not anymore. He'd have to work for it.

He sighed. "Add it to the list of things I need to apologize for... I imagine this list must be staggeringly long."

"I should not have mettled," I admitted. "Even if I'm right, it's not my place."

He let out a weary laugh. "That doesn't sound like an apology."

I turned my head toward him and held his gaze, despite the heat of his causing my body to hum in places it had not hummed for a while... if ever. "It's because it was not meant to be one."

He gave me a half smile, the proud one he always gave me when I stood my ground. "Well, I'm sorry, Lily. Truly."

I tried to keep my face placid, but I was not sure I managed. He called me Lily and apologized! Two things I never expected Alessandro Benetti to do.

He shook his head. "Sometimes, when it comes to Pietro, I can be a little..." He cocked his head to the side as if to think of a word.

"Psychotic?"

He threw me a side look full of exasperation, and I shrugged, turning back toward the ocean I could not see, letting the salty breeze hit my face with its delicious cooling effect.

"I was about to say, *intense*." He cleared his throat. "You will see one day, when you become a mother. Children... They have a strange power over you. They make you feel their pain much more than if it were yours, and you become obsessed with protecting them from everything—even things you know in all conscience you won't be able to because their pain, their fears... you feel it tenfold."

I opened my mouth and closed it again. *It's not your place, Lily, it's not your place. Just let it go*, I repeated to myself as a mantra.

"The thing is..." I winced, sucking my bottom lip between my teeth. Fuck, why could I never listen to my own advice?

"The thing is?" He encouraged me. "Speak your mind, I won't get mad."

I raised an eyebrow with incredulity.

He rolled his eyes. "Okay, I'll try not to, and I'll keep it bottled up."

Yeah, that was more like it. "The thing is, you're expecting people to only see or judge him based on the challenges he's facing, and I say let them." I twisted on the lounger to face him. "These people are not important because they're obviously clueless. Pietro is so much more than his disability. He is funny and kind. *Frighteningly* smart for a boy his age, and he's so resilient and patient. That child is everything someone could hope for in life. And if he has to take over your world one day, then I pray for Chicago because with a man like him at its head, your organization will become an empire."

He cocked his head to the side, letting his eyes trail all over my face as if he was looking for something, but I wasn't sure what. "You're speaking as if you love him."

"That's because I do." I thought that was evident.

He arched an eyebrow with a half-smile. "Should I be jealous of my own son?"

I snorted. I knew he was only trying to ease the mood with his light flirting, but it still made my heart speed up. "Of course not. There's no competition. If I had to choose, Pietro would win every time."

His smile widened, and it felt like I'd given the right answer. "Pietro is a lucky boy to have you in his corner."

"He's lucky to have you, too." And I meant that, because despite his shortcomings, I knew Alessandro only wanted to keep his son safe and happy. "You just need to let go a little."

"You must see me as a monster, keeping him isolated like this. I've never realized that he was hurting so much because of it." He stopped and it was his turn to sit forward. I looked at his profile and his Adam's apple bobbled as he swallowed with difficulty.

"You can hurt even the person you love the most," I offered, grabbing the bottle of water I had and extending it to him. "It doesn't make you a monster; it makes you flawed... human."

He took the bottle and had a sip before turning toward me. "You don't think I'm a monster? After everything you discovered? The things you saw and the ones you rightfully assumed?" His eyes were burning with intensity, his hand denting the plastic of the bottle by how tight he was holding it. It was like my answer was as important as his next breath.

"No, I don't." And I meant that, against all rational thoughts, against all I thought was true before. "You are not a monster in my eyes, Alessandro."

His face softened at my use of his given name, and I stopped breathing as he put the bottle on the floor and reached up, brushing my cheek with the back of his hand, his knuckles barely grazing the apple of my cheek in the softest, almost tender gesture.

"You're wise beyond your years, Lily Matthews. How can you be so insightful about my little boy?"

I knew that if I wanted him to truly take me seriously, I had to open up to him about my whole situation, and it seemed that today was the perfect day.

"Today is Victor's birthday... my brother," I added quickly before looking down at my hands on my lap as I made circles with my thumb and forefinger in my usual soothing gesture. "No one in the world loved me more than Victor did, and vice versa." I let out a little chuckle. "We were the cliché of twins like that, always one with the other. Nobody was forcing us, it was just natural. Victor was..." I looked up but avoided Alessandro's eyes and looked into the starless night, trying to keep the sadness at bay, at least for now.

"You don't have to," Alessandro offered, and I felt the intensity of his eyes on the side of my face.

"I do. Victor was a shooting star. I was so proud of him, you know. He was the star at home, the perfect son, and it was not just an act. Victor was just that good, inside and out. He was the quarterback and the captain of the football team, he had a 4.0 GPA, he was dating the head cheerleader, and was the perfect boyfriend... and what did he do in his spare time? He volunteered at the foodbank and at the homeless shelter." I smiled. "My brother was a saint. And then there was me." I chuckled. "The girl a little socially awkward, who enjoyed books and had one mission: be valedictorian and study physics at Stanford. You could not have found anyone more different than Victor. He was brave and funny and outgoing; and I was always self-conscious, considering things forever, thinking everything through. Vic never judged me for this. He was so proud of me; I was his best friend, and he never left me aside, not once. He saw me for so much more than I was, and I think that's why I ended up dating his best friend, Andrew. It was always the four of us since sophomore year—Victor, Katia, me, and Andrew. We were a package deal." I shook my head, my smile wobbling as I was about to reach the part of the story that contained much more pain than joy.

I was surprised to see his hand appear in my line of vision as he grabbed mine. I kept my eyes on the gesture of comfort. How tanned and big his hand was, how it engulfed mine, and how it made me feel safe. How it eased some of my sorrow, despite knowing they were hands that could also kill.

I turned my hand around and grabbed his as if it were a lifeline.

"Then homecoming came and it all unraveled. One mistake led to so many consequences. Katia... she was young, and Victor and her had been together forever. He was her first boyfriend, and I suspect she'd been his first too, but whilst he was happy in the comfortable situation, she wasn't sure. Over time, my brother stopped showing her as much attention and then another boy came and showed her things she'd been missing..." I shrugged. "It was the homecoming party at a big house by the lake, and we were late because of one of my science projects and Victor refused to leave without me. They had a fight because of this—something that was happening more and more often—Victor said he was not going." I shook my head. "I finished and convinced him to go. When we got there, I went to look for Andrew, and Vic went to look for Katia." I took a deep breath, stopping just for a few seconds. I felt like I was back there again; I could almost hear the deafening music coming from the giant speakers in the room, causing the beat to vibrate all the way to my throat. I could smell the mix of alcohol and what I suspected might already be vomit, and I could feel the heat of so many bodies pressed against each other.

My mind was brought back to reality by Alessandro's soft caress as he ran his thumb back and forth on my inner wrist.

"You don't have to tell me if it's too difficult."

"I know," I replied softly, finally looking up and meeting his eyes full of sorrow, his eyebrows etched with concern. This was for me. This brutal, heartless man felt compassion for me.

I forced a little smile, hoping to ease some of his worry before looking down again, somehow unsure I'd be able to tell him the whole story if I kept looking in his eyes. "I was stopped by a few players from the team... I was kinda like their mascot. They all knew I was Victor's little sister, even though he was only born seven minutes before me, but for him, it was a world of difference." I chuckled despite the aching wrapping my heart in ice. "I stayed with them, knowing I would be safe until Andrew or Victor found me. It was Andrew who found me first, about thirty minutes later. He was panicking, telling me that my brother caught Katia with a guy in the hot tub, and they had a fight. He said that he was now drunk and about to go to war."

"Andrew was a man; he should have dealt with that," Alessandro barked gruffly, his voice full of disapproval.

I winced but kept my eyes on his thumb providing his mesmerizing ministration.

"This is a twin thing, you... you can't really understand. Victor..." I sighed, unsure on how to explain. "I was the only one able to get through to him, no matter the situation. I rushed out as Katia was gripping him, half naked, as he walked to the car, fighting her off. I jumped over the other guy bleeding on the floor and managed to get into the car beside him. He was going too fast, and he was just—" I stopped talking, trying to swallow painfully around the lump of tears in my throat. "We never made it home."

"Lily—"

"Once again, I beat the odds." I grabbed the necklace with my free hand. "I've always beaten the odds," I added, almost wistfully, because at that time, and for a long time afterwards, I'd wished I hadn't. I had wished I'd died with him and didn't go through all the pain and consequences of one poor decision.

He let go of my hand and I felt empty, but it was only for a second as he cradled the back of my head, pulling me forward to kiss the top of my head before resting his forehead on top of it, his nose buried in my hair.

When did this man become so caring? How could he be so tender? How did he know how to comfort me?

"I'm not saying this to seek pity or to make me look weak. I'm just saying that for you to understand that my brother made one mistake—getting in the car impaired—and by doing that, he hurt me in so many ways. Both physically, by causing this lifelong disability, but also emotionally, by taking himself away from me. I lost the only person who loved me unconditionally." I took a shaky breath. "And I'm also telling you all that because you need to know that I understand Pietro. I've been in that wheelchair with little hope to walk again. I've dealt with that pity people didn't think I could see. But Alessandro, we're disabled... not blind or stupid."

Alessandro moved a little and rested two fingers under my chin, raising my head. Our faces were so close that his nose touched mine, but I didn't want to move—much too entranced by his fresh cologne, his body heat, and his eyes that looked as black as onyx under the dim lighting coming from my bedroom.

"I need you to know something, Lily Matthews. There's nothing you can say that would ever make me look at you as weak. You're one of the bravest people I've ever met, which makes you both a godsend and a major pain in my butt." His lips lifted up at the corner, giving him this irresistible rogue smile that I knew brought women to their knees, both literally and figuratively.

I smiled a little at his words. "You're a warrior, woman. One who stood in the office of one of the most powerful CEOs in town and gave him shit for his poor attitude."

"Ah-ha! So you admit you acted like an ass."

"It's all about perspective. So, if today is Victor's birthday, then it's yours too, isn't it?"

I nodded.

He leaned down, closing the distance between our foreheads before brushing his nose against mine in an Eskimo kiss.

"Happy Birthday, Lily Matthews," he whispered before leaning in and brushing his lips against mine.

Once, twice, and as I gasped, opening my mouth a little, I felt his control snap as his fingers tightened on the back of my head. He pulled my face to his, catching my bottom lip between his teeth, and his tongue slid against the seam, making the flutters of my heart morph into a ride of wild broncos.

A small traitorous moan escaped me as he sucked on my lip, and that was enough to encourage him as he crushed his lips to mine, his tongue invading my mouth with the same dominance that exuded from him with everything he did.

My whole body tingled as I gripped his shirt, my thoughts completely clouded by the taste of him, his warmth, his scent.

He groaned with approval against my mouth as one of my hands let go of his shirt and wrapped around his neck to play with the soft short hair. His kiss turned even more intense and hungrier as I felt his fingers slide under my shirt and slip up my stomach to cup my aching breast. His touch was a perfect mirror of his lips—fierce, passionate, and possessive.

I knew it was a mistake, that we would probably both regret it in the morning, but I was too caught up in him, in this passionate inferno I'd never experienced before. I was going to drown in him and be left broken, but right at this moment I didn't care.

And as suddenly as he kissed me, he broke the kiss and stood in one motion, as if he'd just been burned.

He looked away, his chest heaving, and my cheeks burned red as my eyes slid down and stopped on his very obvious erection stretching the front of his pants.

I rested my fingers on my swollen lips and twisted on my seat to look out instead of at his arousal.

I could still feel his lips on mine, could feel the trail of heat his fingers had left on my stomach, and my breasts were still yearning for his delicious attention.

"I... um." He cleared his throat. "Have a good night, Matthews. I still have some things to deal with."

Despite his obvious arousal and the hoarseness of his voice—showing me that this brief moment affected him just as much as it did me—my heart sank at him reverting and using my last name, a clear attempt at putting the distance back between us.

I nodded, not looking at him. I was not sure I wanted to see what was now in his eyes.

"You'll keep me involved, right?"

"Of course," he replied. "I won't do anything without telling you."

I turned my head, but he was already back in my room. "Promise?"

He gave me a sharp nod. "Promise."

And he had lied, right to my face, because the next morning, he was gone.

CHAPTER 7

Alessandro

She was going to be furious. I knew that as soon as I disappeared with the first rays of sunlight to take the plane back to Chicago.

In truth, I had no reason to tell her anything—it was not like I owed her anything. She'd told me she was defying the odds since her birth, and I believed it because for her to survive what she'd witnessed…? It was a bookie's dream.

Despite knowing I didn't owe her anything, I still had to apologize for the cruel words I'd spoken more out of self-loathing than anything. I'd noticed the changes in Pietro, of course I did. It was impossible to miss how my son blossomed in only two weeks with her, and it made it so obvious that he'd been miserable before.

And then Tim, the physio, came, and it really grated on my nerves to see him look at Lily the way he did, how he stayed longer than usual just to give me an in-person update, but I knew better. He stayed behind to have time with Lily. Well, not on my watch; she was here for a reason, and he was here to take care of my son, only my son. My assistant was off limits.

However, no matter how annoying he had been in his failed attempts at flirting with Lily, he was one of the best physios around—one I paid a fortune for—and he'd confirmed what I'd also suspected. Pietro was a completely different boy, trying much harder and making more progress than he had in the last several months.

I didn't tell her I was going to Chicago because I knew she would have insisted on coming with me, and there was no point, at least not yet. It was not secure, and I was going to interrogate a couple of thugs who may know where Byrne disappeared to. Besides, I was not ready to take her away from Pietro, no matter how unfair it was to her.

I wanted Pietro to be happy for just a little while longer.

Pietro... I sighed, leaning back against my seat as my pilot announced we'd be landing in the next thirty minutes.

I'd made a complete mess of the situation last night, I knew I did. For her, for me, and for Pietro, too.

The thing is, when I teased her about her attachment to Pietro, she'd said words I'd never expected.

'There's no competition. If I had to choose, Pietro would win every time.'

And I believed her, I saw it in her eyes. Despite her laughter, she had meant it, and it was the way it should be. The unadulterated love that woman was showing my son was enough to crack my heart even more, allowing more of her to slide in.

It has been enough from taking the bludgeoning attraction—or maybe the recently acknowledged one—to another level. I just meant to give her a small chaste kiss, just to remind myself how soft her lips could be. I guess it was the masochist part of me wanting a memory of something I shouldn't have or ask for.

What I didn't expect was once I started kissing her, I wouldn't be able to stop. And then she melted into my arms as if she belonged there and kissed me back with the same unbridled passion I was kissing her.

That almost immediately drove my thoughts to the darkest, wickedest corners of my mind, where I kept speculating how the proper looking Lily would be in bed. If her kiss was any indication, then I knew making love to her could kill me, but I wanted to try more than anything else.

I shook my head as I felt my dick harden at the thought. A thought I was sure I'd expunged from my system last night in the cold shower.

I was grateful for the familiar jolt caused by the tires hitting the tarmac. I had too much to do now, and I couldn't obsess over that kiss, her response to it, and what it could mean for her and me.

That question would have to wait until I flew back to the island.

Well, if I made it back alive which was not certain based on who was waiting to greet me.

I should not have expected anything different, yet I still paused at the top of the stairs seeing the slick black car waiting for me on the tarmac. The car was not mine, and the driver—who looked more like a mercenary than a driver—standing at the front of it with a shiny gun visible in his jacket, was not my driver.

The tinted rear window slid down slowly, revealing Matteo, his face his usual cool mask. His cruel eyes stayed on me, a silent invitation to come to my execution meeting.

I let out a small sigh, taking the steps slowly enough to show him that I was not one to be led.

His driver circled the car and silently opened the door for me.

I took my seat beside Matteo and looked at his hand as he played with his insignia ring. I'd only seen him do that when he was deep in thought, and a Matteo deep in thought was far more dangerous than any other version of himself.

His thoughts, directed to anyone other than his wife, were usually dark and torturous.

"Thank you for coming to pick me up, but it was not necessary."

He threw me an exasperated side look. "Don't push your luck, Alessandro," he said with the calmest voice, which again, didn't mean he was not absolutely seething with anger inside.

Matteo Genovese was unreadable, which was probably why he was so dangerous.

"You may be the *capo dei capi*, but you're not the boss of me, at least not in this way."

Matteo let out a low chuckle that sounded more like a threat than a genuine show of mirth. "It's cute that you think so, but deep down, we both know it's not the truth, don't we?" He gestured forward. "We'll just have a little chat, and then we can both go on our merry way. I'll leave this town and go back to where I belong."

"With Gianluca?" I couldn't help but taunt. It was a sort of point of jealousy with all the North American *capi*. Montanari has always had Matteo's favor, no matter how much he fucked up, and some of us wanted to be daddy's favorite.

I always thought it was ridiculous, even when my own father puffed his chest when Matteo was around like a pathetic pigeon. I had always known it was best not to be in Matteo's line of fire because his positive vision of you came with a lot of obligations and rules I'd rather not be attached to.

"With my wife," he replied. "And the sooner, the better, but it all depends on you and the outcome of our discussion."

"Ah, I see." I nodded, looking out of the window as the driver took the exit to the docks. That was not the greatest sign. "It all depends on if you have to kill me and get rid of the body. It will delay you, for sure."

Matteo snorted. "Don't be silly. I wouldn't be the one doing the cleaning, but it's true, replacing you would cause some work and it would be annoying."

My death would be... annoying. Yep, that was Matteo in a nutshell.

We drove for a few minutes on the docks in silence before the car stopped in front of a gray hangar away from the others. I knew this one quite well; I used it on a few occasions, and usually the person I took in didn't make it out with his heart beating.

Matteo opened his door and gestured for me to do the same. I did and followed him into the hangar, and I hated that an apprehension—very akin to fear—had settled in my stomach. Worse was that this fear was not really linked to my own fate. Death was death—there was nothing to truly fear, at least not for me. No, what I feared was the fate that would be bestowed onto Pietro and Lily. Fuck, since when did Lily's future became a main source of concern?

A muffled voice pulled me out of my thoughts, and I noticed a man gagged and bound to a chair. Blood covered his shirt, running down his left brown pant leg.

When my eyes connected with his—well, his right eye specifically as his left one was swollen shut—his eyes widened and he started to scream against his gag, squirming on his chair.

I frowned as we passed him to go to the little office that was usually used for nothing other than waiting for the person to deal with or waiting for the cleaning team to arrive.

Matteo took a seat on the depressed blue office chair that was way past its prime and gestured to me to sit on a three-legged chair in the corner.

I twisted my mouth to the side, doubting that gravity would allow this chair to carry my two hundred and twenty pounds.

"You know what? I'll stand," I said, leaning against the wall facing Matteo. It was ludicrous, almost comical for both of us to be in this decrepit guard cubicle instead of our luxurious offices with comfy leather chairs and well-stocked bars.

"He seems familiar," I started, jerking my head toward the glass window behind Matteo.

"A present for you... depending on how today's conversation goes."

Of course, nothing came free with him.

"And he is...?"

Matteo let out an exasperated sigh. The conversation was not taking the turn he was expecting. What did he think would happen? That I'd cower with fear and fall on my knees, begging for forgiveness for whatever he thought I did wrong? If he did, he was in for a heap of disappointment.

"He is the one you are looking for. The *yakuza* couldn't touch him but I could. I..." He cocked his head to the side with a half smirk. "Let's just say I was bored and annoyed waiting for you, so I played with him a little. I'm sure he will tell you everything you want to know."

I didn't ask how he knew who I was looking for or that I involved my brother-in-law or even that I was on my way back. He would have gloated, and I would have known nothing more.

"You know," he continued when I remained silent. "Of all the *capi* I'm in charge of, you're the one I didn't think I'd ever have to remind my authority to. I thought you were smarter than that."

"I told Dom to tell you," I replied, crossing my arms over my chest, getting a little irritated at having to defend my actions to him, even if he had every right to ask.

He nodded. "I know. He pleaded your case like a good little messenger."

I didn't miss the hint of bitterness in his tone, but I didn't dare speculate. Matteo's relationship with Dom was a clusterfuck I would never touch.

"Your honesty on this is the reason you are still breathing and she is still on that island with that son of yours."

My blood ran cold in my veins at the threat. This island was my haven, a place very few people knew about, and having my safe harbor threatened put me in an uncontrollable rage.

"Matteo, if you—"

"Don't be a fool, Alessandro. Don't start throwing threats that will cost you a lot more than you have. I said I wanted to talk to her, and you took her away... You went against me Alessandro, and that's not something I look at kindly."

When had Matteo Genovese ever looked at anything kindly?

"I needed time. It was just too fast, I have... had things to figure out. As you know, there is more at—"

"It was *not* a request, Alessandro, it was not a choice. I demanded you bring her to me, and you didn't."

I didn't because I was scared of what he might do to her if she let her sassy attitude get the best of her. I might find it more endearing than annoying most of the time, but Matteo was not the type. If she dared disrespect him, he'd hurt her, and I knew I would not be able to just stand on the sidelines and watch. I was terrified to admit it, but part of me suspected that I'd be ready to start a war with my own *famiglia* for her, and that was not a theory I was too keen on testing.

"You know I've always been on your side, Matteo," I started, trying to relax my posture. "You know I am one of the few who stood by you and refused to take part in the little rebellion."

He nodded slowly, his blue eyes scrutinizing every movement of my face, speculating, looking for a clue of what my words could be hiding.

"I always kept my faith in you, in your decision-making, even if they didn't seem to make much sense. I'm just asking you to extend the favor to me."

He sighed, twisting his ring again, and I knew that my words affected him, even if reluctantly. There wasn't much Matteo valued more than loyalty, which was something I always showed him "This is different. My actions didn't risk our way of life, my family... my *wife*. This girl is..."

Ah yep, Elena Genovese. That would do it. There was nothing in this world Matteo valued more than his wife.

"How could Lily affect Elena? She didn't even see Dom. All she saw was me kill a man. A man whose body has long been dissolved in hydrofluoric acid and is now part of the city sewer system." I shrugged. "The only life Lily would endanger is mine, and no body, no crime, right?"

How could I tell Matteo I was not worried because Lily loved my son? She would never do anything that would take me away from him, that much I was sure about. She was a lot of things, Lily. She was stubborn, defensive, and hellbent to prove she didn't need anyone, to the point of hurting herself in the process. But above all, she was intelligent, kind, understanding, and patient... well, with anyone else but me. She would never take me away from Pietro because she realized the danger of my life and she wouldn't want to leave him unprotected.

He would never understand this kinship; he would never believe her attachment to Pietro was enough. For Matteo, all that worked were threats.

He shook his head. "See, that is where you're wrong. We're a *famiglia*. If you're taken down, then there's the risk for me. Not that you'd talk, I'd have you killed before you could get out of custody."

Charming.

"But the other *capi* will look at me and think I'm not fit to lead. That I made the wrong call and allowed you to be caught, that *I* made a mistake; and Alessandro, I do *not* make mistakes." His Italian accent thickened, and I knew that his irritation had reached its peak. "Your decisions impact me, and I cannot tolerate this."

"She is on my island; you said it yourself. She's not a danger, she has no contact," I insisted, hoping he was too preoccupied to see through my lie.

His eyes narrowed, he was like a fucking lie detector and suddenly, the light in his eyes changed as if he caught something.

I tensed, uncertain of what he thought he saw in me.

"Why do you even argue so much for her? She's just an insignificant assistant. You had dozens of them before and will probably have dozens after. Why does it matter? Why does *she* matter?"

"She's n— She is an innocent," I finished rather lamely.

"It never stopped you before. I warned you before about keeping her too involved in your business. If you'd let her go, as I advised you to do, we wouldn't be having this conversation now."

"Lily is…" *Important to me. Well, for Pietro's sake.* "She won't be a problem."

Matteo nodded, but I could see he was still lost in his thoughts and speculations.

"Are you going to claim her?" he asked, finally meeting my eyes again.

My heart squeezed in an unfamiliar and uncomfortable way at the mere thought of claiming Lily as mine. "No, absolutely not!" I snorted.

Matteo laughed. "I see. Why? You're not into the shy, librarian type?" He shrugged. "I know from experience that the most unassuming women make the best wives."

Matteo misunderstood my reluctance. It was not because Lily was not good enough, it was because she was *too* good. Too good to condemn her to a life with me.

He looked at his watch and let out a sigh. "Listen, either I speak to her and get satisfied or..." he paused for a second, "I won't let her walk away like that."

"And I won't let you kill her," I finally admitted out loud.

He stood, arching an eyebrow. "Don't antagonize me. I enjoy challenges and I may just do that to prove my point." He waved dismissively before snapping his fingers in the direction of his driver, who was waiting by the car and made a rolling gesture to him. "I'm going home now; I stayed in this *place* long enough." His mouth tipped down in the corner. "Just claim her, marry her, breed her; do whatever the fuck you need to convince me she is not a threat."

My cock jolted at the thought of claiming her. "I'll deal with it."

"You do that. Oh, and when you find out which one of us was working with that CFO of yours, let me know. I'd love to come and play."

I shook my head. "With all due respect, Matteo, whoever betrayed me will be dealt with by me. This is my territory, my responsibility."

His mouth lifted in a half smile as he nodded. "That's fair. Don't make me come back about the girl, Alessandro. Neither of us will enjoy the outcome."

I felt that peculiar fear again, not for me but for her. Damn it, when did she become such a liability? I could not afford weaknesses, pressure points. Pietro had been the only one until Violet entered my life, but she was protected by a man just as lethal as I was, but now there was Lily. Shit! She was a weakness I truly couldn't afford.

"See you soon, Alessandro. Don't make me regret giving you the trust you requested." He turned and walked briskly to his car as he snapped his fingers to the man standing beside the thug tied to the chair.

The man immediately moved and joined Matteo in the car, leaving me alone with the guy in the chair.

I exited the small office and walked toward him. The man's face morphed and his whole body relaxed as if he was relieved to see me. Was he delusional?

I picked up my phone and texted one of the only people I trusted within the *famiglia*, and it was only because he didn't care enough to actually backstab anyone, Oda. My half-Italian, half-Japanese spy who proved his loyalty enough for me to know he had no play in this, despite his flagrant lack of concern for my authority and his obsession with text over calls.

He texted me with his aggravating reply I barely understood.

K bts bfckg -Gime 20

I shook my head with a sigh and ripped the gag off the man's mouth.

"Mr. Benetti! Thank you for saving me. I'm not sure what the *capo dei capi* wanted, but I swear, I—"

I raised my hand, stopping him in his tracks. "You're Giacomo Lombardi, aren't you?"

"I... Yes, sir, but I'm not—"

"*Stai zitto*!" I ordered, crossing my arms on my chest. "I only want to hear answers to my questions, nothing more. *Capice*?"

He looked at me, his eyes wide with fear.

I rolled my eyes. "You can answer now."

"*Sì*."

"Do you know why you're here?"

"Is it because of Mr. Byrne? I did as you asked, I swear."

I opened and closed my mouth, taken aback by his words. Of all I would have imagined, that was not it.

"I asked you to do something?"

He nodded vigorously.

"I, as in *me*?" I asked, pointing at my chest. "I came to you and asked you something?"

"No, but Byrne said you did. He gave me the password."

"The pass—" I shook my head. "What the fuck are you talking about? Are you playing mind games or are you plain stupid? Do you think we're in some spy movie, like the *Da Vinci Code*? *Dì la verità, sei stupido*?"

He opened his mouth to reply, but a chuckle interrupted whatever he was about to say.

"I don't think anybody is that stupid, boss," Oda replied as he stopped beside me.

I threw him a quick look and did my best not to roll my eyes at his ripped jeans and bright pink Henley. Frankly, I'd never understood anything about his generation, and I didn't even want to try.

The saying says, '*Dress for the job you want*.' Well, Oda looked more like a punk than a made man.

"Thanks for showing up." I made a point at looking at his clothes. "Also," I got my phone out of my pocket and showed him his text, "*ma che cazzo*?"

"What do you mean, what the fuck?" He shrugged. "The text is clear. It said, 'Okay, be there soon. Busy fucking. Give me twenty minutes.'"

"Is that wh...?" No, seriously, I was too old for this shit.

Oda turned to Giacomo. "So, tell me, what was your password? Did he promise you Narnia?"

Giacomo threw me a look, and I gestured my hand for him to answer.

"He said you were in on it. That the IRS was looking into it, and he needed to hide."

"So, you think I was in on him stealing from my company?"

"You might have been onto something before," Oda offered, burying his hands in his pocket. "I think the man is retarded."

"I-I questioned it too, but he said it was to finance the other side of the business."

I looked heavenward. Did he even know what the other side of the business was making? Enough to probably buy my legal business ten times over.

"He gave me a *lealtà moneta*!"

That made me falter for a second, and I was impressed on how impassive Oda looked as well. We both knew what a *lealtà moneta* was, but we also knew how rare they were as a generality. It was a coin you gave to another high member to prove you owed him a favor. They were of high value to trade, and for Byrne to have one could only mean that he worked with one of our men from Chicago or another region, but it was not a simple made man.

"*Lealtà moneta* is just a myth," I scoffed. "He played you."

"No, *da vero*, look into my pocket!" He jerked his chin toward his left pocket.

"Swear to God, if it's to get your peen touched, I'll cut it," Oda muttered, taking a couple of steps forward and reached into the pocket. He turned it over and laughed. "That's fake, man. Even in this darkness, you can see that." But once he turned toward me, I could see the truth in his eyes. It was real, and it was big.

I extended my hand and looked at the coin engraved with '*Imperare sibi maximum imperium es*t.' To rule yourself is the ultimate power. This coin was one of the rarest but unfortunately, not limited to the Chicago camorra. I needed Byrne more than ever now—his greed and idiocy were not even that important anymore. I needed to find who he was working with and cut the head of the snake before he poisoned the whole nest.

"Where is he?" I asked, slipping the coin into my pocket.

"Mr. Benetti, liste—"

"Where is he?" I shouted, making him recoil on his chair.

"I don't—"

I got my gun out. "Three seconds or I swear, I'll shoot." I cocked it, aiming it to the center of his forehead. "One."

"I didn't know I was betraying you. I..." he rambled, getting more and more agitated.

"Two."

"I didn't even get that much mon—"

"Thr—"

"Boston!" he cried, closing his eyes tightly. "I helped him get to Boston."

I nodded. "Goodbye. I'll see you in Hell," I replied before pulling the trigger.

I stood there silently, staring at his limp body as the blood started to drip from the fatal wound on his forehead. Heads always bled the most, but it was the most efficient way to get rid of someone and to stop whatever annoying begging came from their mouth.

Giacomo had been a traitor. He'd known the coin was not mine; he just thought he could get rich and be protected by whatever powerful traitor was working behind the scenes.

I turned to Oda, who looked serious for once. "I'll take care of it."

"Thank you." I turned and walked out, pleased to find my car waiting for me.

I sat in the car and let out a weary sigh as I rested my head on the headrest. *Boston...* Fuck, now I had a real fucking problem to deal with. Worst of all, I had to make a deal with Killian Doyle, the psycho, short-tempered pure Irish blood who was in charge of the Irish mafia.

I just needed to figure out how.

CHAPTER 8

LILY

Three days. He had been gone for three days and he didn't bother to answer any of my calls, not a text. I heard him speak with Pietro a couple of times. Mario, the guard who was following Pietro like his shadow, told me gruffly that Alessandro would be back soon, and I could ask him whatever nonsense I had to ask him when he returned.

I was pretending to be fine for Pietro, since he didn't deserve to feel or see any of my irritation.

I wiped the counter furiously, letting my irritation take the marble to a shiny level never seen before.

I was not sure what I was the angriest about, to be honest—that he kissed me, basically destroying every other kiss

I ever had, and then just walked away like it was nothing to write home about or if it was because he lied to my face and kept me away from something that was basically my life. Yes, that was it, of course. I ignored the little taunting voice in my head that kept saying it was the kiss.

"Lily?"

I stopped mid-wipe, grateful that Pietro got me out of my thoughts.

"Yeah?"

"Do you have a minute? Aunt Vi would like to chat with you."

My heart jolted in my chest. "Be right there!" I took a couple of deep breaths before looking at my reflection in the microwave door and groaned at the messy bun on top of my head that barely contained the heathen mess my hair became in this tropical heat. It was too late to try to do anything to make me look presentable. Taking care of my curls in this weather would take an hour.

Why do you even care how you look? You've met her before. Why should her opinion even matter? My reason sternly reminded me. *Nothing has changed!*

I took another deep breath, squared my shoulders, and walked down the corridor to Pietro's room.

Except, it wasn't true, though, wasn't it? Everything had changed. I knew who Alessandro was now, and being part of his life, staying at his secret haven had allowed me to see a side of him that uncovered the feelings I had for him, and now I was not completely certain I could ever put them back in the denial box.

When I walked in, Pietro was showing the Jedi costume we'd been working on to Violet on the screen and they were laughing. I couldn't help but laugh, too. I just loved this little boy's laugh.

His head jerked up and the bright smile he gave me made all the worry and frustration evaporate to give room for the joy I felt at seeing him reacting to me that way.

"I told Aunt V about our *Star Wars* evening, and how you're dressing as Princess Leia."

I couldn't help but blush at the level of nerdiness he revealed to his aunt, and I walked to stand behind him, providing a little discreet support as he leaned on his standing frame. I didn't want him to overdo it, but I also didn't want to smother his efforts—nobody knew his limits better than he did.

"I think trying to tame this mess into two rolls will need the use of the force," I jested, looking at the stunning, dark-haired young woman on the screen.

She waved at me, a big friendly smile on her face, and it was still hard for me to believe she was related to a man as closed off as Alessandro.

"I'm sorry for hijacking the end of Pietro's Japanese lesson, but I wanted to see how you were doing?"

"Oh, I..." I looked down at Pietro and ruffled his hair. "I rarely get holidays, and in a paradise island even less!" I hoped I sounded cheerful enough.

Pietro switched his stance and I moved, pushing his chair toward him.

"Don't overdo it," I said gently.

"I'm okay. I just need the toilet."

"Ah, sure." I watched him move from his stand to his wheelchair and had to use all my willpower not to help him when my whole body was screaming for me to. Once he was seated, I turned toward the screen again, relieved that it was now the end of conversation with Alessandro's sister. "Well, it was nice talking to you. You have a—"

"Why don't we chat for a little while?" she asked, her friendly smile still firmly anchored on her face despite my dismissal that I knew was bordering rudeness.

"I... um, maybe Pietro wants to do something or has another class?" I threw a pleading look to Pietro just before he took the direction of his bathroom.

"No, it's fine." He directed his chair to the other side of his gigantic room. "I've got my book to finish anyway, take your time."

"Okay." *Traitor.* I took a seat in his chair and started tapping my fingers on the desk. "We've been introduced before," I reminded her, just in case she could not place me and that was the reason for her desire to chat. I would not blame her if it was the case; I was usually pretty forgettable.

"Oh, I know." She laughed and it sounded so warm and friendly. I couldn't help but wonder again how she could be so different from her brother. "But things are different now, aren't they? You're not only Sandro's assistant anymore."

I tensed, feeling my smile waver. How much did she know about the situation? How much did he tell her?

"I'm not sure I understand..." I trailed off, throwing a rapid glance toward the bathroom. How desperate was I to look for a ten-year-old child to come to my rescue?

"You're Pietro's best friend, too. I'm a little jealous, you know. I've been trying to get that spot for years and it only took you days."

"Ah, yes!" I exclaimed, relaxing on my chair. "He's an exceptional little boy, and I'm privileged to be in his company."

She nodded thoughtfully before looking over the computer screen then back at me. "Hoka explained everything. It must not be easy to be isolated like that, but I wanted to offer my ear. I know Sandro can be a little…" she cocked her head to the side as if she was trying to ponder her words, "*unreasonable* sometimes."

I couldn't help but let out a little snort, which made her laugh even more.

"I know, I know. I was trying to be nice, but you know this side of them comes with the territory," she added, looking up again.

I heard the faint rumble of a deep male voice, and despite my inability to catch what he said, her blush was enough to let me know it had not been anything fit for my ears or the little boys' who had just exited the bathroom.

"Pietro, why don't you go see if Mario can get an order for more baking supplies? I left a list on the counter but forgot to tell him. We need to bake some more Halloween treats for our party."

"Yes! I love baking cakes!"

I raised an eyebrow. "You especially love eating them!"

He giggled as he passed me.

"Oh, and don't try to get additional ingredients than what the list says," I shouted after him. I shook my head as he didn't answer. "He's going to pretend he didn't hear me, you'll see." I tried to sound stern but failed miserably. I just loved seeing him so carefree, acting like a real little boy. I would give in to almost everything he wanted, just to make sure the heaviness and tiredness I'd seen in his eyes when I'd first met him would never resurface.

"He's different. Speaking with him these past few days." Her smile turned tender. "He can't stop talking about you. He's a fan."

"I am, too."

She nodded thoughtfully. "You're good for them."

My heart jumped at the word 'them.' "I... umm, yeah."

She waved her hand dismissively. "I know Sandro is not the most forthcoming man there is, and I won't pretend to be an expert on him, because Lord knows, these men are a different breed but," she shrugged. "This island is his sanctuary, you know. The only place he's truly himself. He never brings anyone there, and he left you with the person he loves the most."

"He didn't really have a choice."

She raised an eyebrow. "We both know he did."

Yes, he could have killed me like he was supposed to. It would have made his life much easier.

"Mario is here. He's protecting Pietro."

"He does, and he protects you, too. I know you're probably not happy about the situation, but Sandro... he cares."

"I know he does." I could not deny that. He cared about a lot of things, too much even, and I realized, despite my anger, that all the weight he carried on his shoulders must have been exhausting.

"You know, men like him have a weird way to say they love people. To prove he loved me, he thought that blackmailing Hoka with a war and throwing money at me would do the trick."

Love? No, that was a whole different story. She had mistaken the hint of human decency he showed me for something a lot deeper that didn't exist. "He cares about me, I'm a good employee."

"Is that really what you think?" she asked with laughter in her eyes. "You know since you've been working for him, he's been—"

"Some things are better left alone, sweetheart." I heard the deep male voice much closer now.

A fully tattooed arm appeared on the screen, and he cupped her cheek. She turned her head and kissed his hand. This caused an expected yearning in me—his closeness, the tenderness from a man I knew was just as ruthless as Alessandro.

"Fine," she said with a reluctant sigh.

The man leaned in, and I saw her husband for the first time. I couldn't help but let my mouth hang open at the specimen of a man on the screen. Lord Jesus, who was that? His bare chest made of tattoos and muscles was a work of art you only saw in movies, and his hard face belonged to a warrior but with a softness in his eerie golden eyes that I suspected was only there when he was in the safety of his home.

"I'm sorry for my state of undress, but I am ready to go train. I just wanted to prevent my wife from being nosy and trying to force things that need to be worked out on their own." His words were chastising, but his tone carried nothing other than love and a little amusement.

"I-I..." I ran my fingers under my mouth, hoping I was not actually drooling.

My gesture made him grin and Violet slapped his shoulder. "Hoka, stop dazzling women. Besides, this one is not for you to dazzle! She's Sandro's!"

That brought me out of my lust-infused fog. "I'm not sure I understand what you mean."

"Sure, you don't," Hoka replied, his grin widening. "It's nice to finally meet you in person, Lily. I'm sure we'll be seeing plenty of each other in the future."

I opened my mouth to reply that it was unlikely—that once Alessandro uncovered whoever wanted me dead, I would go home, back to my boring but safe life—except I didn't want to correct him.

If just for a few more days, my crazy brain wanted to imagine what a life with a man like one of them could be.

"Now say goodbye, wife. There's someone who needs you."

"Yuko is napping..."

"I never said it was Yuko..." His voice had dropped to a purr that made me wonder how she could ever keep her hands off him.

Her eyes widened and her face blushed red before she turned toward the screen.

"Goodbye, Lily, I'll speak to you soon," she said quickly, and I didn't even have the chance to say goodbye before the call disconnected.

I stayed seated for a minute, replaying that weird discussion. I needed to tell Alessandro to speak with his sister if he ever had the decency to come back. She was making the gesture of him taking me a lot more than it really was.

But what if it really is something? the voice that belonged to my stupid heart asked. *What if you truly matter to him?*

I stood and winced, the chair Pietro used was much lower than normal chairs and my damaged muscle screamed in pain.

I hissed as I started to massage it through the fabric of my wrap skirt, trying to ease the pain.

I'd almost forgotten the pain here. It wasn't raining too much, and the heat really helped, but this was a bitter reminder. A reminder that no matter how much I tried to ignore it, the physical limitation was there. A physical limitation Alessandro was well aware of, which was also the probable reason why he decided to spare my life.

Why kill the poor, crippled girl? I was sure that even a mafia boss like Alessandro would have second thoughts about killing someone like me.

I sighed with relief as the muscle finally loosened under my deep massage.

I had to stop speculating and letting my mind drift into useless dreams. This was not a *Lifetime* movie, it was real life, and the sooner I got back to my gray and rainy reality, the better it would be for me and my heart that seemed to be more than inclined to fall for a man who would only break it into a million pieces.

This is not a life for you, Lily Matthews. Keep your feet grounded, because all that could be waiting for you at the end of the road is endless disappointment.

"Lily, I'm ready!" Pietro shouted from the kitchen.

I chuckled, grateful for the little ball of sunshine taking all my attention.

"I'm coming!" I called back, closing the laptop and getting ready to give this little boy a taste of Halloween he would never forget.

"Is my dad a bad guy?" Pietro asked me the next morning as we watched *Maleficent.*

I swallowed the piece of cake I had in my mouth and started to cough. I tapped the top of my chest and grabbed the hot cocoa on the side table. It was too early for this.

"What?" I asked, throwing a look toward the terrace, where Mario was sitting, having a cigarette after muttering that the blasting AC was going to make his balls drop off.

How else were we supposed to get into the Halloween vibe on an island where it was eighty-six degrees all day long? We needed the November coolness to get into the vibe and the blasting AC took us down to a nice fifty-two.

Pietro turned back toward the screen. "My dad... he's a bad guy." He said it as an affirmation this time. His tone was surprisingly detached for something so serious.

I pressed pause and pulled the knitted blanket higher, turning on the sofa to face him on the other side.

"Why do you say that?" I asked gently, not wanting to deny something before knowing how much he knew. I'd always suspected Pietro knew more than he said or let us see. He was seeing the world from the bubble people placed him in.

I knew that because I'd been there, and when I was sitting on my wheelchair, I'd noticed a lot more things than I did before—a lot more than I actually wanted to see, including Andrew's desire to fly away while being weighed down by his own guilt. Ultimately, I unburdened him of this weight, and he'd gone faster than anyone could have anticipated. It had stung badly back then, I was not going to deny that, but it had been for the best.

Nobody wanted to be a charge, a liability or a commitment made out of obligation, guilt, or any other feeling that wasn't unadulterated love.

He shrugged and kept his eyes forward despite the image being frozen on the scene where Maleficent got her wings back.

"Pietro," I encouraged him. "You can talk to me."

He looked toward the closed French doors leading to the balcony.

"He can't hear anything," I reassured him.

"I'm not stupid, Lily."

"No, you're not. I think you're too smart for your own good," I admitted.

He turned on the sofa to face me. He was absolutely adorable in his pumpkin flannel pajamas and bed hair.

I looked at him silently, holding my cup of hot cocoa as he tapped his fingers on the side of the blanket, probably organizing his thoughts.

"I'm bored here," he admitted on a sigh.

It broke my heart to hear him say that, even though I'd suspected it from the start. What ten-year-old would enjoy being ostracized on a tropical island, no matter how luxurious it might be? He wanted to be like any other boy, and he should.

I felt a new wave of irritation at Alessandro, adding to the already impressively growing pile, but I kept my thoughts for myself and gave Pietro an encouraging smile. It was his time to be heard.

"I- I know I shouldn't, and my dad told me to never do it, but I listened at the doors and I heard him talk on the phone a few times. Sometimes, when I am in California at Uncle Hoka's house, I hear things and…" He shrugged, his face reddening a little in self-consciousness. "I heard you two argue when you first came here. I heard you say he kidnapped you. He didn't hurt you, did he?" His eyes widened, full of concern, sadness, but still full of an innocence I'd rather die than take away.

"I—" I opened and closed my mouth a couple of times. It was not really a discussion I planned to have with him, or one I could even have. I knew close to nothing about Alessandro's life and the mafia. I also felt guilty for causing this beautiful boy some unnecessary worry. "No, your dad didn't kidnap me... at least, not really," I added quickly as his eyebrows dipped and his mouth twisted in disbelief. "I thought so at first, but your dad was only protecting me." *For witnessing a murder he committed.* I added to myself, but this was not really constructive right now.

"He was?" Pietro asked, his voice full of hope.

I nodded, my smile growing as I relaxed on the sofa. "Your father is not perfect, Pietro. No one is. But you saw it in *Maleficent* today, didn't you?"

"Saw what?" he asked, leaning toward me.

"Maleficent. Do you think she is the bad guy?"

He shook his head slowly, visibly confused by my change of subject.

"That's because she isn't, but if you ever watch the original *Sleeping Beauty*, she really is the worst."

"Is she?" he asked, arching his eyebrows. "Why?" His beautiful dark eyes were wide and full of wonder.

My smile widened. "You see, we are taught the distinction between good and evil, hero and villain, savior and captor, but what if the only difference is who is telling the story?"

His mouth morphed into an 'O' of surprise. "So, you're saying my dad is a good guy?"

God no! "What I'm saying is that you are a very bright boy, but you are making assumptions on the little you heard or *think* you heard. I say you need to talk to your dad and ask him to explain."

Pietro's shoulders slumped. "He won't," he said with a huff of defeat. "I'm not good enough to be his son."

My breath stalled at the turn this conversation was taking. "What do you mean?"

He tapped the side of his head with his forefinger. "I'm defective here. I looked on the internet and I read that cerebral palsy means there is something wrong with my brain. My... my dad keeps me here because he's ashamed of me, but he will not tell me."

If I thought my heart was broken before, this conversation took it to a whole new level. No child should even feel like they are not good enough, that they are more of a weight than a joy. I'd felt something similar for a couple of years after the accident, and it left scars I wasn't sure would ever heal. Just imagining this little boy feeling this way from such a young age...

Before I thought better of it, I pulled at the blanket he was wrapped in until he was in my arms. I kissed the top of his head and wrapped my arms around him as I rested my chin on top of his head, trying to wrap him in a cocoon of love.

"Oh, Pietro, you couldn't be more wrong about your father. You have no idea how proud he is of you, how much he loves you." I tightened my hold around his tiny body.

He moved his head and I reluctantly moved mine to look into his eyes while keeping him secure in my arms.

"I know he loves me, I just—" He twisted his mouth to the side, something I'd seen Alessandro do whenever he was looking for words, which was, admittedly, quite a rare occurrence.

"You can tell me anything." I kept one of my arms around him and brought the other one up to move the mop of black hair that was falling in his eyes. This boy needed a haircut.

"Why does he keep me here if he is not ashamed of me?"

I knew why, or at least, I knew why he thought he needed to, even if I didn't think it was the right thing to do. Alessandro had been right; I knew nothing about the world he lived in. I also knew that, misguided or not, everything he did was to protect his son, who was the person he loved the most.

"You are everything to your father, Pietro. He is terrified to lose you and for you to be hurt." I offered evasively.

His face crumpled a little and his innocent, wide eyes started to shine with unshed tears. "He thinks I'm useless, that I can't take care of myself." He sniffled as a tear escaped the corner of his eyes.

I brought my thumb up and dried it softly. "I don't think so, but you know what, it wouldn't matter *even* if it was the case."

He cocked his head to the side, detailing me as if I'd lost my mind, and I let out a little laugh because I'd take any look coming from him instead of the sadness.

I tapped the tip of his nose. "You can do so much more than you think, Pietro. Only you can limit yourself. I mean, it's true, you were born with some challenges, we can't deny that, but have you seen how strong you already are? How wise? I know you don't know many ten-year-old boys, but Pietro, you are spectacular."

He arched an eyebrow with incredulity, and I could see Alessandro again in his face.

"You think so?" The hope and awe in his voice made me feel like a hero.

I nodded. "I know so. I'll show you something." I pulled away from him and pulled up the wide leg of my flannel pajamas to show him my scarred thigh.

I held my breath as he kept his eyes trained on it, hoping I was not making a mistake.

He brought his hand up and gently ran his fingers on the scars. "Does it hurt?"

"Sometimes. Less when I'm with you, though." And it was true, being with Pietro kept my mind busy and seeing him navigate his challenges really put my own issues into perspective.

He beamed at that. "I feel better with you, too."

I ruffled his already messy hair and his revelation was bittersweet, especially since I knew our time together was temporary, no matter how much I wished it wasn't so and we could continue like this. But I couldn't hide on this island forever.

"A lot of people didn't believe in me or were trying to do everything for me because they thought I couldn't do things by myself, but they were wrong. You will fail sometimes, that's the way it is. You will fail over and over again, but the important thing is to not let this define you. Failure teaches you so much more than success ever will. You take what you learned, and you try again. In the end, I can assure you, you will not remember how many times you tried and failed; you will only remember the times you succeeded."

He looked at me for a second before leaning back against me silently, resting his head against my collarbone.

I wrapped my arms around him, and we stayed like that for a few minutes, each of us probably lost in our own thoughts. Meeting that little boy had changed me, seeing Alessandro as a father had changed me, and I worried that when I went back to my life, I would not fit in anymore because the Lily Matthews who came here would certainly not be the one who left. The two Benetti men had taken significant spaces in my heart, and I was not sure I would ever have space for anyone else.

"My dad says if you wish for something very hard, it can happen," Pietro said, not moving from his spot on my chest.

"Yes, I agree with him. Your brain is much more powerful than you think. Tell me, what are you wishing for?"

"I wish you were my mom."

Yep, that did it! I looked at the ceiling, rapidly blinking back my tears. How could a child slay me like that? How could I ever walk away from him?

I tightened my hold on him. "And I wish I could have a son just like you one day." It was not a lie; Pietro was everything I wished for in a child, and irrationally, I wished he was mine.

I took a deep breath and tried to shake away the blues that seemed to be reigning in this room now. We were supposed to have some Halloween fun, not feel sad about not being a family.

"What do you think about going for a swim?" I offered, still a bit confused on why, even during his physiotherapy sessions I'd never seen him in the pool.

It was something I had meant to ask his physio; why he didn't do any sessions in the water with Pietro, but I hadn't had the chance yet and worried that I would, once again, overstep the boundaries and make Alessandro angry. My own physio back home has sworn by it, and the water has always been a source of fantastic relief during my own rehabilitation journey. I'd done my research last night and read that aquatic therapy was one of the greatest ways to improve mobility for children like Pietro. The physio was coming back tomorrow and if, as I expected, Alessandro was still away, I'd ask him the reasons why.

"I'm not allowed," Pietro replied a little wistfully.

I moved back to look at him. "What do you mean?"

"I used to swim with Tim, but I tried alone and I almost drowned. My dad saved me, but he was very angry with Tim and me. I never saw Tim again, and I am allowed near the pool."

I nodded. I couldn't even imagine the fear Alessandro had experienced, but still, it was not a reason to deprive him.

"How old were you?"

"Five," he replied sheepishly. "He told me never to go alone in the pool. I should have known better."

No, you shouldn't have. You were just a baby. "Do you enjoy it? Swimming?"

He nodded with enthusiasm.

"Okay." I stood up. "Let's go for a swim."

"Really?!" he shouted, bouncing on the sofa with excitement. "But Dad..." His excitement dimmed as his brows puckered. "He's going to be angry."

I waved my hand dismissively, pretending to feel a lot braver than I was. "I'll deal with your dad when he's back. And what he doesn't know can't hurt him."

"Okay!" He moved from the sofa to the wheelchair, and I couldn't help but notice how much easier it was for him to move and use his legs. Now that he was willing to do his exercises, his progress was amazing.

I was not sure if I was not making a mistake, but it was making him happy and after the revelation he had just shared with me, I was ready to face Alessandro's wrath for his joyful smile.

Or so I thought...

CHAPTER 9

Alessandro

The clusterfuck of shit that was coming out from this embezzlement was only getting worse.

Finding out that Byrne was in Boston was not even the cherry on top of the shit cake that hit the fan while I was back in Chicago.

Lorenzo was riding my ass, questioning my two-week absence as if I owed him any explanation. He wanted to know too much all the time, and part of me couldn't stop but suspect him. How could I not? Only a handful of people knew I'd be in the basement at that moment and of those people, only few had access to the company computer system.

Which Lorenzo hadn't, but he was in this office often, charming enough women to have gained access without my knowledge.

I'd looked into him, but he didn't seem bright enough to pull off something like this, but maybe it had been all an act, maybe he was actually a genius who played us all.

Not trusting the people around me was exhausting—not that I'd ever been of a particularly trusting nature. Men in my position couldn't really afford to trust easily, but this level of doubt would take a toll on anyone.

I was also annoyed with the finance teams of Datasole Corp, with whom I had to be Alessandro Benetti, the businessman, and not Alessandro Benetti, the mafia boss. I was sure I would have gotten the information a lot faster if I had been able to threaten them with physical damages, including death, instead of immediate dismissal and a bad reference.

It was because of their incompetence that the trip that should have lasted twenty-four hours lasted four days. I couldn't even imagine how angry Lily was going to be once I set a foot on the island. I also knew avoiding talking to her, ignoring her texts and angry voicemails were only putting fuel on the fire, but I thought it was better to wait until I could explain in person and give her news that would help calm her.

Except that everything I was bringing back was just as muddled as it was when I left. I still hadn't talked to Byrne, I had not yet spoken with Killian Doyle, and the whole auditing team was at a complete loss as to how long it had been going on for and how much money had been taken.

I was angry, tired, and frustrated, yet I couldn't help but notice that my heart felt a little lighter when I saw the shore of the island get clearer and clearer. I was always happy to come here and spend time with my son, let my armor fall and be just me, without apprehension or agenda, but I had to admit that some of the trepidation had to do with the fierce woman who was there now, treating my son as if he was her own, loving and caring for him in all the ways he deserved.

I glanced at the shopping bags as I pulled the lever to reduce the speed of the boat to maneuver by the dock. I hoped all the presents I bought would help pacify her a little. I even got her the summer version of the ugly shoes she liked so much.

My two island guards waited for me at the post by the dock. "Anything unusual?" I asked as they approached me to take care of the boat.

"No. The cleaning crew was here yesterday, and the food was delivered early this morning. Mario came and took it all."

I nodded. "*Bene.*" Only Mario was allowed inside the house and around Pietro and Lily, while the other guards ensured the security of the island itself, not that it was really necessary. Only a few people knew it existed and who I was hiding on it, and those were people I trusted not to invade my space.

One of the guards from the private security company reached for a bag and I stopped him. "What are you doing?"

He frowned. "Helping."

"I don't need your help. Your access to the island stops at the palm tree line there." I pointed to the line around the end of the beach. "Don't cross the line." I looked at the other guard who had been assigned on the island for much longer. "Don't cross the line," I added more firmly.

He nodded briskly, pulling the other man by the arm. "He's new, sir. I'll remind him."

I threw a suspicious look to both men. They were highly vetted and highly paid to do next to nothing. It was a perfect gig, but one that could cost them their lives should they break the rules. I was not forgiving when it came to the safety of my son and now Lily. Breaking the rules meant death, and a couple of previous guards over the years had been demoted to shark food for that.

I grabbed the bags and put everything in the golf cart I used to go from the house to the dock.

By the time I parked at the bottom of the stairs that led to the house, the weight I felt when I was the boss had faded, replaced by a longing I rarely experienced—a longing to be home, in this house, with my stubborn boy and the insufferable woman who had taken over my life.

I missed a step at the realization. *Lily Matthews represented a part of home? How was that even possible?*

I reached the house and was surprised to find the main room empty but in complete disarray.

It's not disarray, Sandro, it's lived in, the voice in my head that sounded a lot like my sister taunting me. There were two empty mugs on the coffee table with a half-eaten waffle, a blanket thrown carelessly on the back of the cream leather sofa, and the TV was paused on some kind of dark movie where a battle seemed to be happening.

I put the bags on the floor and heard Pietro's unmistakable giggle come from the back terrace, quickly followed by Lily's melodic laugh.

By the time I reached them, I was laughing too, hoping my presence would not dim the mood.

However, everything changed when I stepped outside and saw Pietro in the pool. Every rational thought fled my mind, replaced by the flashback of Pietro's accidental drowning and the absolute terror I'd felt that day. The terror was quickly followed by an anger so powerful that I couldn't breathe or see straight.

"What the fuck do you think you're doing?!" I shouted in Italian, making Pietro stop immediately, and Mario took a step toward the pool.

That fucker had been there the whole fucking time, knowing full well Pietro was not allowed in the pool or even near it.

"Get him out now, or I swear, you will not live to see another day." I continued my rant in Italian, the vein on my neck and temple beating so hard under the influx of blood, it felt like it was going to rip at any second. "Now!" I bellowed.

Mario grabbed Pietro from the pool, who screamed like a banshee.

"Please, Dad, no. Don't be mad! Dad, don't do this! Look I—"

"Bring him to his room!" I ordered Mario. "And you!" I pointed an accusing finger at the woman standing in the pool, who was lucky not to be in front of me or I would have strangled her with my bare hands.

"Alessandro—" she started with a pacifying tone that angered me even more.

"It's Mr. Benetti to you," I roared. "How dare you take liberties with Pietro. He is *my* son, it's *my* family! You are *not* a part of it." I snorted. "Is that what you want? To play the part of his mother and warm my bed? Are you so incapable of creating your own family that you need to borrow from others? You have no place in this story, no decision to make. He's *not your* son, I'm not your husband. This is not your family. You want a family? A kid? Go find a pathetic loser, like your pathetic Andrew, and have him fuck a baby into you that you can mess up all you want! It's not my fault nobody wants an opinionated, crippled, old shrew. Don't start poisoning your way into our life." I took a few heavy breaths, feeling like a bull staring at the red cloth.

I let out a scream that was more animalistic than human. I grabbed the pitcher on the table and threw it with all my strength. It crashed onto the floor, shattering into a million pieces.

I heard her gasp, but I was too furious to even care what caused it, and I swirled around, disappearing in the house, ready to murder Mario.

I found him slowly walking down the corridor—probably to get back to his side of the house—and the image put more fuel on my fire. How dare he just walk away as if his betrayal didn't deserve death.

I reached him in two steps and shoved him against the wall, pressing my forearm against his windpipe, not enough to cut the oxygen just yet. His life depended on how the next few minutes played out.

"Why didn't you stop her?" I asked through gritted teeth.

"Why would I?" he asked with a raspy voice, my arm probably causing a little more discomfort than I anticipated.

Good! I only wanted to press harder and squeeze the life out of him.

"I'm here to protect your son and Lily... and neither were in danger."

I pressed just a little more. "You don't know that."

"Of course, I do." His voice was barely louder than a whisper, so I reluctantly eased the hold I had on his neck. "She took all the precautions, sir. She made him wear a lifejacket, and she wore one too, just so he didn't feel different."

Fuck, I'd been so angry I hadn't even noticed the lifejacket. That was not the point, though. The problem was, she made decisions she had no place making.

I had not realized I had let go of him until he stepped to the side.

"I may be overstepping, b—"

"You are," I clipped, throwing him a dark look. I was not yet completely sure I was not going to kill him. He knew what had happened to Pietro in the pool, and he knew how strict I was with the rules.

"But I've been keeping your son safe for over five years now, and I've never seen that little boy happier or more alive than he has been over these past few weeks," he continued as if he had nothing to fear. "You said that his wellbeing and his safety were paramount, but what you did today went against all that."

I snorted. "Thank you, Dr Phil."

He shrugged. "I'm no expert in children, but I can see that she makes him happy."

I know that you little shit! "I didn't hire you to have your opinion."

"No, you're getting that for free."

"Mario..." I warned through gritted teeth. "I advise you to get out of my sight right now, because I swear-" I didn't have to finish the sentence; I knew my glare conveyed enough of the underlying threat for him to understand.

He nodded once and turned, walking faster down the corridor.

I walked up to Pietro's room and stopped in front of his door. I'd scared him, I heard it in his voice when he was shouting as Mario grabbed him out of the pool. Now that some of the anger and fear had started to fade, I could think a little more rationally and couldn't help but wince as I replayed my son's words and how fearful he sounded.

I rested my hand on the door but thought better of it. My boy was a lot more like me than I'd like to admit, and I knew that he was not scared anymore. He was probably angry, and I needed to give him time to calm down before I went in there.

When I went back into the living room, I found the bags where I left them—one had tipped over, revealing the summer dress I had bought for Lily. It was the first time in my life I actually bought something for a woman by myself. Usually, when I wanted to thank a fling for their services that were no longer needed, I called my usual jeweler and they handled everything for me.

But yesterday afternoon, I was frustrated with the incompetent accountants and decided to go for a walk to clear my head. I had stopped dead in front of a store and saw this dress on a mannequin. It was not the right season to have something like that in the window, yet as I looked at it, I could imagine Lily wearing it—I also couldn't help but imagine getting her out of it.

I let out a little whistle of frustration as I turned toward the terrace again. The words I'd said to her... I shook my head. I could be a cruel, heartless man; I'd been one more than once, not caring who was on the receiving end or how they would take my words. But today was different, today it was directed at Lily. Usually, all the words I said were the truth but again, my words today were all lies. I said all the things I knew were going to hurt her because, in my moment of pure irrationality, I saw her actions as a betrayal of my trust. Today I wanted to hurt her, just as her betrayal had hurt me.

I grabbed the bag to go give it to her, knowing it was my cowardly way to find out how much trouble I was in with her and how much I would actually need to fix it.

I stopped on my tracks when I saw her unruly red curls in the kitchen. I hesitated for a second. I was not ready to face her yet; I needed the extra few seconds to get ready and figure out what I planned to say.

I took the moment I needed watching her, as she had yet to notice me since she was way too engrossed in her investigation of the kitchen cabinets. She was wearing one of the long dresses she had ordered, but it appeared she had put it back on without taking the time to dry herself based on how the fabric clung to her like a second skin. She truly had a figure many women would die for, and yet, she was always going out of her way to hide it.

My hesitation to speak vanished when I noticed the couple of droplets of blood on the floor as she retrieved the bright orange first aid kit from under the sink.

"Are you okay?" I asked, taking a couple of steps into the kitchen.

She tensed at the sound of my voice, and I could not blame her after the horrors I'd spit at her.

"I'm fine," she replied coolly, keeping her back to me. Her voice held a coldness I was not accustomed to, though I shouldn't have been surprised after the things I'd said to her.

"Are you hurt?" I insisted.

When she remained silent, hunched over the box, my previous good intentions to see how things went flew out the window and I reached to turn her around.

She briskly turned, slapping my hand away, leaving me both surprised and aggravated by her visceral reaction to my touch—even a little hurt if I was being completely honest with myself.

I opened my mouth and closed it again when I noticed the little cut on her cheekbone. I reached up to touch her face, but she jerked away again, and I couldn't contain my groan of frustration. This was bound to become very old, very fast.

"What happened?" I asked, ready to kill whoever made her bleed.

She threw me a side look with her lips pursed and I realized I would have to kill myself. It was a shallow cut and I finally connected the dots with her earliest gasp. I was the one who did that, albeit not voluntarily, when I smashed the pitcher outside.

"A piece of glass?" I asked.

She nodded silently and turned around again, opening an antiseptic wipe before cleaning the cut. She glanced at her reflection on the silvery platter on the counter.

"I'm sorry." I sighed in surrender. "I shouldn't have said that." I seem to be doing that a lot these days—saying things I don't mean and then apologizing.

"It's fine." She shrugged, continuing to take care of her cut as if I was not even there. "You were right. He's not mine, and I don't belong in this equation. It was not my place to get involved in anything. I had lost my focus, but you reminded me why I was here."

"No, I was wrong." Did she even know how much it cost me to say that? I couldn't remember the last time I ever admitted being wrong about anything.

It's probably because you never did, you conceited asshole. The voice in my head, which usually sounded low and mellow like Violet's, sounded more silvery and authoritative like Lily's. "You belong in this—"

"Have you found out what you needed to find out?" she asked as she applied a thin coat of cream to the cut.

I leaned against the counter, giving her a questioning look.

She finally turned to face me completely, and I wished she didn't. Her face was not angry, which I would have preferred. No, she looked resigned, unbothered; her eyes holding mine with a cool disinterest that unsettled me.

"You went back to Chicago, didn't you? Have you found out what you needed to do?" She reached for her necklace again—a habit of hers, as if touching it gave her comfort.

Now that I knew it was her brother's gift—a brother who caused her all the pain—it made no sense to me why she would reach for something of his to give her a sense of comfort and security.

It was probably because she had a high capacity for forgiveness, and that gave me a little hope that I could make things right again.

"I'm ready to go home now," she added, smothering my bludgeoning hope.

I was not sure why, but that cut deep, as if she was betraying me by dismissing… whatever this was.

I shook my head. "I can't take you home just yet. Byrne is still in the wild, and Matteo ordered to see you as soon as the plane touches the ground."

"That's fine." She shrugged again. "Take me to him and let's have a talk."

I let out a laugh that died pretty quickly when I noticed the determination on her face. "You're not joking?" I shook my head again. "Meeting with Matteo is never just meeting with Matteo. If he's not happy with your loyalty, you may not leave the room alive." And then I will have to start my own fucking vendetta.

"I'm willing to take the risk."

"The fuck you will." I gritted my teeth. "Is death really better than being here?"

"I think so, yes."

It was her turn to be cruel, and even if I knew she didn't actually mean that, it stung like a motherfucker.

"You didn't say that when you were enjoying all the luxury this house brought and you spent time stuffing your face with Pietro." I sneered. That was my stupid defense mechanism; I always had to give back the unwanted feelings tenfold.

"As I said before, I seemed to have forgotten my place, which will *not* happen again." She turned around, breaking eye contact, but somehow it didn't feel much like a victory. She put the kit back where she found it and cleaned the counter of the things she'd opened. Even angry, she was still so composed, and I realized her anger was very different from the fiery one I usually saw at the office—the one that used to amuse me like nothing else. This was deeper, scarier.

She walked past me, and I had to use all my self-control not to grab her arm and stop her from leaving. My hand shook with my intent, and I buried it in my pants pocket.

"Please let me know when you have something new and," She stopped just as she reached the exit and hope once again crawled to the forefront of my emotions.

"Yes?" I prompted, trying to sound more casual than I felt.

"I will not wait forever. I will take my chances with the sharks, should it come to it... *crippled* or not," she added quickly before leaving. The acid that dripped from her words was another side of Lily I'd never witnessed before—one I didn't particularly like.

I shook my head before running a wary hand over my face. It was a gift I had, it seemed. I was perfect at pulling the worst out of people.

I grabbed a cool beer from the fridge and decided to go to the office and concentrate on work for a while. Maybe if I let her and Pietro cool down for a while and gave her some good news, then maybe she'd be more inclined to forgive my latest outburst until the next one.

How many times could good people forgive? I was not too keen to figure it out.

I sat behind my desk and listened to the voicemails I had. How was it possible that in only five hours of turning it off, I already had sixteen messages? Fourteen were from Lorenzo, complaining about everything and anything. One was from Oda, telling me that he was on the verge of killing Lorenzo and needed immunity. It made me chuckle, but it also concerned me since Oda was probably the most laid back man I had. If he was having a hard time... I tapped my pen on the desk in thought. It was a conversation I didn't particularly want to have, but once I was home, I needed to remind Lorenzo that his diva attitude had no place in the mafia. I also planned to remind him that his position was only secured because my father appointed him as his *consigliere*, his right-hand man, at his father's death. Something I could not explain to this day. It was not going to be a pleasant chat, but I had to remind him that he was not irreplaceable; he was, in fact, very much replaceable and I had a list of men who would be so much more suitable, starting with Moreno Caprese, who had always been one of my father's most trusted *caporegime*. I had actually expected Moreno to take over after Lorenzo's father's death. If it had been the case, I could have named him my underboss when my father died, but things had not been going that way and I'd been stuck with Lorenzo, who still hoped to become my underboss one day. Didn't he see he was more trouble than he was worth? It was also the reason why, even after four years in the position, I had not yet named an underboss.

The other message was from a business associate, his voice trembling with fear as he explained that he would not be able to accommodate us anymore should Lorenzo continue to act the way he was.

Fuck it! I was gone merely weeks, and everything was going to shit.

I couldn't leave again, not that early anyway, and certainly not with how things were with Lily. I froze at the realization that I'd just picked Lily over the *famiglia* without thinking about it, and that was a problem in itself.

I picked up the phone. I had to deal with one problem at the time.

"Boss." Came the hard voice of Moreno, which was somehow comforting. The man was older than me, yet he always addressed me with the reverence that was due to my rank.

"I have a problem."

"How can I help?"

"Lorenzo seems to be making a mess of things, and I can't come to deal with the situation. I would have asked Oda to help, but he's too young, too low in the hierarchy for Lorenzo to listen to."

"Yes, he is. Lorenzo is no *consigliere*," he replied with the same firm tone.

"I need you to help me refocus him while I'm away."

He was silent for a moment. "I need the authority."

"You do," I agreed. "I will name you temporary underboss until I'm back. What do you say? It will only be for a couple of weeks." I couldn't and wouldn't make that permanent, anyway. The underboss would replace me in the event of my death, and I didn't trust anyone enough not to be the one killing me for the spot, even if Moreno was the closest to an underboss I had.

"He will hate that," he said with amusement.

"He will, but let me deal with that, okay? He won't kick up a fuss; he would hate for people to know that I appointed him a babysitter."

Moreno let out a low chuckle. "*Da vero.*" He sighed. "I'll handle the mess while you're away. Don't be too long."

"If you need help, ask Oda; he's trustworthy."

"I don't need any help."

I rolled my eyes. He was extremely old-school for a man in his late thirties, and once again, I tried to understand why my father had chosen Lorenzo over him. The only thing I could think of was that Lorenzo and his father knew something damaging about my father.

"I'll deal with Lorenzo." He added gruffly.

"I'll make it up to you."

"Don't worry, helping the boss is an honor."

"*Grazie.*" I hung up, thinking more and more about creating the scandal one more time and appointing Moreno as my underboss until Pietro was old enough to take over.

Pietro... Just the thought of my son being exposed to the sharks in the *famiglia* made my stomach turn with fear. Yet it was his legacy, his birthright. I knew the longer I waited to introduce him to our lives, the worse it would be, but I was not ready yet.

I called Lorenzo, who, of course, made a full drama of everything—accusing everyone to be the source of whatever misunderstanding as it was impossible for him to do anything wrong. He was seething when I announced that Moreno would be in charge while I was away, but he calmed just as quickly when I told him that should he make things harder for Moreno, I'd have no other choice than to make this announcement official, and he'd have to deal with the consequences himself.

By the time I was done with all the business, it was much later than I had anticipated, and I only had an hour or so before Pietro would go to bed.

I found Mario alone on the terrace, the living room back to its spotless state, and I was wondering if he had been the one cleaning or if Lily came out and did that.

Lily. Of course, it was Lily.

"Where are they?" I asked Mario as I joined him on the terrace.

He took a drag on his cigarette, looking at me warily. I could not really blame him for this.

"Isn't it time for Pietro's show?" I may not have been here often, but I knew my son by heart, and he never missed an episode of his kid science show.

Mario shrugged, dropping his cigarette in his almost empty Coke bottle. "The kid didn't seem like himself. Well, not like his *new* self." That was a jab I didn't miss. "He said he was tired and took his sandwich to his room. As for the little miss..." He shrugged. "I'm not her keeper."

I pursed my lips. He was doing this on purpose.

"*Stai attento, Mario. La mia gratitudine si sta esaurendo.*" I was grateful for his protection of my son, but his attitude was getting a little too much.

I softly knocked on Pietro's door, already expecting him not to answer. He was a good kid, perfect really, but he was also stubborn—yet another infuriating trait he got from me—and I was sure he was mad at me for today. If it had only been anger, I would have left him for a while until he forgave me like he always did, but I knew I'd hurt and scared him, and that wasn't something I could let sit through the night.

I opened the door, and the room was dimly lit by the couple of nightlights he used to get around his room at night. I looked at his back for a minute, knowing he was not asleep as his breathing was not deep or slow enough.

"*Buona notte, cucciolo.*"

I sighed and rounded his bed when he remained silent. His eyes were wide open, and I was grateful he was not faking being asleep, but I hated seeing his little nose all red and his eyes wet, as well as the dark spots on his wizard pillowcase, proof of his silent tears.

I had been the one who hurt him, making him cry when the only thing I wanted was for him to be happy and safe. I'd bleed myself in a second if it was necessary, yet I seemed to always be the source of his torment. How could I be such a bad father?

I crouched by his side, and he kept looking at the nightlight plugged by his bathroom door. That child was really pigheaded.

"I'm sorry, *polpette*. I never should have shouted and scared you like that. I..." I sighed, running my fingers through my hair in frustration. I, what? I was a fucking beast, end of story, and once again, I let my irrational temper take over.

"I got scared when I saw you in the water, and I shouted because I love you." We were quite cheap on the L-word in the world I lived in. I couldn't even remember either of my parents ever telling me they loved me, but it probably was because they didn't. To my father I was nothing more than a duty, a necessity to ensure continuity. I was no better than a tool for him. I was an asset first, a son second. For my mother, I was nothing more than an unwanted child, born from a loveless marriage—someone she forgot existed as often as she could as she kept her facade while popping pills and drinking her expensive wine.

I'd promised myself when I saw my little boy—who looked so fragile and defenseless as he fought for his life in the incubator—that I wouldn't be like my parents had been, that I would be his source of love and safety. How much had I failed him already?

He sniffled but kept his eyes away, locked into a mutism I hoped wouldn't last.

I rested my hand on top of his soft hair for a minute, hoping there was something, anything, I could tell him that would make what I did okay, but I knew there was none.

I shook my head with defeat as he sniffled again. "Sweet dreams, my boy. *Ti voglio molto bene.*" I stood with a huff, the emotions and mistakes of the day starting to weigh me down.

"I love you, too," he said as I reached the door and the sadness in his voice stopped me on the spot. "But sometimes... I don't like you very much."

I turned around and looked at his back. "Sometimes I don't like myself very much, either," I admitted softly.

He sniffled again and his unsteady, deep inhalation showed he was trying to fight back more tears.

"Lily says I can do anything, become anything I want to. She said that only I know what my limits are and-and-and..." He let out a soft sob and I pursed my lips, tightening my hands into fists to fight my need to go to him.

I couldn't stop him now that he was in the middle of his explanation; I needed to hear it and take the cuts if it made him feel better. I deserved nothing more.

"I want to get better because I'm sorry you had me, a son who's broken. I'm sorry you can't be proud of me, and that you have to hide me here. I'm sorry that no matter how much I try, I'll never be good enough." His voice cracked, and I felt my knees buckle as a wave of nausea hit me.

"Sometimes I wish I'd died with my mom," he added with a weariness and finality that took away my ability to breathe.

That had done it. His raw pain was my fault, my doing, and it finally broke me.

I leaned against the doorframe and slid down until I sat there crying for the first time in ten years.

I took a shaky breath, trying to ease a pain so overwhelming, I could barely think straight.

"You're enough, my son. No, that's not true. You're not enough; you're *everything*. My moon, my sun, my life, my heart. I could not be prouder than I am to be your father, Pietro. I swear to God." I opened my mouth again but closed it, not knowing how I could make it better, but all my instincts were shouting for me to go get Lily. She would know how to help, she would help him heal, and she would help me breathe again in the process.

Lily was not just a piece of this puzzle; she was a central piece, and for all I knew, I'd destroyed it.

CHAPTER 10

LILY

Today I realized something I had probably felt for a long time but did my best to deny. I was in love with my boss. I couldn't really say when it started, probably when I saw him at work—his raw masculinity and charisma would have tricked even wiser women—but I'd known better. Men like Alessandro didn't consider women like me, small-town girls with trauma and scars, as worthy of them.

Then, contrary to all logic, these feelings only grew over the past few weeks on the island. Seeing him more relaxed, being a father to Pietro, made me fall deeper, and then there was that kiss. A kiss that obliterated any other kiss I'd ever received.

I also realized how deep I was in when he said those cruel words and how much they'd affected me. I'd never been particularly sensitive to insults or criticism—at least I rarely let them hurt me—but Alessandro's words had hurt me in a way that few things did. It felt almost as painful as when I woke up in the hospital with my body completely broken.

A rasp at the door got my attention, but I remained on the cozy chair I pulled by the opened windows. I knew it could only be Alessandro and frankly, I was not in the mood to hear anything he had to say.

I touched the cut on my cheek, and despite it not hurting physically anymore, it was a reminder of his heartlessness that had never really been directed to me before. His words hurt even more because I knew a lot of what he'd said was true.

I came to think of him and Pietro as my family without having the right to, and no matter how much I worked, I did have some physical limitations and would always have them, even if I'd forgotten recently.

"Lily."

I turned briskly, almost expecting to find him in my room. He had the keys, I knew that, yet the room was empty.

"I know you don't want to talk to me, and I can't blame you. It's just—"

I stood and walked to the window, closer to the voice, though I remained hidden from view as I imagined he had rethought his strategy and was now on a nearby balcony.

"I'd almost lost Pietro so many times in the few months after he was born, and every time I felt agony because I loved that baby from the moment I set eyes on him. I brought him here to keep him safe, and when I saw him lying in the swimming pool, lifeless, when he was five... Lily, I thought I was dying." His voice cracked and I had to stop myself from stepping onto the balcony to comfort him. He had hurt me deeply, and I needed to be strong.

"When I saw him in the pool again, I didn't think; I lost my mind and said many hurtful things that are in no way how I feel." He stopped for a second, and I was tempted once again to step on the balcony and look at him.

I rested the side of my face against the wall and waited.

"I'm just not good at this." He let out a frustrated groan that made me smile. "I just never really had to worry about how people dealt with things, and I don't know how to express when I care. It's... baffling."

Baffling? It was a way to put it. It was messy and hurtful. Welcome to the human realm, Alessandro, feelings suck.

I couldn't help but wonder if it meant that he cared about me or... *No, don't start, Lily, nothing good will come out of this.*

"You belong in this equation, Lily. You belong in a way that is astonishing and aggravating, and part of me can't really deal with the fact that—" He stopped abruptly, and I cursed every god that was willing to listen.

I needed to hear the rest.

He let out a little laugh, but it sounded tired and washed out. "I don't even know if you're listening; you might already be asleep with your earbuds in, and here I am, pouring my heart out into the night. Ah well, it's probably for the best. I'm probably making a mess of things like I always do."

No, you're not. You're strangely good at it... in a clumsy, endearing kind of way, I thought as some of my anger and hurt started to fade.

"Admitting things to no one in particular is strangely cathartic, and there's no one to mock my failed attempt."

There's nothing failing about your attempt, I admitted begrudgingly.

"The thing is, Lily, I have a hard time accepting the importance you have in many areas of my life. I started to depend on you as my assistant. I trusted you, which is something that, you can probably guess, is quite rare in the life I'm leading, and then I realized this trust went deeper, and I took you here, to the person who's the most precious to me. I let you into my real life and that's just..." He let out a long exhale. "I'm not sure how I'll deal with it when it's all fixed and you leave, because you are part of this family, in a very unconventional way, in a way that I can't even name. But you are, Lily, and it will be hard, not only for Pietro, but for me, when we can't see you every day, when you're gone."

A feeling of deep sorrow submerged at the thought of walking away from this broken man and his extraordinary son, even if I knew it would be for the best.

The best for whom?

"You matter to me, Lily. I care," he added with so much defeat that the rest of my anger vanished.

I took a couple of breaths, trying to figure out how I could answer but the words failed me. I took a step onto the balcony, hoping that a smile would be enough for now, but he was nowhere to be seen.

I looked at all the darkened empty balconies and wondered for a second if all these beautiful, yet terribly clumsy, words had been nothing more than my imagination.

"I care, too." I gazed at the bright full moon. "I care too much," I added before walking back into the room, hoping sleep would come after this day full of emotions.

I gave up on sleep just as the sun started to rise, giving the night an increasing golden hue.

How could Alessandro break my heart and fill it with joy all on the same day? It was insane.

I looked at the clock, seeing it was not even five yet—much too early to run around in the house and risk waking up Pietro. The kid was good but waking him up earlier than was agreed didn't let out the best part of him.

I changed into the bikini set I was sure Alessandro bought just to annoy me, but I didn't have much choice as the other one was forgotten in the laundry room and I was not going to risk walking past Alessandro's room.

I needed a little more time to decide if I wanted to forgive him and give it another chance. His words had been hurtful, and despite what he thought, not everything slid right past me.

I put on one of the summer dresses we ordered, despite my desire to wear the one I'd found in front of my door last night. It was a guilt present I had been too angry to consider.

I grabbed my towel, put on the flip-flops, and left the house from the side door as quietly as possible to go to the little creek with the waterfall I'd discovered a few days ago. The cool water was absolute heaven and helped my muscles. I was sure that some time there would also help my busy mind figure out what I was supposed to do.

I walked for a few minutes through the trees until I reached my newfound oasis. The sound of the waterfall, combined with the gentle scent of flowers was just as calming as any fancy spa.

I removed my dress and shoes, and gasped as I stepped into the cool water. I held my breath as I walked to the middle of the creek until the water touched mid-stomach, then I dove under, enjoying the weightlessness I felt as I was under the water.

"I thought you were trying to leave." I heard as soon as I broke the surface.

I turned around with a gasp to find Alessandro standing on a high stone at the edge of the creek.

He looked magnificent, wearing nothing more than a pair of loose dark blue linen pants, his hair still tussled with sleep. I'd never thought of him like that before, but how fair was it that this man was even more stunning when he was not even trying?

It seemed his presence stole my ability to speak or think straight for a second, and all I could do was stare at him and take in all the details. The big expense of this chest, and his skin looking even more golden in the rising sun, the light dusting of dark hair peppering his chest, his flat hard stomach, and the little trail of hair that disappeared below his pants, leading to... I blushed when I realized where my eyes had focused and jerked my head back up to look at his eyes.

"Where would I go?" I asked, and I didn't miss the way his mouth pursed at the jab I didn't really mean as such.

"You said you were ready to take your chances with the sharks."

"I think we both said things we didn't really mean, and I would never leave like that, not without saying goodbye."

His face softened. "To Pietro or to me?"

"Does it matter?" I asked, my heart starting to hammer in my chest as his face took on the intense look I saw before in the boardroom. The fierce Alessandro stood in front of me, and when I usually saw him like that, there was nothing he couldn't achieve. His determination was so intense that everything bent to his will, and I suspected that it would include me if he really put his mind to it.

"More than you think."

"B-both," I replied, cursing myself as I felt my skin heat despite the coolness of the water.

"I'm taking Pietro back with us to Chicago, I'm done with the island."

My head jerked back toward him in surprise, my embarrassment gone.

"Really?" I stood up straighter in the water. "Oh, Alessandro, this is so amazing! Pietro is going to be so happy."

He nodded, his eyes dipping to my chest and stomach, and I realized that under my excitement I'd started to show a lot more skin than I intended, including some of the scarring on my side. I crouched back in the water, somehow annoyed by how self-conscious I felt under his gaze.

"I'm terrified, and so out of my depth with all this. The life I lead in Chicago is very different from here, and I just hope I'll be enough for Pietro there."

"I can help," I blurted before thinking better of it, but knowing it was the right thing to do regardless.

"Help?"

I nodded. "I mean, we both know I can't work as your assistant anymore." For so many reasons, one of them being my feelings for him. "But I can work for you and take care of Pietro, not that it would be that much of a job, to be honest."

"So, you'd be living at my house with me and my son?" he asked. Hearing it coming directly from him sounded exactly like what he accused me of doing yesterday, and I couldn't help but wince in mortification.

"N-no." I shook my head vehemently. "It doesn't have to be, of course. I understand you wouldn't want me in your space of cou—"

"I would love you in my space," he interrupted, the tone of his voice pressing on the double meaning.

My eyes widened with surprise, but then I shook my head with a little smile. He was joking; of course, he was.

"Having you under my roof every day... It would be like taking the lamb to the wolves' den."

"Oh!" It made sense now. "Because of the... *mafia*?" I whispered the last word, looking around.

He let out a tired laugh. "No, beautiful. It has nothing to do with the mafia and all to do with me being a man who has had a hard time controlling his urges around you recently."

"You don't have to say that. I know you didn't mean all the horrible things you said yesterday."

"You think I'm lying?"

"Not lying exactly, but—"

"Come here." His order lacked the condescension it usually carried, but something else filled his tone that made my skin heat and my lower stomach tightened embarrassingly.

I shook my head.

"Matthews..." the warning sounded almost playful, "come here."

The command caused shivers to race down my spine, but it was not from fear. No, unfortunately, it was from something a lot more complicated and unwanted desire. God, why was my body reacting like that?!

"No," I squeaked embarrassingly.

The look on his face was predatory, but not in the sense that endangered your life, more in a sense that endangered your virtue.

It was irrelevant how experienced you could be; I was sure that a man who looked like Alessandro could take a virtue you didn't know you still had.

"Fine. I'll come to you."

It took me a second to understand as he reached for the waistband of his pants and pulled them down.

"Oh!" I swirled around, my face burning with embarrassment. He went commando under his pants, and I caught a glimpse of a part of him I'd only been imagining late at night. This quick view—merely a second—of the real deal showed that my imagination, even if generous, didn't render him justice.

Would it even fit? *Damn it, Lily, don't think about that now!* I cursed myself.

I felt the water ripple against my back and caught my breath, knowing he was there. I could feel his presence.

I gasped when I felt his fingers brush the side of my neck to the ball of my shoulder.

"Turn around, Lily Matthews." His voice was so low and hypnotizing, it almost sounded like a purr.

"You're naked!" I let out on a breath.

"Yes, I am," he replied, the smile evident in his voice as he trailed his fingers up and down my shoulder.

I scowled at the boulder in front of me, getting annoyed at his mocking.

"Wh— Why are you naked?"

"Um, so many reasons."

I let out a shameful sound that was a mix of a cry of surprise and a moan of pleasure as I felt his teeth replace his finger, gently biting at my skin, quickly followed by a long lap of his tongue.

"You taste like pineapple... and I love pineapple."

Lord have mercy! I begged, closing my eyes. I was so grateful I was in the water and that the heat and wetness between my thighs could be attributed to it.

"You're naked," I repeated, but it came out as a whine. I almost hoped my legs would give out and I'd drown.

"I think we already established that," he murmured against my skin as he trailed his lips up my neck to stop against the shell of my ear. "If you came to me like a good girl, then I wouldn't have had to take off my pants and come to you."

The words '*good girl*' made me weak in the knees, and I had to grip the rock in front of me for support.

"Ah." He laughed. "I'm lying. The pants would have had to come down anyway." He wrapped his free arm around my waist, pulling me back against his hardness.

"How else could I prove to you that I meant all the words I just said."

"Oh god!"

"Ah, I'm sure it's not the first cock you've seen or felt... is it?"

"No." But the only one I ever saw or touched didn't come close to the size of the thing poking in my back.

"I want you, Lily. Do you believe me now?"

How could I not when his anaconda was pressed against my back?

"Alessandro, people could see us," I whispered urgently as I still had a little control over my libido, which I expected would only last for a couple more touches. But even now, when every logical part of me screamed for him to stop, I didn't, too scared that he would actually listen and break the spell we were both under.

"No, they can't. I just want to touch you. Feel your body hum under my touch."

As if on cue, I shivered as his hand trailed down my shoulder to cup my breast over the thin black material of my bikini.

"I didn't imagine the attraction the other night on the balcony, did I?" he asked, and there was a twinge of uncertainty in his voice I was not familiar with. "You want me too, don't you?"

I didn't want to think anymore; I didn't want to be the analytic Lily—at least, for now in this creek. I didn't want to think about the reasons why this had no future, why it was a mistake. I just wanted to enjoy this man's touch, getting lost in the sweet oblivion of pleasure that I'd only read about. My heart had been broken many times before, not only by romance but also by life, despite always being careful. I was okay to have it broken for being reckless for once.

I leaned back against him, pressing my back against his erection and letting my head fall against his shoulder, keeping my eyes closed to concentrate only on his hands on my skin.

He let his hand travel down my side, and I held my breath as his fingers trailed over the raised skin of the scars on my flank. He didn't stop or even linger on the scarred skin, and he kept on going until he reached the waistband of my bikini bottom.

He kissed my neck again softly as he let his finger slip inside just an inch and waited as he trailed his lips along the pulsating vein at the side of my neck.

I knew that he stopped to give me time to say no, and even with my lust-filled brain, I appreciated the concern, but there was no way I would stop him now. I was way too gone, and it had been way too long. In fact, I had to stop myself from grabbing his wrist and pushing his hand deeper so his fingers could finally ease the growing ache.

"Alessandro," I whispered with a tone akin to a prayer.

His hand on my breast tightened as his other hand finally slipped in. I couldn't contain the soft moan that mixed with a sigh of relief as his fingers brushed softly down my slit.

His fingers were gentle, searching for the first couple of strokes as if he was tuning his caress to the way my body responded, getting his erotic touch attuned to what my body wanted...

This man was an artist.

He pressed his thumb against my engorged clit, and I let out a cry of pleasure.

"Mmm, that's right, Matthews, tell the world how much you enjoy my fingers on you," he purred against my ear.

I started to move my hips as his fingers turned more demanding, more rapid, firm, pressing on my clit with every back-and-forth movement.

He kept going faster and faster as I felt myself getting closer to the edge. My hip movements turned completely erratic as I felt myself about to tip off the ledge.

"Come for me, beautiful," he commanded as he pinched my nipple and inserted two fingers inside me.

That did it. The fullness created by his fingers and the pleasurable pain of his pinch had sent me flying, and I came shouting his name into the wilderness of this island with the most earth-shattering orgasm I'd ever experienced.

It was blinding, all-consuming, and body-numbing all at the same time, and it lit all my nerves ending on fire. It was all fire and ice. So insanely contradictory, but I could feel it everywhere, making me question if I ever had an orgasm before.

I blinked as he touched the underside of my jaw and pushed my head up so I could look at his face.

My vision was still a little fuzzy, but I saw how he detailed my face, his hand still cradling my jaw, his thumb running back and forth on my lips.

"Pleasure suits you, Lily. You should be given orgasms more often... preferably by me."

I opened my mouth but closed it again as my brain was still humming from the satiation of my needs.

I looked at his face clearly now. He had this look of male pride that I would have normally wanted to smack away, but it was more than justified right now.

I opened my mouth again as his thumb passed in the middle, and I sucked it in, the only thing I wanted to do.

His nostrils flared and his eyes narrowed, but it was not from his usual irritation or anger—this was desire, pleasure... want. Something I had never truly seen from Alessandro Benetti, and certainly not something I ever expected to see directed toward me.

"*Dio aiutami*," he muttered under his breath before removing his thumb from my mouth. He leaned down, giving me a possessive kiss—different from the one on the balcony that had started soft and sweet. This kiss was demanding and hot and carried a tinge of desperation as his tongue invaded my mouth and I went lax in his arms, completely surrendering to his masculine dominance I never expected to crave like I had.

I let my hand roam behind me and surprised myself with my own boldness as I trailed my fingers along his hard cock, not able to contain the gleeful thrill and feminine pride to be the reason for it.

I circled his length, or at least, I tried to. I squeezed, making him hiss against my mouth.

"No," he growled, pushing back from me, his breathing heavy, as if letting go had been physically impossible. "Not here, not now." He spoke through his teeth, his gaze seemed to be going right through me.

He was not talking to me; he was talking to the beast inside him.

I took a step back, leaning against the stone for support as I pressed my thighs together, shocked by my reaction at seeing his barely contained control starting to slip, seeing all his muscles tense up and his nostrils flare like a bull ready to strike.

I'd been used to clumsy, gentle lovemaking when I was with Andrew—nothing compared to what this ruthless man could do and how he already possessed me with nothing more than a kiss. I knew that if his control was broken, he'd likely take me roughly, mount me, show me who I belonged to... and instead of terrifying me as it should have, the thought almost made me come again.

I frowned, unsure why he was fighting so hard. Surely, he knew I wanted it too, right? He had to know I wanted all he was ready to give me.

I took a step toward him.

"Don't. Come. Closer." Each word seemed to come out with great difficulty. "One more step, and I'll ravish you right there on that stone." He jerked his head toward something behind me. "And come what may."

I glanced at the stone and looked back at him. "That doesn't sound too bad to me," I said breathlessly. "I'm not breakable, I can take it." My voice conveyed much more bravado than I felt at the reminder of the sight of him.

"This is not the place. I would kill anyone who saw you like that. I need time to—" He swirled around, moving much quicker than I thought possible.

He helped himself up and I ogled him, not even trying to hide it. He stood on the edge with his back still toward me, and he was ever more glorious than in all my fantasies. Strong shoulders, narrow hips, round muscled ass, and thick powerful thighs.

He stepped back into his discarded pants and walked away without another look to me.

I watched him leave wordlessly. I was still too overwhelmed by how powerful my reaction had been to him, but I also felt destabilized by his sudden mood swing and his rapid retreat.

I didn't take it as a rejection, at least not really. I didn't think I could have resisted him the way he managed to resist me, but there were factors he had to take into account that I couldn't—Pietro's wellbeing being one of them.

I sighed, looking at the waterfall. I knew the water hitting the creek was really cold as I swam toward it. I needed to cool myself down so I could think rationally again.

I needed to figure out if what I was feeling right now was only due to the pleasure he'd just given me or if it was something much more terrifying... and something I suspected was true.

I had fallen in love with Alessandro Benetti.

CHAPTER 11

Alessandro

I panicked when I saw her sneak away so early. I thought she was really making good on her threats about taking her chances with the sharks to escape the island.

I'd jumped into a pair of trousers and followed her deeper into the wilderness and the worry morphed into something a lot stronger—animalistic, a deep-rooted jealousy I was not entitled to feel.

I frowned as I slowed my steps. She was easy to follow with her bright red dress... I speculated she was going to meet one of the guards. Was she meeting Mario? Did they get closer while I was away? Was that why he let her break the rules with Pietro? I turned toward the house, but I could barely make it out through the overabundant foliage. I tightened my fists as an image of Mario taking her flashed in my mind, and I wanted to kill him for it. Was she meeting the new guard? The one who clearly had a death wish if he took what was mine.

She's not yours, Alessandro, my conscience tried, but I smothered it. In real life she wasn't, she deserved a good, safe life, but within the mafia world? Fuck if I let anyone steal her from me. In this world, she belonged to no one else but me.

I turned toward her and took a few more steps before stopping. My body tensed as I watched her shimmy out of her dress, revealing the tiny bikini I bought her just to piss her off.

Well, the joke was on me, because my cock was waking up with a vengeance and the influx of blood was painful.

That woman's body was nothing like I expected the little angry prude to be. Well, I did have a glimpse of her figure when I took her to the island in her tight dress, but my mind was much more occupied by all the shit that would follow this one insane decision than to take the time to admire her. But now, I could feast my eyes on every inch of her, and it was worth the early morning walk in the fucking jungle. Fuck, I was sure it was even worth a swim with the sharks!

She was all soft curves and silky skin. She had full, perky breasts and a small waist that flared to rounder hips and a shapely backside. She had a lot of scars, but it didn't make her any less sexy or attractive, at least not to me. This woman was a warrior, a woman who experienced a world of pain I could not even start to comprehend, and she was here, standing, laughing, giving love and care to the people around her. Her battle scars made her even more attractive and caused so many conflicting emotions inside me. I wanted to worship her and protect her, but I also wanted to pleasure her and dominate her in ways I hoped she would enjoy.

I should have walked away when she stepped into the water—there was no threat, no attempt to escape—yet I had to show myself to her.

I saw the lust in her eyes as she'd detailed me. I'd already guessed it when she'd kissed me back, but now I knew for sure that she was as attracted to my body as I was to hers, and when she implied I pretended to be attracted to her for ulterior motives, I snapped. I had no reason to fake anything; she'd already offered to stay for Pietro, and once again, I gave in to my most primal need and did all the things I knew I shouldn't have done.

But when she came undone in my arms, with my fingers deep in her tight heat, I felt a string snap around my heart—something more than just sexual attraction, more than simple care. It was something deeper, making me run as I always did.

My phone vibrated on my desk, and I looked at my brother-in-law's name flashing on my screen. For once, I had to admit I was quite grateful for the interruption.

"Hoka."

"Do you ever check your voicemail?" he asked angrily.

I removed my phone from my ear and glared at the screen. Who the fuck did he think he was talking to?

"I don't remember you being the boss of me," I replied coldly, putting the phone to my ear.

"No, but your sister is the boss of *me*," he admitted without shame.

It was something I would have teased him about just a few weeks ago, but now...? I didn't find that as funny anymore, and I was not really sure why.

"She's been riding my ass to come to the island, and I promised to do it if I didn't hear your voice by the end of the day." He sighed. "You know how much I enjoy being the one riding her-"

"Don't!" I shouted down the phone.

He let out a little laugh. "Seriously, I was starting to worry, too. You left that cryptic message about needing to contact Boston, and then nothing else."

I felt a pinch of guilt at leaving them high and dry, especially Violet, who didn't need this stress in her life.

"Things took a turn I didn't really expect."

"I see. With the matter at hand or with the fierce redhead?"

I cleared my throat, not really pleased that he was so close to the truth. "I need to speak with Killian Doyle."

Hoka took a sharp breath. I knew I took him by surprise, and I could not blame him. We all stayed far away from the Irish.

"What do you need from the Irish? I can help," he finally said, his voice suddenly lower. I knew it meant that my sister wasn't far, and he didn't want to worry her.

"Why would you meddle in that? I thought the *yakuza* didn't mix in other people's mafia."

He snorted. "I know, but I sort of made a commitment when I married your sister, and she'd be mad if I didn't help. She loves you."

"I'll owe you one."

He scoffed. "Like I'll ever need anything from the Italians, please. Just take the favor and move along."

"You don't need anything from me? Are you sure?" I smirked, knowing I was about to hit way below the belt. "Who was the man who got drunk and cried pathetically into his glass no more than six months ago because his wife was mad at him and hadn't given him any for weeks." I shook my head. "I saved you from your everlasting case of blue balls when I pleaded your case."

Hoka was quiet for a moment. "I thought that was not to be mentioned again. You agreed."

"I reserve the right to mention it when you think you're so much better than your brother-in-law."

"Wait until you meet her; the woman who will make you reconsider everything you believe in, the woman who will become so much more important than your pride and your ego."

I turned toward the door almost subconsciously and thought about the little woman who was now probably bonding with my son.

"God protects me against such a plague," I prayed, fearing deep down that it was already too late.

"It may be a little too late for that, don't you think?" Hoka expressed my unspoken thoughts. "I met your woman a few days ago. I like her, she's bold."

I couldn't help but smile at that. "Lily is unaware of her power, but she's a force to be reckoned with."

Hoka laughed.

"What?"

"It's funny how you didn't deny she was yours, and how you knew exactly who I was talking about."

Fuck.

"I need to get Doyle to give me Byrne. He's hiding there."

Hoka sighed. "Seriously? See what happens when you hire another mafia?"

I threw my head back in exasperation and looked at the ceiling. "For my legit business, it didn't matter! The man was a brilliant accountant! He flew under the radar for years, cleaning accounts, but I know it's not for him. He was not working alone, and he's not the reason why Lily has Matteo over her head. I need to know who he did that for so I can take him out."

"Doyle is psychotic on his best days, and he's such a protector of the Irish blood. I don't think you can get him to hand anyone over."

"I can."

"How? Magic? Sexual favors?"

I grimaced. I had not planned to give away my only card to Doyle unless it proved critical, but Lily's life was in danger and that was worth it.

"I have the thing he wants the most."

"What is that? A pot of gold?"

I took a deep breath. "The location of his brother."

Hoka cursed under his breath. "How long have you known?"

"Long enough," I replied evasively.

"You know how much that's worth?" he asked slowly. "There's nothing he wants more than Finn back. He'd give almost anything to get revenge on his betrayal."

"Yes, Hoka, I'm well aware of that," I replied with a sigh of irritation. "I'm not a newbie in this world. I was born into it, just like you were."

"And you'd give that wild card up? For *her*?" The disbelief in his tone aggravated me more than it probably should have. How could he be so dismissive when he had been ready to give away his whole fucking kingdom for my sister.

"It's not just her. It's my business, too. I can't have traitors in my ranks."

"Ah." Hoka laughed. "A man in love is often the last one to know it."

I heard my sister's muffled voice in the background.

"No, sweetheart, not yet," Hoka replied, his tone shifting to a soft, warm undertone as it always did whenever he was speaking to her. "I know." He chuckled. "I've always told you your brother was a little slow."

I glowered at the phone. *Fuck off stupid Japanese thug!*

"What is she saying?" I asked through gritted teeth.

"She asked me if you realized you were in love with Lily yet."

"I'm *not* in love with her!" In lust? Probably. In awe? Indubiously. But in love? I snorted internally. That was completely stupid.

"Okay..." Hoka sighed. "Well, I better let you go deal with the situation and the woman you *don't* love."

I let out a little growl of frustration, causing him to laugh. Why did people enjoy torturing me so much?

"Jokes aside, you know you'll always have a safe haven here," he said seriously, his tone taking the fierce protectiveness he used for his family, which by a play of fate, I was a part of. "Pietro and Lily are welcome here and will be protected as if they were mine."

My previous irritation drained at once, replaced by recurring gratitude. "I know. I might take you up on that but..." I looked at the door and grimaced at my earlier decision. "I'm taking them back to Chicago. Pietro needs to be in his environment, in his home. I can't keep him hidden forever."

"No, you sure can't. Something that Violet and I have been telling you for two years now, but I guess Lily had other, um, *attributes* to make you listen."

"She has nothing to do with this, and this is not a life she'd want or deserve. Once we're back—" I stopped talking and shook my head. Talking was pointless. "I need to fix this mess."

"You do," he confirmed, his voice no longer mocking. "But thinking they can't handle it is how we lose them. I'm not saying you want to keep her, but whatever is happening between you two on the island doesn't have to stop. Speak to her, be honest, and let her make her own decision."

I closed my eyes and nodded, despite the fact that we were on the phone, too tired to try to deny it.

"I'll let you know when I've spoken to Doyle. Give a hug to my beautiful sister and nephew for me."

"Of course. Give a hug to my nephew and my future sister-in-law," he rushed out before hanging up.

"Asshole," I muttered, putting my cell back on the desk.

I tapped my fingers on my desk, looking at my closed office door.

Sister-in-law. I shook my head. This was ridiculous. We had no future. I could make no commitments, at least not the type she deserved. She thought she knew what she was getting into because of what she witnessed, but she wouldn't have a clue and I wouldn't even know where to start.

I ran my hands over my face and even if I should be picking up my phone to speak to Doyle, all I could see was

Lily's body, feel her tight pussy squeezing my fingers, and hear her call my name as she came. Her soft cries of pleasure were like a spell on me, and I knew I would not be able to concentrate on anything until I spoke to her. I had to either make her mine—at least for now—or make her keep me away.

I was not strong enough to stay away, but maybe she was?

I stayed in my office a little longer, staring at nothing in particular. I knew the solution would not fall into my lap and that the only way to quench this obsession with Lily would be to surrender to it.

I sighed and gave up. I planned to go see her and give her an actual breakdown of where we stood with our problem and what I had to do next. I also wanted to see how mad she was at me running away again.

Seriously, if I were her, I'd punch myself in the throat… and the dick.

I stopped in front of her door and knocked softly, not even sure she was there or with Pietro.

I heard her soft voice from inside, and I opened the door and froze as she exited the bathroom in nothing more than her panties and bra—a set I'd picked for her, imagining what the royal blue would look like against her pale skin.

Mouthwatering, that's how.

She let out a shriek and I cast my eyes down in politeness when all I wanted to do was to keep on staring.

A gentleman would have stepped out and closed the door, but I was no gentleman—something we'd established a long time ago, so it shouldn't have come completely as a shock to her when, despite keeping my eyes downward, I closed the door, staying in the room.

"Alessandro, wha-what are you doing here?" she asked breathlessly.

I looked back up. Fuck it. I enjoyed the view and it was not anything I'd not seen and touched just a few hours earlier.

"I knocked, and I heard you speak. I thought you were inviting me in."

"I..." She blushed, and I could see it was not only her face that took the lovely shade of pink, but her chest, too. "I was singing."

I nodded, having a hard time keeping my eyes on her face when all I wanted to do was let them dip down and stare at the swell of her breast and the rest of her body.

She turned slightly to the side, a small movement, but it was more telling than a thousand words. It was something I saw Luca do sometimes—more rarely now that he was married with kids, but she was trying to hide her scars. She was uncomfortable under my scrutiny and that was not acceptable.

She reached for the chair where her wrap-on dress lay.

"Don't." I didn't mean for my voice to sound so hard, so commanding, but it did the trick, and her fingers froze an inch from the fabric.

She threw me a confused look.

"If I had half a mind, I'd request... no, I'd demand you be half-naked every time it was just you and me."

She let her hand fall to her side, and she chewed on her bottom lip. "You don't have to say that."

Here she goes again. Her self-doubt irritated me. She was always so sure, so fierce... So why couldn't she believe me?

"Do I need to show you I mean it again?" I rested my hand on the waistband of my pants and she raised her hand.

"No! I believe you," she exclaimed, her face a shade redder than before.

I removed my hand from the waistband, somehow annoyed that she so vehemently refused. Would she actually be strong enough to say no to me? That wouldn't work at all.

"I want you, Lily. I wanted you last week on the balcony; I wanted you this morning at the creek. I want you now, and I know that when I wake up tomorrow, I'll want you then, too."

"I..." She sucked her lower lip between her teeth. "You ran away pretty quickly."

Ah, so my actions had affected her. How could they not?

I ran my hand through my hair with a weary sigh. "You've become a distraction I can't afford," I admitted with a tone full of reproach, as if it were her fault. Well, in a way, it was. Why did she have to be so smart, so sweet, so kind and understanding? Why did she have to challenge me, and be funny, and at the same time, be the perfect role model my son crucially needed. And above all, how did she dare to have curves to damn a saint? Yes, it was her fault after all. "But lord forgive me, I'm willing to pay the price and make you pay it, too."

She took a couple of tentative steps toward me, her brow etched in confusion. It was enough to show me that she wanted me, that she was willing to give in.

"I'm not a symbol of honesty, but with you, I need to be. We have too much to lose to do something, anything under misconceptions. Before we go further, I need to say that I don't know where this," I pointed from her to me and back again, "will lead. Once we leave this place, once we're back in the cold, bloody world that is mine. I can't make any promises or commitments to you. I—"

She quickly closed the distance between us and rested her fingers on my lips, and for that, I was grateful. "There is no reason for this to follow us once we leave the island. This, us, can stay here with all the other sweet memories."

I reached for her and pulled her closer, until her body was flush against mine, and I could feel her breasts press against my chest and my semi-hard cock press against her stomach.

I trailed my finger over her collarbone, doubting that I could leave this memory behind. I knew after the little I had already experienced with her that she was a bad addiction, but that was the thing with addictions; we were aware we had them, but we were rarely strong enough to say stop until it was much too late.

I leaned down and brushed my lips against hers and she wrapped her arms around my neck. I felt her tongue tentatively run along the seam of my mouth, and I opened, allowing her to hesitantly explore me as I used the little self-control I had to give her this bit of control. But as I started to suck on her tongue, tasting the fruitiness of the juice she'd probably just drank, she pressed herself more into me with a moan, and that little control snapped completely. I grabbed the back of her head and took control, burying my tongue in her mouth as I walked us backward toward the bed, undoing her bra on the way and only breaking the kiss just long enough to discard my T-shirt.

I wanted—no, I needed—to feel her skin against mine. I laid her gently on the bed and crawled over her, staring at her face for a second to make sure there was no doubt, but her hazel eyes were hazy, her pupils wide, and her breathing frantic. She was just as wrapped up in the lust as I was, and I thanked every god willing to listen for that.

I pulled away her bra and marveled at her beautiful breast and pink nipples. She arched her back slightly under my gaze in a silent invitation.

I couldn't help the proud smile as I lowered my head and caught a hard nipple in my mouth and sucked on it.

She moaned loudly, parting her legs and allowing me to nestle between them, my cock pressing against her warm heat.

I rubbed myself against her as I let go of her nipple and reached for the other one, licking it before closing my mouth around it.

She buried a hand in my hair, scraping her nails against my scalp, and this simple gesture gave so much pleasure.

"Alessandro, please... I want you," she said, raising her hips and causing so much friction.

"I want to take it slowly," I growled against her nipple before lapping at it, "but I won't be able to if you keep rubbing yourself against me like that."

"I'm not going to break." She sighed, trailing her short nails down my back. "I know I look broken, but I'm not."

I looked up at her face, her comment bringing a little of my rationality back.

I gave her a deep bruising kiss. "I don't see a broken woman when I look at you. I've never seen you as a victim, Lily—dressed or undressed, even if now I'm more partial to your nakedness and would always like to see you naked." I kissed her plump mouth again. "Yes, I see the scars, but Lily, they are part of you and they are beautiful." I let my hand trail to the ones on her flank and slowly ran my fingers over the raised skin. "In my culture, we're different. *La mia bella guerriera*, scars are badges of honors we wear proudly to show that we survived what life threw our way. You can try to beat us, kill us, but like the phoenix, we will rise from the ashes and rain motherfucking revenge on you."

She raised her hand and cupped my cheek. The tenderness I saw in her eyes brought me to my knees.

"I know you're not going to break, but I want to give you only pleasure, no pain." I started to make my way down, kissing her along the way. Lips, chin, throat, collarbone, each round breast, her breath catching in her throat every now and then, and I tried to memorize her most sensitive zones.

I stopped when my lips reached the waistband of her panties. "The thing is, this morning, I felt how tight you were, how snug my fingers were inside the heaven of your body."

My cock jerked at the thought of burying myself in her tight wetness, knowing that, once I was inside her, all rational thoughts would vanish. I also knew that once the beast took over, there would be no gentleness, no softness.

"I want you to be ready for me." I pulled her panties down slowly and kissed her pussy before taking them down completely. I grabbed the back of her thighs, and as

I kneeled on the floor, I pulled her to the edge of the bed, making her squeal.

"Alessandro, wh-what are you doing?"

"Shh!" I ordered, putting her legs on my shoulders so my face was in line with her beautiful pink pussy, glistening and swollen with desire. "I haven't had dinner yet. Time for me to eat."

Slowly, I trailed the flat of my tongue up her slit.

"Oh god!" she let out in a breath, her back arching.

I smiled against her clit. "Not quite, but close enough." I pressed the tip of my tongue against her clit, and she let out a sound that was not quite human.

I couldn't help but wonder as I gave open-mouthed kisses on her tasty heat if anyone ever did that, and a part of me wished they didn't—I wanted to be the first.

I sucked on her clit as I buried one finger inside her, going in and out slowly before adding a second one. I continued the slow thrusting as my tongue and mouth continued to worship her.

Her walls squeezed around my fingers as I raked my teeth over her bundle of nerves.

I raised my head. "Tell me, beautiful, did anyone ever eat you like that?"

She shook her head frantically as she fisted her pastel-colored bedspread.

"No, no, no," she repeated over and over again. "Don't stop. I can't… It's just—" She was so lost in her pleasure, she could not form a coherent thought, which boosted my ego.

"So tight," I groaned as her thighs quivered on my shoulders, squeezing my face as if to stop me from moving.

She had nothing to fear; I was not moving until she came on my tongue.

I removed my fingers and replaced them with my tongue as her thighs started to shake even more. Her soft moans turned into muffled cries as she brought her hand to her mouth, trying to keep quiet. I regretted not hearing the full extent of the pleasure my mouth was giving her, and I knew I'd have to have her again one day—when Pietro would be out of earshot so she could scream to her heart's content.

Her thighs locked around my head as her free hand reached out to grab at my hair. She pulled my face deeper into her spasming pussy as she came, and I feasted on her as if I'd been a starving man. I lapped at her hungrily until she went lax and her thighs relaxed.

I gently removed her thighs from my shoulders and reached for her waist, pushing her back up the bed as I stood.

I met no resistance as she just laid there, her legs still slightly parted, her eyes unfocused as she was high from the bliss I just gave her.

I wished I could take a photo right now and keep it for my lonely nights. I'd fucked my fair share of women, but none had looked as stunning as my Lily did right now.

You also never tried to please a woman as thoroughly as you pleased her, my brain—which was now on life support as all my blood seemed to have migrated to my cock—managed to remind me.

I pulled down my pants and she moved her head a little, licking her lips as her eyes locked on my cock.

You'll suck it soon, beautiful... You'll choke on it, and you'll enjoy it. I know that much already, I thought darkly, already seeing it. *But not now, now I need to be inside you so much more than I need my cock hitting the back of your throat.*

I rested a knee on the bed, and she widened her legs in a silent invitation to take what I wanted so badly.

I grabbed my cock, rubbing it against her heat while keeping my eyes on hers before I finally pushed forward slowly. I let out a hiss as she moaned, her walls molding around my length like a tight glove, and despite the blissful feeling, a doubt insinuated in me, making me stop only a couple of inches in.

She let out a frustrated cry as she reached around, resting her hands on my ass and pressing, trying to force me down.

"You've done this before, right?" I asked, knowing that the answer didn't really matter. Even if she'd been a virgin, I was going to take her tonight. Maybe I was strong enough to pause, but I knew I was not strong enough to pull out now that I had a taste of heaven.

"Hmm?" she asked, pressing on my ass again.

I slid another inch in. "You've done this before, haven't you?"

"Had sex with a mafia boss who had a giant penis?" She shook her head. "I'm afraid not. But I'd love to."

"Little vixen," I muttered. "Sex. It's not your first time, is it? I won't stop, but I'll take it slow." I pushed in a little more.

She arched her hip as she squeezed her walls, trying to swallow me, but I had all the power in this position. She could not do anything, and it was the way I loved it.

"I have, but it has been a while."

"How long is *a while*?"

"Long enough." She raised her hips again. "And with nothing this big."

I smirked and she rolled her eyes. I didn't have a monster dick—at least nothing that would cause more pain than pleasure—but I had been gifted and I was pleased with the way she looked at my cock with a little apprehension and how snug she felt around me.

I felt the perspiration start to form on my forehead at the force it took not to slam the few remaining inches inside her.

"I can't..." I let out through gritted teeth.

"I'm stronger than I look. Give me everything," she said before raising her head and kissing my bobbing throat.

I lost the fragment of control I still had and slammed into her with a relieved moan as she arched her back, throwing her head back, her mouth opened in a silent cry.

I hissed as she squeezed her walls. "Don't or I'll come." I felt like a boy getting his first taste of a woman's body.

I closed my eyes and leaned my head down, trying to focus on the slow thrusting motion of my cock in her wet, inviting pussy. I needed to keep control; I was not ready to come yet. I was not ready for this moment to be over.

"Oh, Alessandro." She wrapped her arms around my neck. "I can feel you everywhere. Oh, this is... Oh!" She gasped and fisted my hair as I increased the pace. "Faster, harder," she breathed, and I thanked God for this woman.

I kissed her deeply before withdrawing to the tip and slamming back inside her in one swift motion, earning a sharp cry of pleasure.

I licked her neck, marveling at the fact that she liked the roughness of my thrusts. She really was a gift from the gods. I unleashed the beast completely, pumping harder and faster into her, the only sounds in the room being our moans of pleasure and the rhythmic sound of our skin connecting.

I kissed her again, something that was not familiar to me. This was, for me, far more intimate than the pure sexual act. Kissing was a connection, a tender moment between two lovers, and something I'd never been tempted to do until her. Now I wanted to devour her mouth, make her already plump lips swollen and red with the force of our passion. I wanted the world to see what I was doing to her.

I was on the edge, my thrusts turning erratic, my balls drawing together, announcing my impending orgasm.

"Touch yourself, beautiful," I let out breathlessly. "I want you to come with me."

She reached between our bodies and rubbed her clit as I gritted my teeth, trying to hold on for a few more seconds.

I felt her reach the edge as her thighs squeezed my hips and her eyes widened. Her walls gripped me so tight that I could only let go and come calling her name in complete rapture.

I fell heavily on top of her, catching my breath. I knew I was heavy, but as I tried to move, she wrapped herself around me tighter and kissed my temple.

It was unexpected and really threw me off. It was such a tender, gentle, and dare I say, loving gesture—something that had never been given freely to me like that before, and never without ulterior motives.

I smiled despite the fact that she couldn't see my face buried in her neck.

She ran her fingers through my hair, caressing it. It was terrifying how good it felt, how comforting it was. I had never thought I would need these types of interactions, but now I knew I could easily become addicted to this... to *her*.

"Did you come?" I asked after brushing my lips against her neck. I had come so hard that I'd lost sight of her orgasm.

"Harder than I've ever come before," she admitted before kissing my temple again.

I wanted to stay like this forever, in her loving arms, but no matter what she said, I knew I was heavy and reality would be calling soon in the form of Killian Doyle, no matter how much I wanted to delay it.

I sighed and rolled to the side, reluctantly leaving the warmth of her body and reached down for the light spread at the foot of her bed to cover us. I grabbed her hand, intertwined our fingers, and kissed the back of it before resting it on my stomach.

I turned my head to the side to look at her and she was looking at the ceiling, chewing at her bottom lip. She was deep in thought, and I wasn't sure if it was a good thing. Was she second-guessing what we just did now that the lust had subsided? I opened my mouth to ask her what she was thinking about, but all I could think about was what she meant by *'a while.'*

"What happened to Andrew?" I asked before I could stop myself.

She turned her head to the side to look at me. "What?"

Way to go, Sandro! Bring up the ex, post-orgasm. What better way to kill the mood?

"Andrew," I repeated. "He never came to Chicago; you never mentioned him."

I knew that for a fact because I'd looked into each man's name I ever heard her utter. I always justified it by my need for safety, but based on recent events, I was obviously delusional.

"Oh." She let out a little wistful laugh I was not sure I liked. Did she miss him? She took a deep breath and let it out in a loud huff.

She rested her arm on top of her head and shrugged. "I don't think it was anything particular, really," she admitted. "No bad breakup, no tears. You know what it's like… high school romances rarely last."

I nodded absentmindedly, even though she wasn't looking at me. In fact, I didn't know what it was like. We didn't really date when we were at the private school. Dating outside the *famiglia* was frowned upon, even before you swore allegiance, and dating within the *famiglia* was just as risky. One mistake, one virginity taken, and you'd end up in front of the altar with a gun to your head. *No, thank you!*

Most of the guys secretly dated both in and out of the *famiglia*. I'd never been tempted to go steady then, and I took everything life was ready to offer.

She turned her head toward me and smiled, it was a little nostalgic somehow and I was wondering if she missed that time or him.

"You know, after the… accident." She stumbled on the word as if it hurt her to talk about it.

A better man would have told her to drop it, but once again, I was not that man and I needed to know how much attachment she had to her past.

"I think we realized the only thing we really had in common was Victor." She was still looking at me, and I saw the nostalgia in her smile fill her eyes and give them a hint of sadness that didn't belong there after what we shared.

"Andrew was the co-captain of the football team with Vic, and I was my brother's sidekick. We were fusional, Vic and I." She reached for her necklace and let her graceful fingers trace the sides of the dice.

I brought her hand up to my mouth and kissed the back of it—a tender, comforting gesture that was foreign to me, yet it came as second nature with her.

She squeezed my hand. "After Victor, after he was gone, I think we both realized that it was never really meant to be, but he stayed—mostly out of guilt and I didn't want that, so I let him go." She shrugged. "Last I heard, he was engaged to a cheerleader. It made more sense really, because without Victor, it was just the jock superstar and the math geek." She let out a humorless laugh. "Something straight out of a bad *Hallmark* movie."

I wanted to tell her that he had every reason to feel guilty, and that he had been a fool to walk away from her, but I had already killed the mood enough for today.

"Yeah? *Hallmark?* And what kind of movie are we?" I asked with a playful smile.

"The mafia boss and the assistant?" She gave me a half smile. "Based on what and how we just did? At least *HBO*."

I laughed and pulled at her arm so she moved closer to me.

"Okay, so let's give the cable-paying pervs their money's worth," I added playfully before crushing my lips on hers and showing her again how much I wanted her.

CHAPTER 12

Alessandro

I picked up my phone to call Doyle. I'd waited longer than necessary, I knew that, but when I'd woken up after having sex with Lily a second time, I just didn't feel like ending our time here.

When I opened my eyes, I was wrapped around Lily's body, as if I was trying to protect her even from bad dreams. I couldn't remember waking up with a woman in my arms, even Pietro's mother. She'd been my only poor attempt at a relationship, but I'd always woken up on the other side of the bed, as if I was trying to escape her and the chains she was trying to force on me.

But now I woke up in a sort of peace that was unusual and not warranted in the state of shit my reality was these days, yet just looking at Lily deep asleep, her face in total relaxation—probably due to the state of exhaustion our two rounds of sex put her—put me at ease.

I smiled at the thought and looked at her a little longer than socially acceptable, probably taking me from smitten lover to perverted creep. I let my eyes trail down her side to her beautiful round breast that escaped the thin cover.

I licked my lips as I kept my eye on her nipple, trying to fight the irrepressible need to suck it into my mouth and give in to my lust again.

If I had thought that giving in would have dimmed my desire for her, I'd been truly wrong.

I sighed before leaning down and brushing my lips against her curly hair, taking in the scent of her flowery shampoo.

I left her bed with a reluctance I could not really place and kept my eyes locked on her naked form as I slid into my pants, picked up my shirt off the floor, and walked to the door.

I stopped for a second, with my hand on the handle, a pinch of doubt insinuating itself into my mind. *Would this be over now?*

She said whatever happened could stay on the island, but was that what she wanted? I couldn't blame her if it was the case, and it was probably for the best.

I hesitated most of the morning, trying to find excuses as to why calling Doyle could wait, but knowing, especially based on Moreno's text about Lorenzo's piss-poor attitude, I had to go back home sooner rather than later.

I dialed the number of the *Rose of Tralee* club I knew Doyle used as headquarters.

"Yeah?" a woman's voice said, followed by a loud popping of gum.

I rolled my eyes. She was a classy Irish, as always.

"I need to speak to Doyle."

"There ain't no Doyle here."

He was there, it was clear if only by the way she pronounced his name a little louder than the rest. She was alerting whoever was around.

"He will be here for me. Tell him Alessandro Benetti wants a word with him."

"Listen, Alessandro Bene-whatever, I can't tell him shit. There's no Killian Doyle here."

"Funny how I never said his name was Killian, though."

She didn't reply, and I heard a click at the end of the line. I expected her to have hung up, and I was about to do the same when I heard some low jazz music on the line.

"Alessandro Benetti..." he crooned, his voice sounding more like a late-night radio host than a crime lord. "To what do I owe the immense honor of your call?"

"Don't lay it on so thick, Doyle. We both know you despise me." *Just like I despise you.*

He laughed. "Ah, that's not really true. I despise all of you." I heard the familiar sound of ice against glass. "A little birdie told me you'd be reaching out soon."

Fuck, Byrne! He has been smarter than I thought, announcing his need for protection to Doyle.

"I want Byrne," I announced coldly. Fuck diplomacy, I could be a raging asshole, too.

Doyle laughed. "And I want a summer house on the moon."

"Doyle..." I let out with a threatening tone that was pointless. I had no power there, and he knew it just as well as I did.

"Oh, I'm sorry... I thought you were playing at asking for something fucking impossible."

I shook my head, losing the little hope I had to negotiate Byrne without giving him my most precious card. "He stole my money."

"He said he didn't, and even if he did, that's not my problem. It's only money; Irish blood is much stronger."

Ah, and so it started—his ode to the Irish legacy. "It's not him I want. He worked with another Italian."

That kept Doyle silent for a second.

"Possibly, but you'll kill him, anyway."

Obviously. "How would you know that?"

He let out a little laugh. "Because I would."

That was a fair argument. No member of any mafia would let Byrne live after that.

He sighed. "Listen, Benetti, it's not like I don't enjoy this riveting conversation, but there's nothing you can say that will change my mind. I've got way more money than I need, and you can't offer me more power. We Irish are different from you; we actually value blood more than anything else."

I pursed my lips, trying hard not to tell him that he knew nothing about the honor of our families. We valued blood, but we also knew that it could be tainted, while he believed that Irish blood made you perfect.

"Blood, you said? What if I can give you what you want the most, Killian Doyle?"

"And what is it, pray tell, that's worth so much that I'll betray one of my own for?"

I looked at the ceiling in defeat. Here was my precious card… "The location of your brother."

The line went silent, except for the faint jazz music in the background. He finally shouted something in a language I didn't understand and the music died.

"Do you have him?" he asked darkly.

"No, Finn is happy and living his best life away from you." I sighed. "I wanted to be a good man and leave him to his freedom."

"His freedom is *my* decision, *my* prerogative," he snarled on the line. "If it's a trick, Benetti—"

"No trick. Do we have a deal? Byrne for your brother's address?"

He hissed on the phone, and I knew how much it must have cost him to yield. "You would have to come and collect him, and I want to look into your eyes when you tell me where my brother is."

"Fine."

"Who told you Byrne was a thief?" He asked after a second.

"Someone."

"Someone?" He laughed. "Bring the girl with you."

I cursed Byrne for opening his mouth. How did he even know it was Lily who ratted him out? I'd kill him just for bringing her into more of this mess. She had Matteo's assessment to go through. There was no way I'd let her walk into the same room as Doyle in a territory I had no control over.

"I want her to look me in the eyes when she tells me how she knows. I want her to look at me when I explain to her that her words will serve as a death warrant for the man in question."

I heard Lily's soft laugh from the open window and shook my head. "I can't do that."

"Can't or won't?"

"I won't put her in danger."

Killian laughed loudly. "Oh! Is Alessandro Benetti in *love*?" he taunted before laughing again. "Oh, that's the best thing I heard all day! Now I definitely need to see her. Brother or no brother, if you don't bring her, Benetti, there's no deal."

"I believe you are a man of honor." I did not believe that, but a little ass kissing was sometimes necessary.

"I'm Irish, we do not break our vows."

Yea right. I sighed "Will she be safe?"

"As safe as she could be between two heads of families."

Yea, that was not the answer I was looking for. So many things could go wrong in this scenario.

I sighed, running my hand over my face.

"As long as she is truthful, no harm will come to her… At least not from me or my men."

"That woman has more integrity in her little finger than we both have in our bodies combined."

"Young love. Oh, young love…" he sang tauntingly. "Do we have a deal, Benetti? I don't have all day—"

"I'll ask her. I'll give her the full picture, and if she decides it's too dangerous, then I won't force her," I replied stubbornly.

"Then I have no concern she'll say yes. If that woman is stupid enough to get into bed with an Italian mob boss, she'll come. She obviously has no sense of self-preservation."

I opened my mouth to deny it but closed it again when I knew so intrinsically that it was the truth.

"You've got until the end of the week to show your face, Benetti. If not, I'll send Byrne so far away, you'll never find him, and then we'll both have a secret. And before I forget, if you lied about Finn or if you hurt him in any way... neither you nor your redhead will escape Boston alive. Did I make myself clear?"

"Crystal." I didn't get a chance to add anything as the line died. A chill ran down my spine as I wondered... How did he know she was a redhead?

I stood and slowly walked to the back porch where I could hear the happy discussion going on between Pietro and Lily.

I stayed in the shadow of the house for a few more minutes as he sat on his wheelchair across from her seat. She was wearing the beautiful blue dress I'd bought for her on an impulse in Chicago, and I realized how right I'd been, this dress was made for her.

She started to laugh at a joke he'd just made that I didn't understand, and my heart squeezed painfully in my chest. She understood him so effortlessly, and instead of feeling jealous, I was sad at not being able to be the father he deserved.

She turned toward the open French doors as if she felt me there and jerked her head a little, the only sign of her surprise.

"Oh, Alessandro, just in time! Why don't you come try the strawberry lemonade Pietro made? It's amazing."

Her bright smile directed toward me made me forget the doom from the call, if only for a moment, and I felt a lot lighter when I stepped onto the covered patio to take a seat on the other side of Pietro.

He gave me a wary look as I reached for the pitcher of pink lemonade.

"You don't have to, you know," he said, his face serious.

We'd not discussed what had happened the other night—the heartbreaking things he admitted and my own breakdown as I sat on his bedroom floor, crying for almost an hour at all the pain I'd caused him.

I wanted us to talk about it, but I had no idea how. I was not born in a world where we shared feelings, it was the opposite. You kept any feelings you may have buried until you smothered them.

I had no idea where to start, and I was ashamed to ask Lily for help—having to admit to her the extent of the hurt I'd caused my son, even if I suspected she somehow already knew and it had been the reason why she'd fought me so hard.

"I know I don't, but I want to." I sat back in my seat. "Why should Lily be the only one to enjoy what you made?"

He looked at me silently as I brought the glass to my lips and drank a few sips, the taste of strawberries so delicious, I didn't have to fake it.

"This is delicious, *cucciolo*!" I exclaimed before taking another sip. "You'll have to make some more when we're back in Chicago."

"Lily helped me—" He stopped mid-sentence, catching up to what I'd just said.

I couldn't help but smile brightly as his eyebrows shot up and his mouth morphed in an adorable 'O' of surprise.

Lily leaned forward on her seat, grinning at the shock tainting with happiness on his face.

"Chicago?" he repeated, his voice high with disbelief.

I nodded, taking another sip. "Yes, I think it's time for me to bring you back home. It's long past due, actually. It will be winter soon, but you'll get used to it and—"

"Oh, *Papà*! Thank you!" he shouted and put his feet on the floor, throwing himself into my arms.

I caught him in a huff as he wrapped his arms around my neck, hugging me a lot tighter than I would have expected.

I looked up at Lily, who was looking at us with her hand on her heart. Her eyes shone with emotion and a tenderness I dared hope was not only directed toward my son.

I gave her a smile I hoped reflected all the gratitude I felt. I tightened my hold around Pietro's back, knowing Lily belonged in this hug, in this family picture of joy, but also knowing it was too early, too selfish, and that we needed to clean this mess first.

"When are we going?" he asked, pulling back. I could feel his muscles twitch with excitement.

"Tomorrow. We'll need to stop in New York for a couple of days first, but then we're going home."

He turned his head to look at Lily. "You heard that, Lily? New York!"

"I heard!" She clapped her hands. "It's going to be amazing!"

"And after, we're going home. I..." He stopped, his eyebrows dipping as he thought. "You're coming home with us... right, Lily?"

Lily threw me a helpless look, unsure of what to say, and I didn't know, either. I didn't know much until we spoke with Matteo and Doyle.

I patted his back gently. "Why don't you go see what we need to take with us now? I'll have the team get the rest later."

"Okay! Lily, will you help me pack?"

Lily nodded and part of me was a little peeved. I had wanted a few minutes with her. I stood and helped him back into his chair.

"I need to organize everything, but I'll see you later."

I gave a long look to Lily, who gave me a quick nod.

"*Papà*?" Pietro called just as I was about to walk back inside.

I turned my head and looked at him.

"Thank you. I'll make you proud."

My heart squeezed in my chest, his comment making it all bittersweet.

"You don't have to make me proud, *cucciolo*. There's not a day that I'm not immensely proud of you, and that's been true since the day you were born." I took a deep breath. "You are the best thing I've ever done."

After I called Luca about stopping in New York for a day or two and asking him to take care of Pietro, I decided it was time to face Lily and tell her about Doyle's request.

I softly knocked on her door and waited, even if I would have loved seeing her in her underwear again, but this would have probably led to another round of sex—which, again, I wouldn't have minded—but we needed to concentrate on the issues first before giving in to our desires.

"Come in."

"See, I waited this time," I said jokingly.

She laughed as she crossed the room to pick up some clothes in the chest of drawers to put in her newly-acquired suitcase. "Yes, you're learning."

I closed the door and leaned against it, watching her pack with a certain longing. This little interlude was over, this life in a cocoon far from everything.

The dress flowed with every movement, showing her leg with every step.

"I picked well," I said out loud.

She turned around with the tiny bikini from the day before in her hand. "Pardon?"

"The dress."

"Oh!" She looked down at her dress before looking back at me. "You picked it?"

I cocked my head to the side with a startled laugh. "Who else would have?"

She shrugged. "I don't know. I reckoned you hired someone to pick clothes for me. I know you often asked me to buy presents for disgruntled mistresses..."

I winced. I'd walked right into that one, but what bothered me even more was the causality of the tone when she mentioned the mistresses, as if she didn't care. Wasn't she a little bit jealous? I was already aggravated before, whenever a man got close to her, but now that I had touched her, that I had made her mine... I was not sure I would ever look at a man touching her with anything other than murder in my mind.

I waved my hand dismissively. "That was the past."

She gave me a small smile—the type you gave to indulge a stubborn child—before she turned and put the bikini into the case and resumed her packing.

It rubbed me the wrong way that she didn't believe my words, as if she didn't believe I could be serious, committed.

Do you want to, Sandro? Do you want to add a weakness to your list and force her to become part of a world she probably had no intention to be in forever? I shook my head as she leaned down to pick up a pair of ballet flats, the dress molding to the curve of her ass, making my dick stir in my pants. *Yep, I chose exceptionally well.*

"You know, I don't think one suitcase will be enough. You really spoiled me."

"As I should. You deserve the world, Lily Matthews," I blurted out before thinking.

She stumbled on her step as she turned her head toward me.

We looked at each other for a few seconds in complete silence, and as if she was a magnet, I took a few steps toward her.

She opened her mouth and closed it again a couple of times. It would have been funny if I'd not felt just as confused as she seemed to be.

Suddenly, a gust of wind caused a plastic cup on her dresser to fall to the wooden floor, breaking the spell.

She shook her head and turned her back to me again. "Thank you for letting me witness your announcement to Pietro. Seeing his happiness made me the happiest woman in the world."

"Yes, I just regret it has to be when there are so many uncertainties, but I could not leave him here again... not after everything."

She nodded and I knew that she understood, like really understood, once again proving how priceless she was in my life.

She closed the lid of the suitcase and turned toward me. "I suppose you spoke with the Irish guy?"

I nodded, burying my hands into my pants pocket as I walked in the middle of her room. "Yes, but it didn't go exactly as planned."

"Oh?" She sat on the stool in front of her vanity. "He's not giving you Byrne?"

"No, well, yes, he is, but – " I sighed and sat at the foot of her bed, facing her. "He has some conditions that he says are mandatory. One of them..." I detailed her beautiful face, her little pert nose peppered with light freckles giving her an innocent, youthful look that caused a huge wave of protection in me.

"He wants me."

God, how could this woman read me so well? It was terrifying and so dangerous.

"He wants you to come and tell him what you found out," I admitted, still unsure I could risk her like that, even if she wanted to.

"Okay, I'll go."

"You'll go?"

She nodded. "Yes."

"Lily, I don't think you understand what you are agreeing to here," I said slowly. She must have lost her mind; she didn't even think about it. This was pure craziness!

She leaned forward on her seat, resting her forearms on her legs, causing her top to gap and showing me her beautiful cleavage. "Tell me, then."

I blinked a couple of times, pushing away the thoughts of my mouth on her nipple. "What?"

"Tell me what I'm agreeing to."

"Doyle is just as psychotic as Matteo is, except we'll be in his territory. I'll have no power there."

"Okay." She nodded. "But tell me something. You said that Byrne was working with someone within your organization, correct?"

"Yes..."

"And this person is an issue, right? He's the reason I should be dead."

"He is," I reluctantly agreed. I was wary of where her argument would be taking her. She had that fiery determined look on her face that I loved, but right now, I was not confident I wanted to see it. "Because of him, you witnessed something you never should have seen, and he knew that." I didn't add the little fact that I'd been to blame in this one too, because I'd been advised by Matteo and Luca to let her go many times in the past. I only started to understand now why I'd been so opposed to the thought.

"He is a risk for you, and especially for Pietro, and that alone is worth me going there."

I frowned, not liking her logic at all. "Are you seeing yourself as a pawn I can carelessly dispose of to ensure my son's safety?" I could not contain the bite of anger in my voice. How could she even think that? "Do you really think you don't matter?"

She huffed and stood with a dismissive gesture as she resumed her packing, carelessly stuffing bottles that were on her vanity into a small pouch.

"I never said that. I know I matter. Pietro is attached to me, and I wouldn't want to cause him any harm, and

I know you want to shield him from pain as well. I know you'll keep me safe."

Sudden realization made me stiffen, and I stood up slowly as what she'd told me the night before, about the useless piece of shit Andrew and her brother, came back to my mind.

"Is that why you think I care? Because of Pietro? Because he is the common factor?" I took a step toward her as she kept her back to me, her silence confirming my question. "Lily, do you think what has transpired between us is only due to the attachment you share with Pietro and our forced close proximity?"

I stopped a couple of steps behind her as irritation and a hint of sorrow and hurt mixed together. How could she think so little of me? So little of *herself*? I wanted to shake some sense into her and find this Andrew and cut his dick off just because he had her first.

"Matthews, turn around," I ordered, unsure if it would work, but what I had to say needed to be said face to face. "Matthews..." I used my best boss voice.

She sighed and turned around slowly.

"Is that really what you think?"

She shrugged. "I know you care, Alessand—"

"No." I shook my head. "That's not what I asked. Do you really think what's happening between us and my concern for you is caused by Pietro's feelings?"

"It doesn't mat—"

I took a step closer. "Yes, it does! Do you know how difficult it was to invent a fake job in the London office just to get that stupid accountant away from you?"

Her eyes widened in surprise, and I couldn't help but grin.

"I knew it!" she gasped, slapping my arm playfully. "Head of the special accounting projects..." She rolled her eyes. "That sounded completely made up, and you gave me so much grief about it!"

She tried to slap my arm again, but I grabbed her wrist and pulled her against me, wrapping my arms around her securely to stop her from going anywhere.

I chuckled. "I'm quite proud of that one, to be honest." I leaned down and brushed my lips against hers. "I may have been slow, but I think this attraction has been there for a while. I just decided to stop fighting it. Doomed if I do, doomed if I don't."

She sighed, relaxing in my arms. "I appreciate the honesty, but I also want to make sure Pietro is safe. I'll be there with him after everything is over, and I want to be able to breathe, not feel paranoid every step of the way. His safety will also be up to me."

I opened my mouth to reply that as the head of the Chicago outfit, hers and Pietro's security were entirely my responsibility, but she cupped my cheek and once again, I was lost in her touch and gentle eyes.

"I'm not a victim, remember. Sandro, please, don't make me feel like one."

My heart tightened at her calling me Sandro, and I sighed. "Fine, you'll come, but you will do as you're told, okay?"

She nodded eagerly.

I leaned down and brushed my lips against hers again. "Because no matter what you think, you matter to me... a lot. A lot more than is safe for both of us," I whispered against her lips before catching her plump bottom lip between mine and sucking at it.

She let out a moan and it was enough to give me the green light as I deepened the kiss, exploring her hot mouth, taking possession of her again. The more I took, the more she pressed her body against mine. She loved that dominance and fuck me, did I love how she yielded for me in the bedroom and not anywhere else. I loved her warrior side she had in every aspect of her life, but I loved it even more when it was mixed with this submissive, soft nature she only showed when I was possessing her body with my mouth, my fingers… my cock.

She was a delicious and perfect contradiction I was rapidly becoming addicted to. So addicted that I feared that when the moment came for me to do the right thing and let her fly away, I wouldn't be able to and I'd cage her, damning her to a life she never asked for.

But for now, I left those concerns behind as I swirled around, never breaking the kiss and walking her backward to the bed. Tonight was the last night we'd share in this haven, and I intended to make it count and brand my touch and the pleasure I could give her in her memory forever. I wanted her to never doubt how powerful my desire for her could run, and I wanted her to become so inebriated with pleasure that she'd beg me to stop.

So I did, four times during the night, every time drowning in her cry of pleasure, knowing that these would stay with me until my dying breath.

CHAPTER 13

LILY

Pietro had been nothing more than a complete ball of electric energy since the moment I'd stepped into the kitchen the next morning.

I'd woken up alone and even if I shouldn't have expected anything, it bothered me a lot more than it should have.

He had not said anything about love or a relationship last night —the only thing he'd talked about was caring for me, and knowing Alessandro, it probably was the best I could get from him.

However, Pietro's excitement had switched any of the spotlight from Alessandro and me to him, and for that, I was grateful.

Well, until the moment he'd admitted that he'd barely slept last night.

Alessandro and I exchanged a quick glance as we settled into the boat that would take us to the mainland and the private airfield. I felt the apprehension of the discussion that would ensue until Pietro admitted that he'd spend the night listening to podcasts about Chicago and researching the city online.

At that moment, Alessandro and I shared a relieved huff and earned a side grin from Mario. Yes, Pietro was clueless, but Mario wasn't.

Pietro started to enumerate in scarily exact details all the things he was going to do in Chicago over the next few weeks. He also asked about the school he was going to attend, letting Alessandro know the top five schools he would consider and why.

I couldn't help but be happy, despite the events looming in front of me, things I had no knowledge about and that I knew could cost me my freedom and my life. Seeing Pietro so excited and alive made anything worth it.

However, the sleepless night and excitement soon got the better of him, and before we were even flying for an hour, he crashed in a dreamless slumber.

I stood and asked the hostess for an extra blanket and pillow.

"You know you don't have to stand for that, right?" Alessandro said with a side smile. "We're the only four passengers on this plane. I'm sure she could bring you what you need."

I rolled my eyes. "It's good to stretch my legs and besides, they are not for me." I took the pillow and placed it between Pietro's legs before adding the second blanket on top of him.

Alessandro remained silent during all this, drinking his coffee.

"He's pressing on his legs in this position, and I'm not sure what it could do to his muscles and joints. I..." I shrugged. "It can't hurt."

Alessandro rested his cup on his table and patted the seat beside him in silent invitation. "I doubt you would ever be able to hurt him without hurting yourself in the process."

"Yes, this little boy is so incredible." I sat down and looked at Alessandro. "You are so lucky to have him."

He looked at me and the light in his eyes caused my stomach to fill with running broncos and I was not even sure why. "Yes, I know. I thank God for him every day."

"Would you like some food?" Alessandro asked and gestured to the hostess before I even got the chance to reply.

"How long is the flight, exactly? I could probably wait until we get there."

Alessandro looked at his watch. "Another three hours, but I doubt we'll have time to eat for a few hours after we land." He ran his hand through his hair with a weary sigh. "I suspect Matteo will be waiting for us at Luca's house."

"Oh." I felt my hands grow clammy with apprehension as Alessandro asked the hostess for a selection of mini sandwiches and pastries, as well as a latte for me.

He grabbed my hand and didn't let go, despite the perspiration. "Don't worry too much about Matteo."

I kept my eyes on Pietro. "What if I can't convince him I'm not a threat?" And for the first time, I felt genuine fear seep through the cracks of my brave armor. It was easy for me to ignore the reality while I was on the island—all threats and potential dangers were so far away that they seemed unreal. But that was not the case anymore; I'd be facing my reality in mere hours, and I had not prepared for it.

"It's okay," he said, squeezing my hand, his voice so certain, it took some of my apprehension away. "If we can't convince him, I'll marry you. It's simple."

That had the effect of a slap, and I tensed so much that he threw me a questioning glance.

Didn't he understand how insulting that was? How could this man treat something like marriage in such a trivial way?

I forced a smile as the hostess rolled the food cart toward us and put everything on the table in front of us.

"I'd rather not," I replied, and his hand tensed almost painfully around mine. I kept my eyes on the food in front of me, though any hint of hunger had disappeared under his dismissive comment.

I pulled my hand from his grip with certain difficulty and reached for a mini croissant on the table.

"I'm sure we can figure out another solution. We are full of resources."

"Yes, indeed, we are," he replied sharply before getting his tablet open and starting to work on something.

I looked at him and his lips were pursed, his jaw tight. My reply had obviously annoyed him, and I wasn't really sure why.

I forced myself to eat a couple of mini sandwiches and drank my latte before going back to my seat and pulling it down to lay flat. I'd planned to just pretend to sleep, to avoid any further awkwardness and hurtful proposals, but my lack of sleep must have been more potent because I was suddenly startled awake by a gentle brush of fingers on my cheek.

I let out a little gasp as I opened my eyes and saw Alessandro leaning over me, the annoyance from before gone.

He brushed my cheek again. "Sorry to wake you, but we'll be landing in thirty minutes. I thought you probably wanted some time to freshen up first."

I nodded silently as I pressed the button to sit up and noticed the blanket wrapped around me as a wave of tenderness for Alessandro filled me.

I gave him a questioning look and he shrugged, rubbing at his neck self-consciously. "I didn't want you to get cold."

"Thank you," I said, my voice thick with sleep and emotion as I kept my eyes locked with him.

"We'll see New York soon, Lily!" Pietro said, or at least I assumed he said with his mouth full of food.

I laughed, breaking eye contact with Alessandro and looking at Pietro, who was sitting there with an impressive amount of food in front of him. He had been eating a lot more since I met him, and he'd increased his exercises.

"I can't wait," I replied as I stood and walked to the door Alessandro had pointed out to me.

I walked in and couldn't help but look around with surprise. It was an actual bathroom in a plane, with a shower and everything! I let my eyes trail to the counter where my makeup and toiletry bags were waiting.

I turned toward the closed door as another wave of tenderness hit me at the thought of the man on the other side of it.

He was just so attentive with me, so attuned to my needs and my desires. I blushed again at the memories of our lovemaking. I understood he was a mafia boss, and that being with him would have been a mistake, even if he genuinely wanted to commit. The truth was, I was in love with him, and the thought caused me a lot of sorrow, even if I knew it was never his intention.

Alessandro Benetti had been nothing less than perfectly honest with me, clearly telling me that he could not make any commitment and probably never could.

It was my own fault that I let myself fall in love with him, but how could I not? How could I resist the man I had been on the island with? The proud father, the loving man, the caring protector. How was I supposed to be immune against this? Against his playful smile and tender touch?

A little turbulence made me lose my footing, bringing me back to the now. I would have all the time in the world to wallow in self-pity like a silly high school girl when this threat was not hanging over our heads. For now, I really needed to be logical Lily and bury my emotions deep—something I had quite a lot of experience doing.

I quickly washed my face and applied some light makeup before brushing my hair and disciplining it into a braid.

"Lily, look! New York!" Pietro shouted as soon as I walked back into the main part of the plane before turning his face back to the window.

I leaned down and looked at the city and apprehension caused my stomach to squeeze again.

I probably didn't hide it as well as I wanted as Alessandro reached for my hand and pulled me, so I sat beside him.

"Time to fasten your seatbelt," he said softly, running his thumb back and forth over my knuckles.

I nodded and did it with one hand, not wanting to break from his comforting touch just yet. "I'm sorry, it's apparently only sixty degrees here, and I didn't plan for clothes, but I'm sure Cassie, Luca's wife, will have a few things to lend you until tomorrow."

"Don't worry about it. I'm Michigan born and raised, so the cold doesn't bother me." Or at least, it didn't until the accident and the damage that followed.

He turned toward me. "Lily, look at me," he whispered, and the secrecy of his tone made me curious.

I turned and met his fierce eyes. I was met with a look I didn't see often, but it was the one he wore when he was about to enter a negotiation battle, he knew he'd win.

"I will never let anything happen to you, do you understand? I will protect you with everything I have. Nothing will hurt you."

Other than my feelings for you. I smiled. "I know."

He quickly glanced around us before leaning down and giving me a quick kiss. "Sorry, I'd wanted to do that since this morning. No, actually, scratch that, I'm not sorry."

The pilot announced we were about to land, and I closed my eyes until I felt the jolt of the tires hitting the tarmac.

I let out the breath I was holding. Now was the time to face the music.

Once the plane came to a stop, the hostess and Mario jumped into action, dealing with all the logistical things.

I threw a quizzical look to Alessandro as he muttered something under his breath after looking outside the window.

"The welcome committee is here..." he said cryptically. "Though I expected more friends than foes."

I looked out to see two black luxury cars stopped close to the plane, and a stunning man dressed in an impeccable three-piece suit was waiting beside one of them.

Alessandro groaned, "Maybe wipe the drool off the side of the mouth. Just know the man you're lusting after is Matteo Genovese... You know, the man who wants to put a bullet in your head," he hissed close to my ear.

His words should have terrified me, but as I looked at him and met his scowl and pursed lips, I couldn't help but smile.

"Jealous much?"

He grunted with an eye roll and my smile widened. "Don't worry, Alessandro Benetti, one mafioso is more than enough for me."

He snorted but I saw him relax, and I shook my head at the small ego boost.

"Come on, *cucciolo*," Alessandro said, reaching for Pietro to carry him down the steps of the plane.

"No!" Pietro said, pressing his legs against the seat.

Alessandro's cocked his head to the side. "Don't you want to come to New York?"

"I want to walk down the stairs, please, *Papà*." He threw a begging look to Alessandro. "I want them to see me as strong." He looked down at his legs, glaring at them as if they were offensive. "I don't want them to think I'm broken."

That broke my heart, and the sharp intake of breath from Alessandro allowed me to guess it was the same for him.

"Pietro, son. No one will think you're broken, but it's been a long flight and your legs have been resting for long. I think that—" He sighed and shook his head.

"*Papà*, please, I need them to see who I am."

"I..." I closed my mouth and looked down. I knew better than to intervene in his education.

"Lily?"

I looked up, startled.

"What do you think?" Alessandro asked, his eyes begging me for help.

I looked from him to Pietro a couple of times and shook my head. "This is... I'm not—"

"You are part of this family. Lily, please."

I nodded with a sigh. "Do you remember what we worked on with the physio? One step at a time. Are we okay if we do it like that? Can you?"

Pietro straightened in his seat and gave me a sharp nod, his face taking a determined look that made him look just like his father.

That boy was a force of nature and there wasn't a thing he couldn't do; of that, I was certain.

"Okay, let's do this." I turned toward Mario. "Could you give me Pietro's crutches, please?"

Alessandro stood to the side as he watched us get into action. I could see how tense he was and how he pursed his lips when Pietro struggled to stand.

I couldn't help but shiver as a gust of wind entered from the opened door, but I kept concentrating on the task at hand as I zipped Pietro's jacket before sliding his crutches up his arms and tightening them securely.

"Allow me." Alessandro's deep voice came from so close behind me that it made me shiver, but not from cold this time.

He rested his suit jacket on my shoulders. "Arms in," he ordered, and I did, his warmth and spicy cologne engulfing me.

"It's a little big." Pietro giggled.

I looked down and had to laugh, too. It was like wearing the dress of a giant. "I'd say so."

"It's only for now. I'm sorry, I didn't think," Alessandro added apologetically.

I turned my head to look into his dark eyes. "It's fine. I enjoy the comfort of it." I turned around before I could see his expression as he realized what I meant.

Pietro walked to the door of the plane with me close behind and as soon as he reached the step, he turned to give me a nod.

I looked at Mario, who nodded as well, and took the first step down, waiting there as a buffer in case things didn't go the way we would have wanted.

I quickly counted the steps as I stood behind Pietro and wrapped my arms around his chest, resting my feet between his feet and his crutches. Eight steps, it was double what we tried to do at home, but I knew he could. We shared that fire, him and I.

I kissed the top of his head. "You move, I move."

"One, two." He started the rhythm going down a step at a time.

The closer we got to the tarmac, the prouder I was of the boy and the more relieved I was to have suggested this solution. One misstep could take him so far back, and I wouldn't have anyone to blame but myself.

I let out a little huff of relief as my ballet flat touched the hard ground.

"We did it, Lily." Pietro marveled with a certain sense of awe that proved he didn't really believe it.

"*You* did it, Pietro. This victory is all yours."

Alessandro stepped beside me, and I saw the light shine in his eyes as he looked down at us.

"Is there anything you cannot do?" he asked me under his breath, as if he was talking to himself.

"Good coffee, apparently," I teased, reminding him of all the times he bitched at me for his coffee.

He gave me a little smile and straightened up. "Come on, let's face the music."

We walked slowly, side by side, matching Pietro's rhythm and the man just remained beside his car, his face a perfect mask of bored indifference. I was grateful that our slow progression didn't cause any visible frustration.

We stopped a couple of steps from the car, and I took an instinctive step back. I was not part of this narrative; I was the help. I didn't belong in this family picture, no matter the lies Alessandro told himself.

"Alessandro," the man said solemnly before looking down at Pietro.

I tensed, though I was not sure why. I was just not a fan of having such emotionless eyes on such a special boy.

Alessandro wrapped his arms around Pietro's shoulders. "Matteo, let me introduce you to my son, Pietro."

"Nice to meet you," Pietro said, standing straighter, and I couldn't be prouder of him than I was at that moment.

"Pietro Benetti, it is good to finally meet you. It was long past due," he said with his deep, slightly accented voice.

"*Posso solo scusarmi, ma meglio tardi che mai,*" Pietro replied with a tone that also reminded me of his father.

Matteo's eyebrows shot up and he nodded. "It's true. Why don't you go wait in the car?" He jerked his head toward the black sedan parked in front of his. "Your father will be joining you in a minute."

Pietro was smart enough to know it was not a suggestion and nodded, taking the direction of the car.

All three of us looked at him as the driver opened the door and Pietro refused his help to get in, undoing his crutches and helping himself into the car.

"That boy has the brain of a genius, the courage of a warrior, and the determination of an Italian man," Matteo said with a nod of approval. "You have a worthy heir, Alessandro. The Benetti line is well-represented." He turned toward Alessandro, but his eyes rested on me instead, and I couldn't help but flush under his scrutiny.

"Matthews, why don't you go sit with him," Alessandro said with a detachment that took me off guard. It had been so long since he'd taken that tone with me and called me Matthews.

I nodded mutedly.

"I don't think so," Matteo replied coldly. "Ms. Matthews will ride with me. You go with your son, Alessandro. I'll see you at the compound."

Alessandro stood taller as he stiffened. "I thought I was going to Gianluca's."

"Plan changed. It's best for the kid to stay in the city with me, and you know that."

Alessandro remained silent, unmoved. "She's not getting in a car with you."

"Defying my authority now, Alessandro. My, my... *Continua a ripeterti che non sei innamorato.*"

Alessandro hissed and Matteo sighed. "Be careful, Alessandro. Remember your place."

Cold sweat formed at the back of my neck, and I stepped forward to stand between Alessandro and Matteo. "I'll come with you, no problem. I've got nothing to fear."

"Well," Matteo cocked his head to the side, "I would not say that, either. I'm known to be a man with a temper."

Alessandro wrapped his arm around my waist and pulled me against his body.

Matteo rolled his eyes. "You know Lena would have my head if anything happened to her. She's really looking forward to meeting Pietro and the infamous Lily."

Infamous? I looked behind me at Alessandro, who was doing his best to look anywhere but at me.

Alessandro's hold on me tightened for a second before he let me go with a weary sigh. "Just…" He looked down at me, his eyes full of indecision. "Just…"

I gave him a tentative smile I hoped carried more certainty than I felt.

Matteo snapped his fingers. "*Andiamo*!"

Alessandro reached for my hand and squeezed it before walking to the other car without a backward glance.

Matteo opened the back door and gestured for me to go in. "After you."

I nodded and walked in, sitting down and taking in the luxury of the interior and the comfort of the seat before finally realizing I was sitting in a car across from the highest authority of the Italian mafia.

I looked at Matteo, who had his icy blue eyes trained on me. He didn't look older than Alessandro, though I always expected the big boss to be old and decrepit.

"What are you thinking?" he asked, cocking his head to the side.

I knew better than to lie to someone like him. "I'm thinking that you're much younger than I expected the big boss to be."

"Ah…" He let out a little chuckle. "That is probably due to my natural talent for torturing and murdering people. It helps you get up the ranks very fast."

It was my turn to cock my head to the side. "Are you trying to scare me?"

He arched his eyebrows. "If you were smart, you would already be. I've heard you are terribly smart, so wouldn't that be a wasted effort?"

"Ah, then my intelligence must have been overestimated because I might be scared, but I'm also intrigued."

He looked out of the window for a second before turning toward me. "I've got a dilemma, you see. You've witnessed something that you never should have witnessed, and you now know things you should never have known."

Any curiosity I might have felt before faded, replaced by nothing other than genuine fear.

"It's not my fault... I never intended to know anything."

"It's true, but it's irrelevant here, isn't it? It doesn't lessen the threat you cause and we, the *Cosa Nostra*, didn't stay at the top of the food chain for as long as we have by being careless. I've seen criminal organizations come and go faster than they imagined by making the type of mistakes we don't."

"What does it mean for me?"

"The easiest way would be to put a bullet through your skull because the dead don't talk."

My stomach squeezed and a wave of nausea hit me. I was grateful I had nothing to eat since the small sandwiches earlier during the flight or I was pretty sure that man's shoes would now be covered with it.

"But the thing is, the kid is fond of you, Alessandro is obviously smitten, and it seems that my wife likes you without ever meeting you." He let out a sigh of frustration. "All of which forces me to find an alternate solution, which complicates my life."

I'm sorry that keeping me alive is such a nuisance for you, I thought as I pursed my lips to stop myself from saying it. If there was a day in my life to have a filter, today was the day.

"What are my options?"

"Is your allegiance only because of the kid?"

I arched an eyebrow, the question was so random.

"I adore Pietro and I would never do anything that could hurt him, if that's what you're asking."

He gave me a side smile as if he could read right through me.

"This is not what I'm asking, Ms. Matthews. Please, don't pretend to not understand as I have zero patience for liars and fools."

"Why are you asking? Does it solve your problem to know who I am attached to?"

He shrugged. "The simplest way to fix the problem other than killing you is marrying you to Alessandro."

I jerked back in my seat. "What? I..." I shook my head.

He waved his hand in a dismissive gesture. "Don't play the blushing virgin, I know what happened between you two."

"He told you?" I gasped, reddening both in shame and anger. I was going to kick him in the balls. Who kissed and told past the eighth grade, seriously?

"No, he didn't." He leaned forward with an amused glint in his eyes. "But I suspected that much. Nobody gets that protective of a woman without an investment in her vagina."

I grimaced at his crude words. "Or in her heart."

He shrugged. "If you'd like to think so, be my guest."

Of course, Alessandro didn't love me. He liked me, yes; he loved how his son responded to me, and it may have been enough for them to marry, but not for me.

I shook my head and looked down at my hands on my lap.

He muttered something in Italian under his breath. "What's so bad about marrying one of us; you could marry an Irish or worse, an *accountant*."

"Ah, that's a shame. My ideal husband is an Irish accountant."

His lips lifted on the corner with what I suspected was a genuine smile. "I like you," he admitted begrudgingly, then looked out the window.

He turned toward me again with a sigh as the car slowed, then stopped in front of iron gates. "I won't be able to let you walk away without the satisfaction that you are not a danger to the *famiglia*."

"I know, but you also have to understand that I can't commit for less than I deserve."

"Even if it means losing your life in the process?"

He sounded dumbfounded, and in a way, so was I—it was like choosing death.

"Wouldn't I lose it either way?"

He looked at me for a second, his face a perfect mask of cool indifference.

"I expect your answer to be very different once you face the barrel of my gun, but only time will tell, Lily Matthews... only time will tell."

The door abruptly opened as soon as the car stopped, and Alessandro detailed me from head to toe before letting out a little huff of relief.

Matteo threw me a knowing side look before letting out a mocking chuckle. "Don't worry, Alessandro, I did not hurt your booty call."

I cursed that man internally and looked down with a blush.

"You took a really long way back," Alessandro told Matteo, his eyes narrowing a little.

"I enjoyed the company; I wanted a little more time to chat."

"Are you okay?" he asked, still standing in front of the door, blocking the exit.

"I'm perfectly fine. It was a lovely moment." I gave Matteo a big smile.

He shook his head once more and gestured at Alessandro to get out of the way.

He exited the car and then turned to help me out, which, based on Alessandro's puckered eyebrows, couldn't be a common occurrence.

"I do like you," he said once I was out, and he buttoned his suit jacket. "Don't make me kill you." He swirled around and went up the stone stairs. "*Sbrigati*, Alessandro. *Abbiamo molto da decidere*."

Alessandro rested his hands on my shoulders. "Are you sure you're okay? Don't worry too much about what he said, it's just words."

"I'm really okay, and no, it's not the words, but in a messed-up way, I kind of see his point. He only wants to keep his family safe. If it wasn't my head on the block, I'd even say it's commendable."

Alessandro snorted, "Matteo is a lot of things, but commendable is not one of them."

"Where's Pietro?"

"He's with Matteo's wife; those two hit it off immediately." He looked up and sighed. "Listen, I need to discuss strategy and tomorrow's trip to Boston."

"Of course! You do what you need to do; I'll be with Pietro." I pulled his jacket tighter around me.

"Alessandro!" I heard Matteo call from inside.

"Come on, let's go," I offered, stepping to the side and taking the stairs up to the house. "We wouldn't want you to get in trouble with the principal."

He let out a groan of exasperation behind me. "You don't even know how accurate that is."

I walked into the house and didn't even have the time to detail the hall as a heavily pregnant woman exited a room from the left with a bright smile on her face.

"Lily! Welcome!" she exclaimed, gesturing me forward as if we'd been friends all our lives instead of just meeting. "Why don't you come with me to the library? There will be hot chocolate and cookies in a minute." She gestured toward the direction Alessandro had just taken. "Just leave the boring discussion to them."

I smiled and went to her, immediately at ease. She was the exact opposite of what I had imagined Matteo's wife to be. I expected a tall, thin, expressionless, model-like woman, like the ones you saw in the Hamptons magazines or in a season of *Real Housewife*.

This woman was short, probably as short as me, with a round young face and a friendly demeanor. She was also wearing a pair of wide-legged maternity pants and a long-sleeved T-shirt that wrapped around her round belly. The T-shirt was an Iron Man theme with a little Iron Man figure in the fetal position on top of the belly with the text 'Superhero cooking.'

I chuckled at that; it was very cute. She rubbed her stomach and I saw her engagement and wedding rings. Her engagement ring was a copy of Iron Man's heart.

"*Marvel* fan?" I asked as we both entered the library, and I felt the immediate warmth of the majestic open fireplace at the end of the room.

"How could I not?" she replied playfully, gesturing me to the cream-colored sofa.

I removed the jacket and took a seat as I kept detailing her as she walked to her maternity armchair.

"My name is Elena, but you can call me Ele. That's what all my friends call me, and after all the things I've heard about you, I'm sure we'll become fast friends."

"You shouldn't believe everything you hear."

"Oh! I hope it's all true. You're probably wondering how it is that I'm Matteo's wife." She chuckled without offense.

"No! Well, yes... maybe a little." I felt my face warm under her amused gaze, but I hoped she'd think it was due to the fireplace.

"We couldn't be more different," she agreed with a quick nod. "For example, I know these shirts annoy him, yet he always buys them for me."

I cocked my head to the side, having a hard time reconciling the cold, threatening man with this adorable woman's loving husband.

"Mafia men have many faces. There is the cold and unforgiving one they show the world, and then there's the man he is in private with his loved ones, and I can assure you, it makes it all worth it." She rubbed her belly lovingly as a man entered with a tray and set it on the coffee table. "Thank you, Jeffrey."

"Any time." He bowed to her and me before exiting.

"Where's Pietro?" I smoothed my clammy hands on my dress and looked around.

"I took him to the room he'll use. There is a gigantic half-built Lego set on the table that Jude works on whenever he stays here. His eyes just lit up and he asked to work on it."

"Ah, Legos. We've lost him."

"It will give us some time to chat. It's not often I meet new additions to the *famiglia*."

"I'm not—" I shook my head, unsure how much I could tell her of what was happening. I stood and winced as my leg muscle seized up. Ah yes, cold and wet was a stark reminder of my limitations, especially when the clothes I was wearing did nothing to protect me from it. I reached for a cup of hot chocolate and extended it to her. "Cookies?" I asked, extending the plate toward her.

"Always," she replied, taking two.

She really was my kind of person.

She looked at my dress and sighed. "I was informed of your arrival too late to make sure clothes would be delivered for you. Mine won't fit, I'm way too chubby."

"You're pregnant."

"Ah, well yes, I'm pregnant now, but trust me when I say that pregnancy only affects the stomach and boobs... the rest was all there before." She laughed, visibly happy with the way she looked, as she should be. "Cassie, my brother's wife—who you'll meet soon enough—left a few things here, and you're both about the same size it seems. She said you can take whatever you want, and I'll have a few things delivered for you tomorrow."

I shook my head, quite uncomfortable with that much generosity from a woman I'd just met.

"Oh no, thank you, but I could never."

"Nonsense! You'll need to get used to it very soon. The mafia wives are quite a close-knit club. We're more like sisters than anything else."

I frowned, resting my hand on my chest. "I'm... I'm not a mafia wife."

"Yet," she replied with a little smile.

"Ever. Alessandro is not a loving anything."

"I heard he proposed."

I let out a startled laugh. "He said, 'If we can't fix it, I'll marry you.' How romantic! And I'm not interested, anyway."

"Ah." She nodded, taking a sip of her chocolate. "We are at that stage..."

"What stage?"

She bit her cookie and stood. "Never mind. But just FYI, our men suck at this romance thing. Matteo didn't propose to me; he told me we were getting married, whether I liked it or not. And Dom? India proposed to him."

"I don't see how it relates to me."

She threw me a side look as her mouth quirked up into a little smile. "Do you want me to show you your room? It's just across Alessandro's, not that it matters, right?"

My face reddened as I looked down at the table, taking in the silvery tray as if it was the nicest thing I'd ever seen

She chuckled again.

"It's complicated," I finished rather lamely, feeling bad about lying to her.

"The best things often are."

"Do you mind if I go see Pietro first? I want to make sure he's okay. Not that it's not nice here or anything," I added quickly, fearing that my words may have offended her.

"Oh, don't worry, it makes complete sense!" She pointed down the corridor. "I have my doctor coming for a visit in a bit, just go check-up on Pietro. Your room is on the first floor, your suitcase will be in front of it, and please, take all the clothes you want, Cassie has so many."

I nodded. I was a little too desperate to refuse, anyway.

The next few hours passed in a bit of a blur between helping Pietro with the Lego version of the Death Star and having dinner with Pietro and Elena before retreating to my room. Nervousness for tomorrow and the discomfort of not seeing Alessandro since we arrived continued to pile up on the pain I already felt in my leg.

I took a shower and slid on a long nightshirt before looking at the bed longingly. I only wanted to get under the covers and sleep, but my leg screamed for some relief that I knew I had to give or I probably wouldn't be able to walk tomorrow. I didn't know anything about Killian Doyle—the man I was going to meet in Boston—but I knew I didn't want to show any weakness.

I took the tube of cream that Elena had given me, it was not exactly the strong type of stuff that the doctor prescribed, but it was probably enough to be okay for a couple of days to keep the pain to a manageable level.

I rested my foot on the velvety ottoman at the end of the bed and rubbed some cream in my hands before rubbing it on the scar tissue and into my sore, spasming muscles.

I let out a hiss of both soreness and relief as I dug deeper into the knotted muscles.

"Are you okay?"

My heart skipped a beat in surprise, and I turned my head sharply to see Alessandro standing in my room, dressed in a simple gray T-shirt and loose, dark gray sweatpants.

"You really need to learn how to knock, you know," I said, trying to mask how I always reacted to his presence.

His eyes trailed to my leg, and I realized how visible my scars were. I reached for the nightgown to pull it down, even if I knew it was irrational. Alessandro had seen, touched, and kissed my scars, but having him witness my moments of discomfort and pain was a completely different story.

"No, don't." He closed the door behind him and walked toward me. "What's wrong?" he asked, resting his warm hand on the middle of my thigh, this simple touch giving me goosebumps from the top of my head to the bottom of my feet.

"Ah, it's nothing too bad." I let out a little laugh. I wanted to sound derisive, but I knew I sounded uncomfortable. "I've just forgotten over the past month on the island that the cold and humidity affected my muscles. And..." I shrugged. "It's not a big deal, just some cream, a warm bed, and some rest, and I'll be like new."

He kept his hand on my leg as he nodded slowly, letting his eyes move from the scars to the ibuprofen tube on the ottoman a couple of times.

"Allow me." I didn't even have time to ask what he meant because he gripped my leg behind the knee and moved it to sit on the ottoman before placing my foot between his open legs.

"What..." I stopped as he grabbed the cream and mortification hit as realization smacked me in the face. "Alessandro, no. I'm okay now, I—"

"Stop it, Matthews," he ordered, grabbing my ankle as I tried to move my leg. "Let me take care of you." He leaned down and kissed my knee, making me shiver again. "Please."

I sighed and looked away as he put some cream in his hands and started to massage the top of my thigh.

I sucked my bottom lip between my teeth, trying to stop myself from moaning at the magic his hands did on my muscles.

"I think we're passed Alessandro, don't you?" He smiled up at me. "Call me, Sandro."

I felt a little thrill, as if it meant I was part of his circle. "Sandro." I loved the sound of it on my lips.

He smiled with a small nod before looking down again. "I'm sorry for disappearing all day; I didn't think it would take so long," he said, keeping his eyes on his task.

I looked at his strong, tanned hands working on my leg with such methodical precision it was almost professional. Who could have predicted a month ago that I'd end up being Alessandro Benetti's temporary lover? That he would be the one taking care of me.

"Where did you learn all that?" I asked with an embarrassing groan of relief.

He looked up and winked playfully. "I was pretty sure we established on the island that I was good with my hands... but maybe I need to remind you again."

I wanted to flirt back, but I stifled a yawn instead.

His eyes changed from playful to concerned in a second. "You're tired."

I shrugged.

He sighed. "I know things are concerning right now, and I'm sure it's taking a toll on you."

"It's not a big deal. It will be over soon."

"Yes, soon you'll be able to go back to a life that is more normal."

I didn't think he meant it as such, but it felt like a hidden way to make me understand that we had no future together.

I removed my leg and let my nightgown fall back down to my ankles. "Thank you. It feels better," I admitted truthfully.

I yawned again, and both Alessandro and I turned toward the old-fashioned alarm clock on the nightstand. It was close to midnight.

"I think you need a good night's sleep." He stood and pulled the cover back as if I were a child.

I wanted to tell him that he shouldn't baby me, that whatever guilt or apprehension that transpired from his discussion with Matteo wasn't his fault, not really, but it felt so nice that I didn't have it in me to refuse.

I nodded and walked to where he was standing and laid down, letting him pull the cover on top of me. I closed my eyes, unsure that sleep would actually find me, despite my tiredness mixed with weariness.

"Goodnight Lily," he whispered before brushing his lips against my forehead and rounding the bed to exit the room.

I turned to my side, facing the window as the light turned off, but I knew, despite the lack of noise, that he was still in the room, and I could feel his presence in every nerve ending in my body.

I waited, barely breathing for a few minutes as I started to think that it was probably my mind playing tricks on me. Just some wishful thinking.

However, a few seconds later, I felt the cover move and the bed dip as he slid under the covers. He came closer to me and wrapped his arm around my waist, pulling me against him, spooning me.

"Just for tonight. Just for tonight," he muttered as if he was trying to convince himself.

I rested my arm on top of his and slid my fingers through his as I remained silent.

I felt my body relax as his skin warmed mine and within minutes, I fell asleep, soothed by his gentle breathing and the impression of safety I felt when I was in his arms.

There was no going back for me, I was sure of it. Alessandro had transformed me, and I knew there would be a before and after him. Alessandro was the type of man, and gave the type of love that you never really recovered from.

CHAPTER 14

Alessandro

I sat on the plane for the one-hour trip to Boston while watching Lily talk to Dom as if they'd known each other forever.

It was aggravating to see how at ease she was with him, how easy it had been for him to make her open up. I knew it was a sort of gift with him, but jealousy still reared its ugly head.

Last night had destabilized me much more than I'd expected. If I was completely honest with myself, I'll admit that the main reason for my visit to her room had been to make sure she was doing okay, but the lusty part of my brain was praying for some sex with her. I was still craving her as much, despite having given in to my desire a few times.

But when I went in and saw her tired and in pain, my wish—no, it was much deeper than that—my need to comfort her, to ease her pain changed everything. I wanted to be here just for her, and I realized that just making her feel better was making me feel like a champion.

I couldn't really accept how important she was, how much I cared about her, far beyond her relationship with Pietro and my physical desire. No, there was an emotional connection here, too. There was something much deeper than we probably both wanted, and it was something that was bound to complicate everything, no matter the outcome we reached.

I'd been unable to leave her room last night, and the yearning to sleep with her in my arms had been so strong that it shook me to the core. I'd told myself as I settled in her bed that it was just for one night, but I wasn't sure I believed myself.

"So, you're studying to be an accountant?" Dom asked.

"Part-time. It's something I started when I worked for my uncle." She chuckled. "It was something he crucially needed."

"Ah." Dom nodded. "Explain how you went from a promising University chemistry student to a part-time accounting student."

I wanted to intervene—it was too personal, too blunt—but I also felt guilty for never asking myself.

She shrugged. "The accident happened, and then I stayed home for a year because of the rehab and everything." She sighed as she reached for her necklace and fidgeted with the dice. "I can't really say why I walked away.

I went there, but I was not the same person anymore. I was being favored due to my disabilities, you know... *quotas*," she added as she threw me a side look.

I felt the jab right through my bones and wanted to apologize for all the things I'd told her back then. She'd not mattered then, and she'd not changed me yet.

"Sororities begged me to become a member, professors treated me differently." She shook her head. "I didn't want to be poor little Lily Matthews, the girl who lost her twin in an accident that left her permanently changed inside and out. So, I went home and after a couple of years there, suffocating just the same, with pity looks and whispers about my past. I decided to call it quits and move to Chicago where nobody knew me and nobody cared." She smiled. "It was the best decision."

Dom shook his head. "People are *stronzi*."

"Stronzi?"

"Assholes." Dom grinned and she laughed. "But I'm not sure I agree with your decision."

I frowned and threw him a dark look, ready to punch him.

"Calm your tit, Sandro," he said, raising his hand toward me. "I just think she could have chosen a better city than lame-ass Chicago. New York for example... now that's a real city."

"*Vaffanculo*!" I barked, flipping him the finger.

Dom chuckled and as Lily laughed too, I realized his goal had been to keep her mind from the stress of what she was about to face.

That was something else I found irritating with Dom. He was very intuitive and managed to make husbands and boyfriends feel like losers—which was exactly how I felt now.

The pilot announced our approach to the private airfield and the conversation died as Lily started to fidget with her necklace even more.

I reached up and grabbed her hand, giving it a comforting squeeze.

I cleared my throat to attract their attention. "So, as we discussed, Rémo will be waiting for us when we land. We'll take the car straight to Doyle's club, and you two will wait outside while Lily and I go in." I was pleased with how sure and steady my voice sounded, despite all the variables and the number of things that could potentially go really wrong, really fast.

"That's the plan," Dom replied, but there was a slight edge in his voice. It was something so subtle that I knew Lily wouldn't pick up on it, but I also knew that it was a reminder of what he had said yesterday. If I didn't text him with a passcode every thirty minutes, he would come in, guns blazing.

But I knew that despite Doyle being a hot-headed Irish, he was not stupid and he would never start a war with the Italians.

Lily looked at me questionably.

"It will be okay. Doyle is not stupid."

"And then what?" she asked, straightening in her seat.

"Then we'll take Byrne back to New York for Matteo to have a chat." *A chat*. It was almost laughable. Matteo would take him down to his 'playroom' and torture him until he gave us all his secrets or until Matteo got tired of torturing, which rarely happened. "And after that, we'll go home to Chicago."

"Home to Chicago," she repeated softly with a nod.

I wanted to ask why she was saying it like that and what doubt she was harboring, but it was not the type of conversation I wanted to have with Dom or anyone nearby. It was an *us-only* conversation.

We remained silent until the plane touched the tarmac and finally came to a stop.

I was grateful when Dom jumped from his seat to get out, leaving us alone for a couple of minutes.

I grabbed her hand as she started to walk down the aisle and pulled her against me. She looked adorable today, dressed in a long green woolen sweater dress and leggings.

I pulled gently on her braid with a playful smile. "It's going to be fine, Lily. I would not take you somewhere I thought there were risks."

"We're also a little desperate," she added with a little grimace.

"True, but I would have rather found another way if I thought you'd be harmed."

She stood on her toes and kissed my cheek. "I know, and as you said, as long as I remain truthful, it will be fine."

"Exactly." I followed her to the door. "How's your leg?" I whispered just before we reached the last step.

"Much better, thank you. I never should have doubted your skills."

"Let's not forget that."

"How could I?" she asked. I wanted to question the light bite of sorrow in her voice, but we were already stepping into the car.

The drive to downtown was quite short thanks to the location of the airfield, and we stopped in front of an unassuming black and gold building that appeared to be an Irish pub, but I knew it was so much more.

I exited the car first, quickly eyeing my surroundings and not missing the man at the corner of the street who grabbed his cell phone as soon as I exited the car. Doyle had eyes everywhere in Boston, and downtown was his kingdom.

I helped Lily out of the car and rested my hand lightly on her back. "Don't be fooled by appearances, nothing is truly as it seems," I whispered into her ear.

"Okay."

We walked in the pub, and for anyone other than us, it would look like nothing out of the ordinary—and to be fair, it was a pub, but it was also so much more.

I looked at the barmaid as she stared back at me while she wiped a beer glass, chewing her gum loudly. She was definitely the classy chick who took my call the other day.

She jerked her head toward the back, and we took the direction until we faced a plain wooden door.

I knocked once and it opened to show that it was actually a heavy security door made to look unassuming.

The guard closed the door behind us.

"Follow me," he ordered, taking a set of metal stairs down.

"Oh dear!" Lily muttered as we walked past big two-way mirrors showing scenes of depravity. The one she had just looked at was a naked woman wearing a white rabbit mask in the middle of pleasing three men in wolf masks.

"We're down the *Rabbit Hole*," I told her reluctantly.

I didn't think Doyle would make us walk through his kingdom of dark fantasies, but at the same time, I should have known better—he lived for the shock factor.

This never-ending basement was Doyle's own version of Amsterdam's Red-Light district but way, *way* more twisted, and for the right amount of money, any and all of your fantasies could be satisfied... no matter how fucked-up they were.

"That's, um, yeah," she added, looking down at her feet as she kept on walking. It might have been for the best based on some other scenes that were going on.

We both let out a little sigh of relief when the guard stopped in front of a door and knocked twice.

The man waited a second before opening the door. "Get in."

We walked into Doyle's office and found the man sitting behind his desk with a grin on his face.

The light was dimmed with a slight red hue. I wondered if it was always like that or if he did that especially for us.

However, despite the poor lighting, I didn't miss the slight marks on the dark wooden floor where the chairs must have been not too long ago.

He'd removed them, forcing us to stand, to remain on edge.

"Alessandro Benetti and Lily Matthews, the Chicago troublemakers in my office," he let out with a teasing tone, leaning more comfortably on his seat.

Lily took a step to the side, standing closer to me, and neither I nor Doyle missed it.

He shook his head a little with a mocking smile before he turned toward me and locked his blue eyes with mine challengingly.

If you didn't know who Doyle was—if you were an unsuspecting bastard lucky enough not to be in his universe and just crossed his path on the street—he would look like the typical businessman with his short-cropped blond hair, his well-trimmed beard, and his blue eyes. Perfectly Aryan for an Irish, but also seemingly so safe; it was the perfect contradiction like wolfsbane. Stunning on the outside, but deadly.

"Tell me, Benetti, how long have you known where he is, and how can I know you're not lying?"

"How long I've known and how I found out don't really matter. I'm here to settle a deal, not to chitchat." I shrugged and checked my watch. I had fifteen minutes before I would text Dom. "I've got to text my men every thirty minutes with a code," I explained as he raised a questioning eyebrow.

"Covering your back." He nodded. "I respect that, even if it crushes me to see how little you trust me."

"Probably just as much as you trust me."

Doyle laughed. "That's abysmal." He turned toward Lily and rested his chin on his hand. "Why are you staring at me, princess? Are you reconsidering your choice of criminal?" He smirked. "Spoiler alert... the Irish do it better."

"Lord Jesus, no!"

The outburst made Doyle pucker his eyebrows into a scowl, and I had to look away to hide my smirk.

That's my girl.

"I just," She shook her head. "Nothing."

"No, no, please tell me."

She glanced at me, and I gave her an encouraging smile. It was not like he would hurt her now.

"I just—" I saw the light flush of embarrassment taint her cheeks. I loved it when she did that, and I used to either anger or embarrass her just to see it on her skin. "I just didn't expect you to look like that. I... with all the stories I heard about you, you're the devil."

He smiled as if being called that was a compliment.

"And yet, you look a lot more like an angel."

"I see. Never forget that Lucifer was once an angel, little girl." He leaned forward on his seat and rested his forearms on his desk. "So tell me, Lily Matthews, how did you convince your boss that Byrne's a thief?"

And then she started to explain everything, calmly, methodically, and with a steady voice. I was so damned proud of her.

Doyle must have been impressed as well, because he remained silent during the explanation and after she was done, he turned his head to the side and I finally noticed a man with thick glasses who gave him a little nod.

"What you said checks out."

"I know," she replied, standing straighter, and I had to smile at her bravery. She truly was my queen.

He nodded. "And you do also know that lover-boy right here is going to kill Byrne, right?"

I stiffened. I knew that Lily saw me kill someone, but I was not overly fan of her being reminded of what I could do.

She looked at me for a few seconds before turning back toward him. "Yes, I knew it was likely."

"So, you're okay with condemning a man to his death? Can you live with this guilt hanging over your head?"

"Doyle—"

He raised his hand to stop me, keeping his eyes on Lily.

"It is not on my head. He did what he did, knowing who he worked for. I was not the reason he stole that money, nor did I know what I was looking for when I uncovered the truth. However, he knew he could condemn *me* to my death when he tried to hide his secret, and that's on him, not me."

That was Lily's black-and-white view on life I'd witnessed before, and it was also why I knew I couldn't force her into a life in my world. She might think that she was going to be okay, but her moral compass was too strong for this.

Doyle sighed. "I'm bored now." He snapped his fingers and the door behind us opened to throw an unconscious Byrne at our feet.

I looked at the ruffled and bruised man on the floor. "He's still able to speak, right?"

"Of course, he's just heavily sedated." Doyle rolled his eyes. "That man is such a whiner, and as for the bruises, it's nothing too dramatic. I just don't appreciate being lied to. You do know that, don't you, Benetti?"

I nodded and turned toward him. "Your brother is living his best life in Little Italy in Montréal, and in particular, the Midnight Café."

Doyle made a grimace. "Canada? Montreal?" He let out a sound of disgust. "And on top of everything, *Little Italy*?"

"I think that was the point. Go where you would never think to look."

Doyle snapped his fingers at the men standing by the door. "Help them with this," he said, jerking his head toward the unconscious Byrne.

"Doyle, I'd like to say it was a pleasure, but we'd both know I'd be lying."

Doyle smiled. "Same." He turned toward Lily. "However, meeting you, Lily Matthews, was a *pleasure*. I am always looking for unassuming smart people to join my team, so if you're interested, you know where to find me."

"I..." She smiled. "I'll think about it."

"No, you won't."

She smiled at him. "No, Mr. Doyle, it appears I won't."

He sighed. "Well, it was worth the try."

We turned around and followed the men dragging Byrne down another much shorter corridor that took us straight outside, which confirmed my suspicion that our way down was just for show.

"That was not as bad as I expected." Lily let out with a huff of relief as we reached the street.

"No. At the end of the day, we're businessmen, except we sometimes deal in crime rather than assets," I replied, trying to sound far more detached than I felt.

She hadn't known how easily it could have gone to shit or how much it actually cost me and how I just condemned Finn Doyle—the good one, who never hurt anyone—to a lifetime of punishment for simply wanting to be free. And the worst part of it all is how I did it without an ounce of regret or guilt because when it came to protecting mine, I was as heartless as could be. Lily Matthews was mine, whether we acted on it or not.

"She's lying, I swear!" Byrne spat some blood on the concrete floor of Matteo's torture room.

"Oh, is she now?" Matteo murmured, walking around the chair Byrne was sitting on.

Matteo was wearing his heavy-duty plastic apron as Dom and I were standing a few steps away while we let him play his favorite game.

Matteo looked at the clock on the wall. He'd bet one dollar that he'd make Byrne talk in less than fifteen minutes. He only had five minutes left, and I was already laughing at how it must have killed him inside.

"I see... So now you're telling me that members of my family are liars, are you?" Matteo asked, picking up the shears on his table.

"What? No, no! I said the bitch is lying! The only thing she was good at was sucking cocks around the office."

I took a step forward, ready to smash his face in, but Dom caught my forearm. "No, it's what he wants. He wants you to kill him before he's forced to cave. Don't give in," he hissed.

I gave him a curt nod, pursing my lips and staying back, but Dom knew better than to let go of my arm.

"The thing is, *idiota*, the woman you called a bitch is Alessandro's, and Alessandro is family, so in turn, *she's* family."

That pleased me, even if I knew that it complicated things more. Matteo seeing her like mine would take her freedom away, and I could only imagine how much she would resent me if she was forced into a marriage she didn't want. I'd seen how fast she rejected the idea on the plane, and even if, at the time, it had been an offer made to reassure her, the plain rejection didn't feel nice.

"I stole the money. I did it for me," he spat quickly, and Matteo threw me a startled look from behind Byrne.

It made little sense. We all knew he didn't do it alone, if only for the trap set to keep Lily quiet.

"Is it?" Matteo nodded and put the shears on Byrne's little finger, cutting it off.

Byrne let out a howl of pain as blood squirted to where we stood.

"We've got nine more fingers to go through, so, please... keep on lying." Matteo rounded the chair and stopped on the other side, trapping his left little finger in the shears. "Okay, let's try again, shall we? Who have you been working with?"

"Please, don't. He'll kill my family. I just—" He let out a scream of pain as Matteo cut off the finger.

"*Figlio di puta*, I'll kill your family! Fuck, I'll ask my men to retrieve them right now and shoot them in front of you."

That wasn't true. Matteo didn't kill innocents... Well, not anymore; not since he married Elena, who seemed to have given him the hint of a conscience per proxy.

"A name, now!" Matteo demanded, setting the shears on his index finger.

"Lorenzo!" he shouted as Matteo cut his finger.

Matteo looked at me, and I kept staring at him, silently, hardly believing that Lorenzo did all that and yet, it also seemed so evident.

Suddenly Byrne moved his head to the side and impaled his throat on the shears.

"Fuck!" Matteo roared, pulling it out, causing the blood to splatter on his apron as Byrne started to gurgle, choking on his own blood. "The asshole just killed himself? Who does that?!"

Dom and I looked at each other. Desperate and scared people would, and truth be told, suicide seemed a lot sweeter than what Matteo had planned for him.

"Lorenzo?" Matteo asked, throwing his shears into the sink with exasperation. "Does it even make sense? He's not the sharpest tool in the shed."

"No, he's not, but his father was." I let out with a weary sigh. "We could only go so far in the accounts, but it seemed to have started when my father was still in charge and Lorenzo's father was still his *consigliere*."

"Lorenzo..." Matteo muttered. "Always the most unassuming ones, isn't it?" He looked at Dom.

Dom sighed. "Always."

I nodded, already reaching for my phone. "I've got to go back to Chicago tonight. I need Moreno to grab Lorenzo for me, because as soon as the news of Doyle giving us Byrne gets out, he'll disappear."

Matteo wiped his hands on a towel with a silent nod. "We're not done though, you and I."

I sighed. "I know."

Matteo turned toward me. "I can't let her walk away, not like that."

Fear started to settle in my stomach. "I won't leave her here; she needs to be with Pietro."

"For Pietro?" He raised an eyebrow. "Okay." He let out with a snort. "Alessandro, the *famiglia*—"

"I'll go with him. I'll represent you for the Lorenzo issue, and I'll make sure she stays out of public view for the time being."

"Oh, because Domenico Romano is the highest authority now? You think it's enough?" he asked mockingly, still standing beside Byrne's dead body as if nothing had gone amiss.

"We both know it is. *Buon sangue non mente,* right ?"

Matteo sighed and looked heavenward. "Blood won't save you, Domenico."

"I know, but I also know Sandro and I trust Lily, and you know I'm a good judge of character."

"Jury's still out on that one with that wife of yours."

Dom gave him the middle finger. "My wife is amazing, and you know it."

"She won't say anything," I repeated like a broken record.

Matteo kept his eyes on Dom instead of me and finally gave a nod. "It's on you, Domenico; her life is your responsibility." He turned toward Byrne's body. "Now I have a body to dissolve," he muttered, grabbing the pair of heavy-duty gloves on the metal tray and sliding them on. "Want to help?" He turned his head to the side and pointed at the metal bathtub in the corner.

I grimaced and Matteo chuckled. *"Dai, eri proprio un fiorellino delicato!"* He jerked his head toward the door. "Go now but know that I'll come to you soon."

I didn't miss the underlying threat in his tone. Dom may have bought me some time, but I had no idea what to really do with it.

I nodded and exited the room, followed by Dom. "I'm going to call Moreno and have him follow Lorenzo and stop him in case he tries to run before we get there. I'll go tell Lily and Pietro we're leaving now."

"No worries. I'll give India a call to tell her I'll be in Chicago for a few days."

I sighed. "Thank you, Dom, really. I... You didn't have to vouch for us, and it means a lot."

He shrugged. "That's what *famiglia* is for. Don't mention it."

"Still."

He patted my shoulder. "I know how much it sucks and how worrisome it is to love an outsider. Let me help you out like I've been helped," he added before going up the stairs and for once, I didn't feel like denying what I knew was true.

I was in love with Lily Matthews, and it was because I loved her that I would never commit her to this life.

CHAPTER 15

Lily

Being back in Chicago felt as nice as it was familiar, as close to home as I could be, yet it felt different, and I was not sure if it was my new reality that made it so or my new self.

I had changed since that night I witnessed Alessandro kill that man. I'd thought it was only the island and the turmoil of emotions Alessandro had unleashed in me while I was there, but I didn't think it was the case anymore. I feared the irreversible changes my feelings for him and his son would cause, which had happened, and I was not sure if it was a good thing or not.

We came back late last night, and I was much too tired and worried about what our return would bring to fully comprehend the extent of the situation we were in.

I was living with Alessandro Benetti, Chicago's mafia king. It was all so insane.

I looked around the gigantic, luxury bedroom he'd given me and shook my head a little. We were living in the same house, but we were not living together.

I walked to my en-suite bathroom that didn't only have a shower, but a jacuzzi bathtub, and it even had a TV on the wall.

I passed the boxes of clothes that Alessandro had someone pack from my apartment, which apparently, was no trouble as the building was his, but I didn't feel like wearing those anymore. Instead, I settled for wide-legged, high-waisted black pants and a cropped, neon pink sweater that showed a little sliver of my flat stomach as I moved around. Like a silly teenager with a crush, I wondered what effect it would have on Alessandro when he saw me dressed like that.

It was part of the number of clothes that Elena had delivered to the house by their personal stylist while I was in Boston, and even if I imagined it must have cost Alessandro an indecent amount of money, I took it all because I was not the Lily who wanted to disappear into the background anymore, the one nobody looked at. I was Lily Matthew, the woman who stood up—probably stupidly—not to one but to three mafia bosses! A woman who, despite her scars and disability, was desired by one of the most beautiful billionaires in the world.

I was done hiding, no matter what the outcome of this chapter in my life would be.

Today Alessandro was going to deal with the traitor, and as I was on house arrest at least until Lorenzo was found and Matteo decided what to do with me, I'd decided to start on Pietro's bedroom project to keep him occupied as well. I'd promised to take him around Chicago, and I would have a hard time explaining to him why we needed to stay home and for how long.

It was already quite late, and I wasn't sure why Alessandro had let me sleep so late. I was here to help Pietro settle into his new daily life, and I'd slept in as if I had no responsibility.

I rushed downstairs to the kitchen and the housekeeper placed a plate of warm food in front of me and a freshly brewed coffee before informing me that both Alessandro and Pietro had already been down for breakfast and that Pietro took the elevator back to the first floor.

She was looking at me with speculation, but at least there was no hostility. I doubted that Alessandro brought a lot of outsiders into his home and his life. It had to be a lot to get used to, especially with the presence of a child she probably didn't know existed.

"This was delicious, Maria," I said honestly, patting my stomach. "You are an amazing chef. Maybe you could teach me a few things?"

She stood straighter as her face brightened. "Of course, I would love to teach you how to cook. You will need to know how to take care of your family," she said, making a round gesture with her hand. "Mister Benetti loves to eat but do not worry, I will teach you how to be a good chef for him as a good wife should be."

I opened my mouth to correct her; I was not the future Mrs. Benetti, but the little golden cross around her neck stopped me from doing so. She would probably not approve of our relationship status… whatever it was. "Thank you, I appreciate that."

She nodded with a smile on her face. I had conquered her at least for now.

"I'm going to Pietro's room now. Could you please let Mr. Benetti know when you see him? I don't want to intrude."

"*Si,* I will have lunch brought up for you and the *bambino* later."

I simply smiled before exiting the kitchen, not wanting to mess up the points I'd just earned with the older Italian woman, who I knew Alessandro held in high regards.

I didn't have to find any excuse for spending the day at home as I found Pietro in full planning mode as soon as I walked into his room, and we spent the next few hours organizing and designing his dream bedroom like we were in the makeover business.

"Do you think Dad will mind?" Pietro asked after I added the last item of his list on the spreadsheet.

The total amount was astronomical, and more than I made in a year, but I also knew how much Alessandro was worth and he wouldn't even bat an eye, especially if it was for his son. Besides, the man owned an island!

"No, why would he? He wants you to be happy here, Pietro. This is home."

He turned toward the window, which had a perfect view of the garden and the cherry blossom tree, which I could only imagine would give him a stunning view come spring.

"Do you think it's going to snow soon? I've never seen it before, you know."

"Oh yes, I can feel it in the air, trust me." I was not lying to him. Since the accident, I felt the pressure change, especially in my leg. It was something that my grandpa used to compare us with to lighten the mood during the first year after the accident. "You'll have so much, you'll get sick of it," I added lightly, chasing away the nostalgia of my late grandpa. "We'll go make some snowmen or some snow-stormtroopers."

He turned from his seat on the bed and beamed at me. He looked like the little boy he was supposed to be right now, and not like the boy wise beyond his years.

"That's easy. They are all white!"

"Well, we'll see about that!"

"I'm so happy you're here with us, Lily," he added, making me all emotional.

"I'm so happy to be here with you, too."

"You're going to stay here, right?"

"As long as you want me to," I replied before looking down and smoothing my hand over the navy-blue comforter on his bed.

"I want you here for always."

I smiled down at the computer as my eyes started to burn with tears.

His stomach chose that moment to grumble, and I was thankful for the distraction.

"It's getting late. Do you want to get dinner?"

He nodded as his stomach rumbled again. "Do you think we can get some fast-food? Uncle Hoka always gives me a special treat of burgers when I get there."

"Of course, we can!" I stood from his bed and looked at the clock. It was already past six, and Maria would be gone by now, which was a relief because I didn't expect her to really approve of fast-food for dinner. "And what do you say I get us some popcorn as well, and we can do a Harry Potter marathon on that big TV of yours?"

"Yes! It's going to be so much fun."

"It sure will. I'll be right back." I ordered the food and went downstairs to the kitchen to prepare the snacks for the films, hoping I would see Alessandro or Dom. Really, I'd settle for anyone who could tell me how things were going because it felt like they were forgetting that I was serving as collateral in all that too, and I was not pleased to be left in the dark like that.

But the house remained eerily silent, and I even started to wonder if Alessandro and Dom were gone, leaving Pietro and I alone with Mario and the security team.

I was both annoyed and worried by the time the food arrived, and I went back to the room to be with Pietro. Despite all his excitement with his new life and the future schools he could potentially attend, I could not fully concentrate on him and enjoy an evening I would have normally enjoyed.

Pietro started to yawn by the middle of the first film, the excitement of the past couple of days making him tired faster, and part of me was relieved that I wouldn't have to fake an excitement that should have been real. I would now have a chance to confront Alessandro to find out what was going on and to make sure that he would not keep me out of the loop again.

"You're tired, sweetheart. Why don't you go brush your teeth and put your pajamas on."

"But Dad..." he said, rubbing his eyes. "He always says goodnight."

That thawed some of my irritation toward Alessandro. He was a good father, and I knew deep down, the only thing he was trying to do was to protect Pietro and me, but he also had to remember that I was not a child, and I was not his responsibility—at least not to the same level as Pietro was.

"I'll go get your dad now. He'll be up in a minute."

"'K." He yawned as he helped himself to his wheelchair, obviously too exhausted to use his walker tonight but once again, he didn't complain or ask for help.

He didn't want people to find him weak, but he was the most resilient and strong boy I'd ever seen. Even if I didn't know much about the mafia, I was sure that if he took his father's place one day, Pietro Benetti would be a force to be reckoned with.

I went downstairs and even if it made me angry at myself, I couldn't help but stop in the corridor to check my appearance in the mirror before going to his office.

I stopped in front of the door and had my hand raised to knock when the door opened, and I took a startled step back.

Alessandro raised his eyebrows, the only sign of his surprise.

"Lily, hi!" he said, but his voice carried a little confusion.

I flushed a little, fearing that they might think I was spying. "Sandro... I... Mister Benetti, just— Pietro is about to go to bed and, I just thought..." I pursed my lips, stopping the trainwreck before it caused too much damage.

"Yes." He nodded, exciting the office, followed closely by a shorter burly man who kept his dark eyes on me, making me quite uncomfortable under his scrutiny. "I'm sorry, Lily. I didn't realize the time." He turned toward the man. "Moreno, this is Lily Matthews, my assistant."

I smiled despite the little sting that it caused me. It was true, though; I was his assistant but after everything we shared, the title felt wrong.

"Lily, this is Moreno, one of the oldest and most trusted members of my team."

Moreno laughed and reached for my hand. "Alessandro, you make me feel like an old man. I'm only three years older than you." He kissed my hand, letting his lips trail on my knuckles much longer than necessary, and the shivers that it caused down my spine was only due to discomfort.

"I've already seen you a few times around the office," he said, keeping my hand in his.

"Ah, maybe."

"Okay, Moreno, let go of the lady's hand."

Did I actually hear a hint of coldness in his voice or was it just in my head?

Moreno shook his head and let go of my hand. "I will see you around, Lily."

Not if I can avoid it, you won't. "Yes, of course, it will be a pleasure. Have a great evening," I replied as pleasantly as I could with a smile I hoped was friendly enough.

Alessandro stood a little straighter, his shoulders back as he detailed my face. "Please tell Pietro I'll be up in a minute. Have a good night, Lily."

I was a little taken aback by his dismissal, but I knew better than to argue in public, especially when he seemed to be in a mood. It was a side of him I'd been quite accustomed to over the past year and half, and it was not the most pleasurable side of his personality.

Maybe it was best to wait until the morning to have the conversation I wanted to have with him. Having this discussion now would only put fuel on the fire, and we'd both end up saying things we would regret.

"Of course, have a good night," I replied and turned my back to them, walking back up with as much dignity and composure as I could muster.

When I went into Pietro's bedroom, he was already half-dozing. "Your dad will be here soon. Have a good night."

"Sweet dreams, Lily. I love you."

The rest of whatever annoyance I felt just slipped away, and I smiled, leaning against the doorframe. "I love you, too."

I went to my room and called my parents. While I couldn't answer all of her questions, the most insisting one was when I'd come to visit.

I never thought I'd crave home, not really, but right now, knowing that I couldn't go there and that, despite the appearance of freedom, I was still as captive as I had been on the island, somehow brought me down. Except this time, Alessandro was unintentionally my jailer—the true one being his boss in New York and Lorenzo, who I hoped they would find soon.

"Dad and I are worried about you, honey. We've not seen you for so long, and how come you're not going to be Mr. Benetti assistant anymore? And why are you staying in his house?"

I heard my father's booming voice in the background.

"Dad—" She cleared her throat. "We wonder, is something going on with this boss of yours, honey? You know he— he can't use his power over you." She was obviously uncomfortable, and I felt like I was dying just having her imagining that, which was not terribly far from the truth.

"No. Good Lord, Mom, it's *nothing* like that!" *Liar.* "Why would a man like him be interested in a woman like me? Mom, he is a thirty-something billionaire, and I'm... well, *me.*"

She let out a sigh of relief. "Yes, I know! I'm sorry, honey; it's your father. Of course, I know it's not anything like that."

Ouch. Thanks, Ma, for always seeing me as so ordinary.

I was thankful at the knock on my door, even if my heart jumped with apprehension knowing who it was.

"Sorry, Mom. I have to go, but I'll come visit soon, I promise," I rushed out before hanging up. "Come in!"

Alessandro opened the door halfway and popped his head in. "See? I'm making progress. I'm *knocking* now," he said with a sheepish smile.

I shook my head, and I couldn't help but smile, too.

"May I come in?"

"It's your house," I replied, trying to sound detached despite my heart beating faster already.

He sighed and walked in, closing the door behind him. "Not exactly the answer I was going for, but I suppose it will have to do." He leaned against my door and studied me. "How are you?"

I was not expecting that question, and I remained silent, sitting at the foot of my bed for a few seconds, not really sure what I wanted to address first. He had discarded his suit jacket and tie since I saw him in his office a few moments ago, and despite him looking as big and powerful as he has always looked, I didn't miss the dark circles under his eyes, the fine lines on his forehead, and his eyes looking far deeper as they used to. The man was exhausted and suddenly, I didn't feel like piling more on top of everything.

"I'm okay."

"I'm sorry about today... again." He sighed, rubbing his stubble, leaning even more against the door. "I know I dropped the ball with you and Pietro, but Lorenzo has vanished and," He sighed and shook his head. "Dom is tracking him. I should be out with him, but..." He stopped talking and looked at me.

I understood what he was not saying. He wanted to stay close to Pietro and even a little bit to me.

"You look tired."

He sighed again, leaning his head back against the door, and suddenly, I wanted to take care of him, help him as he did for me a few nights ago.

I stood from the bed and grabbed his hand. "Come." I pulled on it and he followed me silently.

"Sit," I commanded as I reached the comfy reading chair in the corner.

"What are you doing?" he asked while still following my instructions as he sat heavily on the chair that seemed so much smaller with him in it.

"Trust me," I replied, rounding the chair and standing behind him. I buried my fingers in his thick, dark hair and applied pressure on the sides of his scalp.

He let out a groan and then a sigh before leaning his head back, which made me smile. I knew the pressure point classes I took at the acupuncture place close to my building were not just a way to occupy my free time.

I kept massaging his head, applying pressure as I looked leisurely at his face upside down while he kept his eyes closed.

I could see his body relax as he leaned more against the comfortable seat.

"You don't have to do that," he said, but his voice lacked conviction.

"I know I don't, but I want to. It's a partnership; you take care of me, and I take care of you."

He opened his eyes suddenly and looked at my face above his. The light was too dim, and his eyes were much too dark to really make out how he felt. It was frustrating, especially knowing that he could read me like an open book.

"I'm sorry for not having answers for you. I don't know how to fix everything," he finally admitted, barely louder than a whisper, and I knew it cost him to admit this. Alessandro was a fixer, and not being in control must drive him crazy.

"It's okay; I'm not worried," I replied as I let my fingers trail down to his temples, and I made some soft circular motions. "And do you know why?"

He closed his eyes and shook his head a little.

"Because I know you, Alessandro Benetti, and you're a force to be reckoned with, mafia or no mafia." I let out a little laugh. "I never admitted it before—I didn't want to be the one feeding your overinflated ego more than it was—but seeing you in those boardrooms was mesmerizing. All those powerful men came in standing tall and proud like they owned the world, and they ended up leaving with their tails between their legs, knowing that their place in the food chain was always below yours." I pressed a little on his temples, making him moan, which enticed my body in ways that were not truly welcome right now.

I pressed my thighs together, begging my body to stop the throbbing.

"There's nothing you can't conquer, and this will be no different. I know it's irrational after everything that has happened but, I feel safe with you, and I know everything will be alright." Before I could stop myself, I leaned down and kissed his forehead.

Faster than I thought was possible, he reached up and grabbed the back of my head as I tried to move back up.

He moved his head to the side and pushed my head down until my lips touched his. He started to give me a couple of chaste kisses, keeping his hand on the back of my head as if there was a single part of me that wanted to stop kissing him, despite knowing it was never going to end the way I dreamed it would.

The pressure of his lips became more insistent and when he caught my bottom lip between his, I let my body relax and leaned even further into the kiss, opening my mouth, and giving access to his tongue. The kiss was not the same passionate, dominating ones he gave me before—this one was soft, his tongue caressing, searching, as if he was making soft love to my mouth, and it almost made me weep.

My knees buckled as I got lost in the taste of him, but his insane reflexes took over again. I let out a shriek of surprise as he broke the kiss, swirling briskly to the side to wrap his arm around my waist and pull me onto his lap, straddling him.

"You are one of a kind, Lily Matthews," he said as he slipped his warm hands under the hem of my cropped jumper, letting them roam softly upward until I raised my arm to help him remove it. "I always knew you'd be."

He wrapped his arms around my bare torso and pulled me closer to trail his lips on the swell of my breast as his deft fingers popped the back of my lacy bra open. "I just didn't know how many things you'd destroy in your wake," he murmured against my skin, his hot breath hardening my nipples to the point of pain.

I wanted to ask him what he meant, but all conscious thought had escaped me as he pulled my bra down and sucked one of my nipples into his warm mouth.

"Sandro," I moaned, sliding my fingers back into his hair, arching my back. "More."

He let go of my nipple and licked it. "I'll give you more, baby. I'll give you everything but let me play with you a little. You taste so good." His voice was low, husky, probably as consumed by desire as I was.

He sucked on my other nipple as I started to move my hips back and forth, trying to get friction I couldn't get.

"Sandro, please."

He growled, and I let out a shriek as he briskly stood, carrying me to the bed. He lowered me there and pressed down on my core, letting me feel his erection where I needed it the most.

I wrapped my legs around his waist and rocked my hips with a little moan—the friction of his cock feeling so amazing despite the layers of clothes.

He trailed his lips against my jawline, and I moved my head to the side, giving him better access to my neck while tightening my legs around his hips, increasing my movements, trying to press him harder against my clit with each shift.

I moaned louder as I felt the orgasm approach, and I was about to come when he bit the soft flesh where my neck and shoulder met—not hard enough to break the skin, but hard enough to make me lose the momentum and delay my orgasm.

"You're not coming before my cock is inside you, do you understand me?" he ordered, his hard CEO voice in action, but instead of causing fear, it made me wetter. He licked the spot he's just bitten, soothing it. "You like it, don't you? The pain, the domination." He licked my neck again and moved a little to the side to pop the buttons of my high-waisted pants open and slid his hand inside my panties.

"Mmm, yes... All yes, yes everything."

He kissed the length of my jaw and caught my bottom lip between his teeth, biting it before sucking as his fingers slowly trailed over my soaked pussy.

"Look how wet you are for me," he whispered against my lips as he pushed two fingers inside me, my walls tightening around them, trying to pull them deeper. "Look how greedy your pussy is; how much it wants me inside you."

"Yes, I want—"

"What do you want, Lily?" he asked, raising his head to look at my face, only entering me to the knuckle before pulling it out again. This mini penetration was not enough to make me come, but just enough to keep me on the verge... He was torturing me.

I closed my eyes. "You, I want you, please," I begged shamelessly, raising my hips to coax his thick fingers deeper inside me.

"Be precise. You've always been so detailed, Miss Matthews..."

I let out a growl of frustration. "I want your big cock inside me," I admitted and felt the burn of self-consciousness at saying those words out loud for the first time in my life. The unhinging desire made me lose the remainder of my inhibitions.

"And how do you want me to take you, Miss Matthews," he asked, stopping his ministrations on my pussy.

"Sandro, please, don't make me say it." I grabbed his wrist, trying to push his hand to move, but of course I was no match.

"Say it!" he ordered and fuck, I almost came right there.

"I want you to take me like the man you are. I w-want you to make me yours."

He growled and moved from the bed, ripping his shirt open, his small buttons flying across the room.

He pulled down my pants and panties and slapped the inside of my knees as I tried to close my legs. "Don't you dare. Open them, wide."

I bent my legs, resting my feet flat on the bed and opened.

"Wider. As wide as possible. I want to see what I do to you."

I opened my legs as wide as I could until the side of my thighs rested on the bed, and I left my slit open.

He licked at his lips, keeping his eyes on my core as he unbuckled his belt and got rid of his pants and boxers to let his thick long cock bob up toward his stomach.

"You're so ready for me." He licked his lips again. "Get on all fours."

I obeyed immediately, though some apprehension slipped in with my excitement. I'd never had sex like that before. Well, I'd never experimented with anything like Alessandro Benetti in any area of my life. My only sexual experiences had been with Andrew, and we had both been virgins, learning as we go.

But Alessandro was something else altogether. He was built for pleasure and almost managed to make me come with just one kiss.

I felt the bed dip as he kneeled behind me, and I shivered as he ran his hand over my ass and up my lower back before slowly letting it trail along my spine before gripping hip.

"I'm going to show you what being possessed by me truly means. What submitting to your mafia boss is really like."

I gasped and shivered with apprehension as I felt him rub his cock through my wetness and suddenly, with a thrust of his hips, he entered me to the hilt with an animalistic roar.

I let out a yelp of pain because, despite my readiness, I was not yet accustomed to his size. However, he didn't give me the time to adjust, not like last time.

The savage part of him had taken over.

He grabbed my other side in his bruising grip, and he started to pound into me with deep, hard, unforgiving thrusts.

After a few thrusts, my hands gave out and I ended up on my elbows, making the angle of penetration even deeper than before. I could feel him everywhere.

"Oh God!"

"Lily, fuck. I won't... Fuck—" He growled before leaning down, covering my body with his, his thrusting slowing and turning shallower. "I won't last, you're so fucking tight. Ah!" He brought one of his hands up to fondle my breast as the other went down to rub at my clit. "Come for me. I won't last much longer."

His thrusts turned more erratic as I felt him grow even bigger and suddenly, as he pinched my nipple between his fingers, I fell off the edge without any warning as the force of the orgasm blinded me for a second.

Sandro let out a guttural sound as my walls tightened around him, and he shouted my name as he followed me into the oblivion of pleasure.

I fell onto the bed, and he followed me down, his weight pressing me into the mattress, his softening cock still nestled deep inside me.

I turned my head to the side and let out a sigh of content.

He kissed the corner of my mouth and left my body, rolling to the side and taking my limp, exhausted body along with him until he had his arm securely around my waist.

"I'd never done it like that before. But I enjoyed it immensely," I added quickly as I felt him tense behind me. I didn't want him to think I hadn't enjoyed it. I wanted more of that, I wanted more of him in this unpolished state.

He ran his thumb across my lower belly. "It was out of this world, Lily. The best sex I ever had."

I was not sure if it was true or not, but it pleased me all the same—and it was true for me.

I sighed and nestled closer to his body. He kept me in his arms as he moved to reach for the side of the comforter and wrap it around us.

He kissed the top of my head and I closed my eyes, enjoying his warmth, his steady breathing, and the soft thumping of his heart against my back. I wanted to soak into this moment, to permeate every single detail into my mind because no matter how much I didn't want to think about it, Sandro and I were on borrowed time.

"Are you sleeping?" I whispered after his breathing turned deeper. I waited a few seconds and when he didn't stir, I closed my eyes. "I love you, Alessandro. I love you so much, I don't think the Lily I am will ever be the same without you." I felt a little lighter having admitted it out loud.

Logically, I knew he hadn't heard me, yet it felt as if he'd just pulled me closer to him.

I was startled awake by a hand brushing my cheek. I blinked a few times and saw Alessandro was dressed in a suit, his hair still wet from the shower, the intoxicating smell of his woodsy cologne soothing all my senses.

"What time is it?" I asked sleepily, turning toward the dark windows.

"It's not even six yet," he whispered, caressing my cheek again. "Dom called me thirty minutes ago. He found Lorenzo. I've got to go, but I didn't want you to wake up and find me gone. Not again."

I smiled, closing my eyes and already feeling sleep pull me back. "Thank you."

He kissed my forehead. "You stay home, okay? No matter what anyone says or does. You stay home."

"Of course, I will stay home."

"Lily, I..." He stopped and sighed. "I'll see you later."

"Later, yeah."

I woke up a couple of hours later, well-rested but sore everywhere. I got out of bed with a groan as it seemed that every single muscle was paying the price for the intense moment I shared with Sandro.

I walked to the bathroom, hoping a hot shower would turn me a little more human.

"Lord," I muttered as I saw my naked reflection in the floor-length mirror. My body was a map of last night's events.

I trailed my fingers to my hips that bore the bruising imprints of Alessandro's fingers. I let my fingers slide up to my breast, reddened by his stubble, to the mark his teeth left on my neck, and the red, chaffed, and swollen lips from our kissing.

And yet, all the physical marks were nothing compared to the marks he'd left on my heart.

I sighed and shook my head, trying to shove the night of passion deep into the back of my mind for now.

I took a long shower and settled for a long skirt and a thermal shirt. I was surprised when I didn't see Maria in the kitchen or Mario in the salon.

Did he leave with Alessandro?

"Pietro?" I called from the bottom of the stairs.

"In the library."

I walked in and stopped when I saw him standing with his crutches and Moreno beside him, too close to him for my liking.

"Moreno, good morning. Is there anything I can help you with?" I asked as my phone started to ring with

Alessandro's assigned ringtone. I cursed myself for forgetting it on the kitchen counter.

"Yes, Alessandro asked me to come to get you and Pietro and take you for brunch downtown."

I nodded. "I thought he was busy looking for his... friend," I said evasively as my phone stopped ringing but started again almost immediately.

"Yes, he is, but he decided to take a break and asked me to pick you up."

He's lying! My instincts screamed for me to get away and take Pietro with me.

I nodded. "Of course." I jerked my head toward Pietro. "Come on, kid, let's get ready."

Moreno laughed and rested his hand on Pietro's crutch, stopping him from moving before reaching behind him and grabbing a gun, cocking it, and resting it against Pietro's head.

"You're not as stupid as I thought you were... What a shame." He jerked his head toward the door. "Step in and close the door behind you."

My heart dropped to my stomach as fear for the little boy I loved so much filled my veins with ice.

"Lily..." Pietro's voice was so small, so scared.

I smiled at him as I took a step forward, closing the door behind me. "It's going to be okay, Pietro."

"Lock the door," Moreno ordered, keeping the gun pointed at Pietro's head.

I reached behind me and turned the lock. "Why don't you let him go?" I asked Moreno, happy at how calm my voice sounded, despite the terror I felt.

"Because," he let out a little laugh, "you must know there'll be no happy ending to this story, don't you?" He sighed with a little shake of his head. "I liked you, Lily; I really did. Alessandro kept complaining about how much harder you were making his life, and I thought *finally*, someone saw him for who he was—a heartless monster—but then you went and spoiled it all when you let him fuck you."

I quickly looked at Pietro, mortified that he'd heard these words.

Moreno nudged the gun against his head. "Don't worry about the kid; he needs to know what blood runs in his veins before he dies, he needs to know why he is paying the ultimate price."

"Why are you doing this?!" I cried with desperation when I saw a dark stain appear on Pietro's pants as he peed himself in fear. He'd never fully recover from that, and I never wanted to kill someone more than I wanted Moreno dead right now.

"Why?" he scoffed, and his voice turned hard. "Benetti took my woman away and destroyed my life. He raped and tortured her when she was barely a woman!"

Bile rose in my throat. I could not imagine my Alessandro doing that to anyone.

"I killed him, but it's not enough. I want him to feel the loss through who he cared for the most... his son, his tainted blood."

"His... son?" I felt like I was having a stroke, nothing made sense.

"Alessandro!" he shouted, the gun shaking with his anger. "His father took everything from me! *Everything!* Alessandro knew how deviant his father was, and he didn't care because the young girls he was abusing were not his to care for."

"Al-Alessandro is not his father, he's ki—"

"Shut the fuck up! Don't defend him, you don't know anything!" His face was red as froth from his saliva formed at the corner of his lips. He was completely losing it, and I felt like he would shoot at any moment. Just the thought of seeing Pietro die both paralyzed me in fear and sprang me into action, wanting to keep him talking, to calm him down, and maybe have him direct his weapon on me instead.

I just need him to want to shut me up more than he wants to kill Pietro.

"Alessandro doesn't need to rape anyone. I was happy enough to let him do everything he wanted to do to me. You're threatening a child! A poor, helpless child. Tell me how does it make you better than Alessandro's father? You're just as deviant." I snorted. "Who's the monster now?"

That worked just as perfectly as I wanted as he turned his shaking gun toward me.

"I'll kill you first, whore! Taking the woman he loves like his father took mine will be the most beautiful act, and I'll wait for him here, with that broken son of his until he comes to find your dead body. Then, when I see the pain on his face, I'll kill the boy."

"You'll never get out alive."

He let out a laugh that sounded deranged. "Don't you see, *puta*? I never planned to make it out alive. This is the perfect vendetta. I have nothing left to lose."

I saw the determination in Pietro's eyes as I saw his hands tighten around the handles of his crutches, and I knew what he was about to do.

He raised one of his crutches and hit Moreno in the balls before pushing him to the side, knocking him off balance and falling to the floor.

The gun went off, and it felt like an out-of-body experience as adrenaline took over and my mind just locked as I sprang into action.

I jumped to grab the gun, but Moreno was already on his feet, roaring insults, and all I could do was kick the gun before the man tackled me on the floor, cutting my airflow as he lay heavily on top of me.

"*Puta*!" he shouted before spitting in my face. He gripped my skirt and pulled it up. "I think I'll just fucking rape you now, before I kill you. I'll show the kid his family legacy!"

I tried to ignore his fumbling fingers as he tried to rip my underwear under my skirt as I extended my hand, trying to snatch the gun that was just out of arm's reach.

"Let her go!" Pietro shouted from behind, and I caught a glimpse of him trying to stand again—the anguish on his face was almost worse than what this man was about to do to me. "Lily, I can't!" His voice broke as I heard the sound of my panties finally give way. Pietro extended his hand and in a desperate last attempt, he reached up to the little side table and threw something my way.

I grabbed the cool metal in my hand as Moreno forcefully pushed two fingers inside me, making me gasp in pain. As he smiled down at me, I tightened my hand into a fist and brought up whatever Pietro threw toward me and stuck it right into the man's eye.

He howled in pain as what I saw was a silver pen stuck deep into his eye. He raised his weight in pain just enough to let me move a few inches, enough for my fingers to touch the cool metal of the gun.

"Bitch!" He pulled out the pen and lay back on top of me as some blood dripped on me as we both fought for the gun.

"Lily!" Pietro shouted as Moreno won and grabbed the butt of the gun. Suddenly, I heard a crash, a gunshot, and blinding pain.

And then everything went black...

CHAPTER 16

ALESSANDRO

Leaving the warmth of the bed and Lily's welcoming body had been harder than I thought it would be.

I was starting to understand now why Luca and Matteo were particularly cranky when they were called in the middle of the night.

If I had a choice, I would never leave her side.

I sighed as I drove through the quiet city to go to the docks. I kept trying to convince myself that I didn't want Lily to have this life, but what if she wanted it? What if she was ready to accept all of this?

Aren't you a little conceited? Choosing a life of blood and death just for you?

But it was not only me, was it? It was Pietro, too. I kept thinking about it; and the more I thought about it, the more real it was in my mind. We could build a family, a life together. I could make her happy.

By the time I reached the familiar warehouse, my mind was made up. Once this was dealt with, I would sit down and have a discussion with her—give her the choice and hope she'd pick me because I was not sure I could just stand back and let her just be here for Pietro. I couldn't let her build a life, marry someone else... have his babies.

The thought brought a murdering rage toward this faceless man who would be stealing my treasure and taking away my only shot of happiness. A man I doubted I would be strong enough not to kill.

I walked into the warehouse to find Lorenzo sitting on a chair with a black fabric bag over his head and Dom leaning against the wall, texting.

I jerked my head toward Lorenzo silently.

"He was just babbling away. 'Please let me go.' 'I didn't do anything.' 'Why are you so mean to me?' 'I'm a delicate flower, I need sunshine,'" Dom added with a high-pitched voice.

I raised an eyebrow as I heard muffled shouts come from under the bag.

"Okay, so I might have paraphrased the last one, but he was so annoying. I gagged him, too."

I removed the bag and saw Lorenzo's face morph with relief. Was he stupid?

I removed his gag, and he took a deep breath. "Oh, Sandro, thank God you're here! This man has lost his mind! I've not done anything! I escaped, and then, I'm here."

I frowned and turned toward Dom, who just shrugged.

"If you've not done anything, then why did you run away when I got Byrne back."

"Byrne? Your accountant?" He cocked his head to the side. "What do I have to do with your accountant? Why did you ask your men to take me?"

"Domenico is not my man," I scoffed at the stupidity of the notion. "He's the *capo dei capi's* brother and New York's *consigliere*."

Lorenzo shook his head briskly as if he was trying to make sense of it all. "I'm not talking about him," he spat. "I'm talking about the three lowlifes you sent to the whore house two days ago when I was balls deep in Catarina!"

I grimaced at the thought of Lorenzo's sex life.

"They just dragged me away, mid-thrust, mind you, saying it was the boss's order and threw me into a crap basement without food or drink! Look at my hands!" he said, looking down at his hand attached to the arm of the chair. "Look at my fingers." He wiggled his scraped and bleeding fingers with pieces of fingernails missing. "It took me a day to use a stupid rusty nail to unscrew the bars of the window and escape. I probably have rabies now."

"Tetanus," Dom replied, keeping his eyes down on his phone.

"What?" Lorenzo asked, turning toward him.

Dom sighed and looked up. "Rust won't give you rabies; it'll give you tetanus... Get your facts right. Fuck, it's like no one's watching *Grey's Anatomy* anymore." He looked back down at his phone and smiled at his screen. "If only you caught tetanus, it would lock your fucking jaw and stop you from talking shit."

I grabbed my phone and called Oda. "Go to *Pleasure Island* and ask to speak with Catarina. Ask her what happened with her client two nights ago."

Oda made a gagging sound. "That place is gross! I'll catch herpes just by walking in."

I rolled my eyes. "Now's not the time to be a smartass; now's the time to do your job. Text when you're done." I shook my head. "I've got no patience left for you, Lorenzo. I know the truth, and if you speak now, I might let you live. But if you don't, I'm not going to kill you... No, you see Dom here?" I pointed toward Dom, who looked up and waved like the asshole he was. "He'll put you on a plane to New York, where Matteo Genovese will use you as the newest test subject for his brand-new torture device. So be very, *very* careful with the next words that come out of your mouth, and for your fucking sake, it better not be a lie."

Lorenzo opened the month and closed it again, doing it two or three times.

"Okay. Fine." I sighed. "Dom, take him."

Dom slid his phone back into his pocket. "Okie-dokie!" He took a step forward.

"No, no! Okay, okay, I admit it. My father and I blackmailed your father!"

I tried to keep my face as impassive as I could under the surprise of this revelation. It never made a lot of sense for his father to become *consigliere,* and even less for this waste of space to succeed him. I couldn't think of a thing my father would want to hide so badly.

"Why would my father care that you uncovered his tax evasion?"

"What?" Lorenzo frowned. "I'm talking about his taste for young girls... very young girls."

I sighed and rolled my eyes. "Nobody would care about a seventeen-year-old stripper!" I scoffed whilst guilt stabbed at my heart thinking about Violet. Her mother was important.

"No, but people would care about Maria Angela Di-Marco."

I opened my mouth and closed it again. "That was what? Twenty years ago? She didn't want the mafia life; she didn't want an arranged marriage. She killed herself the day of her sixteenth birthday, I remember. I was there." How could I ever forget the way she slowly stood, walked to her cake, and instead of cutting it, looked around the crowd and then slit her throat. It was a tragic, cautionary tale, and also part of the reason why I didn't save my sister Violet from her life of poverty.

"No, that is not what happened."

"How would you know? You were what at the time? Twelve?" He could not have been much older than that since I'd only been eighteen when she died.

"Fourteen! And I know because my father told me everything; he told me the dark secret, so when the time came—"

"You'd get his place," I finished darkly. "What's the secret?" I was almost too scared to find out.

"Maria was only fourteen when she came to the US for her introduction party. One young man of only eighteen fell head over heels in love with her, and he asked my father to help him get her promised to him. My father couldn't care less, and he mocked this young man with your father." Lorenzo looked up to the ceiling. "Listen, my father was a power-hungry fucker just like I am, but I'm sure he didn't know what your father had planned. I swear, he didn't."

"Whatever it was, your father didn't have any qualms at using whatever my father did for his benefit."

"What's done is done." Lorenzo shrugged. "Your dad was a young *capo* then and hated being questioned. This young man was too vocal, too determined, so your father waited. When Maria's father finally accepted the young man's offer, your father," Lorenzo swallowed, and I braced for what was to come, "took her for himself and what he did to her that night and so many times after that…" He shook his head. "She was never the same, and my father had proof."

I nodded silently. I'd known for years that my father was a despicable man, the worst kind there was, yet this managed to make me hate him even more.

"And your father used whatever evidence he had to gain power." In reality, his father was no better than mine.

"She was just a random girl—one of many your father stole the innocence from—but this one had a champion who has waited years for his revenge."

"So, you're telling me you are a traitor and worked for—"

"No, not at first, but when he killed your father, I… You hated me, Sandro! You always thought I was beneath you, that I was an idiot! You never showed me even a little respect, so I knew you would kick me out if you knew how I got the job, and he said he would rat me out if I revealed anything!"

I pursed my lips. I wanted to kill him just for being the weak, spineless man he was. He had always been beneath me, and his succession of cowardly actions had proved me right.

"The money... that was not me! I've got no—"

"A name," I demanded.

"He-he said he was going to get his revenge, and once he did, he would die in peace."

"A name!" I demanded, louder.

"He always said that to get peace, he needed to take exactly what was stolen from him."

"Name! Now!" I roared, my vision turning hazy with anger and dread. My father stole the woman this man loved, and Lily's face flashed in my head. No, nobody knew how I felt... They wouldn't—

"Moreno."

Except him! I turned toward Dom, feeling helpless. Moreno, the man who saw too much, the man who pointed out—just last night—with laughter that I looked at Lily as if she belonged to me. The man I told her she could trust...

"Fuck!" I grabbed my phone and dialed her number, letting it ring until it switched to voicemail. "Fuck!" I shouted, getting my gun out and shooting Lorenzo twice in the chest and once in the head.

Dom was speaking on the phone rapidly before hanging up and looking at me. "Matteo's on his way. You call, I drive," Dom said, extending his hand for me to throw my keys at him.

I called every single number, one after the other, for the excruciating long twenty-seven minutes it took to get home, even though Dom drove like a madman on the busy roads.

"If he hurt her, if he—" I slammed my fist on the dashboard as Dom reached the iron gates and the guard was nowhere to be found. I suspected that if we took the time to go into the post, we'd find him dead or unconscious.

As soon as Dom slowed the car, I opened the door and ran with my gun in hand just in time to hear Pietro scream. The fury and adrenaline gave me a strength I didn't know I could have as I broke the library's door. When I saw Moreno lying on top of Lily, her face covered in blood, I reacted and shot him in the head.

I stood there for a few seconds as Moreno fell to the side. Lily remained unmoving, her skirt up, her panties ripped and discarded on the floor, and blood...

So much blood.

"Dad!" Pietro sobbed, half-standing, grabbing at the leather chair to help himself up.

Dom barged in, hitting me on the back, nudging me into action. "Go to your son; I'll take care of her."

"Dom—" I was man enough to admit it sounded more like the broken cry of a little boy than the sound of a man.

"I know," he said softly. "I know. Go to Pietro."

I rushed to my son and helped him up, wiping his tears with my hand. "*Cucciolo*, how are you?"

"Dad, she's hurt. I'm okay, Dad, please. You need to save Lily," he sobbed. "S-she saved me."

I reached for the tissue in my pocket and rested it against the cut on his forehead.

I turned to Dom, who had pushed Moreno's body from hers, and I was relieved to note that his zipper was still up, both for hers and Pietro's sake. Witnessing something like that would have traumatized him, and my Lily... I couldn't even think what it would have done to her.

I swore when I noticed the blood on her side, slowly soaking into her green shirt.

Dom lifted her. "Let's go to the hospital."

I nodded and grabbed Pietro, who buried his face in my neck and cried earnestly.

As soon as we exited the house, Oda parked his car and Dom ordered him into action as he sat in the back, still holding an unconscious Lily in his arms.

"Her pulse is strong," Dom said as I sat in the front. "She'll be okay, Sandro. You won't lose her.

I nodded mutedly, tightening my hold on my son. She had to be alright because I didn't think I could lose her and be the same, yet it was at this moment that I knew with certainty…

I had to let her go.

The next couple of hours at the hospital were excruciating as I stayed with Pietro during his full examination. Oda came back with changes of clothes for him after having taken care of the bodies of Moreno and the guard, who was found dead in his post.

I listened to my son as he told Dom and me the story, his voice breaking, his eyes puffy with all the tears he was shedding. In that moment I regretted killing Moreno; I should have incapacitated him and tortured him as Matteo did.

For the first time in my life, I understood the pleasure one may take in torture because I wanted to do it so badly that I felt like it stopped me from breathing fully.

"Dad, please, I need to know how Lily is."

I nodded and turned toward the door before turning toward Dom.

Dom patted me twice on the shoulder in an unfamiliar touch of comfort. "I'll go check. Give me a minute."

I nodded and sat on the chair across from the examination bed where Pietro was sitting. We'd been more than lucky that he would not suffer any lasting injuries, at least not physically. He had three stitches at the top of his forehead that the doctor assured wouldn't scar. I didn't mind scars—actually the woman who owned me had many, and I loved every single one of them. I just didn't want Pietro to have one that would remind him of one of the worst days of his life.

"I want to go back," he said with a small voice, looking down at his hands that were curled in tight fists on his legs.

I nodded, grabbing the green hospital bag with these things in it. "We will. Once Dom comes back, I'll take you home and—"

"No." He looked up and shook his head. "To the island, I want to go back. I-I don't belong here."

The defeat in his voice broke me almost more than his words did. I wanted to protect him and before Lily, I would have jumped at the occasion to keep him hidden forever, but how could I do that now? She was right; it was not the solution, and I never wanted him to think he didn't belong, because he did.

"No, the island was a mistake from the start," I admitted. "You belong in this life, this is your life, Pietro. You are my son, and you're strong and perfect." I raised my hand to stop him from talking. "I know you think you could have done more, but you couldn't have. You're ten, son, and

Moreno... Moreno was a super trained warrior who fooled everyone, including me. Your challenges didn't change a thing. Actually, your crutches helped you with the diversion."

He looked at me for a few seconds. "He said horrible things."

"I'm sure he did."

"He also said..." He stopped and looked toward the door.

"He said, what?" I asked, leaning forward on my seat, but we were interrupted by Dom announcing, to both my and Pietro's relief, that Lily would fully recover, and that Matteo was here to talk to me.

I stood and turned toward Pietro. "*Cucciolo*, I'll—"

"I want to go to California. I want to stay with Uncle Hoka for a while."

Saying that his words hurt me was an understatement. My son was hurt and traumatized, and he was seeking his uncle for comfort and security instead of me.

"Pietro, California..." I sighed.

"Not for long, just for a little while. Uncle Hoka offered to train me, to make me stronger, but you won't."

I was going to kill my brother-in-law, now I was certain of it.

"Dad, please. I *need* this."

I sighed again. All my instincts were screaming at me to refuse and to protect him forever, but Lily's voice rang in my head. I knew that despite the fear, I had to let him do it.

'He'll never know what his limits are if you don't let him test them. Let him become the man he is supposed to be, let him fly.' I could hear her so perfectly in my head.

I nodded. "Fine, I'll call your uncle and get the plane ready for you."

Pietro's face lit up as if he could not believe his luck. He opened his arms wide, and I hugged him tighter than I should have, but I needed this just as much as he did.

"I'll stay with him, and I'll tell him a little story about a boy I once knew."

I nodded and stopped beside him. "Thank you," I whispered as I knew he was going to tell Pietro his story, and in the process, he'd relive the horror of his youth to help my son.

"That's what family's for," he replied and took the seat I'd just vacated.

I found Matteo sitting in one of the uncomfortable seats in the waiting room, flipping through the pages of a fashion magazine like he belonged here.

I stood in front of him. "We need to talk."

He raised an eyebrow, putting the magazine on the seat beside him, then stood slowly. "I think we do." He straightened his jacket. "Did you know that curls are back in style this winter? I think it will make your woman very happy to be fashionable for once."

I pursed my lips and threw him a dark look.

He rolled his eyes. "Too soon? Oh, come on, she's going to be fine! She's not really part of the *famiglia* if she's not threatened and kidnapped at least once. It's a bit like... a rite of passage if you will."

I wanted to punch him so hard, I could almost feel his face against my knuckles.

He looked down at my tight fist and laughed. "I wouldn't advise it unless you never want to walk or have a hard-on again."

He walked away, and I followed him to an empty room in the corridor.

"I want her free. I don't care how you do it, but when she wakes up, I'll let her go."

"Do you think it's wise?" He shook his head. "Dom said you loved her. Keeping your weaknesses close is the only wise choice to make."

I didn't bother admitting or denying it—my reactions today were enough to lead Dom to the conclusion that she was my weakness.

"She deserves her freedom. What happened to her today would never have happened if she didn't get involved with me. Nothing would have happened."

"Oh please! The self-flagellation act is getting very tiring, very fast. Are you going to blame yourself for her car accident, too?"

"She deserves the best."

"I agree, but unfortunately, I'm not available anymore."

I rolled my eyes. "Matteo, I'm serious. Help me out. I can't force her into this life."

"Bene, I'll figure something out, but if you want my advice—"

"Please don't."

"If you want to give her the freedom you think she's seeking, at least tell her how you feel and let her make an informed decision."

"Okay, Dr Phil, thank you for your input."

"*Cretino*," he muttered with a shake of his head. "Also, I took care of the bodies."

"Mario?" I asked, already knowing the answer.

He shook his head, all his previous amusement gone.

"*Grazie*."

"*Prego.*"

I let him leave and sat down, finally letting go of the fake composure I had held for entirely too long. I ran my hands over my face, trying to settle the fear I'd felt when I saw her lying there. I'd not felt something like that since Pietro's accident at the pool.

I could barely afford one weakness, and now I had two. Losing her would hurt me, but I hoped she'd decide to walk away. I hoped she'd make the right decision and be stronger than I was.

Leave me, Lily, and never turn back, because if you don't, I'm going to marry you. I'm simply too weak to stay away from you.

CHAPTER 17

Lily

I woke up to the familiar sound of the heart monitor and the nose-burning cleaner that was so familiar after spending months in the hospital.

I opened my eyes wide as I remembered what happened. "Pietro." I tried to sit and groaned as I felt a shooting pain in my side.

Alessandro appeared in front of me, grasping my face in his hands and muttering something in Italian. "Pietro is fine. I swear, he is okay," he said, keeping his eyes on mine. "I missed seeing those eyes."

"What happened? How long have I been here?" I looked around. "I want to leave." I hated hospitals, they were synonyms for pain and losses for me, and I'd sworn to myself after the accident that I'd never spend more time than necessary there.

"Calm down, sweetheart," Alessandro said soothingly, brushing his thumbs against my cheekbones. "A bullet grazed you on the side, and when you fell, you cracked your skull, causing you to pass out. You've been out for two days, but the doctors said you'd be fine, and they expect you to be able to get out soon."

"How... Where's Pietro? Is he here? Can I see him?" The heartbeat monitor started to beep faster, and Alessandro threw a concerned look to it before looking back at me.

"Calm down and lay back," he said while gently helping me down.

I took a deep breath as he adjusted the covers on top of me. "Pietro is fine, but he wanted to go to California for a while. He will be back in a few weeks, but I promise, he's okay and you can Facetime him later." He smiled at me, brushing a strand of hair from my forehead.

Did he even know how caring he was?

"He actually demanded that you did so as soon as you were awake." Alessandro let out a weary laugh. "He's strong; he felt guilty for not helping you, but Dom talked to him. Dom, he..." He shook his head. "He went through something a little similar and talking about his experience with Pietro really helped."

"I want to go home... Oh no!" I looked around. "What day is it? My dad... it's his birthday and—"

"Hey, hey! Didn't I say I got everything under control?" He applied gentle pressure on my shoulders, trying to keep me down. "Your parents are okay. I told them you got bitten by an insect while we were away, and it got infected."

I twisted my mouth to the side. The story seemed a little far-fetched. "Did they buy that?"

"Surprisingly, yea." He let out a chuckle. "They spoke with Doctor Dom, who is weirdly knowledgeable about all tropical illnesses. *Juro*!" he added as he saw me raise an eyebrow in disbelief. "He was so good that I almost bought it, and I knew the truth."

"How would he even know all that?"

He waved his hand dismissively. "Something about pregnant Cassie being addicted to TV shows, and someone called Gregory House... I don't know."

I sighed, finally relaxing a little. "I want to leave." I shook my head and gave him pleading eyes. "I can't stay here, Sandro. I can't."

He sighed, running his hand through his hair, and I finally noticed his disheveled state and stubble. Did he stay by my side the whole time?

"Okay, let me go see the doctor." He looked at his watch. "I've got a catch up with Dom, but I'll be back in about an hour, and I'll take you home. I promise."

I couldn't help the wave of warmth that filled me when he mentioned home, but I also remembered how it's been soiled by that demented man.

"Is he..." I trailed off just as he reached the door.

"He is not a problem anymore," he confirmed darkly before leaving the room.

I raised the bed and sat up, despite the pain on my side and the soft throbbing in my head. I grabbed the glass of water on the table and was taking a sip when I heard a knock.

"Come in!" I called, trying to sound far better than I felt, hoping it was the doctor who would allow me to leave.

"Um... Hello?" My voice sounded much more wary when a woman in a black suit came in, followed by a tall blond man in a similar dark suit.

"Ms. Matthews?" the woman asked, coming a little closer to the bed.

I looked at her silently.

She reached into her pocket and showed me her FBI badge. "I'm Agent Riley, and this is Agent Simmons. We're here to talk to you about the attack you were a victim of. Do you mind if we ask you a few questions?" She retrieved a little notebook from her other pocket.

I laid more heavily on my pillow. "I'm quite tired. Can't this wait?" I asked, half-closing my eyes. I needed to speak with Sandro first and put all our ducks in a row. I didn't want to say anything that could jeopardize him.

The woman looked at her colleague again, who nodded silently. What was all this shit about?

She took a few more steps toward me and stood way too close for my liking. "Ms. Matthews, can I be frank?"

"I would much rather, yes."

"We're part of the organized crime unit of the FBI, and we're here because of your ties with the Benetti organization."

Shit, like I need this now. "The company? I'm just the assistant; I don't know much."

She shook her head as irritation flashed in her eyes. "I'm not talking about the company, Ms. Matthews. I'm talking about the underground side of the business. You're one of the first people who was not born within the organization to get so close, and your testimony could change everything and get horrible, heartless criminals off our streets."

"Criminals? Who?"

"We will protect you, Ms. Matthews. We could get you into the witness protection program right now, and you will be offered a new life, a new identity, and you will become a heroine by helping us take down one of the most powerful criminal families in our country."

I realized that denying would only push her more, so I decided to try another strategy. "When you say a new life..."

"Yes?" She leaned forward, victory shining in her eyes.

"Will I get a nice house and money like the people in the films? I'd never have to work ever again?"

She nodded eagerly. "Yes, that is correct. You would be relocated and you would get a generous allowance."

"Oh, that sounds amazing!" I grinned and nodded. "Yes, okay, let's do it. Tell me what I need to say to get that."

She startled. "What do you mean? Just tell me what you know."

I pouted. "I don't know anything worth your time. I didn't even know about that criminal stuff until you told me, but I want that cool life! Tell me what you want me to say, and I'll say it!"

She turned to look at her colleague before looking at me again. "Ms. Matthews, it doesn't work like that. You need to tell me what you know and what you saw to get protection and for us to legally obtain a warrant." She was speaking slower now, as if I was mentally challenged.

"Oh... it would have been so cool, though. Are you sure you can't just tell me what I should know?" I smiled. "I can be convincing."

"This is pointless," the man at the back muttered. "Let's go."

"Ms. Matthews, you're obviously a very nice woman, but you better get out now."

"Seriously, though? What did Mr. Benetti do?"

She sighed and shook her head. "Goodbye, Ms. Matthews."

I sighed happily that playing the eager idiot worked, but I was worried for Alessandro. I had to tell him about the agents.

When he came back, he was with the doctor, who gave endless guidance and medications. He also agreed to sign the discharge paper only after I promised not to stay alone for at least a week or two.

After the doctor left the room, Alessandro helped me dress, and he gave me his arm until we reached his car.

We drove to the house in silence, him seemingly lost in his thoughts and I couldn't help but wonder which issue occupied his mind. Was it Pietro's departure? Matteo's ultimatum? The betrayal of one of his closest men? Or maybe a combination of all three?

He looked tired, worn down, and I almost felt bad about having to tell him about the FBI matter.

I let him help me out of the car, and I was relieved to see Maria open the door for us as he decided to pick me up and carry me bridal style into the house.

"Is it really necessary?" I asked breathlessly as he started to go up the stairs. His presence, his heat, and his smell affected me in all the good, yet devastating, ways.

"Yes, the doctor said to take it really easy, so I intend for you to do just that." He stopped in front of my room. "Open the door please."

I did as he asked, and he gently put me on the bed before removing my shoes and pulling the throw on top of me.

"Rest for a while. I have a few things to organize, but I'll be back up for lunch, okay?" He detailed me for a second and nodded, as if he reassured himself about something.

I couldn't wait any longer. Time could be crucial, and despite my concern about his obvious tiredness, my worry that this FBI matter could make things so much worse, took over.

"The FBI came to see me," I blurted out as he turned to leave the room.

"Excuse me?" He stopped walking and threw me a side look.

"The FBI. A man and a woman—Agent Riley I think her name was. I didn't say anything, of course, but you need to be careful. Maybe talk to Matteo or something."

Alessandro nodded silently. Why wasn't he freaking out about this? It was the FBI!

He turned back toward the door, his hand on the handle but he turned toward me again after a few seconds. "Why?"

"Why, what?" I leaned up on my arm. "Why did the FBI come to see me? I'm sure you can figure out why."

He sighed. "No, why didn't you say anything? After what you went through because of me..." I saw his knuckles whiten as he balled his hands into tight fists. "You should want my head on a stick."

"Sandro! No, of course, not. I'm not blaming you for another man's actions." I shook my head.

"I promised to keep you safe," he said through gritted teeth, his self-loathing almost overwhelming. "I asked you to trust me, and if it wasn't for Pietro and your own fierceness, he would have..." He swallowed loudly. "I want to kill him all over again. I want to rip him limb by limb and let him bleed out and suffer. I want him to feel the same excruciating pain I felt when I thought—" He shook his head. "It's my fault."

"No, Sandro, don't say that. You're not the reason behind his choices, and you are not your father's faults." I tried to sit up a little too quickly, and I winced as I pulled on the stitches.

Alessandro groaned as if he'd just felt my pain. "See, I did all that, too. I destroyed everything you had and—"

"Sandro."

"I have to go. I'll see you later." He swirled around and left the room, slamming the door shut in his wake.

"No, Sandro, wait!" I shouted, but I knew that with the speed of his departure, he was probably halfway down the stairs by now. "I love you."

I laid back on the bed, my mind going at full speed about the whole situation and how Sandro's guilt felt so wrong. I also knew that because of this, he might make decisions with respect to me and our relationship that would not be directed by his feelings, but by his desire to make amends—to set things right—and it terrified me even more than whatever fate I could face joining his life.

I already had a boyfriend who stayed with me much longer than he ought to because of misplaced guilt and remorse. It had hurt me so much back then, and my feelings for Andrew had been nothing compared to the love I felt for Alessandro. It was nothing compared to the burning desire I had to spend my life with him.

I didn't think I could bear him making a decision for us that was based on anything other than the same visceral need I felt.

"Damn it!" I muttered, giving up on any chance of rest after tossing and turning for the next twenty minutes. If I ever wanted to sleep again, I had to speak with him now.

I got out of bed and made sure my balance was alright before going downstairs to his office. Once he would let go of this stupid guilt, I could—

"The FBI, really?" I heard him sigh.

I slowed my pace and stopped by his office door, extending my neck to hear his conversation through the slight crack in the door.

"You knew I was going to test her. What choice did I have? You wanted me to be comfortable with her keeping our secrets." I heard Matteo's reply. "You're never happy!"

"Never happy..." Alessandro muttered. "I wanted you to find an alternative to marrying her. You didn't have to hire cheap actors to play the FBI game."

Matteo laughed. "They were not actors! They are actual FBI agents on my payroll, thank you very much! Who do you think I am? An amateur."

"That's not the point. You didn't need to scare her like that."

"Yes, I did, because now I know she is exceptionally smart, crafty, and most of all, trustworthy. Your problem is settled. You can continue to stick your dick in her without ever needing to commit. Congratulations!"

I grimaced as Alessandro hissed, "Don't be crass."

I started to retreat, my heart breaking in my chest. I had my response, even if it was not the one I had wanted to hear.

I went back upstairs, somehow grieving a relationship that never really existed, because if anything, Sandro had told me many times that there was no future for us, that he was not able to make me any promises. He even said that this was not my family and yet, it felt like I refused to hear all that. I gave so much more power, too much meaning to his few tender attentions, his gentle touches, and our moments of passion.

I could only blame my inexperience and my own naivety for all this. Why would he truly desire me?

When I was back in the safety of my room, I looked at my phone. Even if home was the source of so many painful moments, it was also where I used to feel safe, loved, and cherished. It was where I once felt full of hope, with a thousand dreams to accomplish, and I felt the irrepressible need to be back in my childhood room to heal my broken heart.

I called my mom. "Oh, pumpkin!" she cried as soon as she answered. "Oh, we were so worried about you, baby girl! The doctor said you had a bad reaction to a mosquito bite, and you were sent to the hospital."

I forced a laugh. "Yes, how crazy is that, uh? Only me, I swear."

She let out a little sigh. "I miss you. Why don't you come home for a few days? I know you don't like it here so much, but—"

"Sure. That's actually why I called. I have a lot of time off to catch up on, and I was thinking maybe I could come? Today?"

"Oh! Oh! Marty! *Marty*!" I winced, removing the phone from my ear as her voice turned higher and higher with her excitement, to the point I was sure only bats could understand her. "She's coming home! Marty, she's coming home."

I heard my father in the background, and I almost laughed at how chilled he sounded compared to her.

"Dad is asking if you need him to come pick you up?"

My heart swelled with all the love I felt for them. This was the conditional, healing love I needed. I needed to be sixteen-year-old Lily again.

I smiled, resting my hand on my heart that hurt just a little less. "No, there's no need for Dad to drive four hours both ways for that. I'll take the train. Let me check the times, and I'll text you my time of arrival, okay?"

"Oh yes of course. Oh, I'm so glad you're coming home! I will let Betty and Janet know, and maybe we can have a—"

"No party, Mom. It's not a coming home event; it's just your daughter spending a few days resting after a hospital stay, got it? Lowkey please."

"Lowkey, yes, of course." She took a deep breath. "I love you, pumpkin pie."

"I love you too, Mama. I'll see you later."

I started to pack the suitcase I had on the island with some of the nice winter clothes Elena had purchased for me. They were all so bright, expensive, and so perfectly fitted. Maybe if the people at home saw me as the new Lily Matthews, they wouldn't pity me so much anymore, and maybe they could move on from the drama and let me move on, too.

I was going through the essentials in the bathroom, leaving behind all the things I didn't strictly need, when someone knocked at my door, followed by, "Lily, I'm bringing lunch."

"Come in!" I called as I walked back into the room and put my toiletry bag on top of the clothes.

"What are you doing?" he asked, putting the tray with two plates on the vanity before pointing at the suitcase. "The doctor said you needed rest."

"Yes." I nodded. "And since Pietro is gone for the time being, I decided to go home."

"Home?" He frowned, apparently not like the idea.

"Yes, you know, *home*. What did you call it again? Hicksville?"

"Why? What about m— Pietro? Are you going back on your word?" he asked with a cold edge in his voice.

"I'll be back when Pietro comes back. I'll be here as I promised I would."

"What happened? Why are you running away?"

"I'm not running. I need to get better, and the best way to do that is to be with people who love me."

"People here care about you. *I* care about you."

I couldn't even be mad at him if 'care' was all he could give me, but I realized that I loved him too much for that to be enough. "I need *more*. I need a commitment that you already told me you couldn't make. I want a genuine commitment, not one you feel obliged to give me. I *deserve* more, so I'm going home for a break. I think I deserve it."

"Why now?"

"Because I want to. Don't worry, I won't say anything."

He let out a sigh of frustration as he ran his hand through his hair. "I know that; I always knew that. You love Pietro too much, and you'd never do anything to hurt him."

Was this man really that blind? "Yea, Pietro... just him." *Idiot.*

I closed my suitcase and turned toward him again. "So, there's no need to test me again, okay?"

"I didn't test you; Matteo did."

"But you knew."

"I did, but it was the only way to ensure we would let you walk away."

"And I'm grateful for that, and now I'm taking what you're so generously offering."

"I—" He looked around the room and ran his hand through his hair again as if he was trying to figure something out. "Let me drive you home then, we could discuss logistics on the way."

"No, it's okay. I've booked my train ticket and a taxi is on the way. I'll be okay, but I'll text you as soon as I get there."

"Lily, don't do this. I don't understand. Did I do something?"

No, and that's exactly the problem. I forced a smile I hoped looked genuine. "No, you didn't do anything. I would be grateful if you could help me with the suitcase, though."

He grabbed it almost mechanically and followed me down the stairs and outside into the cold.

"What about when Pietro's back?"

"You call me when you have a date, and I'll arrange my return. Is my apartment still available?"

He tensed, grabbing the handle of my suitcase a little tighter. "Why do you ask? You don't need it. You've got this house."

"Yea... I don't think it's wise. We might end up in the same situation, and then Matteo will force us into choices we don't want. I think it's best I come in the morning and come back with Pietro after school, then leave once he's asleep. I think if we keep work and life well separated, we'll minimize the chance of a repeated ultimatum. We barely escaped once, so let's not tempt fate again."

He pursed his lips, straightening as if my words offended him to the core. "I don't like this option."

"It's the only option," I replied gently as the iron gates opened to let the taxi in.

"I'll figure it out," he added stubbornly.

I nodded, not in the mood to argue further. "Thank you for everything. You take care of yourself, okay?"

The taxi driver exited his car and grabbed the suitcase from Alessandro to put into the trunk.

"Why does it feel like goodbye?" Alessandro asked as I opened the door of the taxi. His voice sounded faint, almost sad.

I felt the lump of emotion build in my throat, and I tried to swallow past it.

"Maybe just see it as a 'see you later'? I will be back, Alessandro. I promised, and I will take care of Pietro until he is able to do it all without me."

"And then what?" he insisted.

"And then?" I shrugged. "And then it will be goodbye," I replied, so proud of how strong and steady my voice sounded, despite the overwhelming feeling of loss I felt.

I sat in the taxi and closed the door before tightening my coat around me.

"Union Station, please?" I asked as my voice broke with my silent tears.

The driver looked in his rearview mirror. "Is everything okay, miss?"

"No, but it will be," I replied as the car went down the alley. I kept on crying, refusing to turn around and look at the man I knew was still on the steps.

Who would have ever thought that I was going back to where I was first broken to heal?

But part of me knew the devastating truth…

There would be no healing from Alessandro Benetti.

CHAPTER 18

LILY

Being home felt strange, as if I once belonged there but didn't fit quite right in this narrative anymore.

At least I didn't feel like I usually did when I was here; I didn't feel the pain and the inadequacy of my disability, or the drama that followed 'poor little Lily' all around town.

No, but I didn't feel comforted and at home anymore, either. I felt like a guest in my own house.

I had changed, and I could see that in my parents' eyes, in the way they addressed me. Even in the way people looked at me on the street yesterday, speculating.

I was different, I'd known that before stepping off the train, but what I had not expected was how much I was going to miss Alessandro. How I felt so much more at home in his stupidly big manor and the house on the island than I did here.

How the petty, childish part of me regretted that he didn't try to change my mind and how he didn't try to contact me.

I was having daily video calls with Pietro, but they were fast, too fast, and every time we ended it, I felt a loss that was irrational but was still there.

I sighed, looking at the ceiling of my childhood bedroom that remained exactly the same as it had always been. Like a museum to who I had been before the accident, as if I'd died then. I guess that it wasn't completely wrong. A part of me had died then, and another part morphed on the island, in the arms of Alessandro, and now I was just here, in the place I didn't belong to anymore, while yearning for a place that was never mine.

I grabbed my phone, letting the anguish settle on me from the painful absence of a text or voicemail, as it has been for the past four mornings.

Scrolling down, I let my finger hover over his name. I could just give him a call… just to see how work was going and if not having an assistant was an issue.

I rolled my eyes and pressed the voicemail button instead, listening to the stupid message he'd left a couple of months ago for a contract he couldn't find.

His deep, commanding voice brought tears to my eyes and caused my lungs to constrict painfully.

I blinked back tears and put the phone back on the nightstand with a growl of frustration. I was my own mental terrorist! Why did I keep hurting myself like that?

I sat up on the bed and moved the curtain a little. At least my mother's car was not in the driveway anymore, meaning that I was finally free to roam around the house without her trying to convince me to either come home for good or take me out to show me off to her friends.

I went to the shared bathroom down the hall but stopped for a few seconds in front of my brother's bedroom door that still sported his football team's stickers.

I continued to the bathroom as I couldn't help but wonder what Victor would have said about the whole situation.

I let out a low chuckle as I stepped into the shower. Victor would have gone and kicked Alessandro's ass, mafia boss or not. He would have kicked my ass too, saying that no man deserved my tears.

But I also knew that if Victor was here today, I wouldn't have met Alessandro. What would my life be like now?

I'd probably graduate from university, be on my way to getting a Ph.D., or maybe a junior physics teacher at the local high school. I'd probably be married to Andrew, who would be back reliving his former glory, at the sweet age of twenty-four, by taking a job as an assistant coach for the high school football team, while still hoping that the Bears would call him.

I wiped the condensation in the mirror and looked at my reflection wrapped in the towel. Would I have been happy in that scenario? I probably would have thought so. I wouldn't have known any better, but I would have missed out on a passion that, despite being a source of heartbreak, had brought me so much more.

I would have probably ended up at forty, choked in a life I finally realized I hadn't wanted.

God, Lily, why so gloomy so early in the morning?! I dressed in a pair of tight blue jeans and a short, V-neck royal-blue cashmere jumper that the stylist had picked. Everything was so beautiful, colorful, and perfectly sized. I didn't think I could ever go back to the clothes I used to wear.

You don't need to hide, Lily. You are beautiful. Alessandro's voice made me shiver and I turned around, almost expecting him to be standing in the middle of my bedroom. But this was not a romantic comedy, and the hero would not appear on my doorstep to declare his undying love for me.

But you want him to, don't you? my heart chimed in. Of course, I did. I wanted that, at least once in my life, for someone to come back to me.

I looked at the ceiling and took a couple of deep breaths, to both settle my emotions and quiet the threatening tears.

I went down to the kitchen to find a box of cereal and a bowl on the counter with a scribbled note from my dad.

'*Mom asked me to make you breakfast. Come in the garage when you're done, I need another pair of hands.*'

I smiled with tenderness at the thought of my dad. He'd never been very demonstrative or very talkative, but he'd always been the rock of this house, the gruff and quiet force that carried us and kept us in line.

I also knew he didn't need help in the garage, especially not from me, who had no clue how anything worked, but it was my father's sanctuary—his equivalent of a confessional and it meant he wanted to talk.

I ate the cereal full of sugar and slipped on my old, beat-up winter boots that my mother would probably keep forever. I grabbed one of my father's fur-lined flannel jackets he used to work from the coat rack and the familiarity of the moment lifted a little of the sadness I felt.

I walked into the garage from the side door and the cold, thick air, foreboding snow, surrounded me as soon as I stepped in.

"Do you think you should keep the garage door open like that? It's really cold, Dad."

His head peeked out from the side of the open hood of the vintage Ford Mustang he has been working on since I was a little girl—and I suspect would never be fully finished. It was his outlet for so many feelings and had been his bonding moments with Victor.

"It's Illinois, sweetheart. It's practically spring today," he replied, disappearing from view again.

I rolled my eyes, tightened the jacket around me as walked closer to him.

"Your mother left," he said without looking up.

"Yes, I know. I checked before coming down."

He stopped his work and turned his head slightly toward me. "Can you give me the wrench with the blue handle?" He jerked his head toward the massive toolbox. "First drawer."

I picked up the wrench and handed it to him.

"You know your mom... she loves you, and she just wants you to be happy. She—" He started once he was back to his task. "It comes from a good place."

"I know that Dad, I do, but I'm not the kind of person to be paraded around like a circus dog." I sighed. "And I know she wanted me to come to her club meeting so her friends could interrogate me about my life in Chicago."

He stopped what he was doing and turned around, leaning against the car, and fixed his hazel eyes on me.

Oh, my dad only did the eye contact conversation when you were in trouble. I tightened the coat around my waist, bracing for a conversation I was pretty sure I wouldn't like.

"You never come here anymore. You're giving all the excuses under the sun, and we pretend we believe them, but we know you're avoiding home. After losing your brother and almost losing you—" He looked away and cleared his throat.

A wave of shame mixed with sadness hit me square in the chest at seeing my father struggle with his emotions. It was so rare, and I hated being the reason for his turmoil.

"It's hard for parents to realize that your home is not a source of comfort for your child, but a source of pain."

"Dad," my voice cracked. "It is not you; it's never been you or Mom, it's—" I shook my head. How could I explain this without hurting them?

"I know that, sweetheart, I do. I'm not mad at you; if anything, I grieve for you. I saw you fade away and slip more and more into that introverted young woman, and I could not help. Nothing is more terrible for a parent than to be helpless, faced with your child's pain."

I nodded, remembering Alessandro's words. It was a universal concept, it seemed.

"But you're different now; you're more alive, and Mom and I are very happy. Your mom just wants to show you everywhere, she's so happy."

"I know."

"Just humor her every once in a while." He chuckled. "It will make everything easier."

I smiled. "Fine. I'll go to her next club thing."

My dad looked at me silently, taking his wrench in the palm of his hand.

"What is it?" I took a step toward him. "Dad, tell me, please."

"You are in love with that man, aren't you?"

I opened my mouth and closed it again, shocked that my father would notice that, and even more shocked that he would talk about it.

"I... Yes, I am."

"Um-hmm. I've got to say, I'm grateful to this man for helping you get out of this cocoon you put yourself in, but I also think he's the most foolish man in the world for breaking your heart."

"I'm the one who left, Dad."

"I'm sure you had good reasons. No daughter of mine would be fickle, and he's an idiot for not running after you."

I felt my eyes sting with unshed tears. "Thanks," I said, my voice breaking.

He let out a little groan, obviously not equipped to deal above a certain level of sentimentality.

"Do you want to come to Langdale with me? I need a few original parts, and Bobby said they may have an unused ashtray for the Mustang."

Langdale was a small town two hours from here, which was basically a complete car junkyard, but the nirvana for car enthusiasts like my dad.

I was also pretty sure he didn't need to go there, but it was something he did with us when we were young and upset. He'd take us on random car trips just to keep our minds occupied, and I had to admit, it seemed like a really good idea right now.

"I'd love to."

"Perfect. Go put on your fancy coat, I'll wait for you by the truck."

And for the rest of the day, I was back at being his little girl, following him around as he picked up parts that would clog the garage and drive Mom crazy. He took me for lunch at the local diner, which considered Friday meatloaf a high-end gastronomy, and I loved it!

It was a great day, but I should have known it couldn't last. My good mood dimmed as we drove up our street in the late afternoon to find a few cars parked in front of our lawn and in our driveway.

"Dad?" I tried as he parked the truck.

"Annie..." he muttered under his breath. He turned toward me, his lips pursed and visibly displeased. "I told your mom not to organize any gathering, but she thought it would be good for you." He sighed in frustration. "I know it's not fair, but I'll ask you to play the part, please, sweetheart. I think your mama needs it."

"Fine." I took a deep breath. "Let's get it over with."

Mom rushed to the door as soon as we opened it and helped me out of my coat.

"Oh, pumpkin, here you are! I know you said lowkey, but it's just a small gathering. It was not planned... it just happened."

"Yes, of course," I replied, eyeing the well-organized platters of food on the table with the plastic glasses and paper plates. "It just *happened*."

My mother's friends were all there, gushing over me like I was the golden child, especially Andrew's mother, who acted like I was still on the list to be her daughter-in-law.

I wanted to be good, but after less than an hour of people detailing me with speculation, it felt like I was suffocating. All I wanted was Alessandro's quiet strength by my side.

I smiled and added to the small talk until I reached the kitchen and grabbed one of my father's discarded jackets to sneak out to the back porch just to take a breather.

I sat on the wooden bench on the patio and looked at the apple tree in the back garden, now bare of its leaves. That tree still carried so many memories, mostly happy, but now they all felt bittersweet.

"Our initials are still on it."

I turned to the side and saw Andrew standing outside the kitchen door.

"Probably." I nodded. "We carved them pretty deep."

"No, I know they are. I helped your father with the grass last month, and I checked." He buried his hands into the pockets of his *Bears* black jacket pockets and jerked his chin toward the bench. "May I?"

I nodded, detailing him. It was strange, but he still looked exactly the same, as if these four years hadn't changed him at all.

"You look well," he said, sitting a bit closer to me than necessary.

I scooted away a little. "So do you. Life in Aurora suits you."

"I'm back here actually, since the new term. I'm working as an assistant football coach at the school. Didn't your mom tell you? I've been seeing her often."

How my predictions had been accurate, and it also explained why my mother was trying to push me to come back.

"No, she didn't. I don't really ask about people, but that's nice." I stood up. "Well, I'd bet—"

"You've changed," he said, though he remained seated. "I spoke to Katia, she has not heard from you for a while."

I sighed. "As you said, I've changed. Katia and I are not in the place we were before and forcing it is not worth it. I called her to tell her why I bailed and she was not happy." I shrugged. "Life continues."

He nodded and detailed me. "I saw you were different as soon as I walked in. You look amazing, Lily... like a real woman."

I flushed a little at his compliment and the heat that lit his blue eyes, but it didn't make me feel like it used to. I felt nothing.

"We all grow up, you know. I've got my life in Chicago, you've got your life here, your fiancée..."

"Angie and I are done."

"Oh no, I'm sorry!" And I truly was. I never wished him anything bad.

"Don't be. I called it off. I realized it was not what I needed. She didn't know me, not really, not like you do." He stood, blocking my way to the door. "And then the other day, I came here and saw the tree with our initials." He let out a little laugh. "This is where we kissed for the first time, didn't we? It was the day of your thirteenth birthday, and I'd forgotten to get you a present, so I panicked and kissed you."

Alessandro had done the same, giving me a kiss on the day of my twenty-fourth birthday... How funny.

Andrew probably misinterpreted my smile because he took a step forward. "We had all our first together, we have a bond, you and I. There's—"

"No."

I froze at the voice. Here I was, summoning Alessandro's memory again.

Andrew frowned. "What?"

I shook my head. "I didn't—"

"I said no. I suggest you take a step back, you're too close. I don't like it."

Andrew stepped to the side and turned away, giving me a full view of Alessandro standing in my garden by the patio steps.

He looked so beautiful in his charcoal-gray coat, his hair perfectly in order.

I couldn't help the feeling of elation at seeing him here, even if it seemed so out of place.

"Who's that?" Andrew asked

"Oh, it's nothing... Just my boss," I said, not in the mood to explain more than necessary.

"Just your boss?" Alessandro asked with an eyebrow raised as he ascended the stairs, keeping his eyes on me. "Okay, though it's a bit reductive if you want my opinion, knowing that I had my dick inside you not even a week ago and you whispered in the dead of the night that you loved me, but you know, that's fine. 'Boss' it is."

I gasped as Andrew hissed.

"Down boy, you don't want to piss me off," Alessandro warned so calmly, he was terrifying.

"You heard me?" I asked.

"No, but I tried my luck. I know you well enough."

Andrew turned toward me. "Lily, it's not true, right? You're not into old men, are you?"

"Old?" Alessandro took a step toward him, and I grabbed his arm, as if I could ever have a chance to stop him if he really wanted to kill him.

However, Alessandro let me keep hold of his arm and stayed close to me. "Let me tell you something, *boy*. I may be thirty-eight, and she is twenty-four, but when she gave you your freedom, you took it and walked away." He pointed a finger toward him. "But contrary to you, I quickly figured out that true freedom is being by her side. She is my freedom, and that's the big difference between you and me. I know what I have, and I'll fight to keep it. You lost her, that's your problem, not mine. Now, I suggest you walk away because adults have to talk, and just so you know, if you ever try to steal what's mine..." He opened his coat and Andrew took a couple of quick steps back.

I cursed him internally, knowing he probably showed him his gun.

Andrew looked at me with wide eyes and I sighed. "Just go, Andrew. I'll be okay."

"Lily—"

"She told you to go," Alessandro growled between gritted teeth. "She is safe with me, and she always will be. You...? Not so much."

Andrew threw me another look before he went back inside.

I let out a little sigh of relief, and Alessandro turned toward me with his cocky smile. "Hi."

"Hi?" I crossed my arms on my chest and scowled despite my heart beating harder than ever. "You didn't need to be mean to him, you know. He didn't do anything to you."

His smile vanished and morphed into annoyance. "Don't be mean? Beautiful, I wasn't *mean*. That boy is a waste of space and deserves a punishment far greater than humiliation. I don't deserve you, at least I know that, but some don't and that's a crime far more unforgivable."

"He was not trying to get back with me."

Alessandro let out a humorless laugh. "Yes, he was, and fuck if I would ever let that happen." He took a step closer, and I didn't feel like taking a step back like I did with Andrew a few minutes ago. I wanted to close the distance and wrap myself around him. "He let you go; he thinks you're convenient. I should shoot him on principle."

I shook my head, but I couldn't help but smile as warmth spread into me. Lord, what kind of woman was I becoming if I found some sweetness in his threats of bodily harm to another human?

"Is that what you thought I was doing? That I was like him? That I wanted you because we were stuck on an island and because of Pietro? That you were *convenient*."

I looked down at my feet and he took another few steps closer until his feet were in my line of vision and the woodsy cologne I missed so much wrapped around me.

I shrugged. "No..." Did my voice sound as uncertain as I felt?

"I made it my life's mission to keep you away from every male in the office. Do you think that was an easy task?"

"I knew it was weird!" I gasped, slapping his arm playfully.

He snickered. "It worked."

I sighed and looked behind him as the curtain quickly moved back. We had an audience. "Why are you here?"

"I knocked on the door, and your father greeted me. I asked to speak to you, and he asked me if I was the idiot."

I couldn't help but laugh as tenderness for my father squeezed my heart.

"I told him that I was, and he sent me out back when I saw a stupid boy trying to steal my girl."

His girl... Butterflies started to make flips in my stomach.

"You let me go."

"I know. You said you wanted to leave, and after everything I've put you through, I thought you deserved that much, even if it made me miserable. I realized a little late, sorry, *amore*. I'm slow sometimes, and I was sinking into depression without you at home. I replayed our last interaction over and over again until it clicked. I realized that when you said you knew I had no play in the FBI trick, that you had eavesdropped again and probably heard what I said to Matteo about marrying you. I have to admit, I love you, but this habit of yours is really aggravating."

I flushed with mortification at being caught again. "I didn't mean to list—" I froze as his words finally hit me. "Wait. You *love* me?" I asked with incredulity.

He chuckled. "Here you go."

"You love me?" I repeated.

He wrapped his arms around me and pulled me against him, keeping his back to the house, shielding us from the world. "More than you can imagine. I think I've loved you for a very long time. I want you to come home with me, and we can have the twelve babies you want."

I choked on air as I gasped and coughed. "*Twelve babies*? Sandro, I don't want twelve babies."

He leaned down and pecked my lips. "We can have as many babies as you want, as long as they are ours. Besides, we both know you enjoy the practice."

I blushed and rested my forehead on his chest. "You know my parents are behind that door, probably listening to every word we say."

"Then let them. I've got nothing to hide. I want you to come home and raise our little boy. I want you to be Pietro's mom because you already are, in so many ways."

I looked up and rested my hand on his cheek. "You want me to be his mom?" My voice cracked on the word.

"Yes. So now you're going to go pack your bag as I try to win your parents over, and then we're going to drive home to our boy and you're going to adopt him. Do you want to be his mother?"

"Of course, I do! More than anything!" I grabbed his face in my hands and pulled it down to kiss him a little more intensely than I should have in this setting.

"I love you, Alessandro Benetti," I whispered against his lips, and his arms tightened around me, crushing me to his chest.

"*Sono pazzo di te.*" He pecked my lips. "I'm crazy about you."

I sighed, leaning against him again.

"You're coming home, right? Pietro said I couldn't come home without you. You wouldn't want me to be homeless, right?"

"Is Pietro home?"

"They all are." Alessandro rolled his eyes. "Pietro came back with Violet and Hoka. My sister thought I sounded depressed and needed a good kick in the ass, which Hoka wanted to be in the first row to witness."

"I see. And what? They kicked your ass all the way to Hicksville?"

"No, she kicked my ass for not going after you and for not giving you all the facts before you left. She reminded me that you deserved at least that, and she was right."

"She is right. You know how I feel about making informed decisions."

"I do. Which was why I needed to tell you that I love you, that my life is not the same without you in it, and it's not a life I want. I want you, all of you. The fierceness, the stubbornness, the love, the selflessness, the patience, the desire, the sensuality." He leaned down. "Your tight pussy..." he whispered, making me shiver. "There's no one else for me, Lily. You're it."

"I'm not stubborn; I'm *opinionated*."

He let out a little laugh that was heavy with sentiment. "You can be whatever you want to be. Just come home with me."

"I love you, Alessandro, and I love Pietro. Being away from you both was so much harder than I could have imagined, so yes, of course, I'll come home with you."

"Say you're mine."

"I'm yours."

"Say you'll stay with me forever, even in the darkness, because I'll keep you warm, I'll keep you safe."

"Forever, yes."

He kissed me again and I felt it then—all his love and devotion. I was unsure how I missed it before.

I grabbed his hand and intertwined our fingers as we both walked back into the house using the backdoor and found my parents leaning shamelessly against the table, not even pretending like they weren't listening.

"We sent the guests packing," my father said, looking at me.

"Yes, we thought it was best to have this discussion in private," my mother added, her eyes shining with anticipation.

"You're leaving," my father said gruffly, keeping his eyes on Alessandro.

My mother had her eyes on our hands, and she was bouncing with excitement.

I looked at Alessandro, who squeezed my hand. "Yes, I need to go home." I smiled, leaning against Alessandro. "Mom, Dad, I'd like to introduce you to Alessandro Benetti, my... my—"

Shit, my what?

"Her newly appointed fiancé," Alessandro added, bowing his head toward my parents. "Mr. and Mrs. Matthews, it's an honor to meet the people who raised this treasure."

My mother squealed and I winced.

"Fiancé?" she shouted. "Oh, Lily, he's so handsome!" She clapped her hands together. "Go prepare your bags. Go, go. I'll keep Alessandro company." She grabbed my wrist and pushed me into action.

I rolled my eyes. *Way to go, Ma!* I looked at Alessandro. "Just so you know, whatever you say will be reported to her church gossip group tomorrow."

"That's not true!" Mom gasped with offense, resting her hand on her chest.

"Oh, it's absolutely true," my father deadpanned. "But don't worry, sweetheart, I'll stay here. I also need to have a word with this man of yours."

The threat in his tone was not even veiled, and I waved dismissively, letting Alessandro deal with my parents. After all, it was his fault for telling them we were engaged.

I packed my bag in record time, and by the time I went back downstairs, Alessandro was sitting at the table with a coffee and a piece of my mother's apple pie.

She was sitting across from him, staring with a sort of awe as if the man was the Messiah.

My father looked at me and nodded. "I approve. He's not as stupid as I thought he was."

"Thank you for the compliment, Marty, it means a lot." Sandro took the last bite of his pie. Mrs. Matthews."

"Please, call me Annie."

Lord, after ten minutes they were already Marty and Annie.

"Annie," he said with his dazzling smile.

Ah, yes, it all made sense now.

"Your pie is absolutely delicious. Thanks again for your hospitality, but now it's time to take my fiancée home, I'm sure you understand. But as I said, our home is your home, and you are welcome to come whenever."

"Oh, you are such a lovely man!" Mom cooed.

My father and I rolled our eyes simultaneously, and we said our quick goodbye using the excuse of the long drive and the late hour. I was both excited and nervous when I sat beside Alessandro in the car to take us back to Chicago.

It was the same, but also very different. We were truly together now, and we were about to be a family.

"Your parents are adorable," he said after a few minutes.

"They are, but let's see if you still feel the same when my mother starts calling us every five minutes and sending us wedding inspiration emails. Why did you tell her we're engaged?"

He threw me a quick look like I was the one not making sense. "Because we are."

"Um, I don't remember you asking or me saying yes."

"I made a commitment to you. I asked you to be the mother of our son, I promised you babies. This is a done deal, *amore*. And as for you saying yes, I'll get that out of you tonight. When you're on the verge of orgasm, you'll agree to anything."

"How dare you?" I gasped in mock hurt. "God, you're so cocky."

"Yes, I am." He lifted his pelvis from his seat. "I thought we established that before."

I shook my head and looked out the window, hiding the smile his confidence always called and also because it was very true. I was not a rational woman when his hands were on me.

"Fine." He sighed. "Marry me, Lily."

"Why?"

"Why?" He let out a startled laugh. "Because there's no alternative to my happiness. Because it's you and me against the world, my love, and I want us to belong to each other, not only for us, but before God, our family, and our friends. I want to marry you because you're the very air I breathe, and because I don't think I could stop the darkness from swallowing me whole without your light. I didn't spare your life that day; you saved mine the day you walked into my office. You saved me from a cold, loveless life, from a heartless future. Marry me, my savior."

How could anyone say no to that?

I turned toward him, not caring that he could see my tears of happiness. "I'll marry you, my heartless savior, because you may seem heartless to the world, but I know you have the biggest heart there is, and I too couldn't imagine a life without you."

"And my dick?"

I burst into laughter. "Yes, and your dick."

"Thought so." He looked down at his lap. "Good job, Colossus."

I snorted but reached across the seat and caressed his cheek. "I enjoy Colossus, but I'm much more in love with that heart of yours, Sandro. Let's go home to our son."

He turned his head and kissed my palm before concentrating on the road again. "Let's go home, *vita mia*, and not waste one more minute of our life together."

I leaned against the headrest and closed my eyes, letting the car soothe me with its gentle motion as we made our way to his house, taking the first step of our life together.

Alessandro saved me just as much as I saved him, and our story may not have started as it should have, it may not have been one for the storybooks, but it was ours and for me, it was perfect.

CHAPTER 19

Alessandro

I'd never been the kind of man to slack at work. I always saw the men leaving early as unmotivated, yet as soon as my lawyer dropped the papers, I left to go home to be with my son, my Lily, my sister and my annoying brother-in-law, who were still at my house after a week. I was really ready for them to leave so we could start our actual life together.

When I walked in, I followed the laughter to the kitchen, where I found Lily holding my adorable nephew, which really kicked my desire for paternity. I could imagine her pregnant with our child, her stomach growing gently.

I never thought I would want that, this ideal family, yet with her, I wanted it all.

"Sandro, I think you have a rival." My sister chuckled as her son snuggled on Lily's chest while she cooed at him.

"I see," I rubbed my chin, pretending to think it over. "At least we know your son has some taste... not like his mother."

"Sandro!" Lily chastised. "Hoka is fantastic."

I rolled my eyes. Violet and Lily were now best friends—something I had expected. They were both fierce, kind, and positive women. They had to become close, and it wouldn't have annoyed me if they didn't gang up against me.

"When are you going home again?" I asked Violet and she laughed.

"Tomorrow, in fact. Hoka is needed back."

"I'll miss you but don't come back until next year."

Violet laughed and grabbed Yuko from Lily's arms. "Actually, we were discussing that recently, and Lily invited us for Christmas."

"If Lily wants it, it will happen." I turned toward my beautiful woman and winked at her. "Do you have a few minutes?" I waved the brown envelope I was holding that I knew would make her ecstatic.

She stood and placed a kiss on Yuko's head before coming into my arms.

I kissed her slowly. "I missed you," I said, letting her go but taking her hand.

She laughed, following me out of the kitchen and into my office. "You say that every time I see you."

"Because it's true." I closed the door behind us, and I had to stop myself from touching her. She was so attractive in her wrap dress. I just wanted to unwrap her like a wicked present and eat her right on my desk until she—

"Hello?"

I looked up and blinked a couple of times as my dick started to harden in my pants. I cleared my throat. "What?"

She laughed and eyed my pants, her eyes darkening. "I said we needed to hurry because Hoka is training with Pietro, and I promised him take-out for their last night here."

"Ah, I'm sure what I have here for you will make it worth it."

She sighed. "I love your dick, Sandro, but—"

I extended the envelope to her. "This has nothing to do with sex, Lily. You really need to stop treating me like a sex object; it's so... reductive."

"Is it?" she asked tauntingly, grabbing the envelope from me and opening it. "I guess you'll suck your own co—" She stopped and looked up at me, all humor gone, replaced by barely contained emotions. "Are these..." She swallowed, her eyes starting to glisten with tears.

"The adoption papers, yes." I took a couple of steps toward her. "Once you sign them, I'll ask my lawyer to file them and it will be official."

She kept her eyes on the papers, sniffling. "Is Pietro okay with this?" she asked, twisting her mouth with uncertainty. "I don't want to impose on him."

"Pietro loves you," I said, walking closer to her and brushing the back of my hand on her soft cheek. "No, he *adores* you, and I'm sure he would love nothing more than to call you mom, but we'll leave that up to him if you prefer." I grabbed the papers from her and put them on the chair beside me. "He has asked me every morning when we will get married, and I keep telling him that we need to give you time, but I think it's time to make an honest man out of me, don't you agree?"

She laughed, and I loved how I could make her so joyous. "I'm not a miracle worker, Sandro. I don't think anyone can do that."

I reached into my pocket and pulled out the ring I had placed there. It was a custom-made, platinum, five-carat, emerald-cut diamond ring, surrounded by light pink diamonds.

"I guess we'll need to see if it works, then. Give me your hand, *amore*. Let me make it official."

She extended her hand, which trembled with pent-up emotions. I slid the ring onto her finger, and all the jokes I had thought of faded as I looked at her slender finger now showcasing my ring.

I felt the overwhelming love for this woman once more, and I wondered if I would ever get used to how much I loved her.

I pulled her hand up and kissed the back of it.

"This ring is stunning."

"Not as stunning as you are, *amore*." I pushed toward her, trapping her between my desk and my body, pressing my erection against her stomach. "I want you."

She looked at me for a second and licked her lips, moving to sit on my desk.

I smiled as I pushed her down and saw her tight nipples peek out from her dress. I spread her legs and stood between them, resting my hands on the hem of her dress, knowing that once I pulled it open, I'd see her underwear soaked with her desire.

I groaned, already tasting her arousal on my tongue, but as soon as I pushed the first side off, there was a sharp knock on the door.

Lily barely had a chance to sit up before the doors opened to reveal Hoka dressed in nothing more than a pair of sweatpants and a tank top that revealed his tattoos.

If he hadn't been so in love with my sister and Lily with me, I would have killed him just because he showed all the things he had no business showing my woman.

He detailed the scene with a half-smile. "Am I interrupting anything?"

"Yes!" I barked as Lily shouted, "No!"

She pushed me away from between her legs and moved to stand.

"Ah, that's karma for all the cases of blue balls you caused me, brother. How does it feel?"

Fucking uncomfortable, asshole, I thought, glaring at him.

"Is there anything I can help you with?" Lily offered so amicably, walking toward him.

"Ah, it's nice to deal with a person with manners. I hope you teach him some," Hoka said with a genuine smile. "Pietro and I are done with the training, but he asked if you were back. Something about the right outfit…" Obviously, he was just as confused as I was, but Lily nodded as if it made sense and for her, it probably did.

Pietro and Lily shared something neither Hoka nor I could understand. She spoke to the part of him that men like us could never understand, and I was more than grateful that he had someone as kind and caring as Lily to fulfill his needs.

"Okay." She turned toward me. "We'll be down soon."

"And we'll finish this discussion tonight," I replied, making her blush before she disappeared out of the room.

"I like her," Hoka said once she closed the door behind her. "She is amazing."

"She is," I agreed, gesturing toward the bar in a silent invitation.

He nodded. "I just can't understand what she sees in you, though."

"You and me both." I snorted as I served us two glasses of scotch. "Though, I suppose I could say the same for Violet."

"Yeah, me too. I guess we should thank our lucky stars and move on." He sighed. "I can't believe you almost let her slip away."

"It was complicated."

"No, it really wasn't. I was trying to stop you from making the same mistake I made. I told you to tell her everything and to trust her judgment, but it took Violet telling you the exact same thing for you to do something."

I let out a little humorless laugh. "No, I just missed her more than anything in the world, and I didn't think I'd last one more day without her. Violet's advice just came at the right time."

"We need extraordinary women to put up with us, and I have to say we're blessed to have them, despite us being so undeserving." He winked at me. "I saw the ring on her finger."

I nodded, sitting on the leather chair behind my desk and gesturing to him to do the same.

"I plan to marry her over Christmas. Since you guys will be here, it's really the perfect time."

"Make her yours before she realizes it's insane?" He chuckled. "It makes sense."

"Does it ever go away? This fear of losing her."

Hoka looked down at his glass for a few seconds, his humor morphing into deep contemplation.

"Ah," He sighed. "I would love to say yes, that once you're married and have the life, the child... That once she saw the darkness and the monster lurking, and still stayed, you won't be afraid anymore, but the truth is, I think you get even more scared, even if it is different."

I ran my hand down my face. "I expected that much because the more I'm with her—"

"The more you love her," Hoka finished for me. "And then it's not her decision to leave you that you fear, it's all the dangers around you, because even if you knew before that you loved her, the longer you are together, the more you realize that she became your life, your reason for breathing. You become concerned about your own safety because you get that irrational fear that if you leave her alone, she will be defenseless and once you know your world truly revolves around her..." He stopped and drank his glass in one go. "Welcome to the club of criminals in love."

"I don't like the word criminal; I'd rather be called 'morally gray.'"

Hoka laughed. "Morally gray? Okay, I like that." He sighed again, relaxing in his seat. "But what you gain out of it really outweighs the fear. Coming home, being with your family... letting your walls down and just being yourself with people who love and accept you completely is beyond the best feeling. When Violet looks at me with her love and trust, despite all the horrors she went through because of me, there's nothing like it, man. You'll see. I can assure you, despite the fear, you will never want to change a thing."

I nodded because I was already feeling it. I felt a rush every time I entered a room and I saw her face morph with a big smile as her eyes stopped on me. How she rushed into my open arms as if I was her knight in shining armor.

"She's my life," I admitted.

"As she should be. Who would have thought that the head of the *yakuza* would talk about love with the head of the Chicago Italian mafia?"

"I will deny it if you ever repeat it, but I'm glad Violet has you."

Hoka rested his hand on his chest. "Oh my god, I'm going to cry. Did we just become best friends?"

I flipped him the finger. "Did Pietro really want to see her, or did you just want to cause me a case of blue balls?"

"He really did. The blue balls are just an added bonus."

"How is he doing?" I asked with a certain apprehension. I was not really keen to let him train, and for him to be faced daily with his limitations. I also resented the fact that he refused to let me attend the training sessions, even if I understood his reasons.

"He is one of the strongest boys I've ever met, your son. He has the will of a whole Samurai army. In Japan, we say that perseverance is strength, and Pietro is leaving me in awe. It doesn't matter how many times he falls, how many times he fails, he keeps standing up, ready to try again. He's getting stronger every day. He knows full well he'll never be exactly like everyone else, but he fights just the same." He turned toward me, and I saw his pride and amazement for my son so plainly on his face. "I hope that my Yuko has even half of the mental strength your boy has. He is going to be a force to be reckoned with, and I can only imagine the boss he will be once he steps into your shoes."

I leaned forward on my seat. "If he so chooses. I will never demand him to follow this path. I know how dark and destructive it can be, and if the Benetti legacy has to disappear after me, then so be it. Pietro will have the freedom I was never offered."

"It's commendable. I don't think I'll be that noble with Yuko." He waved his hand dismissively. "I don't think it will be something you need to think about. Your boy was born to lead, it is in his work ethic, his every gesture. *Keizoku wa chikara nari.* 'Continuance is power', and he carries that power. I don't see anything resisting him once he puts his mind to it. I took Oda to our training yesterday and today."

"I know, he told me."

"I gave Oda a training routine, and I think it would be good for him to train Pietro a few times a week... if it's okay with you. Your son is persistent and will do it with or without help, but I think Oda would be good for him, both physically and mentally."

"Thank you for what you did for him."

"No need to thank me. He's family, and I love that boy. He makes me proud, so proud, and if you don't want him to rule over your legacy, then I'm sure the *yakuza* would want him."

I glared and he laughed.

"You're so easy to bait." He stood up. "I need a shower before dinner and pack for tomorrow. I couldn't escape my responsibilities any longer."

I stood as well. "Is there anything I can help you with?"

"No, I'm good, but I know you're there if I need it, my reluctant ally."

I laughed. "My sister loves you and you love her." I shrugged. "As you said, we're family."

Hoka looked at me for a second. "No bond is stronger than the love of our family. I'm glad you found that too, brother, really."

I helped myself with another small glass of scotch as I reached for the adoption papers and put them on my desk. I drank it slowly, mulling over the revelation Hoka had made while I looked out of the window. The night had fallen, and the garden was only lit up by the bright full moon showing the soft snow that was falling and covering the ground in a white coat.

I enjoyed these few minutes of reflection before exiting the office and joining my family for dinner. We had been having those for the past few days, but it was still so new, so unfamiliar, yet something I couldn't imagine my life without anymore.

As I reached the bottom of the stairs, emotion seized me as I saw Lily holding hands with Pietro as he went down the stairs slowly, only holding on to the banister.

I took a sharp breath and held it as I followed the progression, emotions clogging my throat with every step he took.

Hoka was right—of course, he was. My son was a fearless warrior and the woman standing by his side, his soon-to-be mother, was lending him her quiet strength as love and pride lit her features.

He looked up and locked eyes with me as he reached the halfway point of the stairs. He stopped for a second and my legs twitched with the impulse to go to him and help him the rest of the way.

No, he can do it, the voice in my head chimed. *He'd ask if he needed it.*

He started down again as he kept his eyes on me, his eyebrows etched with determination.

When he took the last step, Lily's shoulders sagged with relief as his mouth broke into a huge smile.

"I did it, Dad. I went down the stairs."

I nodded, way too emotional to speak. Pride, love, and admiration all mixed together so powerfully I could feel tears form in my eyes.

I looked up at Lily for assistance and her eyes reflected my own feelings.

"I never doubted you, my boy," Lily said lovingly before kissing the top of his head. "I'll watch you conquer the world."

He let out a humorless laugh. "Darth Vader style?" he asked her cheekily.

"If it's the dark side you want to follow, then so be it," she replied, tapping her finger on the tip of his nose. "Someone needs to follow in his father's footsteps."

"Hey! I'm not Vader!" I said with mock offense. "I'm much cooler." I detailed his fancy suit. "Why are you dressed so nice?" I pointed at my shirt. "I feel underdressed now."

He bounced a little on his feet, excitement making him unsteady. "I saw the ring!" He beamed. "You're going to marry Lily, and we are going to be a family!"

"We are a family," I replied gently, reaching for his free hand. I looked at Lily before looking at him again. "You know what? I've got a surprise for you, too."

Lily caught her breath, knowing what was coming.

Pietro threw her a suspicious look before he gazed at me again.

"You see, Lily and I have been talking, and she loves you very, *very* much."

"I love her, too..." he trailed off, visibly confused. He looked up to her. "I love you, Lily. You know that, don't you?"

She nodded with a sniffle, her eyes full of tears.

Pietro turned back to me with wide eyes. "Dad?"

"Lily wants to be your mom, officially, *cucciolo*. She wants to adopt you. What do you say?"

Pietro turned toward her, losing his balance, but I held him up. "You want to be my mom?" he asked, his voice breaking.

"More than anything in the world," she replied, sobbing now.

Way to go, Sandro, I cursed myself. *I could have waited until tomorrow.*

"Oh!" Pietro let go of our hands and wrapped his arms around her. "Mom! You're my mom!" He started to cry against her chest.

"Yes, I'm your mom." She kissed the top of his head, tears streaming down her cheeks.

I blinked a couple of times and wiped a few tears at the scene before me. How could I not?

"What's happening here?" Hoka asked, coming down the stairs, freshly showered and holding hands with Violet.

"Lily is going to be my mom!" Pietro beamed, still holding on to Lily with dear life. "She's adopting me."

Violet rested her hand on her heart as her smile turned tender at the scene in front of her.

"Of course, she is your mom," Hoka said with a wink. "Family doesn't end in blood, I told you that."

Pietro nodded. "Family is made of love, truth, and compassion. I remember, Uncle Hoka."

I walked to them and hugged them both, mouthing a silent 'thank you' to my sister and brother-in-law.

Family was love, trust, and compassion, and we had enough of that to last us a lifetime.

Our journey as a family, our life together, was just starting, and as I held my two treasures in my arms, I knew that it would last forever.

I'd been Lily Matthews' heartless savior, and she saved us in return.

EPILOGUE

Lily

Twelve years later

"Your daughter is driving me crazy," Sandro muttered as I was putting the casserole into the oven.

I laughed, discarding my oven mitts and turned to see him leaning against the counter, pouting like a little boy.

"It's funny how she's my daughter when she's aggravating you, but she's yours whenever she's doing something good."

He shrugged with a cocky grin. "That's how it's supposed to work."

I rolled my eyes but went to him when he straightened up and opened his arms invitingly.

He kissed me softly and wrapped his arm around my waist.

"What did she do to you?" I asked, running my fingers through the salt and pepper hair on the side of his head. My husband was the perfect definition of a silver fox, and even at the age of fifty, he was hotness personified. I still had a hard time keeping my hands off him, which, thank God, was mutual.

"She made me stay in her room while she tried on seventeen dresses! *Seventeen*, wife. Why does she have that many dresses, anyway? She's ten!"

I laughed. "Because you keep buying her everything she asks for!"

"Um..."

"Oh, come on." I stood on my toes and kissed him. "She's excited, and you should be happy that it's not for Niccolò Genovese," I taunted, knowing how protective he got every time he thought about the puppy-love crush our daughter had on Matteo Genovese's twelve-year-old son.

"She'll date him over my dead body," he said darkly.

"At least he is in the outfit."

His glower deepened. "Are you really trying to make me angry?"

I laughed. "No, I'm trying to put things into perspective. Pietro is bringing a girl home for the first time, it's big."

He rolled his eyes as my timer beeped.

"Ah, the pie is ready." I wiggled out of his hold.

"Why are you working so hard in the kitchen when you could be upstairs satisfying your demanding husband?"

I laughed and got the golden perfection out of the oven. "I'll satisfy you tonight," I said with a hand gesture. "And our son is bringing the woman he loves home. Aren't you a little bit excited?"

He crossed his arms over his chest. "I think it's a little early in the relationship, and he's young."

"He's going to be twenty-three in a few weeks; he's not that young."

"Bringing a woman here is serious business, Lily."

"I know it is!" I exclaimed, throwing my hands up with exasperation. "Why do you think I'm trying to make sure everything is perfect? Our son is wise and never does anything without considering all aspects. If he is bringing this woman here, then we both know he plans to marry her."

Alessandro sighed and sat at the kitchen counter. "He's too young for that, too."

"I was twenty-three when you took me to the island, and twenty-four when you married me. I don't remember you thinking I was too young when you had your way with me on every flat surface."

He pursed his lips, throwing me a dark look. "That's different."

"How is that different?"

"It was what *I* wanted."

I laughed. "I love you, my stubborn man."

He sighed. "It takes a unique type of woman to accept this life, you know that better than anyone."

"I do," I agreed. It had not been easy, that much was true. The extra security, the fear of losing my husband, the shirts with blood I sometimes had to clean. But there were so many amazing things that came out of this as well. The close unit we created with other mafia wives who were in a happy marriage. Cassandra, Elena, and India became like sisters to me and Violet—my sister-in-law, who was also my best friend and confidant. The protective nature and overwhelming passion my husband gave me every day and the adoration he showed me as he treated me like his queen every day of our lives together, even when we were angry with each other.

"You think it is only me who made it work, but I'm not special, Sandro, my heart. It's our love that made it possible. It was how much I loved you and how much you loved me that gave me all the strength I needed." I smiled. "Our son clearly loves her, and she has put up with a lot already. The extra security, the vetting... Now be honest with me, how much research have you done since he told you he was bringing her back?"

Alessandro shrugged and looked away.

"How much, Sandro?"

"He is our son, I needed to make sure she was okay."

"Sandro, if you don't answer this second, you better remember how my body felt last night, because it will be weeks before you—"

"I did it all, okay? All of it! FBI, CIA, and private detectives on her and her family. I did it all."

I shook my head. "You better pray our son never finds out, or he will be pissed."

He snorted. "Pietro is as protective as I am. Trust me, if the roles were reversed, he'd do the same. Tell him how his sister is all googly-eyed for the Genovese spawn and watch how he reacts. He's his father's son."

It was true. Our Pietro was lethal and already feared by Alessandro's men. He had not yet fully taken his role as Alessandro's *underboss,* which he was supposed to take now that he was done with university.

I looked at the clock and sighed. Pietro's private plane landed thirty minutes ago, and he would be home any minute now.

"And did you find anything of concern?"

"Ah!" Alessandro crossed his arms over his chest. "Look who's not all high and mighty now about respecting our son's private life? How the mighty have fallen," he added with a mocking grin.

"Ah! And look who's going to suck his own cock tonight for mocking his wife." I smirked. I would always win when sex was on the line, and he was stupid to even try.

"It's not fair to hurt Colossus, who's a big fan of your mouth and your pussy," he said in a low voice.

I blushed, still getting worked up by his dirty mouth after all this time.

He sighed in rendition. "She's great. More than great, actually; she's perfect. She's twenty-five, a teaching assistant in history, and she is beautiful."

I beamed, already liking the woman who was making my Pietro happy.

"Pietro is home!" Victoria shouted, nearly flying down the stairs in her velvet purple dress.

She's probably been glued to the first-floor library window, waiting for the car once the gate opened.

"Vicky, princess, wait for us," Alessandro shouted.

"But Daddy…" she whined.

"Victoria Benetti!" Alessandro warned, but his deep, fatherly tone made me swoon. Alessandro as a dad was almost as hot as a naked Alessandro.

I smiled, removing my apron, and extending my hand to him. "Come on, husband, let's go meet our future daughter-in-law."

We walked into the hall where Victoria was waiting, bouncing with excitement in her shiny black shoes. She really went all out today, and it warmed my heart.

This little girl was my pride and joy, and my carbon copy, except for the black hair and the attitude—that was all her father.

Alessandro went to the door and opened it, and we both looked outside as Pietro exited the car and turned to help his girlfriend out of it.

He turned toward us and smiled, the joy on his face making me happier than I could describe. I knew the emotions were getting to Alessandro as well, as he cleared his throat and tightened his hold on my hand.

She took Pietro's arm as he held on to his walking stick. Few people knew that it was a lethal weapon and contained a blade as sharp as a katana. It was a weapon he'd been training with for years and could probably kill an army with.

They walked up the stairs a little slower than most. She naturally matched his steps, and the way she held her arm showed that he could use her for support.

This woman was attuned to Pietro's needs.

"She loves him," I whispered to Alessandro as we moved a little from the door.

"Yes, she does," he agreed reluctantly. "God help us, our son is going to get married."

I was laughing at his words when they entered the house.

Pietro was tall and muscular now, far from my little boy anymore. He was still so frighteningly bright that he could really become the evil mastermind we kept joking he would become.

Pietro stopped in the middle of the hall and looked at me with so much pride. "Mom, Dad, let me introduce you to my Emily." He looked down at her. "Emily, meet my mom and dad."

Emily let go of his arm and came to me, extending her hand. "Mrs. Benetti, it's such an honor to meet you. Pietro is so full of praise for his mother, and I feel like I already know you."

I pulled the short curvy girl into my arms and hugged her tightly. "It's so lovely to finally meet you, Emily. Thank you so much for making my little boy so happy."

"Ma..." Pietro whined.

I gestured for him to come close after I broke the hug with Emily. "I don't care if you're six-foot, you'll always be my baby boy. Come give your mom a hug."

He came forward and swiped me off my feet. "I'll always be my mama's boy," he whispered into my ear before putting me back on my feet and kissing my forehead.

He turned around and winked at Victoria, who was pouting because of the lack of attention. "And I kept the best for last. The little munchkin over there is my little sister, Victoria."

Emily walked up to her and pointed at her own curly hair, which was blond instead of black.

"We match!" she said to Victoria. "You're so beautiful! Pietro told me you were a little princess, but you are even more beautiful than any princess I've ever seen."

Victoria beamed up at her, and I knew she already won her over. "Do you want to come to see my room? I've got the best doll house."

"Vickie, baby, why don't you let Emily rest for a minute?" I tried, sending Emily an apologetic smile.

"No, it's okay." Emily took Victoria's hand. "I would love to see the doll house. Pietro told me how cool it was."

"You did?" Vickie asked with amazement, and Pietro nodded. "You're the best big brother ever!" She beamed at him. "We won't be long. Come, Emily, and you can call me Vickie since we're friends now."

I took Pietro's hand as we looked at them go up the stairs in silence as Victoria started to detail all the dolls she owned and their names.

"You know we won't see her for a good hour, if not two, right?" I told him with amusement.

"I'm going to marry that woman, ma," he said, squeezing my hand.

"I know," I replied with a smile.

He turned toward Alessandro. "I love her to death, Dad. She's my light, she's my support. I… I can't explain it."

Alessandro took his hand and looked at me. "You don't have to explain, son. I understand. When you know, you know. Marry her if it is what you wish. You have my blessing and I can only hope she will make you at least half as happy as your mother has made me."

Pietro kept hold of our hands as he did so many years ago in exactly the same spot.

"It's your love that made me believe it was possible, that everything was possible, and it is because of it that I found my Emily. I wasn't afraid to take the plunge, and if I get to be half as happy as you two are, I'll consider myself blessed because I am already so lucky to have you both in my life."

I hugged him as Alessandro hugged us both, and we stayed like that for a while.

We were so many things. We were mafia, we were husband and wife, mother and son, a family, but what we were most of all was love. And love was the highest power there was. It could conquer anything; it could give you the strength you needed to fight your enemies and your own demons.

Love healed my heartless savior to transform him into the man he was now, and love gave me the strength to step up and become the queen he needed and the mother I was made to be.

This whole life, this adventure, turned out the way it was because of love, and I couldn't wait for the next chapters as I continued to grow old with the love of my life.

Love... I now knew with certainty, was the answer to everything.

The end....for now

The Syndicates series continues with Killian Doyle's story in ***Her Merciless Protector*** coming soon.

ABOUT R.G. ANGEL

I'm a trained lawyer, world traveler, coffee addict, cheese aficionado, avid book reviewer and blogger.

I enjoy writing darkish contemporary romance with heart, heat and a little darkness with strong 'morally grey' alpha heroes and strong heroines.

When I'm not busy doing all my lawyerly mayhem, and because I'm living in rainy (yet beautiful) Britain, I mostly enjoy indoor activities such as reading, watching TV, playing with my crazy puppies and writing stories I hope will make you dream and will bring you as much joy as I had writing them.

If you want to know any of the latest news join my reader group R.G.'s Angels on Facebook or subscribe to my newsletter!

Keep calm and read on!

R.G. Angel

Also by

R.G. Angel

The Patricians series

Bittersweet Legacy

Bittersweet Revenge

Bittersweet Truth

The Cosa Nostra series

The Dark King (Prequel Novella)

Broken Prince

Twisted Knight

Cruel King

The Syndicates series

Her Ruthless Warrior
Standalones

Lovable
The Tragedy of Us

The Bargain

Acknowledgments

Thank you dear reader for giving **Her Heartless Savior** a chance. I hope you enjoyed Alessandro and Lily's story.

It was a very emotional journey for me and I have to admit I fell in love with this little family and I am considering writing a little novella for our Pietro.

I know this book deals with the sensitive subject of disability and I hope I approach it with all the respect that is due. I am a carer for a disabled parent and I suffer from an autoimmune disease as well as a chronic illness that sometimes can be hard to deal with, especially when they flare up. But I wanted to show in this book that whilst your disability is part of you it does not define you, it is not you.

To all my disabled warriors fighting every day with visible or invisible disabilities/chronic illnesses, you are amazing and I love you.

To my Beta readers Liz and Ana - you girls rock!

To Zoe Blake and Willow Winters - You ladies mean a lot more than I can say. Your support, advice and friendship is invaluable and this is my way to tell the world what amazing women with hearts of gold you both are.

Printed in Great Britain
by Amazon